All the Rage

Also by Cara Hunter

The DI Adam Fawley Series

Close to Home
In the Dark
All the Rage
The Whole Truth
Hope to Die

Standalone

Murder in the Family

All the Rage

A Novel

CARA HUNTER

WILLIAM MORROW

An Imprint of HarperCollinsPublishers

ALL THE RAGE. Copyright © 2024 by Cara Hunter. All rights reserved. Printed in the United States of America. No part of this book may be used or reproduced in any manner whatsoever without written permission except in the case of brief quotations embodied in critical articles and reviews. For information, address HarperCollins Publishers, 195 Broadway, New York, NY 10007.

HarperCollins books may be purchased for educational, business, or sales promotional use. For information, please email the Special Markets Department at SPsales@harpercollins.com.

Published as in Great Britain in 2020 by Penguin Random House UK.

First William Morrow paperback published 2024.

FIRST EDITION

Library of Congress Cataloging-in-Publication Data has been applied for.

ISBN 978-0-06-326093-1

23 24 25 26 27 LBC 5 4 3 2 1

To my brother, Mark

All the Rage

Prologue

The night is so warm she has her window open; the net curtain lifts lazily in the bare breath of late-summer heat. There's a light on inside the flat, but only in the living room: that's how he knows she's alone. There's music playing too. Not loud, but he's close enough to hear it. He used to worry about that, at the beginning—about getting too near and giving himself away. But he knows better now; even in daylight vans like this are everywhere. People don't even see them any more. Not even observant people. Like her.

He winds down the window a little further. She must be going out, because the music is fast, energetic, upbeat; not the lazy jazzy stuff she usually prefers. He closes his eyes a moment and tries to visualize what she's going to wear, what she's pulling over her skin right now—skin still damp from the shower he just heard her take. Not the black dress with the beading that fits so tightly he can map her body in his mind: if it was dinner with her tosser of a boyfriend she wouldn't be listening to crap music like that. It's not her parents either: if they were in Oxford he'd have seen the car. No, it must be a night out with the girls. Which means she'll go for something less suggestive—something understated that signals polite inaccessibility. The blue one, perhaps, with the wide sleeves. Tiffany blue, they call it. He never knew that before. It's a nice dress. Neutral. And it's one of her favorites.

She didn't tell him any of this. He found it out. It wasn't even that hard. All you have to do is watch. Watch and wait and deduce. Sometimes all it takes is a few days; but those are rarely the most satisfying. This one has already cost him more than three weeks, but he likes taking his time. And something tells him she's going to be worth it. Like the ads for that shampoo she buys keep on telling her. And in any case, he's learned to his cost that these things can't be rushed. That's when you make mistakes. That's when it all goes wrong.

There's someone coming now. He can hear the clack of shoes against the pavement. High heels. Giggling. He shifts slightly to get a better look, the plastic of the seat sticking and crackling under him. Across the road, two girls come into view. Nothing understated about that pair, that's for sure. Sequins, red gash mouths, tottering about on their tarty shoes; the silly bitches are already half-cut. He hasn't seen either of these two before but they must be friends of hers because they stop outside the flat and start rummaging in their handbags. One of them pulls something free with a flourish and a loud "Ta-da!" A shiny pink sash, with something written on it in glitter he can't quite read. But he doesn't need to. His eyes narrow; he's seen shit like that before. It's a hen party. A fucking *hen party*. Since when did she bother with crap like that? The two girls have their heads together now and something about the way they're laughing and whispering sends a trickle of unease inching up his spine. It can't be *her* party, surely. She can't have—not without him knowing—she's not wearing a ring—he'd have seen—

He leans forward, trying to get a better look. One of the girls is ringing the doorbell to the flat, leaning on the entryphone until the window upstairs shoots up.

"Do you really have to make *quite* so much noise?"

She's trying to sound disapproving but there's laughter in her voice. She leans out and a twist of long dark hair slips over her shoulder. It's still wet from the shower. His throat tightens.

One of the girls looks up and lifts her arms, triumphant. She has a plastic coronet in one hand and the pink sash in the other. "Hey! Look what we got!"

The girl in the window shakes her head. "You promised, Chlo—absolutely *no* tat and *no* tiaras."

The two below burst out laughing. "This *extremely* tasteful piece of decorative headwear happens to be mine, not yours," says the second girl, her words slurring slightly. "We got *this* little number for *you* . . ."

She digs into her handbag and holds something up, and as it catches the light of the street lamp he can see it clearly: a bright-pink hairslide, with the word TAKEN spelled out in diamanté.

The girl in the window shakes her head again. "What did I do to deserve you two, eh?"

She ducks back inside and a moment later there's the sound of the entryphone buzzing, and the two girls stumble over the step into the house, still giggling.

The man opens the glovebox. That bitch is lucky he isn't going to do her right here and now; that'd put paid to their trashy little tart fest. But he won't. He wants the exhilaration of waiting—still wants it, even now. The exquisite anticipation, the detail by detail: how she'll smell, how she'll taste, the feel of her hair. Just knowing he could have that whenever he chooses—that the only thing preventing him is his own restraint—

He sits a while, clenching and unclenching his fists, allowing his heart rate to slow. Then he puts the key in the ignition and starts the engine.

The alarm goes at seven but Faith Appleford has already been up for an hour. Hair, clothes, shoes, makeup, it all takes time. She's sitting at her dressing table now, putting the finishing touches to her mascara, hearinıg her mother calling up the stairs from the kitchen.

"Nadine—are you out of bed yet? If you want that lift you need to be down here in ten minutes."

There's a groan from next door and Faith imagines her sister turning over and pulling the pillow over her head. It's always the same; Nadine is hopeless in the mornings. Unlike Faith. Faith is always ready in plenty of time. Always perfectly turned out. She turns back to the mirror and moves her head right and left, checking the angles, tweaking a lock of hair, straightening the neckline of her sweater. Beautiful. And it's not just showing off. She really is. Quite beautiful.

She gets to her feet and selects a handbag from the cluster hanging on the back of the door. It's suede. Well, not real suede but you have to get up really close to realize. The color is just right though, especially with this jacket. The perfect shade of blue.

* * *

"Is that OK—not too cold?"

I felt Alex flinch as the probe touched her skin but she shakes her head quickly and smiles. "No, it's fine."

The nurse turns back to her monitor and taps her keyboard. Everything in the room is muted. The lights dimmed, the sound muffled, as if we're underwater. Around us, the hospital is brisk with activity, but in here, right now, time has slowed to a heartbeat.

"Here you are," says the nurse at last, swinging the monitor around and smiling at us. The image on the screen blooms into life. A head, a nose, a tiny fist, raised as if in celebration. Movement. *Life*. Alex's hand gropes for mine but her eyes never leave her child.

"This is the first time for you, isn't it, Mr. Fawley?" continues the nurse. "I don't think you were here for the first scan?" She keeps her tone light but there's judgment in there all the same.

"It was complicated," says Alex quickly. "I was so terrified something would go wrong—I didn't want to jinx it—"

I tighten my grip on her hand. We've been through this. Why she didn't tell me, why she couldn't even live with me until she knew for certain. Until she was sure.

"It's fine," I say. "All that matters is that I'm here now. And that the baby is OK."

"Well, the heartbeat is good and strong," the nurse says, tapping at her keyboard again. "And the baby is growing normally, exactly as it should be at twenty-two weeks. There's nothing here that gives me any cause for concern."

I feel myself exhale—I didn't even realize I'd stopped breathing. We're older parents, we've read all the leaflets, had all the tests, but still—

"You're absolutely sure?" says Alex. "Because I really don't want to have an amnio—"

The nurse smiles again, a deeper, warmer smile. "It's all absolutely fine, Mrs. Fawley. You have nothing at all to worry about."

Alex turns to me, tears in her eyes. "It's all right," she whispers. "It really is going to be all right."

On the screen the baby somersaults suddenly, a tiny dolphin in the silvery darkness.

"So," says the nurse, adjusting the probe again, "do you want to know the sex?"

* * *

Fiona Blake puts a bowl of cereal down in front of her daughter, but Sasha doesn't appear to notice. She's been staring at her phone ever since she came downstairs, and Fiona is fighting the urge to say something. They don't have phones at meals in their house. Not because Fiona laid down the law about it but because they agreed, the two of them, that it wasn't how they wanted to do things. She turns away to fill the teapot but when she gets back to the table Sasha is still staring at the damn screen.

"Problem?" she says, trying not to sound irritated.

Sasha looks up and shakes her head. "Sorry—it's just Pats saying she won't be at school today. She's been throwing up all night."

Fiona makes a face. "That winter vomiting thing?"

7

Sasha nods, then pushes the phone away. "Sounds like it. She sounds really rough."

Fiona scrutinizes her daughter; her eyes are bright and her cheeks look a little flushed. Come to think of it, she's been rather like that all week. "You feeling all right, Sash? You look like you might be a bit feverish yourself."

Sasha's eyes widen. "Me? I'm fine. Seriously, Mum, I'm absolutely OK. And completely starving."

She grins at her mother and reaches across the table for a spoon.

* * *

At St. Aldate's police station, DC Anthony Asante is trying to smile. Though the look on DS Gislingham's face suggests he isn't doing a very good job of it. It's not that Asante doesn't have a sense of humor, it's just not the custard pie and banana skin variety. Which is why he's struggling to find the upside-down glass of water on his desk very amusing. That and the fact that he's furious with himself for forgetting what day it is and not being more bloody careful. He should have seen this coming a mile off: newest member of the team, graduate entry, fresh from the Met. He might as well have had "Fair Game" tattooed across his forehead. And now they're all standing there, watching him, waiting to see if he's a "good sport" or just "well up himself" (which judging from the smirk DC Quinn isn't bothering to hide is clearly *his* opinion— though Asante's tempted to ask if Quinn's playing the role of pot or kettle on that one). He takes a deep breath and cranks the smile up a notch. After all, it could have been worse. One of the shits at Brixton nick left a bunch of bananas on his desk the day he first started.

"OK, guys," he says, looking around at the room, in what he hopes is the right combination of heavy irony and seen-it-all-before, "very funny."

Gislingham grins at him, as much relieved as anything. After all, a joke's a joke and in this job you have to be able to take it as well as dish it out, but he's still a bit new to the whole sergeantship thing and he doesn't want to be seen as picking on anyone. Least of all the only non-white member of the team. He cuffs Asante lightly on the arm, saying, "Nice one, Tone," then decides he's probably best off leaving it at that and makes for the coffee machine.

* * *

Adam Fawley
1 April 2018
10.25

"So how's this going to work then?"

Alex settles herself slowly into the sofa and swings her feet up. I hand her the mug and she curls her hands around it. "How's what going to work?" she says, though she's already looking mischievous.

"You know exactly what I mean—the small fact that I don't know the sex, but you do."

She blows on the tea and then looks up at me, all innocence. "Why should it be a problem?"

I shunt a cushion aside and sit down. "How are you going to keep a secret like that? You're bound to let it slip eventually."

9

She grins. "Well, as long as you don't employ that infamous interviewing technique of yours, I think I'll just about manage to keep it to myself." She laughs now, seeing my face. "Look, I promise to keep thinking of two lists of names—"

"OK, but—"

"And not buy everything in blue."

Before I can even open my mouth she grins again and prods me with her foot. "*Or pink.*"

I shake my head, all faux-disapproval. "I give up."

"No, you don't," she says, serious now. "You never give up. Not on anything."

And we both know she's not just talking about my job.

I get to my feet. "Take it easy the rest of the day, all right? No heavy lifting or anything insane like that."

She raises an eyebrow. "So that afternoon of lumberjacking I had planned is off, is it? Darn it."

"And email me if you need anything from the shops."

She gives a joke salute then prods me again. "Go. You're late already. And I have done all this before, remember. I wallpapered Jake's nursery when I was twice the size I am now."

As she smiles up at me, I realize I can't even remember the last time she talked like this. All those months after Jake died, she saw motherhood only in terms of loss. Absence. Not just the want of him but the despair of having any other child. All this time, she could only speak of our son in pain. But now, perhaps, she can reclaim the joy of him too. This baby could never be a replacement, even if we wanted it to be, but perhaps he—or she—can still be a redemption.

It's only when I get to the door that I turn around. "What infamous interviewing technique?"

Her laughter follows me all the way down the drive.

*   *   *

At 10:45 Somer is still stuck in a queue on the A33. She'd meant to come back from Hampshire last night but somehow the walk along the coast had turned into dinner, and dinner had turned into just one glass too many, and at half ten they'd agreed it definitely wasn't a good idea for her to drive. So the new plan was to get up at 5:00 to beat the Monday morning rush, only somehow that didn't happen either and it was gone 9:00 by the time she left. Not that she's complaining. She smiles to herself; her skin is still tingling despite the hot shower and the cold car. Even though it means she has no change of clothes for the office and no time to go home and get any. Her phone pings and she glances down. It's a text from Giles. She smiles again as she reads it, itching to reply with some arch remark about what his superintendent would say if he got sent *that* by mistake, but the car ahead of her is finally moving; Giles—for once—is going to have to wait.

*   *   *

When the minicab driver first spotted the girl, he thought she was drunk. Yet another bloody student, he thought, getting pissed on cheap cider and staggering home at all hours. She was a good hundred yards ahead of him, but he could see she was lurching unsteadily from side to side.

It wasn't till the car got closer that he realized she was actually limping. One strappy shoe was still on but the other had lost its heel. That's what made him slow down. That and where she was. Out on the Marston Ferry Road, miles from anywhere. Or as close to it as Oxford ever gets. Though as he signaled and pulled over alongside her, he still thought she must just be drunk.

But that was before he saw her face.

* * *

The office is all but empty when the call comes through. Quinn's AWOL somewhere, Fawley's not due in till lunchtime and Gislingham's off on a training course. Something to do with people management, Baxter tells Ev. Before smiling wryly and observing that he can't see why the Sarge is bothering: there's nothing about that particular subject Gis couldn't learn from his own wife.

Somer has just got back with a salad and a round of coffees when the phone rings. She watches Everett pick it up and wedge the handset against her shoulder while she answers an email.

"Sorry?" she says suddenly, gripping the phone now, the email forgotten. "Can you say that again? You're sure? And when did this happen?" She grabs a pen and scribbles something down. "Tell them we'll be there in twenty minutes."

Somer looks up; something tells her the salad is going to have to wait. Again. She doesn't even bother buying hot lunches any more.

Everett puts the phone down. "A girl's been found on the Marston Ferry Road."

"Found? What do you mean 'found?'"

"In a state of extreme distress, and with marks on her wrists where her hands were tied."

"*Tied?* She'd been *tied up?*"

Everett's face is grim. "I'm afraid it sounds a lot worse than that."

*   *   *

Adam Fawley
1 April 2018
12.35

I'm still on the ring road when I get the call from Everett.

"Sir? I'm with Somer on our way to the Lakes. We had a call about ten minutes ago—a girl's been found in a distraught state on the Marston Ferry Road. It looks like she may have been attacked."

I signal to pull over into a lay-by and pick up the phone. "Sexual assault?"

"We don't actually know that. But to be honest, right now, we don't know much at all."

I can tell something's off, just from her voice. And if there's one thing I know about Ev, it's that she has good antennae. Good antennae, and not enough confidence in them. Or herself. Something for Gislingham to pick up when he gets back from that HR course of his.

"There's something bothering you, isn't there?"

"She was found with her clothes torn and muddy and evidence that her hands had been tied—"

"Jesus—"

"I know. She was apparently in a terrible state but the point is she refused to go to either the police or the doctor. She made the minicab driver who found her take her straight home and told him she didn't want it reported. Which, thankfully, he ignored."

I poke about in the glovebox for some paper and ask her to repeat the address in the Lakes. And if you're wondering how you missed all that standing water when you did the Oxford tourist tour, there isn't anything larger than a pond for miles. The Lakes is a 1930s housing development in Marston. People call it that because there are so many roads there named after them: Derwent, Coniston, Grasmere, Rydal. I like to think some long-ago town planner was home-sick for the fells, but Alex tells me I'm just being Romantic.

"Do we know the girl's name?"

"We think it could be Faith. The cabdriver said she was wearing a necklace with that on it. Though it might just be one of those '*Live Love Life*' sort of things. You must have seen them."

I have. But not on Ev, that's for sure. As for the cabbie, it seems he wasn't just public-spirited but observant too. Wonders will never cease.

"According to the electoral roll there's a woman called Diane Appleford resident at the address," she continues. "She moved there about a year ago, and there's no crimi-nal record, nothing flagging anywhere. But there's no Mr. Appleford—or not one living with her, at any rate."

"OK, I'm only about ten minutes away."

"We're just turning into Rydal Way now, but we'll hold off going in till you get here."

The Appleford home is a neat bow-fronted semi, with a paved front garden and a low wall made of those square white bricks that look like stencils. Our next-door neighbors had exactly the same when I was a kid. What with that and the frilly nets in the window the house looks landlocked in 1976.

I see Somer and Everett get out of their car and come down the road towards me. Everett is in her standard combo of white shirt, dark skirt and sensible mac, though the bright-red scarf is definitely her little rebellion. Somer, by contrast, is in black jeans, a leather jacket and high-heeled ankle boots with fringy bits around the back. She doesn't usually dress like that at work, so I'm guessing she was at the boyfriend's this weekend and hasn't been home. She flushes slightly when she sees me, which makes me even more convinced I'm right. She met him when we were working on the Michael Esmond case. The boyfriend, I mean. Giles Saumarez. He's in the job too. I can never quite decide if that's a good thing.

"Afternoon, sir," says Everett, hoisting her bag a bit higher on her shoulder.

I reach into my pocket for a mint. I carry handfuls of the bloody things now. Stopping smoking is a bastard, but it's non-negotiable. And by that, I mean between me and myself; I didn't wait for Alex to ask.

"Is that a good idea?" says Somer, eyeing the sweet. "With the teeth, I mean."

I frown for a moment and then remember that's where I told them I was this morning. The dentist's. The universal white lie of choice. It's not that the baby is a secret—people will have to know eventually. It's just—you know—not right now.

"It was OK," I say. "I didn't need anything doing."

15

I turn to Ev. "So anything more before we go crashing in?"

She shakes her head. "You know as much as we do."

The woman who opens the door has dried-out blond hair, white sweatpants and a white sweatshirt with *Slummy Mummy* written on it. She must be mid-forties. She looks tired. Tired and immediately defensive.

"Mrs. Appleford?"

She eyes me and then the women. "Yes. Who are you?"

"I'm Detective Inspector Adam Fawley. This is DC Everett and DC Somer."

She grips the door a little tighter. "Faith was quite clear— she doesn't want the police involved. You have no business—"

"Faith is your daughter?"

She hesitates a moment, as if divulging even so bare a fact is some sort of betrayal. "Yes. Faith is my daughter."

"The passerby who found her was extremely concerned for her well-being. As, of course, are we."

Somer touches my shoulder and gestures back behind her. I don't even need to turn round. I can almost hear the sound of curtains twitching.

"Could we come in, Mrs. Appleford? Just for a moment? We can talk more easily inside."

The woman glances across the road; she's spotted the nosy neighbors too.

"OK. But only for a couple of minutes, all right?"

The sitting room is painted pale mauve, with a sofa and armchairs which are obviously supposed to match but the color's just far enough off to mess with your head. And they're much too big for the space. It never ceases to baffle me why people don't measure their rooms before they buy their furniture. There's a strong smell of artificial air freshener. Lavender. As if you had to ask.

She doesn't invite us to sit down, so we stand awkwardly on the narrow strip of carpet between the seats and the glass-topped coffee table.

"Was your daughter here last night, Mrs. Appleford?"

She nods.

"All night?"

"Yes. She didn't go out."

"So you saw her at breakfast?"

Another nod.

"What time was that?" asks Somer, slipping her notebook discreetly from her jacket.

The woman wraps her arms about herself. I'm trying not to draw conclusions from her body language, but she's not making it easy. "About 7:45, I think. I left with Nadine just before 8:00, but Faith had a later start today. She'd have left around 9:00 to get the bus."

So she doesn't actually *know* what her daughter did this morning. Just because something always happens, doesn't mean it always will.

"Nadine's your daughter too?" asks Somer.

The woman nods. "I drop her off at school on my way to work. I'm a receptionist at the doctor's in Summertown."

"And Faith?"

"She goes to the FE college in Headington. That's why she gets the bus. It's in the opposite direction."

"Did you have any contact with Faith during the day today?"

"I texted her about tennish but she didn't reply. It was

just a link to an article about Meghan Markle. You know, the wedding. The dress. Faith's interested in all that. She's doing Fashion. She has real talent."

"And that was unusual—that she didn't reply, I mean?"

The woman considers then shrugs. "I suppose so, yes."

My turn again. "Does she have a boyfriend?"

Her eyes narrow a little. "No. Not at the moment."

"But she would tell you—if she did?"

She gives me a sharp look. "She doesn't keep secrets from me, if that's what you're getting at."

"I'm sure she doesn't," says Somer, placatory. "We're just trying to work out who might have done this—if it could have been someone she knew—"

"She doesn't have a boyfriend. She doesn't *want* a boyfriend."

There's a silence.

Somer glances across at Ev. *Why don't you have a try.*

"Were you here," Ev says, "when the cabbie brought her back?"

The woman looks at her then nods. "I wouldn't be, normally. But I'd forgotten my reading glasses so I popped back."

Ev and Somer exchange another glance. I suspect I know what they're thinking: if Mrs. Appleford hadn't chanced to be at home the girl might well have tried to hide what happened from her as well. As for me, I'm more and more convinced Ev is right: there's definitely something off here.

I take a step closer. "Do you know why Faith has decided not to talk to us, Mrs. Appleford?"

She bridles. "She doesn't want to. That should be enough, shouldn't it?"

"But if she was raped—"

"She *wasn't* raped." Her tone is unequivocal. Absolute.

"How can you be so sure?"

Her face hardens. "She told me. Faith told me. And my *daughter* is not a *liar*."

"I'm not saying that. Not at all." She's not looking at me now. "Look, I know rape investigations can be traumatic—I wouldn't blame anyone for being daunted by that prospect—but it's not like it used to be. We have properly trained officers—DC Everett—"

"It wasn't rape."

"I'm very glad to hear it—but we may still be looking at a serious crime. Assault, Actual Bodily Harm—"

"How many more times? There was *no* crime and she is *not* going to press charges. So please, will you people just leave us alone?"

She looks round at us, one after the other. She wants us to start leaving, to say Faith can contact us if she changes her mind. But we don't. *I* don't.

"Your daughter was missing for over two hours," says Ev gently. "From 9:00 to just after 11:00, when Mr. Mullins saw her wandering along the Marston Ferry Road in a terrible state—crying, her clothes all muddy, her shoe broken. *Something* must have happened."

Mrs. Appleford flushes. "I gather it was an April Fool. Just a silly joke that got a bit out of hand."

But no one in the room believes that. Not even her.

"If it really was just a prank," I say eventually, "then I would like Faith herself to confirm that, please. But if it *wasn't*, the person who did this to Faith may do it again. Another girl could suffer the same trauma your daughter has just been through. I can't believe you'd want that. Either of you."

Mrs. Appleford holds my gaze. It's not exactly check-mate, but I want to make it damn hard for her to refuse.

"Faith is here at the moment, I assume?"

"Yes," she says at last. "She's out in the garden." For fresh air? For a smoke? Just to get away from all this damn purple? Frankly, I'm with her on all three.

Mrs. Appleford takes a deep breath. "Look, I'll go and ask if she wants to talk to you, but I'm not going to force it. If she says no, then that's her decision."

It's better than nothing.

"Fair enough. We'll wait here."

When the door's closed behind her I start to wander around the room. The pictures are Impressionists." Monet mostly. Ponds, water lilies, that sort of thing. Call me a cynic, but I suspect they were probably the only ones on offer in the right shade of mauve.

"I'd love to go to that place," says Ev, gesturing toward one of the bridge at Giverny. "It's on the bucket list if I win the lottery. And can find someone to go with." She makes a face. "Along with the Taj Mahal and Bora Bora, of course."

Somer looks up and smiles; she's by the mantelpiece, scrutinizing the family photos. "Mine too. The Bora Bora bit, anyway."

I see Ev give Somer a meaningful look that leaves her smiling again and glancing away when she sees I've noticed.

Ev turns to me. "I think it might be a good idea if I went looking for the loo. If you catch my drift."

I nod and she slips quickly out of the room, and almost at once there's the sound of footsteps in the hall and Diane Appleford reappears.

"She's prepared to talk—"

"Thank you."

"But only to a woman," she continues. "Not to *you*."

I look toward Somer, who nods. "It's fine with me, sir."

I return to the woman and adopt my most charming "only here to serve" smile. "I quite understand, Mrs. Appleford. I'll wait for my colleagues in the car."

* * *

Ev pauses at the top of the stairs. To her left, the bathroom door is open. White tiles, a heavy plastic shower curtain and a strong smell of bleach. The towels, she notices (neatly folded, unlike the ones in her own flat), are the same color as the mauve downstairs. It's starting to become a Thing.

Facing her are three more doors, two of them open. A master bedroom with a satin bedspread (no prizes for guessing the color), and what Ev decides must be the younger daughter's. A jumble of clothes and trainers left where they fell. A duvet carelessly dragged across, a scatter of soft toys, a makeup bag. She crosses as quietly as possible to the closed third door, giving silent thanks for the thickness of the carpet. She could never have anything like that in her flat—the cat would have it for breakfast. He loves "shreddies."

The room that opens before her is the polar opposite of the other sister's. Cupboards neatly closed, nothing escaping from the chests of drawers. Even the pile of *Grazia*s is neatly stacked. But that's not what Ev is looking at; it's not what anyone in this room would look at. The whole space is dominated by a pinboard stretching across the full length of the far wall, festooned from top to bottom with pictures cut from glossy magazines, little plastic bags of brightly colored beads and buttons, hanks of yarn, swatches of material, bits of lace and fake fur, notes written in thick red pen on Post-its and, in among it all, a scatter of sketches which must be by Faith herself. Everett's hardly the one to ask about clothes but even she can see the flair in some of these. How Faith has taken a small detail and made a whole outfit turn on it—the shape of a heel, the hang of a fabric, the fall of a sleeve.

"Her mother's right about one thing," she says softly, "she really does have talent."

"Who the hell," says a voice behind her, "are *you*?"

* * *

"This is Faith."

The girl moves forward past her mother, into the light. She is very lovely, Somer can see that at once. Even the tangled ponytail and the smeared mascara can't hide how exquisite her features are. She's as skinny as a rake too— the huge jumper she's wrapped around herself like a security blanket only emphasizes how thin she is. She must have had the jumper for years: there are holes in the wool and the cuffs are fraying.

Somer takes a step toward her. "Why don't you sit down? Is there anything you'd like—tea? Water?"

The girl hesitates a moment, then shakes her head. She moves slowly toward the sofa, feeling her way with one hand like an old woman.

Somer frowns. "Are you in pain?"

The girl shakes her head again. She still hasn't spoken.

Her mother sits down next to her and grasps her hand.

"My name is Erica," says Somer, taking the armchair opposite. "I know this is difficult, but we really are just trying to help."

The girl looks up briefly. There are tears still clinging to the clumps of her eyelashes.

"Can you tell us what happened to you?" says Somer gently. "The man who found you—Mr. Mullins—he says you were very upset."

Faith takes a deep, shuddering breath. The tears start to fall and she doesn't bother to wipe them away. Her mother grips her hand. "It's OK, darling. Take your time."

The girl glances at her and then drops her head again, pulling her hands into her sleeves. But not before Somer sees the grazes on her knuckles and the marks about her wrists. And though her nails are beautifully manicured, one of them is broken; a ragged spike that would draw blood if it caught her skin. She's been home for hours and she still hasn't filed it smooth. And that, more than anything else, with a girl as self-conscious as this, tells Somer something is badly wrong.

"Your mum said you're studying Fashion," she continues. "Is that what you want to do? Design clothes?"

The girl looks up at her. "Shoes," she says, her voice cracking a little. "I want to do shoes."

Somer grins. "They're my weakness too." She gestures at her boots. "As if you couldn't guess."

The girl doesn't exactly smile, but there's a sense of the tension easing. Even if only a little. And then she shivers suddenly. Even though the room is warm—too warm.

"I think," says Somer, turning to Mrs. Appleford, "that a cup of tea would actually be a good idea."

The woman frowns. "She said she didn't want any—"

"I've had a lot of experience in dealing with people in shock, Mrs. Appleford. Whatever it was that happened to your daughter, right now what she needs is hot tea with lots of sugar."

Diane Appleford hesitates, then turns to the girl. "Will you be OK here for five minutes?" she asks softly. "You can tell her to go whenever you want."

Faith nods quickly. "It's OK, Mum. Tea would be nice."

Somer waits until the woman is safely out of the room before speaking again. Faith sits rigidly on the edge of the seat, her hands clenched between her knees.

"You're lucky to have a mum who looks out for you like that," says Somer. "I wish mine had."

The girl looks up at her with a wan smile. "She worries about me, that's all."

"That's what mums are for."

Faith shrugs. "I guess."

"But sometimes that makes it harder to talk about things. Especially difficult things. Because the more our family love us, the harder it is to say something we know will upset them."

There's colour in the girl's face now, two red spots in her pale cheeks.

"So, Faith," says Somer, leaning forward a little, "while there's just the two of us, would you be able to tell me what happened to you?"

* * *

Ev turns sharply to find herself face-to-face with a girl with greasy dark hair and jeans with rips at the knees. A little shorter than Ev, a little heavier too. And without even thinking, the phrase that lodges in her mind is "no oil painting." Everett's own mother once said that about her, when she thought her daughter was out of earshot. Ev couldn't have been more than ten at the time. She'd never even thought about her looks before, but once the damage was done it was impossible to go back. She started to notice how people reacted to girls she knew were prettier than her. She started to worry about what she wore, to feel she mattered less because she looked worse. And here she is now, thinking the same about someone else. She feels herself start to go red, as if she said the thought out loud. Did she judge Faith the same way, without even realizing she was doing it?

The girl is still staring at her, her face surly.

"I'm sorry," Everett says quickly. "You're Nadine, right?"

The girl doesn't bother replying. "Did Faith say you could come in here? Don't you need a warrant or something to poke about in people's stuff?"

"I wasn't poking about—I came up for the loo and the door was open and—"

"No, it wasn't. She *never* leaves her room open. And I do mean *never*."

There's no answering that.

Nadine stands to one side and Everett makes her way past her, doubly embarrassed now. She's never been a very good liar.

* * *

Downstairs in the sitting room, Somer is on her feet, putting her notebook back inside her jacket. When she sees

25

Ev she gives a minute shake of the head. It seems the interview is over too.

Diane Appleford has her arm around her older daughter. "I only left her alone with you for five minutes and you start giving her the third degree."

"I wasn't," says Somer, "really, I wasn't—"

"I told you already," she continues, cutting across her, "Faith said she was not assaulted. And that's what she told you too, right?"

"Yes, but—"

Faith's cheeks are red and she's staring at the floor.

"In which case I'd like you to leave. All of you. I'm sure you have much more pressing things you should be doing. Like investigating some actual *crime*."

Nadine appears in the doorway.

"Darling, could you show the policewomen out?" says Diane. "They're leaving now."

As she passes Faith, Somer makes sure they make eye contact. "You know where I am. If you want to talk."

The girl bites her lip, then gives a tiny nod.

* * *

Out on the street Fawley is waiting by his car, looking at a piece of paper the size of a photograph. But when he sees them approaching, he hurriedly puts it away.

"I'm guessing from your faces that we're not much further forward."

Somer shakes her head. "Sorry, sir. I was just starting to get somewhere when the mother came back with the tea and decided I was being too 'intrusive.' Not sure how

26

I could have questioned her without being at least *mildly* intrusive, but there you are." She shrugs.

"But there was something, sir," says Everett. "Something Somer spotted."

Fawley raises an eyebrow and turns to Somer. "Oh yes?"

"It was as we were leaving," she says. "The girl's hair. She's in such a state I hadn't noticed before, but when we were on our own, I noticed she kept pulling at it. On the right-hand side. I can't be a hundred per cent sure but I think some of it is missing."

* * *

"So what do you want us to do?" says Baxter.

It's just gone two and Everett is briefing the rest of the team on the Appleford case. Or rather the Appleford incident, which is all it's ever going to be, unless and until we get a good deal more to go on. Which is pretty much what I say.

"There's not much we *can* do. Faith is claiming that it was all a misunderstanding. An April Fool's joke that got 'a bit out of hand.'"

"Pretty nasty April Fool," says Quinn darkly, folding his arms. "And doesn't yanking out someone's hair without their consent count as ABH these days?"

"It could have been cut," says Somer. "I couldn't really see."

I intervene. "Either way, Quinn is right: that's ABH. But we're still just guessing. Faith hasn't actually *said* that's what happened. And given she's also refusing to say which of her friends was responsible—"

"Pretty nasty friends too, if you ask me. To do something

like that." It's Quinn again. And I can't be the only one who's slightly wrong-footed by this sudden access of empathy on his part. I see Ev raise her eyebrows but thankfully no one actually says anything. I don't want this promising new development strangled at birth.

"Though it had to *be* a friend, didn't it?" says one of the other DCs. "I mean, you don't get an April Fool's played on you by a complete stranger, do you?"

"But you can be raped by one," says Asante quietly.

There's a silence, then Baxter repeats his question. Stolid first, last and in the middle. "So what do you want us to actually *do*?"

He's frowning, and to be honest, I sympathize. This could well end up being a colossal waste of time. On the other hand, what if it happens again—

"If a big case lands on us tomorrow, all bets are off, but in the meantime, I think it would be worth doing a bit of digging. *Discreet* digging. Let me be clear, Faith has done nothing wrong, and I don't want it to look like we're investigating the victim, but it's possible a crime's been committed and I don't want someone getting away with that just because Faith is too frightened to talk to us, OK? So let's start by talking to that minicab driver again— Mullins. Has he given a formal statement?"

"No, sir," says Somer. "But we have his details. We can give him a call."

"Good. And check the speed cameras along the Marston Ferry Road—see if we can work out where she came from and whether there was anyone with her before Mullins picked her up. And ask that petrol station on the roundabout for their CCTV."

"Someone may have dropped her off," observes Somer. "Mullins said the heel had come off one of her shoes. She can't have walked very far like that. Or very fast."

One of the DCs points at Somer's boots. "Been there, done that, eh, Somer?" he says, grinning.

I wait a moment for the laughter to subside. "And let's have a word with the FE college. See if we can identify any of Faith's friends. Or if she's been having problems with anyone."

"Girls that pretty aren't always popular," observes Ev.

"There could be a bloke in the mix," agrees Quinn. "Even if she really doesn't have a boyfriend, someone else's could have been showing too much interest. I mean, if she's as gorgeous as you lot say." He runs one hand through his hair. He probably doesn't even realize he's doing it, though needless to say it doesn't go unnoticed. Quinn always has put the "I" into "eye candy." Ev opens her mouth to say something, then with truly superhuman effort manages at the last minute not to. But I can see Somer grinning.

Baxter, meanwhile, still has his mind firmly on the job. "I can have a look at her online stuff too. Shouldn't be hard to track down who she hangs out with."

"Good—do that. Asante, can you talk to Mullins, and Somer, I want you and Quinn to pick up on the college end."

Somer looks concerned. "We'll have to be careful though—you know what those places are like. The way gossip gets round."

"I'm sure you'll think of something. Safety on the streets, if all else fails. And Somer—don't change before you go."

Her eyes widen. "OK, if you think it'll help."

I smile drily. "What I *think* is that it's a fair bet Faith's friends are studying Fashion too."

And if that doesn't work, there's always the not-so-subtle charms of Detective Constable Gareth Quinn.

* * *

The FE college reminds Somer of the school she taught at for a few months before joining the police. The same slab of concrete and glass, the same scuffed grass and plasticky shrubs, the same tired old cars that make Quinn's gleaming Audi look like a thoroughbred at a donkey derby. When they were still an item, Somer teased him once by playing that Shania Twain track about the guy who kisses his car goodnight, but wasn't at all surprised when he completely failed to see the joke. Right now, he's making a big show of parking next to a battered old Saab, and then takes an inordinate time locking up afterward. Somer can see the looks they're getting from the students, about evenly divided between the car (boys), and the driver (mostly girls, but not entirely). And that's no surprise either. Quinn is tall, athletic and very good-looking, and he exudes confidence and self-belief. Even now, and despite what a shit he was to her after they broke up, Somer can still see the attraction. Though to be fair, he did eventually manage something as close to an apology as he ever probably gets. She's heard rumors of a new girlfriend lately too.

Quinn finally finishes fiddling about with his car keys and walks around to join her.

"So how do you want to play this?"

"I was thinking about that. How about we start with

the principal to get the background, and if she's OK with it we can tell the students that we're here to talk about taking proper care on the streets. Like Fawley suggested."

Quinn makes a face. He likes Fawley, she knows that, and the DI's had his back more than once, but Quinn's nothing if not competitive and he'd much prefer to come up with an idea of his own. A better one. As if that needed saying.

"How about we ask her?" he says. "See if there's anything that's happened here recently that might justify CID turning up out of the blue. Drugs or something."

And she has to admit, that *is* actually a rather better idea. She looks around for a sign to the offices, but Quinn forestalls her.

"Don't worry," he says. "I'll ask someone."

Five minutes later she's following Quinn and a student up the stairs toward the principal's office. They're taking the stairs because that will take longer and the student Quinn asked for directions just happens to have long blond hair, a very short skirt and an apparently limitless readiness to be immensely impressed with anything Quinn says. He's already talked her through two murder cases Somer knows for a fact he barely worked on, but she's not about to rain on his charade. She just hopes the new girlfriend knows what she's letting herself in for.

* * *

Interview with Neil Mullins, conducted at
St. Aldate's Police Station, Oxford
1 April 2018, 4:15 p.m.
In attendance, DC A. Asante

31

AA: Thank you for coming in, Mr. Mullins.
    Hopefully this shouldn't take too long.

NM: It's OK. It's on my way home anyway. How is
    she—the girl?

AA: She's very shaken up. We're still trying to
    find out exactly what happened. That's why
    we wanted to talk to you again. See if you
    remember anything else. Something you might
    not have mentioned before.

NM: Not as far as I know. It was like I said on
    the phone: I saw her walking ahead of me
    on the side of the road. Well, not so much
    walking—staggering really. That's why
    I thought she was drunk.

AA: She had her back to you?

NM: Right. I was heading towards Marston and she was
    near the turn for that pub—the Victoria Arms.

AA: That's a long way from any houses, isn't it?
    Didn't that seem odd to you?

NM: Yeah. I suppose it did. That's why I slowed
    down. That's when I noticed.

AA: Noticed what?

NM: The state she was in. Crying—makeup all over
    her face, clothes all torn. I thought she was
    bleeding to start with but I realized after
    that it was just mud. It was all over the
    bloody car.

AA: What was she wearing?

NM: Don't you collect people's clothes after
    something like this? They always do that on
    the telly.

AA: It's just for the records, Mr. Mullins. You
    know what it's like.
NM: Tell me about it. I used to spend half my life
    on bloody paperwork—that's why I switched to
    the cabs—
AA: The clothes, Mr. Mullins?
NM: Yeah, right. Sorry. Some sort of blue jacket.
    Denim, I think. A white top underneath but
    I couldn't really see much of that. Those
    sandal things, like I said. And a short
    black skirt.
AA: Did she have a handbag—any sort of bag?
NM: No. Definitely no bag.
AA: What happened when you stopped?
NM: I leant across and asked her if she was OK—if
    she needed any help. Pretty bloody stupid
    question—I mean, of course she wasn't OK—
AA: What did she say?
NM: She sort of staggered towards me and asked
    if I could take her home.
AA: But she didn't mind getting into your car?
    She wasn't frightened of you?
NM: I suppose it being a cab and all that, she
    thought it was OK. And to be honest I think
    she was more concerned about getting the hell
    out of there. Though she wouldn't get in the
    front with me—she'd only sit in the back. And
    she had the window wound all the way down
    even though it was bloody freezing.
AA: So she could call for help if she needed to?
NM: I suppose so. I hadn't really thought about it.

AA: Did she say anything at all about what
    happened?

NM: No. I mean, I didn't like to—you know—be too
    pushy. I said I was taking her straight
    to the cop shop and she started panicking and
    saying no, she didn't want anything to do
    with the police, and then I said the JR then,
    but she didn't want the hospital either. So I
    just took her where she said she wanted
    to go.

AA: Rydal Way?

NM: Right. I thought afterwards that it must have
    been why she was walking that way. She was
    trying to get home.

AA: And was there anyone there when you got there?
    Anyone in the house?

NM: Dunno. She went round the back.

AA: You didn't mention that before.

NM: Sorry. I didn't think it was important.

AA: You said before that she didn't have a bag
    with her. Could she have had her keys in her
    pocket?

NM: I suppose so, I didn't really think about it.

AA: But you definitely think she was able to
    get in?

NM: Oh yeah. She said she could go and get me
    some money if I waited but I said it was fine.
    She didn't need to pay. She was crying,
    when she got out. Poor little cow.

* * *

Sasha Blake puts down her pen and closes her notebook. She's sitting cross-legged on her bed, music on low in the background. The pen has a feather on the end and the notebook is pale blue, with a scatter of white flowers across the front. She likes the sheen of the pages, the feel of the book in her hand, but the real reason she chose it was because it's small enough to fit in her bag. She knows better than to leave it lying about anywhere, that's for sure. She loves her mum, she really does, and she knows she wouldn't snoop deliberately, but no mother has the sort of willpower you would need to stumble across a book like this and not read what's inside. Isabel gets around it by using code, and Patsie sticks everything on her phone, but Sasha likes being able to write things down. It makes it easier to demuddle her thoughts—helps her work through what to do. But her mum wouldn't get that. She'd think everything in the book was true. And it is, in a way. Just not the way her mum would understand.

There's a noise from downstairs now and Sasha quickly leans over and slides the notebook into the pocket of her pink satchel, then sits back against the headboard and picks up her copy of Keats.

"You OK, Sash?" asks her mum, pushing the door open, her arms full of ironing.

Sasha looks up. "I'm fine, just chillin' with my homeboy."

Fiona Blake smiles. "Don't work too hard. You're allowed to enjoy yourself as well, you know."

She shunts the laundry on to the top of the chest of drawers and pulls the door to behind her as she leaves. Sasha opens the book again. *"Awake for ever in a sweet unrest,*

Still, still to hear her tender-taken breath." She sighs. Imagine having someone talk to you like that.

* * *

"So, you can see why we're concerned."

Somer sits back in her chair. The principal of the college hasn't said a word throughout Somer's entire account. She's just sat there, frowning, fidgeting with an elastic band, staring out of the window. Outside, the sky is darkening. It looks like rain and Somer curses to herself. She has no coat, no umbrella and entirely the wrong footwear.

The principal still hasn't said anything. Somer glances at Quinn, who shrugs.

"Mrs. McKenna?" she says, raising her voice slightly. "Is there anything we ought to be aware of? Do you know if Faith has been having problems with any of her fellow students recently?"

The woman turns to face her. "No. Nothing I know of. Faith is very popular with her peer group."

"Do you know who might have played this April Fool joke on her? Do any names come to mind?"

Another, deeper frown. "I hope you're not suggesting that one of our students might be responsible for this—"

"Not at all. But we do know Faith's family only moved here last summer, so she may not have that many friends outside her college circle."

McKenna starts fiddling with the elastic band again. Somer's a hair'sbreadth from leaning over and grabbing it out of her hand.

"Mrs. McKenna? It's quite urgent—"

The principal turns to her suddenly and leans forward. It's like a switch has flicked. She's sharp, attentive, brisk.

"I'm afraid I can't tell you anything about Faith's personal life or what she does outside the college gates. I *can* tell you that she is a talented and hard-working student, and I fully expect she will make a great success of her career."

"But she does have mates, right?" Quinn now. "You must have *some* idea who they are." His tone is short of sarcasm, but only just.

"You want to interrogate my students?" The frown is back.

"Not *interrogate*, no," says Somer quickly. "We were hoping to make it much more informal. Just circulate with the group and get a sense of whether there might be undercurrents—any sense of animosity—"

McKenna raises her eyebrows. "In that case, I dare say I can't stop you. But I would ask you to exercise more discretion than the police are habitually famed for."

"Have there been any incidents lately that might make our presence here rather more plausible? Any problems with alcohol?"

"No."

"Or drugs?"

"Absolutely not."

Somer senses Quinn's reaction but doesn't dare to look at him.

"OK," she says evenly. "In that case we'll just make it something general about personal safety."

"Good idea," says McKenna crisply. "I've had two of my female students in here this week already because they thought they were being followed on the Iffley Road. It's a sad reflection on your constabulary that you see these

37

issues only as a useful smokescreen for something else you evidently consider *far* more important."

"Who the fuck does she think she is?" mutters Quinn, none too quietly, as they make their way down the stairs five minutes later. "Talk about bloody chippy—she's just the head of a poxy FE college and you'd think she was the sodding Master of Balliol."

Who is, in fact, a woman. But Somer isn't about to point that out.

* * *

"You should change those," says Baxter. "It's not a good idea to sit around with wet feet."

Somer looks down. If her boots aren't completely ruined after the monsoon that hit just as she and Quinn were crossing the FE college car park, it will be a minor miracle. Her jeans are wet through up to the knees and she's given up on her hair.

"Seriously," continues Baxter. "If you're harboring any sort of latent cold virus—"

"It's OK," she says quickly. "Really. I'm more interested in what you've found."

He gives her a look heavy with "well don't come crying to me," then turns back to his screen.

"Well, for starters, Faith Appleford does a fashion vlog every couple of weeks or so. *You Gotta Have*, she calls it."

Somer smiles. "Clever."

Baxter frowns. "Come again?"

"You know—'You gotta have faith.' Like the George Michael song."

Baxter is still looking blank.

"Forget it. Go on."

"Right. OK. So she started it last autumn, presumably when her course began. It's pretty damn professional, actually. Technically, I mean. Here," he says, turning to the screen, "have a look."

yougottahave

155 posts   **19.5k followers**   **324 following**

F A I T H Fashion | Beauty | Style
Sharing the passion, learning to love myself

Posted 18.46 06 February 2018

Headshot, interior, direct to cam

Hi, everyone, welcome to my channel about fashion, beauty and style. Lots of people have been asking me about how I create my own look. Basically how I choose what things to put together. Not just the clothes but bags and shoes and all the rest of it, because we all know the details can really make the difference between looking good and looking great. So that's what I'm going to be talking about today.

Everyone always tells me they can't believe that most of the things I wear are just from mainstream stores, but I always tell them it's not about how much you spend, it's about being really smart about what you pick.

Full-length view, by clothes rail

I always start with what I call the "key piece." What do I mean by that? Well, it's easy: the key piece is the thing you build your look around. It might be a fabulous pair of shoes like these [*holds up shoes*].

Headshot, selection of shoes in foreground

These are my favorites for going out in the evening—they're from Irregular Choice and they are just gorgeous—fabulous color and *really* distinctive with all this lovely silver detailing. And yes, they took up a pretty big chunk of my budget but they're going to last for ages and they give me a "signature look" for the whole of the rest of the outfit.

Full-length with dress on hanger

OK, so this is what I mean. This dress is from Zara, and I got it a couple of months ago for £39.99. I really like the cut of it and the fabric is quite nice given it's pretty cheap. It's basically a standard LBD, though with a bit of a twist with these pleats here at the back.

Full-length, modeling dress and shoes

So now you can see what it looks like on. See—those pleats have a great swing to them when you move. And when you add the shoes you can see it's really starting to come together. The silver on the shoes picks up the silver bits on the neckline, and makes the whole thing look way more classy. And if there's one thing that *never* goes out of fashion, it's class.

Full-length, modeling dress, shoes and accessories

And finally accessories. You've heard me say this a *lot*, I know, but this is *so* important. I really love this bag—I got it from ASOS and I've had it ages. I specially love these tassels, and the strap can be detached if you want to use it as a clutch. The earrings are from Accessorize and they're tassels too. Cool, right? And as you probably know, when it comes to jewelry I think less really is more, which is why I haven't put a necklace with this look—with the silver on the neckline, a necklace as well would be too much and probably look a bit blingy, you know?

Headshot, as per opening sequence

So, that's it for today. Hope you liked this video, and next time I'll show you how I did the makeup I wore today. And if you haven't already, do please subscribe to my channel.

This is Faith, signing off the same way I always do: Look good, be kind and love who *you* are.

"See what I mean?" says Baxter as he presses pause.

Somer nods; and it's not just the technical presentation she's impressed with. This girl has more poise than most people twice her age. "What about her more personal stuff? Social media? Friends—boyfriends? Frenemies?"

Baxter shakes his head. "No bloke that I can find. She does a lot on Instagram but it's all just snazzy pictures and hundreds of bloody hashtags."

Somer smiles to herself at the thought of Baxter staring at shot after shot of on-trend shoes and brow tattoo products. She can't even remember the last time she heard anyone use the word "snazzy."

Meanwhile Baxter is still talking. "But she doesn't appear to be on Twitter at all and the Facebook account has barely been used. Seems she's more into broadcast than dialogue."

Somer nods. "That's the impression we got at the college too. Everyone knows her but no one knows her very well. One of the girls described her as 'nice but really really private.' I just can't see her pissing anyone off enough for them to play a joke on her—especially one as elaborate and cruel as that."

Baxter's face is grave. "If it actually *was* just a joke. Sounded a lot worse than that to me."

Somer nods. "I know."

"But if it really was a sexual assault, why the hell won't she report it?"

Somer sighs. "She wouldn't be the first. Not by a long way."

They sit there a moment, staring at the girl's face on the screen. Faith is frozen mid-smile, confident, happy, self-assured. She's barely recognizable as the girl Somer saw earlier.

"There was one thing I found a bit odd," says Baxter eventually.

"Oh yes?"

"All Faith's social media—the Instagram, the Facebook account—none of it goes back further than last year."

Somer glances across at him. "Nothing before that? Couldn't she just have deleted the old ones and started again?"

Baxter shakes his head. "I don't think so. I can't find anything."

Somer frowns; this doesn't feel right. "And why would she want to do that anyway?"

He shrugs. "Search me. But what do I know about teenagers?"

Somer turns back to the screen. The video must have been filmed in Faith's bedroom. Somer can see the pin-board Ev told her about, and underneath it a white side table with makeup bags and toiletries, and half-a-dozen framed photographs.

"Can you enlarge those?" she says suddenly.

Baxter flicks her a quizzical glance but says nothing. He taps the keyboard and the photos fill the screen.

"It's just a bunch of old family snaps," he says, sitting back again. "Faith isn't even in them."

But Somer is on the edge of her seat, staring, and when she turns back to Baxter her eyes are bright.

"Exactly," she says. "She's *not in them*."

*   *   *

Sasha is lying on her back on the bed, staring at the ceiling. Years ago, when she was little, her mum stuck little silver stars all over it that glow in the dark. And her mum being her mum, she didn't just stick them up any old how, she did proper constellations—the Great Bear and Cassiopeia and the Pleiades. She got the idea from some TV program about Grand Central Station. Some of the stars have fallen off over the years, and these days Orion has to manage without a head, but Sasha still loves it. She's promised herself that she'll go to New York one day and see the real thing. It's on her list, in the back of her notebook, along with—

Her phone pings and she rolls over and picks it up from the floor. Patsie. A selfie with her poking two fingers toward her mouth, then a photo of a saucepan full of diced carrot.

Sasha types *Gross* and gets a string of green puking-face emojis in reply.

Are you back in school tomorrow? she writes.

The text pings back at once *If I can b arsed. Rather watch the telly.* There's a photo underneath of her feet propped up on a cushion in fluffy slippers. In the background the *Jeremy Kyle Show* is on the TV. A burly security guard is trying to keep two teenage girls from scratching each other's eyes out. The subtitle at the bottom says, "You slept with my boyfriend and I'm going to prove it!"

Look at those stupid mares, writes Patsie.

Sasha laughs and texts back, *WTAF?*

There's a pause then, and Sasha thinks Patsie must have tuned out until suddenly there's another text. *Bloody Lee's here*, it says. *Prancing about showing his rancid tits again.* There's another line of puking emojis. *I wish Mum would just wake up and dump that loser.*

Sasha frowns. *You on your own?*

Mum shd b back soon.

Don't know what she sees in that perv, writes Sasha. *Sure you're OK Pats?*

There's a kissing emoji now, then *Awww U R the best. I told him to fuck right off. See ya tomorrow babe Xxx.*

The stars above Sasha's head are just starting to glow and she gets up and goes over to close the curtains. There's a white van parked up on the opposite side of the road. A man is sitting inside, but Sasha can't see his face.

* * *

"Do you see what I mean?" says Somer. "Faith's not in any of these photos, and she wasn't in any of the ones I saw in the Applefords' sitting room either."

Baxter is frowning. "So?"

"There were a couple of the mother, and some of a little girl with dark hair, but that's definitely Nadine, not Faith."

"Still not sure what you're getting at. Perhaps she just doesn't like pictures of herself. Some people don't. Especially bloody baby photos. Mine just make me look like Shrek."

Somer suppresses a smile. "But there might be a reason why she doesn't have any pictures. What if she's adopted?"

He shrugs. "But even if she is, what difference does it make? No one's going to attack her because of that—"

"Can you pull up the General Records Office database?"

Baxter gives a heavy sigh but he's seen that look on Somer's face before. When she's in this mood it's best to just let her get on with it.

He taps the keyboard and a new screen opens. He turns to Somer.

"So, what do you want to know?"

"Can we look up Faith's birth certificate? She's eighteen so she must have been born in '99 or 2000."

Baxter clicks through the search facility, then frowns.

"What? What is it?"

He points at the screen. "That can't be right. Can it?"

But Somer is nodding. "I think it can. In fact, I think it might explain everything."

*   *   *

It's gone 11:00 when Everett gets the email from Somer, telling her what they found. And only because she forgot to turn off the phone before she collapsed into bed. The beep and flash of light has her wide awake and seizing the phone before she's even conscious she's doing it. At the end of the bed, the cat stirs and resettles. Everett can feel her heart pounding as she unlocks the phone and peers at the screen. It can't be good for your health to be jolted bolt upright like this.

Then she lies back down again, staring at a ceiling she

can't see. Her heart is still pounding and, this time, being woken up in the middle of the night has nothing to do with it.

* * *

Adam Fawley
1 April 2018
23.07

I'm stacking the dishwasher when my mobile goes. Somer. And she doesn't even bother apologizing. And that, take it from me, is not like her at all.

"I'm emailing you something, sir. Can you call me when you get it?"

"What is it?"

"It's a birth certificate. From 1999."

The line goes dead. And then the phone pings.

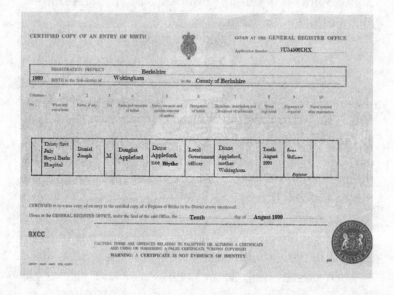

46

"Problem?" says Alex, seeing the look on my face.

"I'm not sure."

But I don't like it. And when I see what Somer's sent me I like it even less.

"Please tell me this isn't what I think it is."

I hear Somer sigh. "I wish I could."

"And you're sure? There's no chance we got this wrong?"

"We double-checked. The Applefords only have one other child. Nadine, born 6th June 2002."

"So Faith isn't their daughter. She's their son."

"That's not how she would see it, sir. I mean, yes, that's what's on the birth certificate, but I think Faith would say she was always a girl inside."

And, of course, everything now falls into place. Why she didn't want to be examined by a doctor. Why she didn't want to talk to us—why she didn't even want to report what had happened to her. Why her mother is being so protective. It may even explain why the Applefords moved here in the first place. It was a fresh start; a chance for Daniel to leave his old identity behind and begin a new life. As a girl.

"There's no record of a change of name—no application for a Gender Recognition Certificate?"

"No, sir."

"So legally speaking, Faith is still Daniel."

"Quite possibly. Which would mean she probably had to apply to the college in that name. I think that's why the principal was so cagey. She told us she 'couldn't tell us anything' about Faith's personal life. We assumed that meant she didn't *know* anything, but looking back now, I think she chose that phrase very carefully."

I take a deep breath. Alex has gone back to the sitting room. I can hear the sounds of the TV, the rain on the glass lantern above my head. I know what I have to do; I'm just not looking forward to doing it.

"OK, Somer. Leave it with me. I'll call Harrison and tell him we want to escalate this. To a possible hate crime."

*   *   *

> Hey did anyone see Faith today? She wasn't in class and I don't think I saw her all day. Bit worried given the police were here

>> No I didn't c her. Try Jess? They're sort of m8s aren't they?

> I tried her already but she said no. Have you got her mobile no?

>> No sorry. Perhaps try through the Insta acct?

> Good idea. I'll try. It's weirding me out that noone saw her.

*   *   *

It's late, but there's no way Somer is getting to sleep any time soon. She picks up her phone and hesitates, wondering if

48

she'll wake him. But she knows he doesn't go to bed early and, right now, she'd really like to hear his voice.

He picks up at the second ring: he wasn't asleep.

"Hey, I was hoping you'd call. How's it going?"

"The case? Better, I think. We may have made a breakthrough."

"You have—or *you* have?"

She smiles; he's good at that: making her own up to her own achievements. It never comes naturally to her, not even now.

"You're not too shabby at this detective lark, are you?"

He laughs; he has a good laugh. "Well, I think I may have inside info on this particular suspect."

She sits back in her chair and draws her feet up under her; she can hear the faint murmur of voices in the background.

"You watching TV?" She isn't really interested—she just wants to talk. About anything, nothing.

"Uh-huh."

No need to ask what. For a DI with over ten years' experience Giles has an endearing addiction to true crime. TV, books, podcasts, you name it, he does it, as the recordings now racking up in Somer's Sky box testify. And she gets it—up to a point. She watched *The Staircase* with him and it was completely riveting, but Giles runs through the whole range, all the way from serious documentary to things like *Wives with Knives* and *Southern Fried Homicide*, which she'd initially assumed had to be spoofs. But as far as Giles is concerned, it's all equally fascinating. "Helps me understand why," he'd said, when she quizzed him. "Why, after ten thousand years of human evolution, we're still doing such appallingly shitty things to each other."

"How was your day?"

She can hear him stretch now. "OK. Not exactly exciting."

"Have you heard from the girls about the summer?"

Saumarez has two daughters who live with their mother in Vancouver. Somer hasn't met them, but they're due over for the long school holidays. She's been trying not to let the prospect completely freak her out.

"Still waiting for confirmation on the flights."

She tries to think of something to say, but the long day is taking its toll.

"It'll be OK," he says, reading into her silence. "Really. They're nice kids. They just want me to be happy."

And you make me so.

He doesn't say it, but perhaps he doesn't need to.

"Can't wait to meet them," she says, realizing, suddenly, and with a jolt of happy amazement, that she actually means it.

* * *

Adam Fawley
2 April 2018
09.15

There are different types of silence, in this job. There's the silence of anger and impotence, when we have absolute knowledge but absolutely no evidence and can't do a damn thing about it. There's the silence of pity, at the terrible things people go through, even—or especially—at the hands of those who are supposed to love them. And there's the silence of failure and regret, when we've done everything we can but it just isn't enough. But when Somer pins up the copy of Faith's birth certificate it's a different sort of silence entirely. You can almost smell the dread. At where this might go, what it might turn out to be.

"So you think it could be a hate crime?" says Gislingham, turning to me.

I nod. "I hope not, but yes. It has to be a possibility."

Everett is looking uneasy. "But she's still insisting she wasn't attacked. How can we even start investigating it properly if she won't tell us what actually happened?"

"We'll just have to hope she changes her mind," observes Baxter, who appears to be taking over Gis's old role as Principal Stater of the Bleeding Obvious.

There's another silence. A silence of evaluation. Of deliberation.

"So how do you want us to play it?" Quinn now.

I take a deep breath. "We start by re-interviewing Faith. Formally, this time, and as a matter of urgency. I'm sure I don't need to remind you that this needs to be handled extremely carefully, but there's no getting away from it: we need to know who else besides her family knows about her status."

"I can check her social media again," says Baxter. "See if there's anything online—if she's logging on to any discussion boards for trans kids. Nothing popped the first time but I wasn't exactly looking for it."

"That's an excellent idea, Baxter," says Gis, who's clearly putting his recent "Giving Feedback" session to good use ("be positive, use their name"; I should know, I was sent on that damn course myself).

"Yes, I agree," I say. "And let's see if we can track down the father as well."

Gis nods and makes a note.

I glance around again. There's only one person who hasn't said anything.

"Any thoughts, DC Asante?"

He considers, and he takes his time doing it. Evidently he, at least, isn't afraid of silence.

"No," he says eventually. "I think we've covered everything."

* * *

Everett and Somer are in the car, across the road from 36 Rydal Way. There's no sign of life inside. The postman knocked five minutes ago but no one answered. They can still see him, a few doors along, talking to an elderly woman with a chihuahua barking tetchily in the crook of her arm. Somer makes a face; her grandmother had one of those when she was a child. She's hated crabby little dogs ever since.

She looks at her watch. "The college said Faith had called in sick, so she should be here. And surely the mother must have left for work by now."

"And taken the delightful Nadine with her," says Ev heavily. She pushes open the car door. "So let's just cross our fingers we have more luck than the postie."

The two women walk up the path to the front door. The street is now completely deserted, apart from a couple of jackdaws scrapping over some raw and unidentifiable roadkill. It's not the happiest of omens.

Ev rings and waits. Then rings again, longer this time. "I can't hear anything."

"Give it a minute," says Somer. "She's probably trying to see who it is. I would be, if I was her."

And sure enough, they eventually hear the sound of footsteps inside, and the door opens. But slowly and not very far.

"What do you want?" Her face is scrubbed clean now, but there are still red rims around her eyes. She has the same ragged old jumper wound about her like a straitjacket. "Mum's not here."

"It's you we wanted to talk to, Faith," says Somer. "On your own, if that's OK. It's quite important."

"Doesn't Mum have to be with me?"

Ev shakes her head. "You don't need anyone with you unless you want them to be. You're a victim. Not a criminal. You haven't done anything wrong."

She leans on those last words, trying to get the girl to meet her gaze. *We're on your side—we want to help.*

"We can do this whichever way makes you feel more comfortable," says Somer. "At the station with your mum or someone else you trust, or here, with just us. We thought that might be easier, but seriously, it's entirely your call. We'll do whatever you prefer."

Faith hesitates. "I told you—it was just a bad joke." But her eyes are wary all the same. Because she can see something in their faces; something that wasn't there before.

Somer steps forward. "We know, Faith," she says softly. "We know about you—about Daniel."

The girl bites her lip and her eyes fill with tears. "It's so unfair," she whispers. "I never did anyone any harm—"

"I'm sorry," says Somer, reaching out and touching her lightly on the arm. "I wouldn't have brought it up if I didn't have to. But you can see why we're worried. What you do with your own life is no one else's business and we're absolutely with you on that. But we don't want this to happen to another girl. Someone else in your position. Something like this—it's not OK. Even if it was 'just a joke.' And if it wasn't—"

She leaves the sentence unfinished. She knows the power of silence. Silence in a good cause.

The girl takes a deep breath and blinks the tears away. "OK," she says at last. "OK."

* * *

Tony Asante is in a café on Little Clarendon Street. One of those achingly trendy places with displays of muffins and shiny cakes and sourdough bread. The place is packed, and a couple of students taking up space with laptops are getting side-eyes from people in the queue. As is Asante, though he's too absorbed to notice: the cup of coffee in front of him is long since empty, but he's still sitting there, staring at his phone, switching every minute or so between different web pages. Baxter may have been the one assigned to social media, but he won't be doing what Asante is doing. Or going where Asante has gone.

* * *

Faith takes the two women through to the kitchen at the back of the house. Ev had been steeling herself for yet

54

more mauve but it proves to be just anonymous cream cupboards and worktops that look like granite but probably aren't. The fridge is barnacled with Post-its and to-do lists and jolly little magnets. A woolly sheep, an enamel cat, three ducks in formation; a large pink heart saying *Daughters start as your babies but grow up to be your friends*, and another, square and yellow with a sprig of daffodils, *Just be yourself. That's plenty wonderful enough.*

Somer feels her throat tightening. Diane Appleford might be prickly and defensive with the police but when it comes to her kids her heart is definitely in the right place. She's going to support her children, whoever they turn out to be. And Somer wonders suddenly if her husband wasn't, in the end, able to do the same—and whether that's the reason he's no longer around.

"You want tea?" she asks, moving toward the kettle. "Coffee?"

Faith shakes her head but Everett indicates yes. She'd have done the same even if she'd had four cups already and was wired with caffeine: it's not about the drink, it's about the domesticity. The reassurance of routine. There's only instant in the cupboard but the aroma fills the small room. Not for the first time, Somer wonders why it always manages to smell better than it tastes.

She pulls out one of the stools at the breakfast bar and slides Ev's mug across to her. They're waiting to see if Faith speaks first—they want her to feel she's in control.

"So," begins Everett, having strung out the process of sugar and milk (neither of which she takes) as long as humanly feasible.

"I'll talk to you," says Faith at last. "But I don't want any of it coming out. In public, I mean. About me. Who I am."

The two women exchange a glance. They know the perils of a promise like that. Especially if this is a hate crime. Somer takes a deep breath and makes a decision.

"Until we know *who* did this we won't know *why*. If he did it because of your status, then we'll have to charge him with that offense and it'll be almost impossible to keep your name out of it entirely."

Faith starts to shake her head but Somer plunges on. "*But* if he attacked you because you're a beautiful girl—and *you are*—then that's different. Either way, I *promise* you I will do everything I possibly can to protect your privacy."

She reaches out for Faith's hand, forces her to look up, to believe her. Their eyes meet and slowly the girl sits up a bit straighter and lifts her chin.

"OK. What do you want to know?" she says.

"Why don't you start at the beginning?" says Somer. "You had breakfast with your mum and sister then left for college? Let's start from there."

Faith takes a deep breath. "I left the house at 9:00 and walked down towards the bus stop on Cherwell Drive. That's where it happened."

"Someone took you—abducted you? Is that what you're saying?"

Her head drops and she nods.

"It's usually quite busy along there at that time of the day, isn't it?" says Ev. She makes it a question, hoping it sounds less confrontational like that, but there's no getting away from the fact that Rydal Way is a rat run and no one reported any sort of incident along there that morning. The idea that a young girl could have been snatched off a busy cut-through in the middle of the rush hour and no one saw anything—

Faith looks up briefly. "It had just started raining. Really hard."

Which could—just about—explain it. The road is suddenly awash, windows get steamed up, drivers concentrate more on where they're going and less on what's around them.

"I'd stopped to get out my umbrella," says Faith. "I'd propped my bag up on a wall to look for it. That's when it happened. Someone put a plastic bag over my head and started dragging me backwards. I tried to fight them off but they jabbed something in my back. Something sharp. I thought it was a knife."

"You didn't see his face?" asks Somer, keeping her voice steady. It's her own personal wake-at-dawn terror. Not being able to breathe, not being able to see. "No one went past just before? No one was hanging around?"

"I had my earphones in, so I wasn't really concentrating."

"And then what happened?"

"He started dragging me round the back towards the garages. I couldn't see but I could tell—it's all gravelly in there—it's different to the pavement."

"The garages?" asks Ev.

"Yeah, you know, at the bottom of the road."

And Ev does know, now she thinks about it. You hardly ever see that sort of thing any more, but Rydal Way has a separate area for garages just before the junction with Cherwell Drive. And now Faith's story is starting to make more sense: if the attacker was lying in wait around there he wouldn't have been visible from the street and it would have taken only a few seconds to bundle Faith out of sight.

"And then he shoved me against the van and I heard him open the door."

"He had a van?"

Faith nods. "Oh yeah, he had a van."

"What happened next?"

"He pushed me forward and I fell into the back. That's when he tied up my hands."

"In front or behind your back?"

"In front."

"And you're sure it was a van? It couldn't have been an SUV? Some other sort of car that opens at the back?"

Faith shakes her head. "I never saw it but it was too low for an SUV. And it wasn't that big. When we went round the corners I got thrown against the side. There was some sort of plastic on the floor—I could feel it sticking to me."

Somer nods and makes a note. However traumatic it was to get to this point, now Faith has made up her mind she's proving to be a surprisingly good witness. Accurate, observant, attentive to detail.

She's playing with her necklace now; the one that bears her name.

"Just now you said 'they,'" says Somer. "And then you said 'he.' Is it possible there was more than one person?"

Faith shrugs. "I don't think so. I'm not sure."

"But no one spoke to you—you never heard any voices?"

She shakes her head. "The whole time, he never spoke. He never said a single word."

* * *

58

I'm halfway home when I get the call. I curse under my breath when I see who it is. I promised Alex I'd be there to meet the health visitor, but I was rather hoping to get back to the office before any of the team realized I was AWOL. Some hope, clearly.

The line is breaking up but I can still just about hear.

"Sir? It's Tony Asante."

I could have guessed it'd be him. He's been with us a few months now and thus far I can't fault him. Diligent, intelligent, technically excellent. He does what he's asked and he takes the initiative when he should. And yet there's something about him I just can't get a handle on, and I don't think the rest of the team can either. Every time I think I have him worked out, he manages to wrong-foot me. It's almost as if he's playing a role; going through the motions. As if his real agenda is elsewhere. Alex says he's probably just extremely ambitious and not very good at hiding it, and I suspect she has a point. It would certainly explain why Quinn has taken such an obvious dislike, and let's face it, he's not that good at hiding it either. But unlike Quinn, Asante seems to get on better with the women on the team than the men, which still isn't that common in this job. Perhaps it's just that, like them, he knows what it's like being in the minority.

"What is it, Asante?"

"Sorry to bother you, sir. I think I've found something."

I frown slightly. "What—Douglas Appleford, you mean? You've tracked him down?"

A slight pause. Embarrassment or calculation?

"No. It's not that. Look—it'd be easier to explain face-to-face. I could come to you if you're off-site."

Of course I'm bloody well "off-site." He wouldn't be calling me otherwise.

I can hear the sound of traffic in the background; he must be on the street somewhere.

"I'm not in the office. I had to go home. Briefly."

"That's Risinghurst, right? I can come there."

I don't know why him knowing that annoys me, but it does. It's not as if people from the office haven't been to the house before. But not that often. And not since Alex has been pregnant.

"I'll only be an hour or so. Can't it wait till I get back?"

I hear the intake of breath. "Actually, sir, I don't think it can."

* * *

"We drove off really fast. Not for long though—just a few minutes. Then we stopped again and he dragged me out of the back. First we were on something hard and then on grass—it was uneven and all squishy in the rain. I could feel my feet getting wet. And then he pushed me inside somewhere and I heard a door shut and it went dark."

"It must have been completely terrifying," says Somer softly.

Faith looks down, her lips trembling. "I thought he was going to kill me."

There are tears spilling down her cheeks, and Somer reaches across the table and takes the girl's hands in her own. "You are being *incredibly* brave. Not much more, I promise."

Faith takes a deep breath. "He pushed me on the floor. On my back. It was cold. Gritty. Then I felt him pulling my skirt up. I was screaming and kicking but he grabbed hold of my legs and held them down while he dragged off my knickers."

The tears are falling fast now and her cheeks are red.

The two women exchange a glance. It's what they feared. And they have no choice: they have to press her.

"Faith," says Somer gently, "I'm about to ask you something very sensitive. Very personal. I'm sorry I have to ask, and please believe me that I wouldn't if it wasn't absolutely necessary."

There's a pause; she holds the girl's hands a little tighter. "Can you tell me—have you had gender reassignment surgery?"

Faith isn't looking at them. She shakes her head. "Not yet. Later, maybe."

"Do you think the person who did this—do you think it's possible he knew?"

Faith looks up at them now. Her eyes widen. "You mean, was he *surprised*? You're actually *asking* me that?"

Somer feels her face flush hot. "I'm so sorry, Faith—I didn't mean that to sound as crass as it did. But you know why I'm asking—it would make a difference. To what sort of crime it was. To how we narrow down who might have done it."

Faith wipes her tears away with the back of her hand. They wait, give her time. Somer can hear barking, somewhere outside. High-pitched. Petulant. Probably that bloody chihuahua again.

"Who else knows you're transgender, Faith?" says Everett at last. "Apart from your family?"

Her voice breaks a little. "No one here. I haven't told anybody."

"Not even your friends? Your best friend?"

She looks away. "I don't want people looking at me and seeing a boy dressed as a girl. Staring at me trying to work out which bits give it away. I want them to see *me*."

"What about where you used to live. Basingstoke, wasn't it? Did you keep in touch with anyone there?"

She shrugs. "I wanted to start again. Leave all that crap behind."

She doesn't need to explain: both women can imagine what it must have been like.

Faith is fiddling with her necklace again, running her fingers along the letters of her name.

"It was a great choice," says Somer, gesturing toward it. "It's a lovely name. Unusual." She almost says *like you*, but stops herself. She'd have meant it as a compliment but it might not have sounded like that.

The girl blushes a little. "Mum would have liked Danielle. Or Dannii, like Dannii Minogue. She said it'd be easier if it wasn't such a big change. But I *wanted* it to be a big change. I wanted everything to be different." There's pride in her face now. And defiance. "That's why I chose Faith. It was about being true to who I really am."

"And there really isn't anyone in Oxford who knows?" says Everett. "No one who could have targeted you because of your past?"

Faith shakes her head, "No. No one."

The two women are avoiding each other's eyes but they're both thinking the same thing. Was the attacker as convinced as everyone else by the way Faith looks? Or did he know her secret and target her for that very reason? Either way, does Faith know how close she came—how much danger she could have been in?

But the look on the girl's face answers that question. She knows full well. She's known all along. This is a reality she's lived with half her life.

"So can you tell us what happened next? After what you just told us?" Even Ev, who's been doing this sort of thing for years and has specialist training in dealing with the victims of sex crimes, shies away from the actual words.

Faith slips her arms around herself, pulling the jumper tighter. Her hands are shaking.

"Did he hurt you, Faith?" says Somer softly.

Faith shakes her head. "Not—like that. But I thought he was going to. I felt him coming close—I could hear the breathing and then he grabbed at my hair and it really hurt and I could feel some of the extensions ripping out and I started kicking again and I felt it—the knife—on my skin—running down my stomach—and—"

She's crying again.

"It's OK, take your time."

She blinks away the tears, wipes her eyes and looks up. Her lip is trembling but she holds their gaze. "I wet myself, OK? I thought he was going to hurt me—down there—and I wet myself."

*　*　*

Alex pours me a glass of juice and leans back against the worktop. The remains of her lunch are on a plate on the draining board. Chicken salad: brown rice, lean protein, leafy greens—she's ticking all the boxes. But there's too much left on the plate and her face looks thin. Thinner than I'd like.

"The health visitor just texted me to say she's running late so as long as the mysterious Mr. Asante is on time, we may just wing it."

She's goading me now. She's been curious about Asante ever since I first mentioned him.

"He's not *mysterious*, Alex. He's just not that easy to read. Not like Gislingham—"

Her smile broadens; she's very fond of Gis.

"Or Quinn."

A grimace this time. "Thank the Lord for that. This town ain't big enough for more than one Quinn."

I move over to the kettle; Alex's current beverage of choice is cherry bakewell green tea. We must be draining Waitrose dry.

"I'd just prefer not to have anyone from work coming here right now. I haven't told anyone yet—about the baby."

Alex squints down at her belly. "OK, I'll make sure I stay sitting down." She makes a rueful face. "Let's just hope he's not much of a detective."

"I'm sorry—I know it's a bloody pain in the neck, but he insisted on coming—"

She reaches out and touches me gently on the cheek. "Don't look so worried. I was *joking*."

64

By the time the doorbell rings Alex is curled up on the sofa with her tea. She grins at me as I go past, and pulls a cushion on to her lap.

Asante is on the doorstep. He has a laptop under one arm. Immaculate suit, white shirt, deep-red woven silk tie. I can see the edge of the label: Burberry. It occurs to me suddenly that a lot of Quinn's dislike may be nothing more than preener's envy.

I step back to let him in, and he waits, courteously, for me to close the door.

"We'll go through to the kitchen."

I steadfastly refuse to look at Alex as we go by, but I sense a minute slowing of his pace behind me, and then he says, "I'm sorry to disturb you."

"Occupational hazard," she says; I can hear the laughter in her voice.

In the kitchen Asante refuses tea but accepts water, and I find myself reaching for the bottle in the fridge rather than just running the tap. I suspect he has that effect on people quite a lot.

He sets up his laptop on the island and the screen opens to the same bland factory-issue screensaver I have on mine. Gislingham has his toddler son, dressed in a Chelsea strip; Ev has her cat; Quinn has some tropical beach he'd like us all to think he's been to. But Asante's is quietly and deliberately anonymous. Another fact for my mental file.

He pulls up a stool and I realize suddenly that I've left the ultrasound picture the midwife gave us on the island, barely three feet from where Asante is now taking a seat.

I reach for it quickly and put it in my back pocket. If Asante notices, he gives no sign.

He finishes with his keyboard and turns it toward me. It takes a few minutes for it to hit me, what exactly it is I'm reading. But when it does it's like an iron bar to the throat.

* * *

The wind has got up again by the time they park the car. Everett turns around and looks at the girl. She's in the back seat, looking out of the window. She'd agreed to come, but now they're here she looks less sure. Though at least there's hardly anyone else around: it's the middle of the day and the Marston Ferry Road allotments are practically deserted. The only life Ev can see is two elderly chaps in almost identical caps and sweaters, sharing a thermos and a vape on a bench by the skips.

"Are you still OK to do this, Faith?" she asks.

"It's fine," she says quickly, pushing open the door. "Let's just get it over with before Mum gets back and I have to start explaining where I've been."

Somer, meanwhile, has got out of the car and is examining the ground. A few yards away there are deep tire tracks where someone has driven off fast. And recently. She looks up at the clouds—they're lucky these marks are still here and they'll need their luck to hold for just a bit longer: forensics need to get a record of this before it rains again. She gets her phone out and walks a few paces away to put in a call to Alan Challow. The ground around her is thick with sandy red mud. The same mud they found splattered over the shoes they now have sealed in an evidence bag in the back of the car.

Faith is staring. At the upturned wheelbarrows, the ramshackle sheds, the bare earth, the dull twiggy plants. Everything seems either dead or withered.

She shivers suddenly. And it isn't just the wind. "I think I know why he let me go. I remember now—there were sirens—I heard sirens—they were getting closer and closer. That's when he left."

So that explains it, thinks Everett. Out here, with no one around to hear or help, it's little short of a miracle Faith's attacker didn't finish what he started. The driver of that emergency vehicle is an accidental hero.

Somer walks slowly back toward them, her boots crunching on the patches of gravel. She nods a message to Everett: CSI are on their way.

"So what happened after you heard the siren?" asks Ev.

Faith glances at her. "I heard him open the shed door and a few minutes later the sound of an engine and then the van drove away. Fast. Like the wheels were spinning."

"And then?"

Faith takes a deep breath. "I just started screaming, hoping someone would come. I didn't know where I was—I didn't know no one could hear me."

Somer tries not to imagine what that was like—lying there, the bag around your face, no underwear, the panic as you struggle to breathe—

"It wasn't on that tight," says Faith, guessing her thoughts. "The bag." She bites her lip. "I thought, afterwards, that he can't have wanted me to die. Not really. Not if he left it that loose."

Or perhaps he just didn't want it to be over too quickly, thinks Ev. She feels her jaw tighten; they need to find this bastard, and fast.

"How did you escape?"

"I managed to squirm about against the ground and drag the bag off that way. That's when I realized it was a shed. There was garden equipment and stuff. I looked about a bit and managed to find a pair of secateurs. I wedged them against the bench and tried to cut the ties but I kept dropping them. It took ages."

"Which shed was it, Faith? Can you show us?"

"It was that one," she says, pointing. "Over there. The one with the barrow outside."

"What about the bag—do you know where it went?"

"It's probably still there—I didn't take it. It was a Tesco one. If that helps."

Somer pulls out her gloves and starts toward the shed.

"We need to preserve the scene," explains Everett. "There might be DNA. Or fingerprints."

"I think he was wearing gloves," says Faith gloomily. "His hands felt all plasticky."

"Like rubber gloves, you mean, those Marigold things?"

She shakes her head. "No, sort of fatter than that. Bigger. Perhaps gardening gloves or something." She sighs. "So there won't be any fingerprints, will there."

"He'll have messed up somehow, just you wait. And that's how we'll catch him."

"I kept hoping someone would come," says the girl softly. "But no one did. No one ever does, do they? Not when it matters. Not when you really need them."

* * *

68

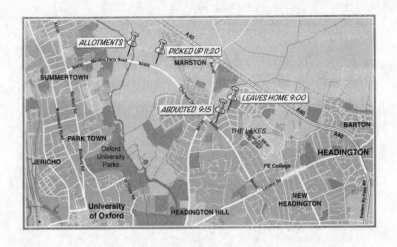

* * *

Adam Fawley
2 April 2018
14.05

When I get back to the incident room there's a map up on the board. Thumbtacks show where Faith lives, where she was abducted, where she was found. Mute but insistent.

Asante is sitting quietly at his desk. I asked him not to say anything until I got back, until all the team are here. But now they are.

I catch Asante's eye and he gets to his feet.

"OK, everyone, can I have your attention, please. There's something we all need to see."

People look up, register the fact that Asante is linking his iPad up to the projector. Ev's curious, Baxter's skeptical, Quinn's downright irritated and doing very little to hide it.

Asante fires up the screen and navigates to the page. I don't look at it; I don't need to. I've seen it already. But

I watch their faces change as they realize what they're looking at.

https://groopz.com/incelsolidarity

Seen that titbitch on TV?—another roastie riding the cocksucking carousel

submitted 2 days ago by supremegentlemen89

17 comments share hide report

Only good femoid is a dead femoid spread their legs ok then no wot I mean

submitted 2 days ago by suckingthatblackpiller

10 comments share hide report

We need to scare these sluts—I mean acid-in-your-fucking-face
TERRORISE the c*nts

submitted 1 day ago by justyouraveragecumpanzeee

35 comments share hide report

The fukking game is rigged from the start—20% of Chadfukkers getting
80% of the fux

submitted 1 day ago by proudtobeaunowot

24 comments share hide report

Dont have to be that way mate—all these whores and feminazis fantasize
about getting raped. Ud be doing them a favour

submitted 17 hours ago by furiousmadomegger

22 comments share hide report

U know whats worse—those fucking shemales that's who—they deserve
everything they get

submitted 16 hours ago by downwiththegynocracy

35 comments share hide report

No kidding—my mate grabbed a hot cunt only to find she was packing a
dick 😡

submitted 9 hours ago by YeltobYob

6 comments share hide report

"How the hell do you get to know about this?" says Gislingham. He can scarcely believe what he's looking at, and I can tell you now, he's not the only one.

Asante shrugs. "We had an incident last year in Brixton. A twenty-three-year-old woman was attacked by a bloke who'd asked her out and been knocked back. He was a bit of a loner, obsessed with gaming, you know the type. Turned out he stalked her for weeks afterwards, online and off, and when we checked his PC he'd been logging on to known Incel sites all that time. I was on the case, so I ended up knowing a certain amount about it. That's how I found this—I knew where to look."

Quinn gives him a look that says *smart arse*, and I give Quinn one that says *takes one to know one*.

Baxter meanwhile is frowning. Thus far the internet has been his uncontested domain and he's clearly more than a little miffed at this sudden incursion.

"Incel as in what, precisely?" he asks.

"Involuntary Celibate," says Asante. "Men who can't get enough sex—or *any* sex—and blame women for withholding it from them. As well as the alpha males who get more than their fair share. That's what the bloke on this board is referring to. Incels call men like that Chads."

Quinn flushes a little at this, but if he starts getting called Chad in the canteen I suspect he's not going to be doing much complaining.

"And of course their own pathetic chauvinist inadequacies have nothing whatsoever to do with it," says Ev acidly.

There are a couple of half-hearted laughs at this, but Asante's face is like stone. "This is way beyond casual sexism." He gestures at the screen. "This is just a sample of what's out there, and believe me, there's a hell of a lot worse if you know where to look. The hosting sites keep closing these boards down, but they just spring up some-where else."

"Don't you just love the internet," says Somer bitterly. "Helping psychopaths make new friends."

"It's worse than that," says Asante, holding her gaze. "Our attacker in Brixton—he wasn't just having a harm-less vent with other losers. It's like any other type of radicalization—these people egg each other on. Each round of replies got angrier and more violent. Right up until the day he threw a can of bleach at the girl, after one of his online pals told him to 'burn the cum-dumpster—let's see how many fucks she gets if she's got no face.'"

Somer has gone pale; Everett has her hand to her mouth. They don't say anything; they don't need to.

"So what makes you think our man is part of this shit?" says Quinn. "I mean, it's disgusting and all that," he says quickly, "of course it is. But the scum who spend their lives on these boards—it's all bloody talk. That story about his 'mate'—it's just a load of bollocks. Doesn't mean he actually *did* anything—"

"Oh, I don't know," says Baxter darkly. "Sounds suspi-ciously like 'asking for a friend' to me."

Asante turns to him. "I've seen at least one Incel talk-ing about abducting a woman and holding her captive to rape and torture. And no, that doesn't mean he went ahead and did it, but the line between fantasy and actua-tion can get very thin here."

Quinn rolls his eyes. He clearly considers the line

between clued-up colleague and pretentious know-it-all tosser is pretty thin too.

"So why do you think this is different?" says Gislingham.

"Exactly," says Quinn quickly. "Even if this tosser did do something, what are the odds it was Faith? It could be absolutely bloody anyone. We don't even know where these wankers live—"

"Look at that last username," says Somer quietly.

They stare at her and then at the screen.

"What, the YeltobYob one?" says Quinn, none the wiser.

Baxter turns to her. "That's just a name, isn't it—like that BBC bloke, whatsisname—"

"Alan *Yen*tob," says Everett. "It's not the same."

But Somer is shaking her head. "It's not a name at all," she says. "It's backwards. Yob is Boy. And Yeltob is Botley."

* * *

At Summertown High the bell has just rung for the end of the period. In the GCSE art class, students are rolling up sheets of cartridge paper and stacking paints and brushes on the long bench that runs underneath the window. Outside, the clouds are racing across a low gray sky.

The teacher stops behind Sasha Blake's chair. She doesn't seem to have heard the bell. Or if she has, she's not as bothered as her classmates about getting to the next class. She leans back a little to scrutinize her watercolor of the still-life arrangement in the center of the room. A white china bowl of plums and lemons, and a pale-blue jug with a sprig of forsythia. Along the side of her sketch she's dabbed swatches of different purples. Reddish mauves, bluish indigos; none of them quite match the color of the fruit glistening in the bowl.

"You're coming along, Sasha," says the teacher. He's perhaps thirty-seven, with sandy hair thinning a little and a check shirt in a thick cotton that's gone bobbly from long use. He's not wearing a wedding ring.

"You have a real eye. You should think about doing A level."

She turns around, finally, and looks up at him.

"There's a book you might like," he begins tentatively, "*Still Life* by A. S. Byatt—it has a wonderful passage about how to describe the precise color of plums—how to capture the bloom on them. In fact, it's why I chose this particular arrangement—"

He's just getting into his stride when one of the two girls lingering at the door calls over.

"For God's sake, Sash! Get a move on, can't you?"

Sasha looks around and gets quickly to her feet. As she reaches for her bag, her long dark ponytail swings forward over her shoulder.

"Sorry sorry sorry!" she calls to her friends, rushing to clear her materials away. "Just got a bit sidetracked."

"Yeah yeah," says the other girl with a smile, "like *that's* never happened before."

Sasha grins and hoists her bag over her shoulder, throwing a half-apologetic, half-relieved glance at the teacher still standing behind her chair. The classroom door bangs shut behind the girls but he can still hear their voices filter back as they go down the corridor.

"Was Spotty Scotty *actually* hitting on you back then?"

"Er, that's like, totally gross! Imagine him actually *kissing* you!"

"He is *such* a creep!"

The man stands there, his cheeks flaming and his fists clenched, as their arrogant young laughter drifts slowly away.

*   *   *

Adam Fawley
2 April 2018
14.35

"OK," says Quinn. "That username *could* mean this bloke is in Oxford. But we don't actually *know* that. For a start, there must be other places called Botley, right?"

"Two I've found," replies Asante steadily. "There's a village near Chesham, in Buckinghamshire, and another one in Hampshire."

I see Somer start a little, and then I remember—her new bloke is with the Hants force.

"Right," continues Quinn. "So that's two to one against for a start. And even if it is the Oxford Botley, we don't know *when* it happened—we don't even know if it happened *at all*."

Asante leans over and presses a key. The comments under the last entry are now visible on the screen.

"Shit," says Gislingham under his breath. "Shit."

*   *   *

At the allotments, it's starting to rain again. Nina Mukerjee parks the forensics van on the far side of the car park and sits there a moment taking in the location. The line of compost heaps, the noticeboard with posters offering surplus plants and second-hand tools, the skips loaded with broken bits of pot and slate. She's been doing the job so long she sees everything as a crime scene. Fingerprints, smears, flakes of skin, tumbleweeds of dust. It makes eating at other people's houses especially trying: the only kitchen that ever looks really clean is her own.

She pushes open the door and pulls her kit across from the passenger seat. A few yards away she can see Clive Conway standing by a shed behind a line of blue-and-white crime scene tape. The tape is whipping in the wind and Clive has his hand to his head, keeping his hood in place. She pulls on her protective suit then moves as quickly as its bulk will allow to where Clive is waiting for her. There's no sign of CID, just a couple of uniforms milling about and stamping their feet to keep warm. She wonders who's been put on the case—whether it might be Tony Asante. They discovered a while back that they have a couple of friends in common at the Met and he's bought her a coffee once or twice since. She can't decide if it was just out of politeness or whether he's actually interested. Or what she'd do if he was. She's seen the mess made by relationships at work and she likes that aspect of her life clean too.

Clive doesn't bother saying anything when she reaches him, just pushes open the door, letting her see inside. Her uncle had a shed about this size when she was a child—she remembers the windows thick with cobwebs and sticky with snail trails, the shelves haphazard with rusting implements, the musty, dead-insect smell. But this is different. It's neat enough to live in—well, almost. There are watering cans and plastic flowerpots stacked in lines on the shelves, spades and forks hanging on their own individual hooks, and on the work surface two bags of seed potatoes and a neat line of earth-filled seed trays with small white plastic labels and tiny spikes of green just visible here and there. The floor has been swept, even in the corners, but the dark stain spread across it tells a different story. As does the smell.

"I don't think there's any doubt that's urine." He crouches down and points. "I also found some shreds of hair. But no roots as far as I can see. In fact, I'm pretty sure they're going to turn out to be extensions."

* * *

Adam Fawley
2 April 2018
14.43

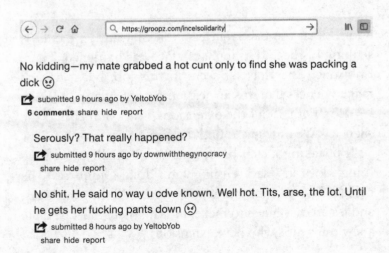

No kidding—my mate grabbed a hot cunt only to find she was packing a dick 😡

↱ submitted 9 hours ago by YeltobYob

6 comments share hide report

  Serously? That really happened?

  ↱ submitted 9 hours ago by downwiththegynocracy

  share hide report

  No shit. He said no way u cdve known. Well hot. Tits, arse, the lot. Until he gets her fucking pants down 😡

  ↱ submitted 8 hours ago by YeltobYob

  share hide report

Fuck me—those chicks with dicks theyr the fucking worst. All come and
fuck me + dont even have a fucking hole

submitted 8 hours ago by letscutthecrappeople7755
share hide report

Too fucking right mate. He said he shd have realized something was
wrong when her fucking hair came away in his hand It was only fucking
EXTENSIONS wasn't it

submitted 8 hours ago by YeltobYob
share hide report

😄 😄 😄 were the tits fake too?

submitted 7 hours ago by KHHVandsowhat88
share hide report

What a cunt. Hope he made her suck him off

submitted 7 hours ago by supremegentlemen89
share hide report

Never got the fucking chance. Anyway, who wants beard burn on your
fucking dick. These tashhags are the worst slags of the lot

submitted 6 hours ago by YeltobYob
share hide report

Someone at the back mutters, "Sick bastards"; Baxter is
shaking his head, Gislingham's face has hardened. There
isn't much they haven't seen, in this job, but it doesn't
make vileness like this any easier to confront.

"He's right about the extensions," says Somer into the
silence. "We only just found out about that ourselves."

"But taking a step back, it doesn't actually prove anything, does it?" says Gislingham. "Like Quinn says, he
could just be making stuff up to impress all the other shits,
and it's an easy guess to make. I mean, there must be quite
a few trans girls who have extensions."

78

But even if he's right, it's still a coincidence. And you know how I feel about coincidences.

Asante looks around. "You can see how it could have played out—if this bloke abducts her off the street, not knowing what she really is—"

Somer stares at him. "'*What* she really is'? Please tell me you didn't just say that."

Asante looks uncomfortable. Now there's a first. "I'm sorry. I was only referring to her preoperative status, that's all. If you're an Incel it's the ultimate betrayal—sex flaunted but then denied."

"Faith doesn't 'flaunt' herself," says Somer coolly. "She goes out of her way *not* to do that."

I cut in. "Did Faith say whether she'd seen anyone hanging around recently, Somer? Anyone acting suspiciously?"

She glances at me and shakes her head. "We did ask, but she said not. Not that she'd noticed, anyway."

But just because she didn't see him doesn't mean he wasn't there. He could have been stalking her for days, and picked that precise moment, and that precise place, because he knew by then that she always passed that spot around that time. On the other hand, he might simply have been parked up in those garages having a fag when she happened to go by.

Gislingham turns to Asante. "Can we track him down through the website or is that asking too much?"

Asante hesitates a moment. "The ISP for the discussion board will have a record of the IP address that logged those posts—we'll just have to hope they're based in the UK—"

"Right, so—"

"—but as I explained to the DI, most of these boards don't even ask for names let alone emails. And he'll probably be on public Wi-Fi rather than his own account. These people use stations, libraries, coffee shops—"

"Not *people*," interrupts Everett. "Shits. Total and utter *shits*."

Gislingham frowns. "So you're saying we won't be able to identify him even if we get the IP address?"

Asante makes a face. "If he's in a public place it'll all depend on whether there's CCTV, and even if there is—"

"Right," says Gislingham. "So we'd better get a bloody move on, and organize a warrant."

"DC Asante's also been monitoring the board," I say, "and YeltobYob hasn't been online since he posted these comments."

Asante looks around the room. "He doesn't post that often but I'm going back through his past activity to see if we can find anything about him that way. Something that might indicate which Botley he's talking about, for a start. But so far, it's all the same poisonous misogynist venting."

"What about registered sex offenders?" asks Baxter. "Shouldn't we be checking all these Botley places in case anything pops?"

I shake my head. "Already done. And nothing doing."

There's a silence.

"It's not just what he says about the extensions," says Somer quietly, staring at the board. "It sounds like he was interrupted. Like Faith's attacker was."

I turn to Baxter. "Have we managed to track down the emergency vehicle Faith heard?"

He nods. "Squad car, sir. There was a burglary reported in Headington High Street and they got stuck behind the roadworks on the Marston Ferry Road."

"But the officers didn't notice anyone entering or leaving the allotments? No van of any kind?"

"Sorry, sir. I spoke to the two guys and they don't remember seeing anything. But I'm getting the footage from the speed camera along there and the petrol station on the Cherwell Drive roundabout. And if he got away in the opposite direction he'd have passed Summertown High so the school CCTV may have picked him up."

"Challow and the CSI team are on-site," says Gis quickly. "And we have the cable ties and the plastic bag. We're also going to question the neighbours in the immediate vicinity of where she was abducted. You never know, someone might have seen something."

And yet they never bothered reporting a girl being kidnapped off the street right under their noses? Some hope. But there are motions to be gone through in this job, and that's one of them.

"And there's the question of Faith's handbag, as well," Somer continues. "Her mum went back that afternoon and found it chucked in one of the bins round by the garages. Minus the valuables, of course." She sighs. "Forensics will check it in case but it's possible her attacker just left it where it fell and someone else came along later and stole the money and the mobile. But no one's used the phone since."

So GPS isn't going to be any use either. Another cul-de-sac.

"What about Faith herself?"

Somer makes a face. "She's reluctant to be examined, sir, for obvious reasons—and in any case she'd showered at least twice before we spoke to her—"

"But what about her clothes? There could be saliva— DNA—"

Somer shakes her head. "She threw the whole lot in the wash. It's only natural, to react like that, but it does make our job ten times harder. The only thing we have is the shoes. We'll get them tested, but I suspect it's a very long shot."

* * *

Interview with Jackie Dimond, 35 Rydal Way, Oxford
2 April 2018, 4:15 p.m.
In attendance, DC V. Everett

JD: I'm not sure what I can tell you, I hardly know the Applefords.

VE: We're speaking to all the neighbors, Mrs. Dimond. Sometimes people have seen more than they realize.

JD: This is about Monday morning, yes? I wasn't even in then.

VE: Yes, you did say that. I was more interested in whether you'd seen anything unusual in the last few weeks.

JD: Unusual, as in?

VE: Anyone hanging around you didn't know? Someone asking about the Applefords? Taking an interest in their house? Perhaps someone parked up in a van?

JD: Sorry, love. I'd have told Diane if anyone was
    snooping about.

VE: I thought you said you hardly know them?

JD: I don't. But she's on her own, isn't she.
    Like me. No bloke to fall back on. I'd
    have definitely said something if I'd seen
    some pervert hanging about.

VE: Do you know the girls—Faith and Nadine?

JD: Not really. Mine are a bit younger so there
    isn't much of an overlap, if you see what I
    mean. Faith is always very pleasant. Smiles
    and says hello. And always looks lovely too. I
    wish my Elaine would smarten up a bit, but you
    know what teenagers are like.

VE: And Nadine?

JD: I can't say I've had much contact with her,
    to be honest. Keeps her head down. Slouches.
    Doesn't make the best of herself, you know?
    It must be tough, though, mustn't it—with her
    sister being so attractive whereas
    Nadine—

VE: Actually, they seem pretty close to me—

JD: I mean—she's not much to look at, is she?

* * *

By 4:30 Andrew Baxter has been staring at CCTV footage for over an hour. In front of him, on the screen, cars
swing in and out across the petrol station forecourt. He's
found six vans so far, along with a horsebox, a vintage
Harley-Davidson he rewound a couple of times just to

admire, two trucks from a traveling circus and any number of yummy-mummy SUVs in the thick of the school run. The chances of their man being there at all are pretty remote, as far as Baxter can see, and even if he was, how the hell are they supposed to recognize him? It's a total bloody waste of time, that's what it is. He pushes the chair back and gets up, feeling a headache lurking in the back of his neck. Must be low blood sugar, he thinks. Better be safe than sorry. Lucky the snack machine is only a few yards down the corridor.

* * *

Adam Fawley
2 April 2018
17.25

"Pull up a chair—if you can find one."

I'm in Bryan Gow's office. Or, strictly speaking, his temporary office, since his building is being refurbished and the Department of Psychology is camped out in a few spare rooms in Plant Sciences. It's a solid 1950s building on the South Parks Road with fixtures and fittings to match—wooden paneling and parquet floors and rare botanical specimens in glass cases. Though most of the potted living versions look in need of a good water and a bit of old-fashioned TLC.

Judging by the books heaped haphazardly on the only free seat, Gow's current roommate is an expert in psycholinguistics, whatever the hell that is. Last time I was here Gow spent the whole time telling me that it's only for a few months and he really doesn't mind sharing, but he isn't fooling me. It seems there's nothing more instinctively human than a desire for our own space. Even psychologists can't talk themselves out of that one.

"I wanted to run something past you," I say. "On Monday morning an eighteen-year-old girl was abducted near Cherwell Drive. I want to know who we should be looking for."

He raises his eyebrows, then sits back and joins his fingertips together. "OK. Shoot."

It takes me a good five minutes to tell him everything, but he's frowning long before I've finished. And even more so when I give him the printout from the Incel board.

"And there's no suggestion, is there," he says eventually, "that it was someone this girl knew?"

I shake my head. "Much as I want that to be the answer—"

"Or someone who's aware she's transitioning?"

"Again, we're looking, but right now we can't find anyone outside the family who knows."

He taps the printout. "So you want to know whether this could be your man."

"And if not him, then who."

He gets up and edges around the desk to a stack of cardboard boxes heaped one on top of the other on a table under the window. He must have packed them a hell of a sight better than I would have managed because it only takes him a few moments to locate what he wants.

"Fairly basic, but adequate for the layman," he says, tossing a book on to the desk in front of me.

Profiling Sexual Offenders: Theory, Research, and Practice in Investigative Psychology. The author is American, if the surname is anything to go by.

"So what's this going to tell me?"

He sits down again. "A lot of what you know already. This sort of crime is primarily about power. Power and fear. This man wants to dominate, and he wants to terrorize. Sexual assault is just a means to that end."

"Even though these Incel boards are all about sex?"

"They're about the *absence* of sex," he says, holding my gaze. "And what that absence deprives them of: status, self-esteem, autonomy."

Sexual assault as taking back control. Jesus.

"In that case, what sort of profile should we be looking for?"

"Tediously predictable, I'm afraid. Almost certainly white, and low-to-middle class. At least average intelligence—perhaps even slightly above." He picks up the printout. "He uses contractions like 'cdve,' but he spells 'realized' correctly, and puts the apostrophe in 'didn't.' And he likes wordplay—YeltobYob, tashhag— that degree of linguistic dexterity suggests the upper end of the educational range generally seen with crimes of this kind."

He puts the paper down again. "My guess is he's holding down a job, though probably not one he considers 'good enough' for him. A female boss is a possibility—someone who doesn't promote or 'appreciate' him. He's likely to live alone and almost certainly struggles to maintain any sort of meaningful long-term relationship with women."

Classic loner misfit. Just what I bloody needed.

Gow is eyeing me now. "Using 'yob' in his username is very revealing. On the face of it, just your typical 'Men

86

Behaving Badly' casual thuggishness, but I suspect it springs from a deep albeit unacknowledged self-loathing."

"Age?"

"Despite the 'boy' reference, I suspect he's more like thirties or forties." He gestures at the book. "Read that. I'm sure you'll find it fascinating."

"And the fact that the assault was frustrated—what difference will that make?"

Gow raises an eyebrow. "Frustrated as in interrupted, or frustrated as in thwarted?"

I shrug. "Either. Both."

He sighs. His face has darkened. "I'm afraid that may well exacerbate matters. To have been so close to getting what he wanted, only to have it snatched from him at the last minute. Things will be a lot more urgent now. And he will be a lot angrier."

I get to my feet. I already knew we were up against it, but there's a cold, sick feeling in my gut now that wasn't there before.

As I get to the door, Gow calls me back. "One more thing, as Columbo would say. I'd get the ever-dependable Baxter to do a search on your man's MO. It wouldn't surprise me at all to find he's done something like this before."

* * *

Graeme Scott turns the lights out in the art room and starts to fumble in his pocket for the keys, then remembers he's forgotten to turn off his sodding PC and has to go back in again. When he finally locks up five minutes later the neon strip in the corridor is still flickering on and off above his head. It's been doing it for at least a month and the caretaker hasn't even bothered to come and look at it. Scott doesn't need reminding that Art comes very much lower down the pecking order than Information Technology or Media Studies but no one likes their inferiority thrust so blatantly in their face.

He rams the jangle of keys back into his pocket then heads out towards the car park. Most of the students have already left, just a few still lingering by the gates waiting for lifts. There are a couple of stringy lads hovering near a group of girls that Scott only now realizes includes some of Sasha Blake's friends.

Scott feels the color coming to his face and is thankful they're too far away to notice. He reaches the car, opens the doors at the back and starts stowing away his materials as fast as he can manage. He can hear laughing now, a sudden gust of guffaws. It might be nothing to do with him—just an accident of timing—but paranoia has become a habit. The piss-taking about his clothes and his car, the nasty hurtful nickname. Just his luck that Scott rhymes with spot; though most of the acnefied little shits who call him that are pots calling the kettle black as far as he's concerned. And as for the car, if they don't have the basic intelligence to realize this is a classic, well, that's their problem, not his. Only it isn't, of course, because they're at it again, right now. He can see the two lads out of the corner of his eye—one is pretending to crank a starter handle as the other makes farting noises. The girls are hysterical with laughter. Leah Waddell with her high heels and Isabel Parker with that ridiculous hair dye she's done to herself. He's amazed the head is letting her get away with it. And as for Patsie Webb with her fuckwit stupidly spelled name. Too clever for her own good, the nasty, vindictive little cow. He doesn't like the idea of Sasha Blake hanging out with the likes of her. She's worth better than that—she actually has some talent, some *potential*—

He shoves a can of paint aside to make way for the rolls of card, then yanks the doors shut and goes around to the driver's side and gets in. He sits there a moment, gripping his keys, willing the damn thing to start first time.

* * *

"My name's Jed Miller, I'm calling from Achernar Internet Services—can I speak to DC Anthony Asante?"

Asante sits up in his chair—this is it, this is what they've been waiting for.

"My boss said you were after some metadata from us, right? For yesterday?"

"That's right."

"I've got what you need right here—though I'm not sure how much help it's going to be—"

"Just send it over, Mr. Miller—the rest is down to us."

* * *

It's gone 7:00 when Gislingham puts his head around my door.

"Just heard back from the team at the allotments, boss. Basically, nada."

Quinn used to say that a lot when he was DS; I hope Gislingham grows out of it before I have to beat his head against a brick wall.

"Only thing they do seem to be managing is pissing off a lot of old chaps who've no longer got a good excuse to get out of the washing-up, by the sound of it." He grins. "I think we should prepare ourselves for some irate compensation claims for parsnips trampled in the line of duty."

"What about the shed Faith was taken to—who owns that?"

Gis whips out his notebook. "A lady called Cheng Zhen Li." He stumbles over the pronunciation then spells it out for me. "No prizes for guessing she's Chinese. Apparently she's lived in Marston for about thirty years and has had the allotment for at least ten. Quite a fixture, by all accounts. Used to be there regular as clockwork every morning and evening with her little trug for a bit of pricking out and potting on."

I'm starting to wonder if Gis might be angling to get an allotment of his own; he's certainly up on all the lingo. Though from what I know of his wife, I can't see her having much trug with that idea.

"What do you mean, 'used to?'"

He makes a face. "That's just it. She's been in hospital. Broken hip. She's back at home now but she hasn't been to the allotment for the last two weeks."

"And the shed—was it locked?"

He shakes his head. "Seems not. It was just on a latch. She doesn't keep anything of value in it, and in any case, she said the allotment owners share each other's stuff. It's the done thing, apparently. In allotment circles."

So that's not going to get us anywhere either. Marvelous. Absolutely bloody marvelous.

"What about the Incel board?"

"Ah, good news and bad news on that one. Turned out the Yeltob bloke *was* using a public Wi-Fi, just like Asante said. He's logged in at the same place every time he's posted in the last few weeks."

"Is that the good news or the bad news?"

He makes a face. "Sorry, boss. It was a Starbucks on the outskirts of Southampton."

So it's not our man.

I take a deep breath. "Have we passed it on to Hants Police?"

Because this piece of shit needs apprehending, even if not by us.

He nods. "Somer's going to call that bloke of hers— he'll know who to send it to. If that Starbucks has CCTV there's a good chance they can narrow down who it was."

* * *

Alex Fawley takes another quick look down the road, then pulls the curtain back in place. Still no sign of Adam. She moves over to the sofa and sits down carefully, feeling the baby move, then settle. She's trying not to worry, trying to carry on as normally as possible, but some days the temptation to crawl under the duvet and stay there becomes almost overwhelming. She's negotiated to work from home for the final few months but now even her own house feels like a minefield—an assault course of inanimate objects out to cause her harm. Rugs she could slip on, steps she could trip over. She keeps telling Adam that she's fine, joking with him in that easy repartee they've developed over the years. But the minute he leaves the house the fear comes down and she spends most of the day too paralyzed to move.

She gets up and goes to the window again. But outside, the road is deserted.

* * *

When Erica Somer gets home she spends a long time under the shower. Something about this case is getting under her skin, and she's not quite sure why. She's met victims who've suffered worse, victims who deserve at least as much pity. But she's never had to deal with a crime against a trans person. She thought she was well-informed, and sensitive, and attuned to the issues—of course she thought that. Every intelligent person probably thinks the same. But she knows now that it's far more complicated, far more nuanced, than she ever allowed for. Even Fawley, who she likes and admires and has gone out of his way to promote and encourage her, seems to be struggling with it. And what about Giles? She tells herself he's not a misogynist, not even a mansplainer, but how can she be sure, when she knows him, as yet, so little?

When she goes back into the bedroom there's a message from him on her phone, asking her to call. She knows it's probably about the Starbucks thing but her heart still lifts—then lifts again as she realizes how instinctive that swell of happiness was. Maybe her unconscious is trying to tell her something. Maybe it really is as simple as it seems.

* * *

It's 8:15 a.m. The temperature dropped to below freezing last night, but according to the station central heating system, April is officially "spring" and the radiators have gone off. Quinn has his scarf around his neck in that loop knot thing that's clearly *de rigueur* these days. Several others are in their coats. And it's pretty obvious the weather has turned inside as well as out. The mood is harder, colder. There's a frown line cut across Everett's brow and Baxter has that stern look to his jaw I've seen far too many times over the years.

I finish telling them what I got from Gow and turn to Asante; this is something I need to do in public. "Good work on the Incel board, DC Asante. Even if it wasn't our man."

He smiles. Not too much, because that would look smug; not too little, because he knows full well that he's done a bloody good job and he's not about to let that be undervalued. Or perhaps I'm reading far too much into it, and he always smiles exactly that way.

"Keep an eye on those boards, though, would you? Just in case something else surfaces."

Somer looks up. "By the way, Hants Police did manage

93

to identify YeltobYob. There was CCTV at the Starbucks so they could see the bloke who was using his phone at the exact times the posts went up. And he paid by card, so they know they have the right man. They're pursuing it as a possible hate crime."

The mood in the room lifts a little: we've achieved something, at least.

I turn to Gislingham. "OK, so where are we with forensics from the allotments?"

"Er, right, there were two usable fingerprints on the Tesco bag," he replies, struggling to find the right notes. "Along with a couple of partials and some smears. Nothing came up in the database though, so they aren't from anyone we know about already."

"And DNA?"

"Several different profiles. No matches on the database there either—it could be anyone—shop assistants, shelf stackers, delivery drivers—"

"But one of them could still be our man?"

Gis shrugs. "Sure, it's possible. But personally I can't see him going to all that trouble and forgetting to wear gloves when he handled that bag."

Neither can I, frankly. But the pathological stupidity of the criminal classes has been our salvation before, and may well be again.

"And we did that house-to-house in the area round the garages," he continues, "but no luck, I'm afraid."

Baxter looks up. "Speed cameras on the Marston Ferry Road didn't turn up anything either so I checked with the school, in case he went that way, but nothing doing: you can't see the road from their cameras."

"What about the CCTV at the petrol station?"

He nods. "Yep, done that too. Over a dozen vans either bought petrol or went past at around the right time—"

"And?"

He makes a face. "Trouble is, you can only see the reg numbers if they actually pull into the forecourt. Most of those going past are just your average white vans with nothing on the side to identify them. Either that or they're half hidden by bloody buses."

"Did you check the number plates of the ones you saw?"

He gives me a look that says *What do you take me for?*

He flips open a notebook. Which, unlike Quinn and Asante, he still uses. "Of those where we either have identifying marks and/or reg numbers we're looking at one plumber, three builders, two self-drive hire vans, a locksmith, a pest control firm, a carpet cleaners and one of those companies that rents out pushbikes."

"Bloody things," grumbles Quinn. "They're all over the sodding place in Jericho—people just chuck them on the pavement and walk off. Bane of my bloody life."

I'm trying to ignore him. I keep looking at Baxter. "And?"

"The pest control guy was on call-out," he says, "as was the plumber. Two of the building vans can account for their movements that morning and I've been able to verify that with ANPR. Same goes for the bike bloke."

He flips the book shut. "That's as far as I've got. A whole heap of sod all, basically."

When I look around the room it seems his apathy is infectious. And I can't afford to let that happen.

"Focus on the self-drives," I say. Firmly. "Our man might be using a hired vehicle. To stay under the radar."

Baxter considers. "OK, yes. I guess that's a possibility. I'll get on it."

"No," I say, looking at Quinn, who's now fiddling about on his iPad. "DC Quinn can do it."

Quinn practically gapes at me. "Oh, come on, surely Asante can handle that—"

"Just do it, please."

If I sound rattled, there's a reason. An email just pinged in on my phone. It's from Alan Challow, and it's marked URGENT. There are plenty of people in this job who up their own importance by marking everything top priority, but Alan Challow isn't one of them.

We go back a long way, him and me. He started at Thames Valley barely eighteen months before I did. We've worked the same cases, made the same mistakes, known the same people. I've backed him up more than once over the years and he's done the same for me. Though I wouldn't call us friends, and he takes an inordinate pleasure in winding me up.

But that's not what he's doing now. I read the email and for a second—just a second—my heart contracts. But I'm being ridiculous. It's just a coincidence—a random accident of chance—

Quinn is watching me, frowning a little. He heard the phone, watched me look at it, just like the rest of them. "Fine," he says eventually. "Fine."

Gislingham glances at Baxter and then at me. "I was also wondering, sir," he begins slowly, "whether we could think about issuing an appeal."

I look up. "What sort of appeal?"

He hesitates. "Look, it's only a matter of time before this gets out. Then it'll be the works—the whole Twitter shitstorm. So why not get in first and issue an appeal for witnesses? We could ask Harrison—"

"Ask him what, precisely?"

"You know, whether he thinks a TV appeal might be helpful—"

I take a deep breath. "If we start announcing that young women are being randomly dragged off the streets and assaulted we'll have panic on our hands, and the odd snide comment on Twitter will be the least of our bloody worries. I'm not about to provoke that sort of class-one mass hysteria unless and until we have completely discounted the possibility that this was a hate crime, perpetrated by someone Faith knew."

I look around the room, drilling in the point. "So where are we with her friends? Her classmates—her wider circle?"

Somer's head goes up. "She doesn't really have one, sir. She's very private. She doesn't seem to have many friends."

"There must be *somebody*—someone she's pissed off— someone with a problem with the whole transgender issue—"

Somer looks bleak. "We have been looking, sir, honestly we have. But she really does keep herself to herself. The picture we've been getting is of someone who goes out of her way to be anonymous, who is careful to the point of paranoia about not upsetting anyone."

"So who have you actually *spoken* to?"

Her turn to flush. "Her teachers, mainly. We've been

circumspect about saying much to other students because she's so concerned about keeping her status a secret—"

"You know as well as I do that her status may be the very reason she was attacked—how the hell can we rule that out if we can't even bloody mention it?"

Somer glances at Everett. I'm starting to lose patience now.

"Look, I'm not about to out anyone for the sake of it, but that's not what we're talking about here—"

"I promised her, sir," says Somer, cutting across me, bright red now, but holding my eye, standing her ground. "I promised her we'd respect her privacy."

I try to count to ten, but only get to five. "And what if it happens again, what then? What if some other poor kid like her gets attacked? And what if next time the bastard who did it doesn't get interrupted? How are you going to explain that to the family? How do you think they'll react when you tell them that we knew there was someone targeting trans kids but did sod all about it because we were too frightened we might upset someone? But it won't be you telling them that, will it? No. It'll be me. As per bloody usual. Well, I'm sorry, Somer, but in future you're going to have to be a lot more careful what promises you make."

I force myself to stop; I'm overreacting, I know I am. I'm pushing this too hard because I'm off-balance. Because I want hatred to be the answer. Because bad as that is, it's better than—

"I could do some work on anti-trans groups, sir," says Asante evenly. "See if there's anything local—anything on social media."

98

"I've already looked," says Baxter quickly, giving him a stare that says *Get off my lawn.* "Nothing doing."

I flash a glare at him. "Then look harder."

I turn to Everett and Somer. "And talk to her friends. And that's not a request. It's an order."

* * *

Sent: Weds 03/04/2018, 08.35   **Importance: High**
From: AlanChallowCSI@ThamesValley.police.uk
To: DIAdamFawley@ThamesValley.police.uk

Subject: URGENT

Not tagging this email with a case number for reasons that will become obvious. I just heard back from the lab—they found calcium sulphate on Faith Appleford's shoes, presumably picked up from the back of that van. There wasn't much, but it was there.

Call me as soon as you get this.

* * *

"What the fuck happened there?" says Quinn, keeping his voice low. He's just joined Everett and Gislingham at the coffee machine. Somer is nowhere to be seen. Asante is a few yards away, apparently reading something on the noticeboard.

"Has Fawley lost it or what?"

Gis shrugs. "Search me. I've never seen him like that before, that's for sure."

"How come he's still flogging the bloody hate crime angle when he knows damn well we can't find shit-all evidence for it?"

Ev makes a face; she's never seen Fawley like that before either, and especially not with Somer. He's always gone out of his way to encourage her—to respect her judgment. So much so that at one time they all thought—

"Could be more trouble with the wife?" says Quinn, a little louder now. "It was only a few months ago that we all thought she'd left him—what do you reckon? More shit in that quarter?"

Gis gives him a warning look and a meaningful glance toward Asante, who's well within earshot. But he still seems completely absorbed in the proposed changes to the Police Service Pension Scheme.

Ev shakes her head. "I don't think it's that—not this time. I saw them last weekend at the Summertown farmers' market. She had her back to me but they looked pretty loved-up."

"So what then—has he got Harrison chewing his ear?"

Gis considers. "Hasn't he always? But whatever it is, I say we just keep our heads down and avoid pissing him off, eh?" He reaches for a plastic cup and presses the button for cappuccino. "Which in your case, Quinn, means tracking down those hire vans. And pronto."

Quinn gives him a sardonic look Gis pretends not to see, and the three of them make their way back to their desks. A few moments later Somer emerges from the Ladies. Her hair is smooth and her face calm, but there's a slight redness about her eyes that only someone observant would see. As she draws close to Asante he turns from the noticeboard.

"Everything OK?"

He says it pleasantly enough but there's something about him that always makes her unsettled.

"Of course," she says, quickening her step. "Why wouldn't it be?"

* * *

You don't need to tell me I didn't handle that very well. I was just a bit wrong-footed, that's all. It's been years—years when I've done my damnedest to lock it away, and now, out of nowhere—

My phone rings. It's Challow. He hasn't bothered waiting for me to call him. And he doesn't bother with informalities either.

"You got the email?"

"Are you absolutely sure—it couldn't be anything else?"

"Unlike human beings, chemistry doesn't lie. It's one reason why I like this job."

"Shit."

"Yes," he says heavily. "I suspect that's probably the most appropriate response. In the circumstances."

There's a silence. Then, "What are you going to do?"

"I don't know."

I hear him draw breath. "You need to tell your team—it's not fair to keep them in the dark—"

"I know. I just need some time to think this through."

I can almost hear him shrug. "Well, that's your call, though it wouldn't be mine. But either way, you have to speak to Harrison. And without wishing to sound like a shit, if you don't, I will."

*   *   *

Everett and Somer have opted to hang out in the canteen at the FE college in an attempt to keep things casual, but even without uniforms they stand out like grannies in Doc Martens. The students buy coffee and Danish and gather chattering at adjacent tables, but all the while you can sense the tension, see the glances thrown in the officers' direction. It's not unease exactly, but disquiet, an awareness that something's up.

"So what do we do?" asks Everett in an undertone. "Pull on our size elevenses and start gatecrashing?"

Somer gestures toward a girl who's just joined the coffee queue; she has a large portfolio on the floor by her feet, a pixie haircut and wide brown eyes. "That may be as good a place to start as any."

"OK," says Everett. "I'll start the other side."

"You're doing Art, are you?" says Somer as she takes her place in the queue behind the girl with the portfolio.

The girl turns and smiles. "Fashion and Design actually. But the bloody sketchbooks are no smaller."

"We've been talking to some of your classmates, but I don't think I remember you?"

The girl gives her order and turns back to Somer. "Yeah, I heard about that. You're from the police, right?"

Somer makes a rueful gesture. "Rumbled."

But the girl seems unfazed. "I had that bug over the weekend, that's why I wasn't around on Monday. I'm Jess, Jess Beardsley. You were asking about Faith?"

"You know her?"

The girl makes a face. "Not exactly *know*, but I don't think anyone here does really."

Somer buys a bottle of water and follows the girl toward an empty table.

"So you're on the same course, the two of you?" she asks as they sit down.

Jess nods. "But she's out of my league. *Seriously* shit hot. No one else is even close."

"And that doesn't make other people jealous? No one likes a swot, do they?"

The girl laughs. "Faith's not like that. She doesn't mind helping you out. You know, making suggestions and stuff. She isn't up herself."

"Does she have a boyfriend?"

Jess shakes her head. "No one here, anyway. Not for want of trying by some of them. But she doesn't seem that interested. Though, frankly, I can see her point."

She glances across at the lads at the next table; they're laughing at something and digging each other in the ribs. "Bunch of overgrown kids, most of them."

Somer returns the ironic look. "How about girl-friends?"

Jess picks up her spoon and starts to stir, a small smile

on the edge of her mouth. "You mean girlfriends or *girl*friends?"

Somer keeps her voice neutral. "Either."

"Neither, in fact." She licks the spoon then puts it down. "And that's not for want of trying, too."

* * *

Harrison must have done some sort of a deal with Facilities because his office is actually warm. He isn't even wearing his jacket, which is on a hanger on the coat stand in the far corner. A proper coat hanger. With satin padding. I suspect there's a clothes brush in his drawer too though I've never actually seen it.

He looks up at me and gestures to the chair.

"Your PA said you wanted a quick chat, sir. About the Appleford assault."

He sits back. "On the hate crime angle specifically. The Area Commander wants an update."

"Enquiries are still ongoing, sir. We've turned up nothing conclusive so far."

"Which reminds me," he says, perking up a little, "I gather the new addition to your team has rather distinguished himself on this one."

I feel my nerves prickling; he has no business knowing that.

"It was good solid policework, sir. What I expect from all my team."

He looks at me, and then away. For some reason, he wants Asante to do well. And not just because he was the one who hired him.

"So," he says, "is there any progress on running down the perp?"

His bloody vocabulary gets more transatlantic by the day. If he starts talking about "unsubs" I may actually have to kill him.

"We've identified several vans that were on Cherwell Drive and the Marston Ferry Road at the right time, sir. We're endeavoring to establish if the drivers have valid alibis, but beyond that we have very little to go on."

Harrison frowns, picks up his pen and starts tapping it. I'm trying not to let it irritate me.

"What about an appeal—asking the public for help?"

So that's it. I wonder, for a tiny moment, if he's been talking to Gis—whether that's where Gis got it from. But he can't have—Gis wouldn't go behind my back—

"I'm not sure that's a good idea, sir. It could cause significant and completely unnecessary alarm—"

His frown deepens. "I'm not sure the quick wins might not outweigh any potential downside."

Jesus. He'll be talking about low-hanging fruit next.

"We can certainly keep it as an option, sir."

"So you'll have a word with the Press Office—tee them up, just in case?"

I get to my feet, glad of any excuse to get out of there—to make this conversation stop. And it's not his turgid bloody lingo I'm talking about now. To paraphrase those immortal words, I do not have to say anything, but it's quite another thing not mentioning it when questioned at point-blank range.

"Absolutely, sir. I'll get on to them right away."

* * *

* * *

Adam Fawley
3 April 2018
12.30

I'm late to the doctor's: Alex is already in the consulting room by the time I get there and the kindly receptionist bustles me through as soon as she spots me.

"They've only just started," she says in a low voice. "Dr. Robbins has had a very heavy morning."

Alex looks up when the door opens and I see the relief wash over her face. She kept saying today is just routine—that I didn't really need to come, not if I was busy—but I know she wanted me here. Just as I know how worried she is, and how much worse that anxiety is getting as her due date draws nearer. And how hard she's working to keep any of that from me.

"Ah, Mr. Fawley," says the doctor, looking up at me over her glasses. She's only been at the practice for a couple of years. Which is my way of saying she never knew Jake. She knows about him, of course. It's in the file, for a start, but even if it wasn't, everyone knows here. It's why the receptionist is always so nice to me, why Alex is getting checkups every three weeks: you get a special sort of compassion if you're the parent of a dead child. A child who died at their own hand.

"I'm sorry I'm late. Traffic." No one questions that excuse. Not in this town.

"I'm glad you're here." She smiles briefly, then looks back at her notes. "The health visitor asked Alexandra to come in today because she was concerned about her blood pressure. As am I. It's rather higher than we'd ideally like." She looks over at Alex. "Are you under any particular stress at the moment?"

Alex opens her mouth then closes it again. "No," she says at last. "Not especially. I'm trying to take things easy. I even got a cab here so I didn't have to drive—"

"But you're still working, I think?"

Alex nods. "Only from home. Well, mostly. I'm not going into the office unless I really have to. You know, for meetings. Sometimes clients insist. If it's a big case."

The doctor makes a disapproving face. "That sounds pretty stressful to me."

"I have an assistant—she's doing most of the basics—"

But the doctor doesn't appear to be listening. She takes off her glasses, as if to underline the point. "I'd like you to take at least a week off—*completely* off—and then we'll check your blood pressure again and decide where we go from there."

I look at Alex and then back at the doctor. "But there's nothing actually wrong, is there? Alex isn't at any risk—"

"No, no," says the doctor briskly. "I'm just being cautious. Perhaps overcautious, but I'd rather err on the side of prudence. In the circumstances."

Alex takes my arm as I walk her back to the car. Perhaps I'm getting paranoid too, but she seems to be leaning more heavily than usual.

"You're sure you feel OK? No dizziness, nothing like that?"

She smiles and squeezes my arm. "No, nothing like that. Stop worrying."

"I *am* worrying. That doctor just ordered bed rest."

"No, she didn't, she just said not to go into work—"

"Well, as far as I'm concerned, that means bed rest. And that's exactly what you're going to get."

She laughs. "OK, you win. As long as it involves tea, chocolate and unlimited supplies of fruit toast."

"I'll even throw in a hot-water bottle. Not literally, of course."

We're at the car now and I stop and turn her to me.

She looks as brittle as a porcelain doll.

* * *

Interview with Kenneth Ashwin, conducted at St.
Aldate's Police Station, Oxford
3 April 2018, 1:25 p.m.
In attendance, DC G. Quinn

GQ: Take a seat, Mr. Ashwin. As I said, this is
    just routine.

KA: I've seen the telly. I know what that means.

GQ: [*passes across an image*]
    Last Monday morning, April 1st 2018, the
    minivan shown in this still was picked up on
    the CCTV camera outside the petrol station
    on the Cherwell Drive roundabout. It's a hire
    vehicle, and when we spoke to the company they
    said you were driving it that day.

KA: That's right, I was. My brother was moving
    house so I was giving him a hand.

GQ: So what were you doing there that morning?

KA: When was it again? Exactly?

GQ: [*becoming impatient*]
    Last Monday. Two days ago. *Like I just said.*

KA: Nope. Don't think that was me.

GQ: It's the same reg number as the van you hired.

KA: I can't help that.

GQ: [*checks paperwork*]
    You live in Barton, don't you?

KA: [*warily*]
    Yeah, so?

GQ: So you might have been coming into the city?

KA: I suppose so. I did pick up some bits and
    pieces that morning—

GQ: So it could be you, after all—is that what
    you're saying?

KA: It's *possible*, yes. But I don't *remember*.

GQ: OK, Mr. Ashwin, I think that's enough for now.

* * *

Adam Fawley
3 April 2018
13.39

"Boss? It's Quinn."

It's just started to rain, and the traffic is slowing to a haul. Beside me, Alex is hunched against the misted-up car window, staring out.

I pull the phone from its hands-free. Alex would normally bollock me for doing that while I'm driving but she barely seems to notice. She's hardly spoken since we left the doctor's.

"Boss—you there?"

"Yes, what is it?"

"Sorry to bother you, but no one knew where you were."

"I had to go home briefly, that's all. What do you want?"

"Just thought you'd want to know. I tracked down the people who hired those self-drives. One was a woman of sixty who was moving some stuff for her church, which the vicar confirmed."

God as alibi. Not bad. "And the other?"

"Bloke of fifty-nine, but I reckon he's a nonstarter."

"Why—did he have a good reason for being there?"

"No, because one) he's about eighteen stone and needed a winch to get him out of the sodding chair, and two) he's

110

effing pond life. Sorry but the bloke's dead from the neck up. Jesus, I ended up wanting to eat my own hands—"

"Doesn't mean he's not guilty, Quinn—you know as well as I do—"

"Seriously, boss, he'd have to be Benedict sodding Cumberbatch to fake it that well."

I take a deep breath; Quinn's a lazy sod but he has good instincts. Despite himself, sometimes. "OK, but don't lose sight of him. Stupidity isn't a defense. Nor is being tedious."

Alex glances across and I smile at her. It's just routine. Nothing for her to worry about. But isn't that what she keeps telling me?

I return to Quinn. "Anything—you know—online?"

Quinn realizes suddenly that I have someone with me. That I can't spell it out.

"Oh, right. No. Baxter's been trawling some of those forums that target trans people but nothing doing yet. Though you wouldn't believe the poison those shits spew out—I only had a quick look but Jesus Christ. Baxter says he's never wanted a hot shower so much in his entire life."

I did a training day once, with the Child Exploitation and Online Protection Command. Hats off to the people who do that sort of work but I felt contaminated for days. I couldn't even look at photos of my own son without seeing other children's faces, other children's bodies superimposed on his.

But I don't want that thought. Especially not now. Even allowing it into my mind feels like a betrayal, a dark jinx over the coming child.

I put the phone down and turn to Alex, who sits back in her seat and reaches for my hand.

"Everything's fine," I say gently. "Let's just get you home."

* * *

Phone call with Julia Davidson, head teacher,
Wellington College, Carlisle Road, Basingstoke
3 April 2018, 2:05 p.m.
On the call, DC V. Everett

VE: I just wanted to have a quick chat with you about one of your former pupils, Mrs. Davidson. Just for some background. The surname is Appleford?

JD: Oh yes? Has there been some sort of problem?

VE: Not exactly—

JD: Because I'd be surprised if either Daniel or Nadine had got themselves into trouble with the police.

VE: [*pause*]
It's nothing like that, Mrs. Davidson. And it's not about Nadine. It's about Daniel. Both were at your school, I believe?

JD: That's right. Mrs. Appleford was keen to move to Oxford, but it made sense to wait until Daniel sat his GCSEs.

VE: What was your impression of him?

JD: I wish we had more like him, if you really want to know. Hard-working, polite, well-mannered. A credit to the school.

VE: How did he get on with his peers? Was there anyone he had trouble with?

JD: Oh, nothing like that, he was very popular. Much more so than Nadine, who, between ourselves, can be rather touchy. Though she's the brighter of the two, if only she'd buckle down and apply herself. But you know what kids that age are like—any sort of academic aptitude is some sort of curse. Sport is different, of course—

VE: Was Daniel good at sport?

JD: No. In fact, as far as I could tell he did everything he could to avoid PE in all its forms. But he wasn't particularly unusual in that. Changing rooms, showers, puberty—it can be a nerve-racking combination for any teenager. No, sport definitely wasn't his thing, but he was hugely talented in other ways.

VE: You mean the design stuff?

JD: Yes. He was exceptionally good at art from Year Seven on. My colleague in the art department said Danny was the most gifted student she'd seen in over ten years.

VE: So studying fashion was a natural progression?

JD: [*laughs*]
Absolutely—he had his heart set on that long before he chose his GCSEs. You may laugh, but I genuinely thought we might have the next Alexander McQueen on our hands.

* * *

I promised Challow I'd talk to Harrison. And I will. Just not yet. There's someone else I need to see first.

I pull up outside a solid brick and flint house a few miles outside Abingdon. Open fields, a high hedgerow and a line of distant trees that marks the river. For as long as I worked for him it was Alastair Osbourne's dream to retire to the country, and last time I came here Project Picket Fence was well underway. Climbing roses, herbaceous borders, the lot. The place looks a lot less loved now, but then again, it's hard to make anything look that wonderful on a gray April afternoon, even if you do have a lot of time on your hands.

I rang ahead so he knew I was coming but he still looks frazzled when he opens the door. He has a mug of tea in one hand and a tea towel over his shoulder.

"Adam," he says distractedly, as if he expected me and yet was still taken on the hop. "It's good to see you."

"You're sure it's not a bad time?"

There's a flicker across his face at that, which I don't immediately understand.

"No, no, not at all," he says. "It's just, well, one of those days." He steps aside to let me in. "Viv's in the conservatory. She likes to be able to look at the garden."

That phrase alone should have told me something, but I'm too wound up about what I'm about to say to hear it. Which is why I'm so entirely unprepared for what I see, when I follow him through to the back. Vivian Osbourne, avid fell walker, former bank manager and no-nonsense

Girl Guide leader, is by the window. She has a rug over her knees and a large black cat curled asleep on her lap, but she's sitting in a wheelchair. I falter a moment then try desperately to pretend I haven't.

"MS," she says, her voice a little halting but still the Viv I remember. "The bastard."

"I'm sorry—I didn't know."

She makes a face. "Well, we haven't exactly been putting announcements in the *Oxford Mail*. It's been pretty shitty, to be honest, but we're getting there. Finding a way forward."

Osbourne puts the mug he's holding on the table next to her. "Will you be OK in here for a bit if I take Adam into the kitchen?"

She flaps her hand at him with a dry smile. "You two go and talk shop. I'm not completely incapable. Not yet, anyway."

When we get to the kitchen Osbourne flicks on the kettle and turns to face me.

"How long's it been?"

"Since the diagnosis? We knew about that before I retired. It's why I went six months early."

I did wonder; we all did. Everyone noticed a change in him, toward the end—a weariness, a sense that he really didn't care much any more. But we just thought it was the job. That it had finally ground him down.

"We weren't doing badly until she started needing the chair. That was last autumn. Since then, it's not been so easy."

I remember the state of the garden, and I try not to make it obvious that I can now see the kitchen could do with a proper clean and there's an over-full bin reeking by the back door.

"I'm sorry—if I'd known, I wouldn't have bothered you."

He shakes his head. "Don't be ridiculous. Life may be tougher but it still goes on. And Viv's the last person who'd want treating like an invalid. You should know that."

He turns and reaches into a cupboard for teabags.

"So what was it you wanted to talk to me about?"

And here we are. No-way-back time.

"Gavin Parrie."

He pours the boiling water, stirs both mugs, puts the kettle back down and then, and only then, turns to face me.

* * *

Daily Mail

21st December 1999

"ROADSIDE RAPIST" GETS LIFE
Judge calls Gavin Parrie "evil, unrepentant and depraved"

By John Smithson

The predator dubbed the "Roadside Rapist" was given a life sentence yesterday, after a nine-week trial at the Old Bailey. Judge Peter Healey condemned Parrie as "evil, unrepentant and depraved" and recommended he serve a minimum of 15 years. There was uproar in the court after the sentence was announced, with abuse directed at both judge and jury from members of Parrie's family in the public gallery.

Parrie has always insisted that he is innocent of the rape and attempted rape of seven young women in the Oxford area between

January and December 1998. One of his victims, 19-year-old Emma Goddard, committed suicide some months after her ordeal. Parrie contends he was framed by Thames Valley Police and, as he was led away, he was heard issuing death threats against the officer who had been instrumental in his apprehension, saying he would "get him" and he and his family would "spend the rest of their lives watching their backs." The officer in question, Detective Sergeant Adam Fawley, has received a commendation from the Chief Constable for his work on the case.

Speaking after the verdict, Chief Superintendent Michael Oswald of Thames Valley Police said he was confident that the right man had been convicted and confirmed that no other credible suspect had ever been identified in the course of what became a county-wide investigation. "I am proud of the work done by my team. They went to enormous lengths to find the perpetrator of these appalling crimes and bring him to justice, and it is absolutely unacceptable that they should be subject to either threats or intimidation. Police officers put their lives on the line on a regular basis to protect the public, and you may rest assured that we take all necessary steps to ensure the continued safety of our officers and their families."

Emma Goddard's mother, Jennifer, spoke to reporters outside the court after the verdict, saying that nothing was ever going to bring her daughter back, but she hoped she could now rest in peace, knowing the man who destroyed her life was going to pay the price for what he had done.

*　*　*

"Alan Challow found it. It was on the girl's shoes."

Osbourne smiles. "How is the recalcitrant old bugger?"

"OK. Bit heavier, bit balder, but otherwise much the same."

He laughs briefly at the memory. But only briefly. "And those test results—there's no doubt?"

I shake my head.

He digs the teabags out and hands one of the mugs to me. There are bits floating on the surface, as if the milk is on the turn.

"But that's not such a huge deal, is it?" he says.

I feel my jaw tightening. "It could be. You know the plaster dust thing was always controversial. We never found any of it in that van of his. Or the lock-up."

"But the brother was a builder, wasn't he? Parrie could easily have borrowed his van if his own was off the road."

Which is precisely what we told the court, and what the jury must have decided to believe, even though the brother vehemently denied it. Parrie always said the plaster dust proved he wasn't guilty, and now there's someone else out there, attacking young women, leaving the exact same thing on his victims—

I take a deep breath. "It's not just that. Faith said he pulled out her hair. Though it's not clear if that was by accident or intent."

Osbourne's face hardens. "Look, Adam, you can't seriously be suggesting that the real rapist is still at large somewhere? Someone who—let's not forget—stopped what he was doing the minute we arrested Parrie, only to start up again now, out of the blue, after all these years?"

"Perhaps he's been in prison. Perhaps he's been abroad.

Perhaps he's been doing it somewhere else all this time and we just didn't know."

"I don't believe that for a minute. Someone, somewhere, would have made the connection by now."

"Not necessarily—"

"It isn't him," he says steadily. "You know it isn't."

"Do I?"

He holds my gaze. "We caught Parrie, Adam. *You* caught Parrie. He's in Wandsworth. The same place he's been for the last eighteen years."

He puts the mug down and takes a step toward me. "We got the right man. I believed that then, and I believe it now."

And I know why. Because there was one thing the jury never heard; one thing the law back then wouldn't let us use. After we arrested Parrie, we discovered he'd been questioned about a similar attack on a sixteen-year-old girl in Manchester two years before, but when they finally got him into an identity parade the poor kid was half out of her mind with terror and refused to identify him. By the time he started on our patch he'd got a lot more savvy. And a lot more brutal.

I look away, out of the window, down the garden. On the horizon, I can just make out Wittenham Clumps.

"We thought we had the right man for Hannah Gardiner too."

Hannah Gardiner who went missing on the Clumps in 2015. Hannah Gardiner who Osbourne thought—we *all* thought—had been abducted by a man called Reginald Shore. But we were wrong.

There's a silence, and when I turn back to look at him his cheeks are red.

"You know how much I regret that, Adam. Especially now."

I take a deep breath. "All I meant was that sometimes we don't get it right. Despite our instincts and our training and all the rest of the crap—even if we're a hundred per cent convinced we have the right man we can still be completely wrong."

Silence again. I can hear Viv talking to the cat in the next room, and the rattle as the wind lifts the corrugated plastic on the lean-to outside.

"I'm sorry, sir," I begin, but he waves it away.

"No need for the apology. Or the 'sir.' If I sounded defensive, then I'm afraid there was a reason."

He goes over to the pile of post by the bread bin and pulls out an envelope from halfway down. Locates it so quickly, in fact, that I know he must have put it there deliberately so it was out of sight. Because whatever it is, he doesn't want Viv to see it.

He hands it to me. A plain brown envelope addressed as "Confidential" to Detective Superintendent A. G. Osbourne, Thames Valley Police (Retired), with a postmark dated two weeks before and a government crest. *Her Majesty's Prison Service.*

I look up with a question and he nods. "It's a psych report on Gavin Parrie. He's up for parole."

PSYCHIATRIC REPORT

Name:	**Gavin Francis Parrie**
Date of birth:	**28th May 1962**
Current location:	**HMP Wandsworth**
Date of report:	**12th March 2018**

Executive summary

This report has been prepared as part of the process of assessing Mr. Parrie for possible parole. I have spent a total of six hours with him, on three separate occasions at HMP Wandsworth. I have had access to police and prison records, and have consulted Dr. Adrian Bigelow, Consultant Forensic Psychiatrist to HMP Wandsworth, who has been responsible for overseeing Mr. Parrie since he took up the post in 2014. In addition, I have considerable personal experience in the assessment of offenders convicted of sexual offenses (a full *curriculum vitae* is attached).

The prison staff I spoke to confirmed that Mr. Parrie has been in every respect a model prisoner. He has taken on a variety of work within the prison environment, and has always carried it out diligently and conscientiously. He has not been involved in any disciplinary or violent incidents, and has successfully completed various training courses which would assist him in obtaining employment, were he to be released. The attached Occupational Therapy report indicates that he is fully capable of carrying out ordinary daily activities and managing his daily routine in a productive manner. He is deemed to be a positive influence on other inmates, especially younger offenders. He has worked hard to maintain contact with his children by letter, and they visit once or twice a year (they currently reside with Mr. Parrie's former wife in Aberdeen so more frequent visits are not practicable). In all the above respects, therefore, I consider him an appropriate candidate for consideration by the Board.

However, there remains one significant issue, i.e., his contention that he is not guilty of the crimes for which he was imprisoned. Such a failure to assume responsibility for offending behavior and express appropriate remorse (especially with offenses of this gravity) is usually deemed to be a significant bar to early release. However, while Parrie continues to maintain his innocence, it appears his attitude has ameliorated considerably in this respect in recent months. Previous to this, he had always insisted that the police "fitted him up"; he now appears willing to concede that while there may have been mistakes in the Thames Valley Police investigation, there was no deliberate attempt to frame him for a crime he did not commit. The abatement of this paranoia is clearly a very positive sign. It must also be borne in mind that he has now served eighteen years, and had he originally entered a guilty plea, he might well have been released before this date.

The Parole Board has a duty to assess whether a specific offender continues to present a risk to the public, and individuals will not be eligible for parole unless the Board is satisfied on this point. However, it is—as is well known—especially difficult for someone in Mr. Parrie's particular position to demonstrate reduced risk of harm, as sex offenders who refuse to admit guilt are not eligible for the Sexual Offenders Treatment Program (SOTP) and the Structured Assessment of Risk and Need (SARN) which follows completion of that program, which the Parole Board look to when assessing these offenders.

At the same time, it is crucial that those who do maintain their innocence—regardless of the nature of their crime(s)—should not be discriminated against, especially where there are other factors that can be brought into play, to assist in the assessment of risk. I would point to Mr. Parrie's proven good conduct, over a very long period, in support of this. In my own conversations with him, he also expressed considerable sympathy with the victims of the crimes (albeit while maintaining that he himself was not culpable), which I also consider to be a positive sign.

I do not consider Mr. Parrie to be suffering either from mental illness or any psychiatric condition such as schizoaffective disorder, within the meaning of the Mental Health Act 1983 (amended 2007).

Dr. Simeon Ware
MBBS FRCPsych
Consultant Forensic Psychiatrist

"I don't believe a bloody word of it. Model prisoner, my arse. It's all just a bloody act."

Osbourne takes the report from me and slips it back in the envelope; he's going out on a limb, letting me see it at all.

"And he's *still* telling anyone who'll listen that he's innocent."

Even now, all these years later. I should have expected it, knowing what I do, but it infuriates me all the same.

Osbourne is watching my face. "At least he seems to have backed off about being fitted up."

"It's not just that, though, is it? This new attack—it's too similar—it's all going to start up all over again—"

"But that's the point, Adam. It's *similar.* It's *not* the *same.* From what you've said, the attack on the Appleford girl is far more likely to be a hate crime. And even if it isn't, there are umpteen ways you could explain any superficial parallels. It could be a copycat, for starters. Someone who read about the Parrie case in the papers. It wouldn't be the first time, now would it?"

I want to believe it. Part of why I came here was to hear him say it. But the unease is still there, snaking around my gut.

"Is that something you're looking into?"

I shake my head. "Not yet. Not officially."

He knows what I'm getting at: looking for a copycat would mean going public. At least internally.

"Might be worth checking who's been visiting Parrie, though," he says carefully.

I nod. That, at least, I can probably do without making too many waves.

"I just think it would be worth ruling it out," he continues. "But I'm sure you have nothing to worry about."

I put down the mug and manage a thin smile.

"Thanks for the tea. And the reassurance."

His smile is a lot more convincing than mine. "Any

time. Though the press are bound to pick up on the Parrie thing sooner or later so best be prepared, eh?"

I get the message. "I'm seeing Harrison first thing."

"Good. And Alex? How's she coping with all this?"

"She's fine," I say quickly. "Busy at work, you know."

He must sense something, because he frowns slightly but he doesn't push it, and then I make a big show of getting out my car keys and we're going in to say goodbye to Viv and shaking hands on the doorstep and I'm trying my best to avoid his eye.

Because I'm not sure which is worse; the lie of omission or the lie I just told.

* * *

"So what do you think—do we still want pizza?"

Patsie is sitting behind Sasha on the top deck of the bus going toward Summertown, her backpack wedged between her feet. She's wearing her red leather jacket, like she always does. Isabel's next to Sasha, listening to music on her phone and fiddling about with her hair. She's dyed the ends pink. Sasha half wishes she had the courage to do that, but only half. It's not just that her mother would flip (to which Iz just shrugged and said it would grow out eventually so no need to get your knickers in a twist); Sasha's always been rather proud of her hair, and her mum never stops reminding her that as soon as you start dyeing it you'll never get the real color back.

Patsie leans forward and digs Isabel in the ribs. "Earth to Parker. *Where. Do. We. Want. To. Go?*"

Iz turns around and pretends to swipe her. "I heard

you honking the first time, you noisy cow. I don't care as long as I don't have to eat my weight in pizza—I am getting SO fat!"

Sasha gives her a sidelong look. "Yeah, right. You're a size six, for God's sake."

Iz blows her a kiss and Patsie makes a puking gesture and they all collapse in giggles. On the other side of the aisle Leah reaches into her bag and pulls out a bottle with a straw in and passes it around. It says Diet Coke on the side, but there's a good glug of her father's Scotch in there too. Not the malt—he'd notice that—just the stuff he keeps for when the neighbors come around. Sasha takes as small a sip as she can get away with then hands it back, feeling the alcohol burn down her throat. She's taught herself not to gag, but really, whiskey is truly disgusting. And as for those bright-green shot things—they just taste like mouthwash—

"So, you going to tell us or what?"

Sasha looks up. Her three friends are staring at her, trying to suppress their knowing smiles. Sasha does her best to look Innocent And Baffled but she can't be making a very good job of it because Leah gives her one of her *yeah, yeah* faces.

"Don't even try and pull that one—we know you've got a new bloke, don't we, Pats? So—give. Who is he?"

Sasha feels herself blushing. "I don't know what you mean."

The girls give her theatrically incredulous looks. "You've been mega secretive for *days*," says Isabel. "What is it—is he married or something?"

She has her head on one side now, scrutinizing Sasha for a reaction, which only makes her blush even more.

"Well, wouldn't you like to know," she says, trying to look playful and teasing. As if she's sitting on a delicious secret. Which she tells herself she is—well, sort of, anyway.

Iz looks archly at Patsie and passes Sasha the bottle again. "Don't worry. Few more of these and we'll get the truth out of her. We've got all night."

Patsie pokes Iz in the shoulder blades. "You, Isabel Rebecca Parker, are all talk. You were totally out of it last week on *two* Cactus Jacks."

She grins at Sasha, who gives her a relieved smile in return. She can rely on Patsie to back her up. She always has—ever since playgroup. The two only became four when they went to secondary school, where the class clever clogs started calling them the LIPS girls: Leah, Isabel, Patsie, Sasha. The others loved it—they even started using it for their WhatsApp group—but Sasha knows irony when she sees it. Especially given how much time the others spend pouting into their makeup mirrors. Either way, the name stuck. And they're tight, the four of them; all the other girls want to be in with their group, but as Pats once joked, the LIPS are sealed. But even now, Sasha and Patsie have something special that Leah and Iz don't share. Though Sasha's realized, these last few weeks, that there are some things she'd rather not talk about to anyone, not even Patsie. Like Liam. Especially Liam—

There's a sudden burst of laughter from the group of lads in the front of the bus, and a man near the back looks up and frowns. He got on just after Sasha and the others, but unlike the boys, he isn't even on their radar. He's not the sort of man people notice, least of all teenage girls. He mutters something about the noise and turns to look out of the window. The boys, meanwhile, are now swiveling glances in the direction of the girls, but Iz has already declared them "like, totally skanky" so talking to them is clearly out of the question.

"What did you tell your mum?" asks Leah. "About tonight?"

Sasha shrugs. "Just that we were going for a pizza and I might stay over with Pats. She's chill about it."

But her cheeks flush a little at the memory. Of her mum smiling and telling her to have a good time. Of the hug she got as she was leaving and the "I love you" that still lays heavy on her heart. She hates lying to her mum; she always has, even when she was little, and she wishes she didn't have to now. But she knows her mum wouldn't understand. She'd be hurt and angry and it's so much easier and kinder right now to let her think she's crashing with Pats. Some day—*soon*—she'll explain everything. She's promised herself she'll do that and she'll hold to it. Just not quite yet.

"Wish mine was more like yours," says Isabel, making a face. "She just will *not* get off my case. I mean, I could actually get *married* in four months."

Sasha's turn to grimace. "God, imagine getting shackled at *sixteen*. I have *so* much I want to do before I get lumbered with all that crap."

Iz grins. "Yeah, yeah, we all know what *you're* going to be doing this summer. That's when you're not walking the Inca Trail and bungee jumping off the Grand Canyon and swimming with dolphins in the Galapagos—"

"It was Australia—I don't think they even *have* dolphins in the Galapa–"

She stops and laughs, seeing their faces. "OK, OK. Perhaps I do go on a bit."

Their mouths drop open, mock-aghast. "No, *seriously?*"

"Anyway," says Patsie, popping a Haribo into her mouth and chewing loudly. "At least it'd be better than no one wanting to marry you *at all*. Like that creep Scott."

Isabel bursts out laughing. "No one'd shag him—imagine that pizza face rubbing all over your tits!"

They're squealing with laughter now, rolling in the seats and clutching their stomachs. The boys are looking around, wondering what's going on and clearly worried the joke is on them, which just sets the girls off all over again.

* * *

Adam Fawley
3 April 2018
19.25

"I'm sorry, I should have said something before. But I didn't want to worry you."

Alex turns back to the chopping board and reaches for another tomato. She's trying to pretend everything is OK but she's gripping the knife so tightly her knuckles are white.

"Osbourne doesn't think there's anything to be concerned about. But there could be something in the press—"

"There's bound to be, isn't there?" Her voice trembles a little and I can see her willing herself to keep control. "It was all over the papers back then, you know it was. It was like—like—the Yorkshire Ripper."

They called Parrie the Roadside Rapist long before they knew his real name. He dragged his victims off the pavement and assaulted them in undergrowth and darkened alleyways and deserted car parks reeking of piss. But that was just the start; we never thought we would end up thinking the first women were the lucky ones. We didn't know, then, what he was capable of.

Alex puts the knife down now and leans against the counter.

"Alex, leave that for a minute, please. You don't need to pretend—not with me."

She turns to face me and my heart contracts at how pale she is. I pull out a chair for her and she sits down heavily.

"We all knew he'd be released sometime. He's done eighteen years."

"It's not enough," she says quickly, her voice so harsh it's as if she's wrenching out the words. "After what he did. The threats—"

I reach for her hand. "Well, let's hope the parole board agree with you."

She pulls away from me and reaches a hand to her hair, pushing it away from her face. Her cheeks are flushed now and I can see a pulse flickering in her throat.

"Try not to let it prey on your mind—it's not good for you—or the baby."

She meets my gaze and smiles weakly. "Easier said than done, I'm afraid."

"I know, but I still had to say it."

"Did Osbourne say when it might happen? If they do let him out, when could it be?"

"He thinks the hearing could be as early as next month."

She gasps. "Before the baby? He could get out *before* the baby?"

"Look, even if he does—there's no way they'll allow him to come back to Oxford. And that's still a very big 'if' as far as I'm concerned."

I'm talking ballsier than I feel, but she knows me too well. "There's something, isn't there?" she says, searching my face. "Something you're not telling me."

I can lie to Osbourne; I can even lie to myself. But I have never managed to lie to my wife.

"The case I've been working on. There are—similarities."

"What do you mean *similarities*?"

"That girl who was abducted—the one I told you about. Faith Appleford. The man who did it ripped out some of her hair. But that's not so unusual," I say, crashing on. "I've seen stuff like that before."

Once or twice, maybe, in twenty years, but that's only a lie by omission. I can forgive myself that.

"You said similari*ties*. Plural."

There are reasons why my wife is an exceptional lawyer. Attention to detail is one of them.

"He used cable ties." I pause. "And put a plastic bag over her head."

"Just like last time," she whispers.

I reach again for her hand and her fingers grip mine. "But that doesn't prove anything, you know it doesn't."

But Alex isn't buying it, and who can blame her. The plastic bag and the cable ties were key elements of the prosecution case.

But not the main one.
I should know.

* * *

Sent: Weds 03/04/2018, 20.35   **Importance: High**
From: Sean.Cameron@hmps.gsi.gov.uk
To: DIAdamFawley@ThamesValley.police.uk

Subject: Prisoner ZX05566 Parrie, G

Dear DI Fawley,
You were enquiring about visitors to the above inmate.
In the last six months Parrie has received visits from the
following:

Ms. Geraldine Hughes (partner)
Mrs. Ivy Parrie (mother)
Mrs. Hazel Cousins (sister)
Mr. David Chandler (solicitor)

Parrie's list of approved phone numbers includes all the above,
with the addition of Mr. Jeffrey Parrie (brother) and Mrs. Sandra
Parrie (former wife and mother of his three children).
   If you require more details as to dates and times, please
let me know.

S. Cameron
Custodial Manager, HMP Wandsworth

* * *

Harrison is halfway out of his office when I get there. He looks distracted.

"I don't have much time," he says. "Meeting with Martin Dempster."

The Police Commissioner. Just my luck.

"Can we go into your office for a moment, sir?"

He gives me a look at that. I have his attention now.

As the door closes behind us, he turns to me. "This is about Gavin Parrie, I take it?"

Sometimes, just sometimes, I underestimate Harrison.

* * *

When the news comes on at 8:00 Fiona Blake switches on the kettle and gets two mugs out of the cupboard. She checks her watch for the fifth time in as many minutes. It's not like Sasha to be this late back. If she sleeps over at Patsie's she always comes home early, so she can change for school. Fiona reaches into the fridge for milk and pours granola into a bowl. Any minute now, she thinks, I'll hear the key in the door. Any minute now she'll be in here like a whirlwind, slurping her tea, downing her food far too fast, out of the door again before Fiona can draw breath.

She's worrying about nothing. Sash will be back.

Any minute now.

* * *

It's the morning meeting. Gislingham is leaning against the one functioning radiator (sergeant's privilege). As for Fawley, he's leading from the front—both literally and metaphorically. Just as he's done ever since they started this bloody investigation. Gislingham isn't about to complain, but this is supposed to be one of his jobs and, to be honest, it's just a bit humiliating, especially in front of Asante. It's not that he thinks Fawley doesn't trust him, but for some reason he just can't let this case rest. Quinn still reckons he's in the middle of a domestic, and says so loudly to anyone who'll listen, but Gis has his own reasons for discounting that one. His wife saw Alex Fawley in the mother-and-baby boutique in Summertown a couple of weekends ago and was convinced she looked pregnant. Which, with the Fawleys' history, would account for any amount of anxiety displacement activity on the DI's part. Not to mention the stopping smoking and the endless Polo mints. He's got through three in the last half-hour alone.

"Did you ask this Kenneth Ashwin if he'd be prepared to give us his prints?" Fawley asks.

"Nothing doing," says Quinn. "Started getting bolshie about not being under arrest and infringing his right to privacy so I backed off."

"What about the other vans?"

"So far I've managed to rule out the carpet cleaners and the locksmith. Both have solid alibis."

Fawley turns to Everett. He's starting to look irritable. "Anything from the FE college?"

Everett shakes her head. "As far as we can tell, no one else apart from the principal has any idea Faith is trans.

134

And to be honest, I don't think it would be an issue even if they did. One of the lecturers we spoke to was wearing blue lipstick and a dress."

"I take it you mean a bloke," says Quinn.

"Yes, I do mean a bloke," she says, over the laughter. "But that's the point. He didn't give a toss and no one else was batting an eyelid either. This generation—they can't see what all the bloody fuss is about. And as for what happened to Faith, I really can't see anyone who knows her doing that. She's just a really nice kid, trying to get on with her life."

"What about the Basingstoke angle?" asks Fawley. Who wasn't laughing.

"I spoke to her old head teacher," says Ev, "and she clearly had absolutely no idea Daniel wasn't still Daniel."

"That's a bit odd, isn't it? Don't trans kids have to live as their new gender for a while before they can be eligible for treatment?"

Ev shrugs. "Perhaps she just didn't want to start doing that until she could make a completely new start. Either way, I think Basingstoke is a dead end."

Baxter mutters something about "dead end" being the nicest thing anyone's probably ever said about Basingstoke, which raises more laughter.

Meanwhile Fawley is trying to get eye contact with Somer but after the car crash between them yesterday she's avoiding looking at him. Gis glances at Ev and she gives a tiny shrug: she clearly thinks the DI's made his own bed on that one.

"Look," says Fawley, "I buy everything you say about this generation not caring which gender people are, or even if they have one at all, but the fact remains that Faith herself *does* care. She's going out of her way to keep her private life private, and that could give someone a motive. Either a motive to out her or—"

"I'm sorry, sir," says Somer, cutting across. There's a flush to her cheeks now. "But I just don't think this is getting us anywhere. I know Faith is incredibly wary about coming out as trans, but so what? We don't all exhibit our personal lives on Facebook for the world to see. People keep all sorts of things secret for all sorts of perfectly good reasons—not just their sexuality but where they come from, whether they're in a relationship, or religious, or pregnant—"

There's an awkward pause. An intake of breath. Gis has a moment of panic—no one else knows about that, do they? And in any case, he knows *he* didn't let it slip. But if anything it's Asante Fawley is looking at.

"So," says Fawley icily. "What do you suggest we do instead?"

Somer flushes again. "I'm not saying we rule out a possible link—of course not, we can't." She stares him in the eye and her chin lifts. "But if you're asking for my *opinion*, I think we should start looking back through our old cases. Because I'm prepared to bet this isn't the first time this man has done something like this."

Gis glances back at Fawley, and for the tiniest moment there's something on his face Gis has never seen before. Not anger now, something else. Something that, in another man, you might even call fear.

The others must have seen it too, because the room is suddenly falling silent.

Fawley takes a deep breath. "There's something I need to tell you. About the Appleford case."

* * *

"Denise? It's Fiona. I just wanted to check—Sasha did stay over with Patsie at yours last night, didn't she?"

She's gripping the phone so tight she can feel her own heartbeat against the plastic. *As long as she answers straightaway it's OK—as long as she answers straightaway—*

There's a silence—an intake of breath. *Please—please—*

"I'm sorry, Fiona, but I haven't seen her. Patsie got back about 10:15 but she didn't have Sasha with her."

Fiona can hear it in her voice. That toxic combination of sympathy and relief. That it's not her daughter who's not where she should be—it's not her world tipping into disaster.

"Do you want to speak to Patsie?"

Fiona grasps at the offer like a drowning woman. "Yes, yes—could I? Is she there?"

"I was just about to drive her in—"

"Could I just speak to her?"

"Sorry, of course. Hold on a minute."

The phone goes mute and Fiona imagines the woman going out to the bottom of the stairs and calling up. Imagines Patsie coming slowly down, looking confused, wondering what Fiona is doing calling her this early—calling her at all—

The sound comes on again. "Yes?" The girl is slightly out of breath.

"Hi, Patsie," she says, forcing casualness into her voice.

"I'm sure it's nothing, but Sasha isn't here. I thought she said she was staying over with you last night?"

"She was going to but then she changed her mind."

Fiona's breath is so shallow she has to sit down. She can't afford to lose it—she has to think clearly—

"So when did you last see her?"

"On the bus. She was still on it when I got off."

"What time was that?"

"Dunno—about 10:00?"

The fist tightens another notch. *It's only a ten-minute walk from the bus stop—she should have been home by 10:15—10:30 at the latest—*

"Have you tried calling her mobile?"

Of course she's tried calling her bloody mobile, she's been calling and texting every five minutes—she must have left a dozen messages—two dozen—

"It's just going straight to voicemail."

"I'm so sorry, Mrs. Blake—I really really want to help but I just don't know anything."

Fiona feels the tears come into her eyes. She's always liked Patsie—ever since she was a little girl with her hair in plaits and scratches on her knees. And these days she seems to spend more time at their house than she does at her own.

"You will call me, won't you, if you hear from Sash? Just get her to ring me? Tell her I'm really worried."

Suddenly she hears the girl's breathing change—hears the gasp of real fear. "But she is all right, isn't she?"

"I'm sure she is," says Fiona firmly. "It's probably just a silly mix-up. I bet she's already at school and will give me a right talking-to later for embarrassing her like this."

But when she puts down the phone there's a fist of ice around her lungs.

* * *

I open the cardboard file in front of me and take out two sheets of paper. A couple of people exchange surreptitious glances, wondering what the hell this is about.

"I spoke to Alan Challow yesterday. He's had the results on Faith Appleford's shoes."

I turn and pin the papers to the whiteboard, hearing the slight stirring behind me.

I take my time, but in the end I have to face them. "Along with soil from the allotment site and bits of gravel and all the other usual crap, he found something else. Something we didn't expect. Traces of calcium sulphate."

They're none the wiser. Of course they aren't. None of them were here back then, not even Baxter. Quinn looks at me and shrugs. "And?"

"It's plaster dust."

"So, you think our bloke is, what—a builder? Decorator?"

The glances aren't surreptitious now; some people are frowning, openly confused. Others are wondering why I've been sitting on this—why I didn't mention it straightaway—and why, incidentally, we've been wasting time with bloody carpet cleaners and locksmiths. But they know better than to say any of that out loud. Asante, on the other hand, apparently doesn't.

139

"When exactly did you speak to Challow about this, sir?" he says as the noise in the room rises. "Only I spoke to him at six o'clock last night and he never said anything to me."

I feel myself flushing. "I asked him not to."

Asante frowns and opens his mouth to say something but I cut across him. "There was another case in this area. Twenty years ago. They called him the Roadside Rapist."

Some of them register recognition; most don't. Somer is staring at me. As well she might.

"He raped six young women and attempted to rape a seventh," I continue. "And he brutalized them. One of his victims lost an eye. Another committed suicide a few months after she was attacked."

"But he was convicted, wasn't he?" says Ev. "The man who did it? I can't remember his name—Gareth something?"

"Gavin Parrie. He's currently doing life in Wandsworth."

She looks bewildered. "In that case, why –?"

"Parrie ripped out his victims' hair. It was one of his signatures."

Gislingham gets the point at once, but he's still reserving judgment. "That doesn't prove anything. Not necessarily."

I look around the room. Slowly. "Parrie dragged his victims off the street, put plastic bags over their heads and bound their wrists with cable ties."

"Even so, sir . . ." begins Ev. But I can see the beginnings of doubt in her eyes.

"The last two women to be attacked were thrown into

a van and driven away. Traces of calcium sulphate were found on both of them."

"So this bloke Parrie was a plasterer?" asks Ev.

I shake my head. "No, he just did odd jobs, house clearance, that sort of thing. But his brother was a builder. Our theory was that Parrie borrowed the brother's van to commit those two assaults, though we were never able to prove it, and there were no forensics in either his van or his brother's by the time we got our hands on them."

Quinn gives a low whistle. "Holy shit."

"But Parrie's never admitted responsibility, has he?" says Asante slowly. "Because if he had, he'd have been out by now."

Asante's sharp, no question.

"No, DC Asante, he hasn't admitted it. He's always maintained that we set him up—that he's entirely innocent, and someone else attacked those women. And given that sex offenders have to admit guilt to be eligible for rehabilitation, that's stood against him with the Parole Board. At least, till now."

Somer frowns. "You said '*we* set him up?' It was your case?"

I nod. "I was DS. Alastair Osbourne was SIO. But it's me he blames. Me he thinks framed him."

They're not meeting my eye now, and I know why. It's every copper's nightmare. A case like this, rising from the grave.

I sweep a look around the room, trying to get them to meet my gaze. "I am absolutely convinced that we got the right man. I was then and I am now. But if the press gets hold of this—well, we all know what will happen then.

Shit hitting the fan won't be in it. On top of which, if Parrie's barrister is even *halfway* competent he's going to use the parallels with the Appleford investigation to raise fifty shades of reasonable doubt about the original conviction."

There's a shifting in the room now, a sense of adjustment, of recalibration. This is not the case they thought it was. It's not the case I thought it was either, and yes, I probably spent far too long refusing to believe what was in front of my face. I'm expecting them to be pissed off with me—for that alone, if nothing else—and for some of them, at least, to show it. Quinn certainly, perhaps even Ev. But she's staring at Gis. And she's not the only one. It's a look that says: *You're supposed to be DS. Say something.* And all at once it hits me that they're going to take their cue from him. And in that realization, I learn something else: what a damn good DS Gis has become.

Gislingham turns to me. His face is completely calm. "We've got your back, sir. I know I don't need to say that, but I'm saying it anyway. We've got your back."

* * *

After his big reveal, Fawley only stays for another ten minutes. Gis decides to take that as a compliment—after all this time with the boss breathing down his neck, suddenly there's nothing behind him but cold fresh air. But at least he understands what all that was about now. No wonder the poor sod was under the cosh—who wouldn't be, with something like that hanging over you. He must have been bricking it. And as Gis well knows, old cases that come back to haunt you are like the undead—it's next to impossible to kill them off again.

As the door of the incident room swings shut behind the DI, Gis turns to face his team.

"Right. Fawley didn't say this, but I'm going to. If anyone has any reservations at all about this Parrie case, then speak now or keep *shtum*, OK? We all know the boss—he isn't just a bloody good copper, he's as straight as a die. There is no way—*no way*—he'd fit anyone up. And if you've even the slightest doubt about that fact then sorry, but you've no place in this team. Do I make myself clear?"

Evidently he does. The energy in the room lifts a level. People look up, stand a little straighter.

"Good. So let's bloody well get on with it, shall we? Because the quickest way to get Fawley out of the shit, and do ourselves a big favor at the same time, is to find the bastard who assaulted Faith and put paid to this Parrie crap once and for all."

Murmurs of "Yes, Sarge," "Right, Sarge."

"OK then. DC Quinn, can you and Everett start with the builders on the petrol station CCTV we still haven't managed to speak to."

Baxter looks up. "And there are two or three other vans going past on the road that look to me like they could be builders."

"OK," says Quinn, "give me what you've got and we'll try and track them down."

Gis turns to Somer. "I need you to talk to Faith—see if the plaster thing means anything to her. It's possible she knows someone in that sort of trade. I don't think it's very likely, but it's a question we have to ask."

"Of course, Sarge. I was going to check how she's doing anyway."

"And when you've done that, help out Quinn and Ev with the builders."

People are dispersing now and Gislingham takes advantage of the distraction to take Baxter quietly aside.

"I don't know about you, but all that stuff about Parrie—it was a bit bloody close to home. I'm not saying the boss got it wrong back then, but the similarities are, well, you know."

Baxter's face is a masterclass of silent eloquence.

"So what do you think? A copycat?"

Baxter considers. "Has to be a possibility. Though he'd have to know a shitload about the MO to be able to pull it off. I mean—plaster dust wouldn't be hard to get hold of, but only as long as you knew about it in the first place."

"Yeah," says Gis thoughtfully. "That's just what I was thinking. Have a look online—see how much you could find out that way."

Baxter nods. "I can dig out the trial transcripts, too."

"Good idea. Best we know exactly what we're dealing with."

He turns to go, then stops and touches Baxter lightly on the arm. "Though let's keep it between ourselves for the moment, yeah?"

*   *   *

At 11:15 Ev parks her Mini in a narrow street off Osney Lane, outside the offices of one of the builders on Baxter's list. Their boards are all over north and central Oxford,

144

outside big Victorian houses bristling with scaffolding and college buildings swathed in plastic sheets, which emerge like butterflies from pupae, gray turned gold and the stone new-shone. The premises is a converted warehouse, a chic conversion in brick and glass and wood that gives its own understated but unambiguous message about the sort of outfit this is. The same message as the carefully consistent branding—the elegant typeface and the dark teal blue that appears to be on every item capable of taking dye—"Make no mistake about it, this is a class operation."

There's no sign of Quinn yet so she wanders up and down a bit; it's not a neighborhood she knows that well so it's an opportunity to be a bit nosy. This was an industrial area once but these days it looks as clean as a film set. From the "artisanal bean" coffee shop on the corner to the über-classy block of flats opposite—that's the sort of place she'd imagine Fawley living in if she didn't already know he has an unexpectedly ordinary semi on the Risinghurst estate, just east of the ring road.

"You all right?"

Quinn's voice behind her takes her by surprise.

"Had to drive round the block three times before I could find anywhere to bloody park," he says tetchily, staring (none too subtly) at where she's left her Mini. She wonders for a moment whether to point out she only got a space because she's been here over half an hour, but decides it isn't worth it.

"Right," he says, pulling the list from his coat and looking up at the building. "This lot are called Mark Rose & Co. Founded by the said Mr. Rose ten years ago and doing pretty well as far as I could work out. They do commercial and residential work and some specialist stuff for the university. Forty-two full-time employees and about the same number of contractors." He tucks the pages back in his pocket and the two of them walk up to the front door.

They're expected. There's a cafetière and a plate of gold-wrapped biscuits set up and waiting in a meeting room on the ground floor, and the smart and efficient (male) receptionist assures them that Mr. Rose is on his way. Ev can see that Quinn's doing his best not to look impressed, but the surroundings are having an impact on him all the same. He picks up one of the glossy brochures on the table and starts studying it with what looks to Ev like more than idle interest.

Rose arrives barely two minutes after the receptionist has gone. He has tan, pale-cream chinos, a button-down pink shirt and an iPad. It's the same model as Quinn's. Ev suppresses a smile; boys and their toys. Rose smiles at them both, holding steady eye contact. "Good morning, Officers. I hope you're being well looked after?"

Ev reaches for her coffee. The mug is blue. The same blue as the vans and the logo and the receptionist's tie. Diane Appleford would give her eyeteeth for color coordination of that caliber. And the coffee is—predictably—very good. Everett also has a weather eye on the biscuits. She isn't going to get caught eating one in public but she might try to snaffle a couple as they leave. It's always worth having something in your back pocket for the next time you need a favor from Baxter.

"My assistant said it was something to do with our vans," begins Rose. "But I've done a quick check and everything is definitely up-to-date. Road tax, MOTs—"

"It's nothing like that," says Quinn quickly. "It's about a young woman who was attacked on Monday on Rydal Way."

"I'm not with you."

"She was forced into a van and taken to the allotments on the Marston Ferry Road."

Rose blinks. A frown is forming. "But there are hundreds of vans in Oxford—"

Quinn nods. "No doubt. But we have reason to believe one of your vans was in the vicinity at the time."

Rose looks a little pale under his tan. "I see."

"Buying petrol at the BP on the roundabout, to be precise."

Rose reaches for his iPad and turns it on. "If you bear with me a moment I'll run a quick check on exactly where our crews were last Monday."

"Seriously?" says Quinn, unable to contain the surprise in his voice. "You can do that?"

Rose shrugs; if you hold as many cards as he does you can afford to be gracious. "The vans are tracked by satnav. And we keep all the records. This is a premium-priced operation, Officer. I can't afford complaints so I need to know where my people are. What time was it you were interested in?"

"First thing in the morning," says Everett, watching the flush spread over Quinn's face. "Before 11:00."

Rose taps the screen for a moment or two, then puts the iPad down and slides it across the table.

"As you can see, one of our vans did travel along that road that morning, but he was en route to a job in Wallingford. Apart from buying petrol, he made no other stops between leaving home and arriving at the site. I also have the receipt for the fuel on his company card. Would you like me to print it out for you?"

* * *

THE CENTRAL CRIMINAL COURT

The Old Bailey
London EC4M 7EH

BEFORE:
THE HONORABLE MR. JUSTICE HEALEY

R E G I N A
v.
GAVIN FRANCIS PARRIE

MR. R. BARNES Q.C. and MISS S. GREY
appeared on behalf of the prosecution.

MRS. B. JENKINS Q.C. and MR. T. CUTHBERT
appeared on behalf of the defendant.

Transcribed from the Stenotype notes of
Chapman Davison Ltd.,
Official reporters to the court

Monday, 25th October, 1999
[Day 7]

ALISON DONNELLY, recalled
Examined by MR. BARNES

Q. Miss Donnelly, I would like to return to the
   events we were discussing yesterday.
   Specifically the assault that took place on
   29th November last year. I appreciate this
   is a distressing subject, but it is
   important that the court is clear about
   exactly what happened. And you will be
   aware, I am sure, that you are still under
   oath. You said the incident occurred at
   approximately 5:40 p.m. that day?
A. Yes. I was on my way home from work. I got
   the 5:15 bus.

Q. And that's the bus you usually got?
A. That's right.

Q. Did you have any sense in the previous few
   days that you might have been being
   followed?
A. One of my flatmates said she'd seen a van
   parked down the street a few times, but we
   didn't think anything of it.

Q. What color was the van?
A. Just one of those white ones.

Q. Your flatmate didn't notice if there was
   anyone in it?
A. No, it was too far away.

Q. On the night of the assault, did you see a
   van?
A. No. I mean, that doesn't mean it wasn't
   there. I just didn't see it.

Q. So you got off the bus, and started to walk
   towards your flat. What happened next?

A. It'd been raining, and this big truck came past really close and sprayed water all over me. I had my new coat on and I was really annoyed. I suppose I just stopped for a minute. That's when it happened.

Q. You felt someone behind you?
A. Yes, first he grabbed me and then I felt a bag going over my head and he was dragging me off.

Q. Do you know where he took you?
A. He put me in the back of a van. He'd tied my hands with something that was digging into my wrists and I felt as if I couldn't breathe.

Q. Do you remember anything else about the van?
A. There was plastic or something on the floor. Some sort of sheeting.

Q. And what happened after that?
A. He took me to a car park off the ring road. I didn't know that then. But that's where it was.

Q. What did he do then?
A. I heard him get out of the van and walk round to the back. He dragged me out and pushed me along a few steps. I couldn't see anything because of the bag. Then he threw me on the ground. And then he pulled off my knickers and raped me.

Q. A subsequent medical examination confirmed that you also received internal injuries from some sort of blunt object. Is that correct?
A. Yes.

MR. JUSTICE HEALEY: I appreciate this is
    extremely difficult for you, Miss Donnelly,
    but I must ask you to speak a little louder
    so that members of the jury can hear what
    you are saying. Do you feel able to go on?
A. Yes, sir.

MR. BARNES: Thank you, my Lord. Miss Donnelly,
    was the rape you described the full extent
    of the assault?
A. No.

Q. What else happened?
A. He beat me up.

Q. I'm afraid I must ask you to be more
    explicit.
A. He did it to make me shut up—I was trying to
    scream so he took hold of my head and beat
    it against the ground.

Q. That was how you sustained the injuries you
    have now? The injuries visible to the court?
A. Yes.

Q. You suffered a fractured skull?
A. Yes.

Q. And loss of sight in one eye?
A. That was when he kicked me. After he'd
    finished.

Q. And he removed your jewelry and some of
    your hair?
A. My earrings. He pulled them out.

Q. Ripping one earlobe, I believe?
A. Yes. And he ripped out some of my hair too.

Q. And where was that?
A. Just here, behind my ear.

Q. How long was it after he left before help
   arrived?
A. They told me afterwards it was about an
   hour. I think I must've passed out because
   it didn't seem that long. But then suddenly
   there was an ambulance and the police were
   there.

Q. How long did you spend in hospital,
   Miss Donnelly?
A. Five weeks.

Q. And have you been able to return to work
   since the attack?
A. No.

MR. BARNES: I have no further questions.

MR. JUSTICE HEALEY: That seems a convenient
   moment to break for lunch. Members of the
   jury, we will resume at 2:15, please.

* * *

"Shall we ask this lot if their vans have satnav tracking
too?"

Ev slides a glance at Quinn. She knows she's probably
pushing it, but it was irresistible. He's so easy to wind up.

He's frowning now, knowing she's taking the piss.
Because if Mark Rose & Co. is a premium service, the second
firm on their list has to be the construction equivalent of
Ryanair. Judging by the rather endearingly amateurish logo

on their website they certainly haven't invested any of their hard-earned cash in a graphic designer, and the offices aren't even offices at all, just an eighties bungalow at the end of a cul-de-sac with paving down one side of the building and a double garage on the other. Ev had to check twice when they arrived, just to make sure it was the right place.

The door is opened by a middle-aged woman in a jumper and baggy track pants. There's a strong smell of cigarette smoke.

"Can I help you?"

"We're from Thames Valley Police. Is this the offices of Ramsgate Renovations Ltd.?"

"That's right." To the woman's credit she doesn't look immediately wary, which is the usual reaction to an unexpected visit from the police.

"Can we speak to Mr. Ramsgate?"

"I'm afraid Keith's on-site. You can talk to me, though. I'm Pauline. His wife. And the manager."

She takes them through to an extension which opens off the kitchen, fitted out with cheap but functional office furniture: a filing cupboard, a couple of desks, a big pin-board with charts of their different jobs. There's a PC as well, but it's obvious Pauline is more of a paper person. There are stacks of files and invoices covering almost every surface. Out the back, two white vans are parked up on the concreted garden. One has the rear doors open and a couple of lads are loading supplies.

"Have you got permission to run a business from here?" asks Quinn, gesturing at the vans.

The woman shrugs. "We're not overlooked, so why

should anyone else be bothered? But if you want to push it the answer is yes. We do."

If Quinn thought it was a good way to get her on the back foot he appears to have misread his woman. They're staring at each other now and Ev suspects Pauline won't be the first to blink.

She decides to have a go at good cop and see if that works any better.

"Mrs. Ramsgate, we were hoping you could help us. There was an incident involving a van on Monday 1st April. So we're talking to all van owners, just to eliminate them from our enquiries."

"What sort of 'incident?'"

"It's just routine, Mrs. Ramsgate."

"Doesn't sound like it to me. And how come you're picking on us? There must be hundreds of vans in this city."

Pauline, evidently, didn't come down in the last shower of rain.

Everett takes out two sheets of paper and puts one down on the table. "This is from the CCTV at the petrol station on Cherwell Drive, taken that morning. We think this vehicle here may be one of yours."

The quality isn't good, and there's a lorry blocking most of the view, but it's just about possible to see the front of a white van with a ladder strapped to the top of it, and on the side a word beginning "RA–."

Pauline's eyes narrow. "I can only see two letters. That doesn't prove it's one of ours."

Everett nods, looking at the second sheet. "You're right. There are actually three builders with names beginning like that in a ten-mile radius from here. Yourselves,

Razniak Ltd. and Rathbone & Sons. We're just working through them alphabetically."

Pauline gives a heavy sigh; a waft of nicotine prickles Everett's nose. "So you want to know where our vans were? Is that it?"

"If you don't mind."

Pauline folds her arms. "I know exactly where they were—everyone was on the same job."

"And where was that?"

"Out at Bicester. Complete hotel refit—we'll be on it for weeks."

"And what time would your people typically start work?"

She bridles a little. "Seven thirty on the dot. It's not a bloody holiday camp."

"So you're saying you can account for *all* your blokes that morning?" says Quinn. "No flat tires, sick cats, dental emergencies?"

Pauline glares at him. "They were all there except Ashley Brotherton. It was his nan's funeral that day. She brought him up after his mum walked out."

"What does he do?" says Ev. "As a job?"

Pauline shoots her a look. "He's a plasterer."

"And where is he today? At Bicester, I assume?" asks Ev, hoping her voice isn't giving her away. And that Pauline doesn't realize Quinn's telegraphing behind her back. "Just so we can have a quick chat and eliminate him from our enquiries?"

Pauline lifts her chin. "He's not due on-site till later so I expect he's at home."

Everett smiles brightly. "Well, if you could just let me

have his address then. And the reg number of his van. If you don't mind."

＊　＊　＊

"She's not in any trouble, I just need to know where she is. I'm sorry to call you on your mobile but I've texted everyone I can think of and spoken to the school and I know she's not there—I'm going out of my mind—please, Isabel."

Fiona hates the pleading in her voice, the desperation. It's like a bad smell.

"But I don't *know* where she is." Isabel's voice rises into a wail. "I *told* you—she got off the bus and I didn't see her after."

"Is there anyone else she could be with?" She can feel the tension in her jaw, the weight behind her eyes. "She told me she doesn't have a boyfriend, but is there someone she likes? A boy who might have stopped and offered her a lift?"

"No, really—"

"Someone she'd have trusted—someone she knew from school perhaps—"

"I'd have told you already—why won't you believe me?"

There's the sound of voices in the background, playground noises; it must be morning break. Fiona takes a deep breath. "So you really don't know where she could be?"

"I'm sorry. I really don't."

There's the sound of a bell now and a moment later the line goes dead.

＊　＊　＊

Every time Everett goes to Blackbird Leys she forces herself to find something good about it. A nice garden or a tree in blossom or even just a particularly sassy local cat. She hates giving in to stereotypes but, no matter how hard she tries, the place always seems to do its best to defeat her. As they drive up Barraclough Road there are two men slumped on a bench surrounded by beer cans, and an overturned bin has spewed rotting food and rubbish halfway across the road. She swerves and Quinn swears. He hates being a passenger, but there was no way he was bringing his car here. And however determined she is not to prejudge this place, she really can't blame him. As they pass, one of the men waves his can at her and shouts, "Fuck off!" And they aren't even in a squad car.

"It's about ten houses further on," says Quinn, squinting at the numbers. "Ninety-six, right?"

The house is on the corner at the end of the terrace. These houses must have been The Next Big Thing once but the seventies architecture hasn't aged well. The windows are too small and the whole of the ground floor is dominated by the garages jutting out from the facade. But all they are now is receptacles for junk: modern cars are too big to even get through the doors. Unlike its neighbors, 96 still has some scrubby grass out the front rather than a concrete parking space, but like the rest, the roof sags as if it just can't be bothered any more.

Ev pulls up and they get out. There's music coming from upstairs; someone's in.

"I'll go round the side," says Quinn. "See if I can spot the van."

Ev nods, takes a deep breath and rings the bell.

The music stops, but there's no other sign of life. She rings again. And a third time. Quinn appears around the corner.

"Did you find the van?"

He nods. He's not smiling. "I could see some cable ties in the back. Looked the same type to me."

"That doesn't prove anything. They're hardly distinctive."

"Just saying."

There's a noise from inside now—the sound of chains being taken off and a bolt sliding back. The door opens slowly. It's an elderly man, breathing heavily from the effort. He's wearing a threadbare cardigan and a pair of brown slacks that hang loosely off his thin hips. His face and hands are freckled with dark age spots.

"Mr. Brotherton?" says Ev, holding up her warrant card. "DC Verity Everett. Could we come in for a moment?"

The man looks suspicious. "What's this about?"

"It's about your grandson. Ashley, isn't it?"

"What about him? He hasn't done anything. He's a good lad—"

"No one's saying he isn't," she says quickly. "We just need to ask him a couple of routine questions. It'll only take five minutes. Is he in?" She smiles. She can see the old man wants to deny it but they both know hip-hop isn't likely to be top of his own playlist.

He sighs heavily. "Through the back."

Ashley Brotherton is leaning against the breakfast bar in the tiny kitchen, drinking orange juice from a carton. The room is tidy but not especially clean; Ev can feel the lino sticking under her shoes.

"Who are you?" he says, wiping juice from his mouth.

He's not tall but he's well built. Very short hair, very pale blue eyes. Handsome, in a rather belligerent way. He pulls out a chair for his grandfather, who sits down slowly, in obvious pain.

"Thames Valley CID," says Quinn. "Just wanted to check on your movements on the morning of April 1st."

Ashley and his grandfather exchange a glance. "That was Nan's funeral," says the young man. "And in any case, what business is it of yours?"

"Where was it held?" says Ev, taking her notebook from her bag.

"The crematorium," answers the old man. "The one in Headington."

"You still haven't answered my question," says Ashley.

"There was an attack on a young woman that morning," says Quinn smoothly. "We think the perp does the sort of work you do."

Ashley walks over to the pedal bin in the corner and drops the empty carton inside. Then he turns to face Quinn. "Like I said, I was at my nan's funeral. Cars got here at 8:30. Ceremony was at 9:00. Wake at the Red Lion at 10:30. You can check all that. Whoever you're looking for, it ain't me."

Quinn offers his most unpleasant smile. "So you won't mind us searching your van, then, will you. Just to make sure."

The old man looks up. "You got a warrant?"

"No," says Everett quickly. "It was just an informal request, Mr. Brotherton—"

"In that case the answer's no. Like I said, Ashley's a good lad. He's got a good job, a proper skill. You've got no right dragging him into this for no good reason. Just because we live on the estate, you people immediately assume we're dirt—"

Ev bites her lip. So much for trying to find something decent about this place; seems she can't even spot it when it's sitting right in front of her. "I'm sorry, Mr. Brotherton. We didn't mean to cause any offense."

The old man gestures to his grandson. "Show them out, will you, Ash. I've got things to do."

On the doorstep, Ev stops a moment and turns. "Ashley—can I just ask—is it at all possible someone else could have used your van that day? Does anyone else have keys?"

She's half expecting him to tell her to piss off, and she couldn't really blame him if he did, but he doesn't. Just looks her straight in the eye. "No," he says. "Only me and the office."

Back in the car, Quinn snaps on his seat belt. "What do you think?"

She puts the key in the ignition and then sits back. "I think we check what he said with the crematorium but I'm pretty sure they're going to confirm it. I don't reckon he attacked Faith. Not least because I just don't think he's that good a liar."

There's the sound of an engine starting now and they look up to see a Ramsgate Renovations van turning right out of the side road. It passes barely three feet from their car yet Ashley Brotherton stares straight ahead, refusing to look at them.

They watch him down the street and out of sight.

"If he really did attack Faith, he'll have that van cleared and valeted within the hour," says Quinn.

Ev shrugs. "Who says he hasn't done that already? And even if he hasn't, the old boy was right—we don't have a cat's chance in hell of getting a warrant." She checks her watch. "Look, we'd better get a move on if we're going to be back in time for the meeting."

Quinn makes a face. "What's the bloody point? Right now, we have absolutely sod all to say."

*　*　*

Adam Fawley
4 April 2018
12.32

"We checked with the crematorium on our way back," says Ev, looking around the room. "Ashley Brotherton was definitely where he said he was at the time Faith was attacked. He was one of the coffin bearers—there must have been fifty people who saw him there."

It's probably just as well I'm letting Gis run this meeting, because I'm struggling to keep my temper. If it was any other case would I really be expecting a major breakthrough by now? Perhaps I just need to be more realistic. More patient. Trouble is, there probably isn't a single person I know who would use that particular adjective to describe me. Least of all my wife.

Gis turns to Somer. "Did you ask Faith about the plaster?"

She glances up. "Yes, Sarge, but it didn't ring any bells."

"What about the other building firms? Did we turn up anything there?"

Somer looks down at her notes. "I spoke to both Razniaks and Rathbone & Sons. Rathbone's vans are green, not white, and Razniak only use transits, so the one on the CCTV isn't either of theirs. But we're basing all this on the ladder on the roof—it might not be a builder at all. It could just as easily be a decorator or a window cleaner or even someone who fits satellite dishes—"

"Wouldn't get plaster dust doing that though, would they," says Baxter stolidly.

"It could still be a builder," observes Asante, "just one from further out of town—"

The door swings open—suddenly and fast. It's the desk officer, wide-eyed and out of breath.

"DI Fawley? We've just had a call transferred across from 999. A woman called Fiona Blake. It's her daughter. She's fifteen. And she's gone missing."

* * *

THE CENTRAL CRIMINAL COURT

The Old Bailey
London EC4M 7EH

BEFORE:
THE HONORABLE MR. JUSTICE HEALEY

R E G I N A
v.
GAVIN FRANCIS PARRIE

MR. R. BARNES Q.C. and MISS S. GREY
appeared on behalf of the prosecution.

MRS. B. JENKINS Q.C. and MR. T. CUTHBERT
appeared on behalf of the defendant.

Friday, 29th October, 1999
[Day 11]

GERRY BUTLER, sworn
Examined by MR. BARNES

Q. Is your full name Gerald Terence Butler?
A. Yes.

Q. Mr. Butler, I would like to ask you some
questions about the events of the evening of
4th September 1998. Could you tell the
court, in your own words, what you saw?
A. I was on my way home from work, walking
along Latimer Road. There's a stretch along
there where there are some bushes and stuff.
It was getting dark so I didn't realize what
was happening until I got quite close.

Q. And what was happening?
A. There was a girl—a young woman—I could hear
noises, like she was trying to call out. Then
I realized there was a bloke there too. He
was on top of her.

Q. On top of her, how?
A. She was on her front—you know, facedown—and
he was straddling her. She had a bag over her
head and he was tying her hands.

Q. Tying her hands in what way?

A. I couldn't see then, but I realized later it was cable ties.

Q. What happened next?
A. I started shouting and he realized I was there and scarpered.

Q. Did you see his face?
A. Not really—he looked up and saw me but he had a hoodie on so I didn't really see what he looked like. And then he pushed through the bushes and ran out the other side.

Q. What is your profession, Mr. Butler?
A. I'm in Security. Used to be in the army, but I've been in Security ever since I came out.

Q. You are, in fact, a bouncer at one of the Oxford nightclubs. Kubla, on the High Street, isn't that right?
A. Yeah, been there four years. I do the odd shift behind the bar sometimes, when they're short-staffed, but mostly it's on the door.

Q. Could you confirm your height and weight for the court?
A. Six two, 220 pounds.

Q. And you keep fit?
A. I work out, I keep in shape. I have to, in my job.

Q. And the man you saw, what would you estimate his height and weight to be—approximately?
A. About five eight, but quite skinny. Say 160 pounds?

Q. So in his eyes, you would have been quite
   intimidating?
A. I guess so.

Q. What happened next?
A. I went over to the girl and asked if she
   was OK. She was in a pretty bad way—her face
   was all scratched and he'd pulled out some
   of her hair. But he hadn't—well, you know.

Q. He hadn't?
A. Raped her. Assaulted her.

Q. Because you turned up just in time.

MRS. JENKINS: My apologies, my Lord, but
   Mr. Butler cannot possibly know the
   assailant's intentions.

MR. JUSTICE HEALEY: Mr. Barnes, perhaps you
   might rephrase your question?

MR. BARNES: Did you see any evidence that
   there had been an attempted sexual assault,
   Mr. Butler?
A. He'd yanked up her skirt—I could see where
   he'd pulled at her knickers. So, yeah, I'd
   say I did.

Q. You proceeded to call 999?
A. That's right. I hung around with her till
   the police arrived. She was crying and that.

Q. And this is the young woman who has been
   identified to the court as Ms. Sheldon?
A. Yeah, that's her.

MR. BARNES: I have no further questions, thank you.

* * *

Gis pulls the sheet off the printer and pins it up on the whiteboard. Behind him, the room is silent. It's a picture of Sasha Blake. Pale clear skin, blue eyes, a swing of dark ponytail.

She looks just like Faith.

* * *

Adam Fawley
4 April 2018
13.45

Windermere Avenue can't be more than half a mile from the Appleford house, and when Somer and I draw up outside the resemblance is even more pronounced. Even the net curtains are the same.

The door opens long before we get to the gate. A tall black woman with her hair in elaborate braids.

"I'm Yasmin," she says, coming toward me, her hand extended. "Fiona's neighbor. She's inside."

There are two more women in the small sitting room, one either side of Fiona Blake. She's rocking slightly. Her face is tight with anxiety.

"Mrs. Blake? I'm Detective Inspector Adam Fawley. This is DC Erica Somer."

The two other women get to their feet. They have that look we see so often in this job—half genuine concern and half immense relief that this particular nightmare

166

hasn't descended on them. They can't get out of the place quick enough. "We'll give you some space, Fiona," one of them says, backing toward the door. "We'll pop back later. You know, just in case there's anything we can do."

When they're gone, we take our seats; me on the sofa, Somer on the only chair. Judging from how she looks—how she smells—I don't think Fiona Blake has even bothered to shower this morning. One of the uniforms must have asked her for a recent photo of her daughter because there's a slew of snaps on the coffee table in front of us. Sasha as a toddler, her hair in jaunty bunches; in school uniform grinning from ear to ear; wearing a leotard, as skinny as a rake, holding up some sort of medal; and older, more contemporary shots on beaches, in the back garden, her arm around her mum. Smiling, relaxed. Happy.

"Can you take us through what happened?" says Somer softly. "When did you last see Sasha?"

The woman takes a breath that buckles into a sob. "Yesterday afternoon. When she got back from school. I made her a cup of tea and then I went to work."

"But you were expecting her to stay at home last night?"

She wipes her eyes and shakes her head. "No. She was going out with three of her friends. Just for an hour or so—it was a school night. But she's very sensible. She wouldn't stay out late."

Somer takes out her notebook. "Can you tell me her friends' names?"

"Patsie Webb, Isabel Parker and Leah Waddell. Patsie's here—in the kitchen—I asked her to come, after I called you. I knew you'd want to talk to her."

"When did you get home last night?"

"Just after twelve. I work at a restaurant in town. We were really busy. There was a group in. Americans. One of those coach tour things."

Somer makes a note. "And did you check Sasha's room when you got back?"

Fiona puts her hand to her mouth; she has a tissue gripped in her fist but it's starting to come apart and fragments of damp paper are shredding on to her clothes. "Yes, I did. But she said she might sleep over at Patsie's so I didn't worry. She's done that for years. But she always comes home first thing. You know, to change and that before she goes to school."

"So it wasn't till this morning you realized there was something wrong?"

She nods. "That's when I tried to call her but her phone was off. And then I rang Patsie and Isabel but they said they hadn't seen her since the night before."

She starts to rock again. "I should have called Sash last night to make sure—I shouldn't just have assumed—"

Somer reaches over and takes her gently by the hand. "It was gone midnight. Her phone would probably have been off even if you *had* called. You mustn't blame yourself."

I get to my feet and walk through to the back. In the kitchen, Yasmin has her arms around a teenage girl, holding her tight against her body. The girl's narrow shoulders are heaving in sobs.

"Patsie?"

The girl looks around and stares at me, pushing her hair away from her face. Her eyes are red.

"This is Detective Inspector Fawley," says Yasmin,

touching her gently on the shoulder. "He's the policeman looking for Sasha."

The girl's eyes widen and Yasmin gives her an encouraging squeeze. "He just wants to ask you some questions, love. It's nothing to be scared about."

I pull out a chair and sit down. Make myself smaller. Less intimidating. "I'm sure you understand, Patsie. We need all the information we can get, right now."

Patsie glances up at Yasmin, who gives her a reassuring nod.

"OK," she says, sniffing and wiping her nose.

"I'll make some tea," says Yasmin.

* * *

Somer sits forward a little on the chair. "Has there been anything worrying Sasha lately, Mrs. Blake? Has anything unusual happened you can think of?"

She wants to ask if they've noticed anyone hanging around—if Sasha might have thought she was being stalked—but the woman is spooked enough already without hearing that.

"She's been fine," Fiona says quickly. "Happy. Busy. Everything's been completely and totally normal. And if there had been anything worrying her she'd have told me. She tells me everything—there's just her and me. We're really close."

Somer wonders if any teenage girl ever tells her mother absolutely everything. But perhaps that's just her own experience talking. And the photos spread out on the table tell their own tale.

"There's no one you can think of she might have gone to see—grandparents perhaps?"

Fiona shakes her head. "My parents are in Portugal and Jonathan's mother lives in Huddersfield. I can't see Sasha going there. She doesn't even like her."

Somer hesitates. "What about a boyfriend?"

Fiona shakes her head. "No. I mean, there are boys she likes, of course. At school. But she's only fifteen. You know what girls are like at that age. They giggle a lot but it's no more than that."

"I see. And she'd definitely tell you? If there was someone?"

Fiona shoots her a look. "I just told you. She doesn't keep secrets from me. She's not that type of girl."

* * *

"Yeah, she's deffo had boyfriends," says Patsie. There's a mug of tea on the table in front of her but she's barely touched it. She has her hands in her lap, and she must be fiddling about with something because I can sense the movement.

"Is she seeing anyone at the moment?"

"I think so. But I don't know his name. Me and Iz—we thought he might be older than her."

"What makes you say that?"

She's still staring at her lap. "Just that she was, like, really cagey about him."

"Do you know where this boy lives? What he looks like?"

She shakes her head. It's like drawing teeth. Yasmin catches my eye and shrugs silently as if to say *Teenagers— what did you expect?*

"And she's definitely had boyfriends before?"

Patsie looks up. "But she didn't tell her mum because she thought she'd be angry. You know—that she's had sex. She thinks Sash's still," she blushes a little and avoids my eye, "you know, a virgin."

"OK, let's leave that for now. Let's go back to last night. You said you went to Summertown to have a pizza and then Leah walked home down the Banbury Road and the rest of you got the bus back towards Headington together?"

A nod.

"What time was that?"

"Nine forty-five? I don't really remember."

"Then you got off first, and Sasha and Isabel stayed on the bus."

Another nod.

"And that was about 10:00 p.m.?"

"Round then, yeah."

"And Sasha would have got off on Cherwell Drive."

"Right."

"But you don't know where she was planning to go when she got off the bus?"

She shrugs. "Up to her house? I mean, where else would she go?"

That, of course, is the whole point of asking. But there's no use getting tetchy with this girl.

"Does Sasha have any other friends who live near that bus stop, Patsie? Someone she could have gone to see after she got off the bus?"

A slow shake of the head. "I don't think so. Nobody *we* like, anyway."

"So you can't think of anywhere she'd have gone, apart from straight home?"

Another shake of the head. She glances up at me briefly, almost shyly, and then stares at her lap again. It occurs to me—as it should have before—that she's been texting on her phone this whole time.

Time for a different tack. "Do you know anything about Sasha's dad?"

She looks up for real this time. "Why?"

"I just need to get the full picture. Do you know if she still sees him?"

Patsie hesitates, then bites her lip.

* * *

"She hasn't seen her father for thirteen years. Not since the bastard walked out on the both of us."

Fiona Blake's tone has hardened and Somer can't honestly blame her. Abandoning a toddler isn't exactly her idea of doing the right thing either.

"Do you know where he's living now?"

Fiona shrugs. "Last I heard he'd shacked up with someone up north somewhere. But that was at least two years ago."

"And he's never attempted to get in touch with Sasha?"

She shakes her head. "No. Not once."

"So if he approached her in the street, she wouldn't be likely to go off with him?"

Fiona stares at her, and Somer can see the hope flare

for a moment then die in her eyes. She shakes her head sadly. "She was three when he left. I doubt she'd even recognize him."

*　*　*

Adam Fawley
4 April 2018
14.09

"He found her on Facebook," says Patsie. "They messaged for a bit and then she bunked off school and met up with him about a month ago. But don't tell her mum—she'd go mental."

"How did the meeting go?"

Patsie shrugs. "OK. Dunno really. She said he was all right. They went to Nando's."

As if that's important. As if it makes any difference at all.

"He told her he's living in Leeds now," she says suddenly. "That she could go up there to see him."

"And is she going to do that?"

Patsie shakes her head. "She said her mum would never let her."

I hold my breath, try not to look too eager. "But if he'd turned up—last night, say, as a surprise—would she have gone with him?"

Patsie stares at me, as if this has only just occurred to her. "I guess," she says eventually. "I mean, she'd never get into a car with a weirdo or anything. But if it was her dad, that'd be different."

*　*　*

"Could I see her room?" asks Somer. "Would that be OK?"

Fiona flashes her a look. "Shouldn't you be out there looking for her? If some pedophile has abducted her what difference will looking at her room make? It's a complete waste of time—"

"We don't know it's a pedophile," says Somer gently. "She may be with someone she knows. That's why we need to find out as much about her as we can."

Fiona looks at her and then away; the flash of temper evaporates as quickly as it came. She starts to cry again.

Somer puts her hand on the woman's shoulder. "And please believe me that we're doing everything possible to find her. We already have a team out searching the entire surrounding area."

Fiona nods, and Somer tightens her grip a little. And when the woman looks up, she asks the question again, silently this time.

"OK," Fiona says at last. "It's upstairs. On the left."

It's like staring at her teenage self. The boy bands may have changed but pretty much everything else about Sasha Blake's room is uncannily like the one Somer left behind in Guildford more than a decade ago. When she helped her parents move house last year, it was all still there, like a time capsule, clean and tidy and dusted just as she left it. And now it's as if she's back there all over again. The mirror draped with pink fairy lights, the dream-catcher over the bed, the box poking out underneath stuffed with shoes and scarves and bits of cheap jewelry, and the row of paperbacks on the shelf by the window. *Pride and Prejudice*, *The Wings of the Dove*, *Look Back in Anger*,

Poems by John Keats. There's a laptop on the desk, with a pile of *National Geographic* beside it and a book called *1,000 Things to Do Before You Die.* There are yellow Post-its purfling the pages.

She wants to seize the book and bury it somewhere. She doesn't want that book staring at Fiona Blake every time she comes in here—because—because—

Five minutes later there's a noise behind her and she turns to see Fawley at the door. He's staring around at the room, just like she did.

"Looks like she's a bright kid," he says eventually. "Henry James isn't your usual fifteen-year-old reading, is it?"

Somer shakes her head and holds up a sheet of paper. "I just found this letter on the desk. It's from *Vogue*—they've offered her work experience for this summer. I can't even imagine how much competition there must have been for something like that."

The flutter of unease Somer's had all morning has sharpened into foreboding. It shouldn't make a difference, that Sasha is clever and likes poetry and is interested in the world, but it does. It does.

"Are those hers too?" Fawley says now, walking over to a cork board hanging by the window. It's thick with photos, but they're very different to the ones her mother has downstairs: Sasha and her friends, grinning, sticking their tongues out, making rabbit ears behind each other's heads. And beside the snaps and selfies, a scattering of sketches: what looks like the view across Port Meadow, a bowl of oranges and pears, a pair of pink stilettos, one lying on its side.

And suddenly Somer sees what Fawley's getting at. "Oh, you mean the shoes?"

He shrugs. "And the *Vogue* thing. And the fact that Faith lives barely a mile from here."

She joins him, and they stare in silence at the drawing.

"An interest in fashion isn't much, by way of a link," she says eventually. "Not when you're talking teenage girls. And Faith is three years older, at college—"

"Just look at her," he says. "Sasha, I mean."

And she knows what he's getting at. It's not just the hair or the facial resemblance. It's only a hunch—an intuition—but something tells her Sasha is the girl Faith has always wanted to be. Pretty in a happy, effortless, unforced way. Confident about who she is, content in her own skin, and barely able to imagine what it might feel like not to be. Even as her anxiety sharpens for Sasha, Somer still finds her heart aching for Faith.

"I'll give Faith a call and ask her if they've ever met," she says at last. "Being so nearby, I suppose it's possible."

"And get me a list of all male employees under thirty at those building firms we've been looking at. It's possible one of them is this older boyfriend Sasha's mother is apparently unaware of."

Somer didn't know about him either, not till this moment. But this is the Fawley she knows—the Fawley they all know. The one who finds unseen connections, the one who gets there first.

She glances at him. "You think there really could be a connection with what happened to Faith?"

"Yes," he says heavily. "I'm afraid I do."

But she can't read his expression. Resignation? Apprehension?

"Update DS Gislingham, please," he says. "And then

176

go through this room with a fine-tooth comb. Look for anything from her father, and any sort of diary. Basically anything that might give us some names—male names. And take that laptop in for Baxter to look at, but make sure you get Mrs. Blake's written permission first."

"Where are you going, sir?"

"To Headington, to see Isabel Parker. The school have sent her home. Let's just hope she remembers something Patsie doesn't."

He stops at the door. "And tell Gislingham I want everyone back at base at 6:00. If there've been no other developments."

He doesn't need to spell it out.

* * *

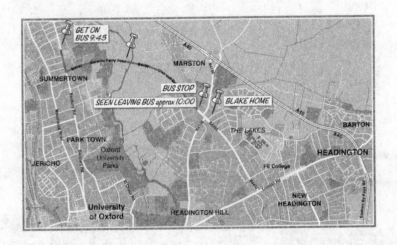

* * *

Back at the incident room, the atmosphere is dense with anxiety. They know the stats—how quickly the clock runs down on abduction victims, how low the chances are of finding them alive once twenty-four hours are passed.

Gislingham is at the front, collating the Sasha material on a whiteboard. A new one, set up next to Faith's. Close enough that they can start drawing lines between them if they need to, but not touching, not yet, because Gislingham is superstitious, and he's not alone. No one wants these two cases to be connected. No one.

"There's no sign of Sasha on the speed camera on Cherwell Drive last night," says Quinn, looking up and catching his eye. "I'm going to call the bus company—see if they have CCTV in that vehicle."

Baxter glances up. "Good luck with that," he says heavily.

Gis turns and looks for Everett. "Anything on her mobile yet?"

"I've asked for the call log," she says. "But the phone is definitely off."

"When was the last signal?"

"Last night, at 9:35 in Summertown. Must have been just before they got on the bus."

"Isn't that rather an odd time for her to turn it off?" says Gis.

Ev shrugs. "Perhaps her battery was low."

"I've trawled her social media," says Baxter, "and Patsie's right—looks like Sasha's father did find her through Facebook. There's a Jonathan Blake living in Leeds listed among her Friends, but he must have contacted her privately after that because he hasn't posted anything on her page."

"What about boyfriends—blokes her own age—anything standing out?"

Baxter shakes his head. "Most of Sasha's feed is about the four of them—the girls, I mean. They call themselves the 'LIPS.' Lots of kiss emojis and stuff. As far as I can see those four are all but joined at the hip. Can't see blokes getting much of a look-in."

Ev looks across at him. "Just because it's not there doesn't mean it wasn't happening. Kids know their parents stalk them online. They'd put stuff like that on WhatsApp or Snapchat—somewhere like that. Somewhere private."

Gis sighs. "I've got that coming too, have I?"

"Oh, I don't know," says Ev with a smile. "Your Billy's only two—I reckon you've got a good ten years yet."

Gis walks around and stands behind Baxter's chair, looking at his screen. Then he bends down, as if to take a closer look. "What about the Parrie stuff?" he asks in an undertone.

Baxter glances up. "There's Wikipedia for starters, but that doesn't have much on the MO. But you can find that too if you're prepared to dig a bit—the usual true crime sites and bloggers who think they know better than we do. And a whole bunch of conspiracy theorist tossers, of course—Parrie's very popular with them."

Gislingham makes a face. "Now there's a surprise. What about the trial transcripts?"

"Just come through. Though I've not found much yet. I've had to drop it *pro tem*, with all this about Sasha Blake."

"Fair enough, but keep on it, yeah? I've got a bad feeling about this, and the last thing we need right now is Gavin Parrie coming back to bite us on the arse."

* * *

At Windermere Avenue, Somer is still working her way through Sasha's bedroom. She's trying to leave everything as she found it, so that if Sasha comes home she won't feel her space has been violated. And all the more—and it's a thought that ices her spine—if she's already been violated in a far worse way. But however carefully she searches, she's still prying, still an intruder, still betraying this girl she's started to like. The clothes in the wardrobe are the same things she wore once—things she could easily see Faith Appleford wearing or talking about on one of her vlogs: the clean lines, the preference for plains over patterns, the one or two retro pieces that must have been shrewd selections from charity shops, the more expensive things carefully chosen to have as many different uses as possible. Every object in the room says something about this girl—a postcard from her grandparents in the Algarve, a picture of a little boy with a bucket and spade tucked into one of the paperbacks, a handwritten note on the back, faded to sepia, *Weston-Super-Mare 1976*. There are annotations in the books too—Keats' "To Autumn" is "unbelievable," "glorious," but *Endymion* only gets "flabby," underlined twice. And there are six gleeful exclamation marks alongside a passage describing how a phrenologist who examined Thomas Hardy's head declared he would come "to no good." All this brings a smile, but it's not what Somer is looking for. There's no notebook, no diary, no secret stash of sexy underwear, no pictures on the board of anyone who might be her boyfriend, and after an hour of searching, Somer is tempted to wonder if such a boyfriend even exists. But as she knows full well, absence of evidence is not evidence of absence. They haven't got Sasha's phone, and they haven't even started on her laptop. And those are fine and private places to hide a love that dare not tweet its name.

She takes one more look under the bed, then goes to stand up but her bracelet snags on the carpet and she has to kneel down again to untangle it. And it's only then that she realizes there's something under the bed after all— what looks like a lipstick, rolled over to the far corner. There's no reason to retrieve it—it can't possibly be relevant to anything at all—but something makes her lie down on her back and reach out an arm.

And that's when she sees it.

* * *

Adam Fawley
4 April 2018
14.55

Isabel Parker's house is unexpected. One of those impossibly gorgeous stone houses in Old Headington, a color-supplement enclave you can barely believe has survived so perfectly, surrounded by the noise and sprawl Headington's now become. But if the house is unexpected, it seems I am not. Or if not me, precisely, then someone like me. The woman who opens the door is probably the same age as Sasha's mother, but Botox and an expensive hairdresser are doing a pretty successful job of masking it. She has a gray marl T-shirt, black leggings, silver flip-flops and bright-red toenails. She introduces herself ("It's Victoria but everyone calls me Tory"; believe me, there really is no answer to that) then leads me through the big slate-flagged entrance hall to a kitchen almost as large as the Blakes' entire ground floor.

The girl at the long wooden table is doing something on an iPad. Outside, in the garden, a man with a long ponytail and a Crocodile Dundee hat is weeding the flower beds.

"This is Detective Inspector Fawley, Isabel," the woman says. "He wants to ask you about Sasha. So turn that thing off and pay attention."

She shoos at the iPad, as if it will just fold itself up and flap away, like some sort of stiff electronic crow.

Isabel rolls her eyes behind her mother's back, and I catch her eye and endeavor to look conspiratorial, but I'm probably just freaking her out.

Mrs. Parker turns to the worktop and the gleaming Nespresso machine. She hasn't asked if I want anything.

"I've just been talking to Patsie, Isabel," I say. "So obviously I wanted to talk to you as well. Perhaps you can take me through what happened last night?"

The girl shrugs. "I already told the other bloke. The fat one."

"I know, but it would really help if you could tell me as well."

"We went for a pizza in Summertown—that place on South Parade."

"Patsie said you got on the bus about 9:45. What time did you leave the restaurant?"

Another shrug. "Nine? Just after? We just hung out for a while after that."

Like teenagers do. Like I did.

"Then Patsie got off the bus in Marston and Sasha in Cherwell Drive?"

"Yeah. And I stayed on till Headington."

"And you got back home when?"

"Dunno. Half ten maybe."

I turn to Mrs. Parker. "We were out last night," she says, flushing slightly as if I've accused her of chronic child neglect. "But we were back by 11:00. Isabel was in here raiding the fridge."

The girl is looking at her iPad again.

"Patsie said the bus was really crowded—a bunch of foreign exchange students, she thought."

Isabel looks up at me. "Yeah, so?"

"Did you see where Sasha went when she got off the bus?" She looks back at her screen and I dip my head, trying to catch her eye.

"Isabel!" says her mother sharply. "This is important—your friend is *missing.*"

The girl looks at her, and then at me. I've seen that look before. And on better liars than this girl.

"OK, Isabel," I say, "whatever it is, you need to tell me. Right now."

She looks distressed. "But I promised—"

"I don't care. I need to know."

She sighs loudly. "Look, I think Sash was going to meet her boyfriend, 'K? She'd told her mum she'd be sleeping

183

over at Patsie's but when we were at the pizza place she changed her mind. I reckon she was going to see him. She didn't actually *say* that, but that's what me and Pats thought. She made us promise not to tell her mum."

I can't say any of that comes as much of a surprise. But it doesn't do anything to shift my unease.

"Did she get a call or a text or something—just before she changed her mind?"

She shrugs. "Maybe. Yeah, actually I think she did."

"What's his name?"

"I *told* you, she never said. She wouldn't even admit she *had* a boyfriend. But there was definitely something going on—she's been super secretive for, like, days and days."

There's a flush to her cheeks now. Her mother smiles. "Don't worry, darling. You're doing *really* well, isn't she, Inspector?"

"Does the name Ashley Brotherton mean anything to you, Isabel?"

Her eyes widen. "No, should it?"

"Or Faith Appleford?"

"No."

I sit forward a little. "Now, this is really important. I know you said before that you didn't see what Sasha did after she got off the bus. Can you think about that again and tell me if there's anything you remember now?"

I hold her gaze. She knows what I'm saying: *I'm prepared to bet you lied the first time, but I'm giving you another chance.*

The flush deepens and she nods. "I think there might of been someone parked there. Meeting her, I mean. We kept asking where she was going and she just kept smiling and saying we'd find out soon enough."

"But you didn't see anyone when she got off the bus?"

She shakes her head. "I just saw her running up the road and looking, just like, really really happy." Her eyes fill with tears. "She will be OK, won't she? I know I should have said something but I promised—"

Her mother rushes to her and wraps her arms about her, stroking her hair. "It's all right, darling, you weren't to know."

I wait a while, and then a little longer, and when Isabel finally seems calmer, I ask her if she still has the bus ticket.

She sniffs a little. "I think I chucked it."

Her mother touches her gently on the shoulder. "Why don't you go upstairs and see if you can find it? It might still be in your bag."

"But I already told him what time it was—"

"It's not that," I say. "The ticket will have other information on it as well as the time. Who the driver was—stuff like that."

She flicks her pink-tipped fringe out of her eyes. "OK," she says eventually. "I'll have a look."

When she comes down five minutes later she hands me a shred of paper.

"This is all I could find."

It's crumpled and the ink has run but it's still legible.

"That's great, Isabel. That's exactly what we need."

* * *

When the lights change, Gislingham signals left and pulls up behind a squad car at the bottom of Windermere

Avenue. He's on his way to meet Ev at Summertown High but he thought he ought to drop in and see how the house-to-house is going. He's not expecting much—he's not expecting anything, frankly, because if there'd been any news on Sasha, they'd have called him to say so—but he doesn't want it to look like CID just hand off all the shit jobs to uniform.

He spots the sergeant in charge a few yards away, talking to a female officer. Gis knows him pretty well. He's a safe pair of hands.

"Anything new, Barnetson?" he says, drawing level.

The man looks up and shakes his head. "We're pretty much done here. We've spoken to everyone between the Blake house and the bus stop. A couple of people recognized Sasha from the photo, but only because they'd seen her round there before. No one remembers seeing her last night or noticed anyone acting suspiciously." He gestures at a clear plastic sack at his feet. "We've trawled the gutters and verges too, but all we've found is the usual crap. I'll get it sent over to forensics but I'm not holding my breath."

Gis looks down at the sack. Fast-food wrappers, beer cans and bags of dog shit. "Alan Challow's going to love you."

Barnetson gives a wry smile. "Oh, I don't know. It might make a nice change from rotting corpses."

"So what now?"

"There's a team starting on the fields either side of the Marston Ferry Road. I'll pop over there later but the last I heard they hadn't found anything either."

Gislingham looks up at the sky. The wind has just got up and there's rain in the air.

"Hope they remembered their wellies," he says.

* * *

Jayne Ayre @NotthatJaneEyre   15.07
#Oxford folk, does anyone know anything about
something happening on Cherwell Drive? There's
a bunch of police cars parked up there.

Alicia Monroe @Monroe51098   15.09
Replying to @NotthatJaneEyre
I live on Thirlmere Road—just saw a couple of officers
talking to people on doorsteps on Windermere Avenue
#Oxford

Mariza Fernandes @Brazilia2012   15.11
Replying to @NotthatJaneEyre @Monroe51098
They have called here also—they are asking about a
girl. I think she is missing #Oxford

Alicia Monroe @Monroe51098   15.19
Replying to @NotthatJaneEyre @Brazilia2012
Oh no—not again. Her poor parents ☹ #missing #Oxford

Jayne Ayre @NotthatJaneEyre   15.22
Replying to @Brazilia2012 @Monroe51098
I've just checked @OxfordNewsOnline and
@BBCMidlandsBreaking. Nothing yet

Oxford's News @OxfordNewsOnline   15.26

Replying to @NotthatJaneEyre @Brazilia2012 @Monroe51098

Do you know the girl's name and age?

Mariza Fernandes @Brazilia2012   15.32

Replying to @OxfordNewsOnline @NotthatJaneEyre @Monroe51098

Sacha I think. I did not recognize her. In the picture she
looks about 15

Oxford's News @OxfordNewsOnline   15.39

Replying to @NotthatJaneEyre @Brazilia2012 @Monroe51098

BREAKING Reports coming in of a possible missing
teenager in the Marston area of #Oxford—residents in
the area believe it may be a 15yo girl. More on this as
we get it

*   *   *

Adam Fawley
4 April 2018
15.45

I'm out at the car when my phone goes.

Harrison. Wanting an update.

"I've just been speaking to Isabel Parker, sir. She thinks
Sasha Blake may have been meeting a boyfriend last night.
Though I'm afraid she doesn't know anything about
him—no name, address, nothing."

I hear him sigh angrily. And I can't blame him.

"And the Blake girl's father—what about him?"

"We've been on to West Yorkshire Police. They're
on their way round. We're still hoping that's where she
went."

"Pretty shitty father to do that and not let the mother know."

"I know, sir. But there's evidently no love lost between them—"

"That's no excuse," he snaps.

If you believe the station rumor mill, Harrison's own divorce was pretty messy. Perhaps that explains it.

"Right now, we're just guessing, sir. It's possible Sasha told him she'd cleared it with her mother. She seems like a sensible girl, but we know she can be economical with the truth when it suits her."

A snort of recognition at this. He has teenage kids; he knows the territory. "Well, either way, I hope to God that's where she is. And not just for her sake, either."

For mine too. That's what he means.

"So what next, Adam?"

"If we have no luck with Leeds I'll arrange a TV appeal with Mrs. Blake."

"Good. And make sure it's in time for the evening news."

*   *   *

Graeme Scott is queuing to get a coffee when the head shows a man and woman into the crowded staffroom.

"Who the hell are they?" asks the teacher in front of him in a low voice. She only started this term—her first job out of training. Domestic science, or whatever they're supposed to call it now. He tried talking to her once, when she arrived, just to be friendly, but she gave him the brush-off. "It's not Ofsted, is it?"

Scott shakes his head. "No—they'd have given us notice. And in any case, those two don't look like school inspectors to me."

But it's something serious all the same. That much is obvious, even before the head claps her hands and asks for silence.

"I'm sorry to disturb you all but I'm afraid I have some worrying news. Sasha Blake of Year Eleven didn't turn up for school today and it's now emerged that she hasn't been seen since last night and isn't answering her phone. This is Detective Sergeant Gislingham and Detective Constable Everett. They'll want to speak to Sasha's friends and teachers, so please can you do everything you can to help them, and to support Sasha's year group at this difficult time. Needless to say, we want to avoid any sort of panic, so it's important we all keep calm. Keep calm and carry on, as they say."

Graeme Scott suppresses a grimace. How bloody clichéd can you get.

The head turns to the man standing next to her. "Would you like to say anything, Sergeant?"

He's stocky, barely mid-height, thinning on top; a bit "jolly," Scott suspects. He's met that type before: classic short-man syndrome. As for the woman, she's positively dowdy. Flat shoes, hair in a mess. There's no excuse for that, he thinks, not in this day and age.

"Just to echo what the head said," says the man, glancing around the room. "We don't want to cause unnecessary alarm, but it's important we gather as much information as we can. And if any of the female pupils would prefer to talk to a woman, then DC Everett is on hand. That's it, really."

The bell sounds now, clanging like an air-raid siren, and the staff start to gather their things. There's the usual sense of too much to do and too little time to do it in. But there's an unease now, a disquiet, which is not usual at all.

And I didn't even get a bloody coffee, thinks Scott as he shoulders his bag. The two police officers are standing by the door, apparently casual. Scott makes sure not to catch their eye.

*   *   *

Telephone interview with Charlie Higgins, driver,
Oxford Bus Company
4 April 2018, 4:15 p.m.
On the call, DC A. Baxter

AB: Thanks for calling back, Mr. Higgins. You got
     the message, I assume?

CH: It's about last night, right?

AB: Specifically the bus that left Summertown at
     approximately 9:45. I believe you don't have
     CCTV in that vehicle?

CH: No, 'fraid not. What is it you're after?

AB: I'm going to text you some photos. Can you
     tell me if you recognize any of the people
     in them?
     [*muffled sounds in the background, then Higgins*
     returns to the phone]

CH: I do remember a big bunch of kids on that
     run. Some of 'em were foreign. And a lot of

them were pissed, even though they didn't look
much more than fifteen, half of 'em. But kids
these days—

AB: So it got rowdy—is that what you're
saying?

CH: Not exactly rowdy—it was mostly girls.
But loud. *Definitely* loud.

AB: Are you sure you don't recognize any of the
girls in the photo?

CH: I definitely recognize the one with the pink
stuff in her hair. Yeah, she was the one who
asked me the time. It was when we was just
getting into Headington.

AB: Do you remember the exact time?

CH: Five past ten? That's right. It was
deffo her.

AB: But you don't recognize any of the others?

CH: Sorry, no. These kids, they all look the
bloody same, don't they?

AB: You've been very helpful, Mr. Higgins. And if
anything else comes back to you, please get
in touch straightaway.

CH: You didn't say—why are you asking about all
this?

AB: One of those girls has gone missing. And
the last time anyone saw her was on
your bus.

CH: Bloody hell. Makes you think, doesn't it.

AB: Yes, Mr. Higgins, it certainly does.

* * *

As soon as I get into the incident room I can tell they have something. The way Somer and Baxter turn to look at me. The expressions on their faces.

"Have we heard from Leeds?"

"Not yet, sir," says Somer. "But I did find something at the Blake house."

It's on the table in front of her. In an evidence bag.

A packet of condoms.

A packet that's already half used.

"It was taped to the underside of Sasha's bed," says Somer. "Her friends were right—she *was* seeing someone. And no wonder she didn't want her mother to know."

"OK, so now we know *what* she was doing—are we any closer to knowing who she was doing it with?"

Somer shakes her head. "If she kept any sort of diary I didn't find it in the room. But there were lots of pens and pencils in a jam jar, so I suspect she probably did have something like that, only she's got it with her."

"What about notebooks? Exercise books, something like that? I remember the girls at my school doodling love hearts with boys' names in all the time. Don't girls still do that?"

Somer smiles, almost despite herself. "Well, I did. But I couldn't find anything like that, I'm afraid."

"There isn't anything on social media," interjects Baxter. "I can tell you that for nothing."

"Did Mrs. Blake give us permission to look at the laptop?"

Somer nods. "But she doesn't have any idea what the password might be."

Baxter sighs heavily and reaches for the machine. "OK, punk. Make my day."

*　*　*

Sergeant Karen Bonnett straightens her uniform and reaches for the doorbell. This wasn't exactly what she had planned for today, but it beats shoplifting. Or school liaison. Or Traffic. Everyone hates Traffic. She can hear PC Mansour behind her, scraping his shoes on the concrete as he shifts from one foot to the other. He's only just out of training and she's prepared to bet he hasn't done anything like this before.

"Don't fidget," she hisses. "Makes us look like amateurs."

The noises stop at once. But there's much more noise, now, from the other side of the door. A baby crying. Full throttle.

The door opens slowly and a woman in track pants and a black T-shirt peers out at them. She has a red-faced baby wedged against her shoulder and she's rubbing its back with that desperate automatic gesture all new mothers develop. Bonnett should know; she's had four of her own. This girl is pretty in a wrung-out and sleepless sort of way, but she can't be more than twenty-five. At least twenty years younger than Jonathan Blake, who is presumably the father of the baby. Yet another second-time-arounder, thinks Bonnett. Yet another middle-aged bloke who's walked out on his past-her-sell-by-date wife for a twenty-something upgrade and a shiny new family to match.

"What do you want?"

"Ms. Barrow? Rachel Barrow? Sergeant Karen Bonnett. Can we come in for a moment?"

The woman's eyes widen. "What is it? Is it Jon—has he been in an accident?"

"Nothing like that. No need for you to worry. We just need a quick word."

The woman steps forward and glances up and down the road. A couple of passersby have stopped on the other side of the street and are watching with undisguised interest.

"OK," she says quickly. "But just for a minute. I need to do the four o'clock feed."

The sitting room has that trying-to-maintain-some-sort-of-order-despite-the-baby devastation Bonnett's seen so many times before. The biscuit-colored sofas aren't going to last the course, that's for sure. And the cream satin cushions are already jostling with a bag of nappies, a packet of baby wipes and a discarded yellow and white Babygro. But give the girl credit; at least she's trying.

Mansour takes a seat without being asked and Bonnett flashes him a look which he doesn't see, largely because he's too busy eyeing up the plasma TV. Bonnett sighs. But when she tries to get Rachel to join her in a complicit smile she doesn't get a response.

"Can you tell me what this is about?"

"It's about Sasha," says Bonnett. "Your partner's daughter."

Rachel frowns. "What about her?"

They call Bonnett "Cawood" at the nick, after the Sarah Lancashire character in *Happy Valley*. And there's no question there's a resemblance. It's not just the hair—though the blond definitely helps—it's all of it: the resilience, the shrewdness, the stand-your-ground-and-speak-your-mind.

"Is she here, Ms. Barrow?"

"What do you mean 'is she here?'" says Rachel. "Of course she's *not here*. I haven't even met her."

Bonnett looks around the room. "But Mr. Blake has, hasn't he? Recently, I mean."

"I don't see how you—"

"The pictures, Ms. Barrow. That one over there, for a start—in the silver frame. That's Sasha, isn't it? Even from this distance I can tell that's not a toddler."

The woman hoists the baby a little higher. "Why shouldn't he have a picture of her? It's not some sort of secret. We talked about it. Jon wanted to see her. He said they'd been kept apart for too long."

"Why now, suddenly? After all these years?"

"It was the baby. Jon thought we should try to be a proper family. That it wasn't fair that Sasha didn't even know she has a brother. Especially now she's old enough to make her own choices."

"Where's Mr. Blake now, Ms. Barrow?"

She flushes a little. "Down south. Berkshire. He's the sales manager for a pharmaceutical company. And you still haven't told me what this is about."

"Sasha Blake is missing. And given she's been in recent contact with her father, Thames Valley Police asked us to check the premises to see if she's here."

The woman's eyes widen and her grip on her baby tightens. The child starts to wail again.

"So could we do that, Ms. Barrow? Check the house? For tidiness' sake?"

The woman hesitates a moment, then nods.

Bonnett gives Mansour a meaningful look and he gets hurriedly to his feet and goes back out into the hall. A moment later they hear his footsteps on the stairs.

"He won't find anything," says Rachel firmly. "I told you—she's not here. She's never even visited. Jon met her in Oxford."

"You just said Mr. Blake is in Berkshire. That's not so far from Oxford. Was he intending to contact Sasha? Perhaps try and see her?"

Rachel flushes again. "Actually, he did say something about that, but I don't know if it came to anything. You'd have to ask him."

"We've been trying," says Bonnett drily. "But the number his office gave us appears to be off."

Rachel reaches over and picks up a mobile from the coffee table. "I've had mine on mute," she says, staring at the screen. "I was trying to get the baby down." She looks up. "There's nothing from Jon but there are four missed calls from his mum. You spoke to her as well?"

"I'm afraid we had to—we needed Mr. Blake's address."

Rachel sighs. "And now she'll be on my case all afternoon."

"Have you had any sort of contact with Mr. Blake today?"

Rachel shakes her head. "He said he had a meeting all morning and to leave him an email if I needed anything. I can call him again now, if you like."

"No, no," says Bonnett quickly. "I'd rather you didn't

do that. We'll make contact ourselves. You don't happen to know which company the meeting is with, do you?"

"It's Dexter Masterson. They're a private hospital group based in Reading. I can find their number—it's how Jon and I met—we worked together—"

I bet you did, thinks Bonnett. "That's fine, Ms. Barrow," she says with a thin smile. "Don't you worry. We'll take it from here."

*　　*　　*

"How are you doing?"

Gis is at the door of the Summertown High secretary's office, where Everett has taken up temporary residence. A line of girls has been trooping in and out to see her all day, and it's starting to feel rather like a confessional box. Not that anyone has anything to confess. The information Ev's collected isn't likely to help them much either. As far as her peers are concerned Sasha Blake is "really nice" and "smart but cool, you know?" She's "really pretty" and "everyone wants to look like her" and she's "really popular, specially with the boys," but no one could name an actual boyfriend, or at least not one at school. Which, given the fact that Isabel and Patsie don't know his name either, is hardly a surprise. In short, everyone seems to like Sasha, but no one has any idea where she might be.

Everett looks up at Gis and sighs. "I've ticked a lot of boxes, but I haven't got anything else to put in them. What about you?"

Gis shrugs. "Not much better. None of the teachers thought she had a boyfriend either, and I've spoken to all of them except one, who's gone home with a migraine, but we can catch them tomorrow."

"Tomorrow?"

"Yeah, just got a call from Baxter. We're going to Reading. To see Jonathan Blake."

* * *

"I've just had Jonathan's bloody mother on the phone asking me what's happened to Sasha—like it's all *my* fault. Why the hell didn't someone tell me you were going to call her?"

Somer bites her lip. "I'm really sorry, Fiona," she says, holding the phone a little closer. "It wasn't actually us who spoke to your mother-in-law, it was West Yorkshire Police."

But that's no excuse; they should have realized that might happen. And right now, Fiona Blake needs to trust the police, not think they're causing trouble for her behind her back. Baxter catches Somer's eye and she makes a face: *Looks like we dropped the ball.*

"I believe West Yorkshire had to speak to his mother to get his address—he doesn't currently own a property in his own name—"

"Presumably because he's sponging off that bloody woman, whoever she is. I bet she's younger than him—I'm right, aren't I—"

"I'm afraid I'm not able to—"

"I'll kill him—if he's taken Sasha after all these years not even acknowledging she exists, I swear, I'll bloody kill him—"

199

Somer takes a deep breath. She's trying not to let on that Sasha's already seen her father, because that's the last thing Fiona Blake needs to hear right now. Or perhaps the second last.

"She's not there, Mrs. Blake."

"What –?"

"She's not there. West Yorkshire searched the house. Mr. Blake wasn't there either."

"So where the bloody hell is he? He's got her, hasn't he—he's abducted her—"

"There is absolutely nothing to suggest that. Mr. Blake was at a business meeting in Reading this morning. We've confirmed with the company concerned that he did, in fact, attend that meeting, and we have two officers on their way there right now to speak to him."

She can hear the woman's ragged breathing, can imagine the pain in her chest, the rawness in her throat.

"Mrs. Blake—Fiona—I know this is easy for me to say, but please do try to stay calm. When Sasha gets back she's going to need you. She'll need you to be strong."

Fiona takes a deep breath. "OK. But you'll call me? As soon as you've spoken to Jonathan?"

"Of course. Of course I will."

* * *

Even though the Dexter Masterson reception is crowded, Gislingham and Everett don't need to ask the woman on the desk to point out Jonathan Blake. The man is on his feet and in their faces before the revolving door has even closed behind them.

"I've been sat here over three hours. What the hell's all this about?"

Gis glances around, and steers Blake to an empty sofa in the far corner. He's wearing a slim-cut gray suit, a white shirt and a pale silk tie, along with just a hint of stubble. Trying a bit too hard, aren't you, mate, thinks Gislingham, who, like Karen Bonnett, has seen this type before.

"Let's just sit down, shall we, Mr. Blake? Shall I get you a glass of water?"

"I don't need a bloody glass of water. I want to know what's going on. Do you have any idea how embarrassing it is to be told by a *client* that you need to stay in their building because the *police* want to talk to you?"

"Sorry about that, Mr. Blake," says Gislingham, who doesn't look sorry at all. "I can have a word with them if you like."

"No thanks. You've done quite enough damage already."

Gis takes a deep breath. "It's about your daughter, Mr. Blake. I'm afraid she's gone missing."

Blake gapes at him. "*What?* Sasha's gone *missing?* When was this?"

"Last night, around ten. She was last seen getting off a bus at the bottom of Windermere Avenue."

"Why the fuck wasn't I told about this before?"

"She wasn't reported missing till this morning," says Everett. "And it's taken since then to track you down."

Blake has gone white. He's staring at the floor now. The two officers exchange a glance and Everett raises an eyebrow.

"Apparently Sasha was due to stay over at her friend's last night," continues Gislingham. "But then she changed her mind. Her friends don't know why. Do *you* know why, Mr. Blake?"

He glances up at them briefly and then drops his gaze back to the floor.

"Yes." He swallows. "She was meeting me."

* * *

At the Marston Ferry Road, the search team is taking a breather in the allotment car park. Someone's passing around a thermos of tea, and a couple of people are chewing chocolate bars, though without any particular sign of enjoyment. It's been an arduous day, up to their ankles in mud half the time. Even the terrain seems against them, the wet clay sucking down their feet and sapping their energy. The Cherwell has burst its banks at several points and half of them are now wearing waders. There's talk of getting divers in. Sergeant Barnetson looks up at the sky; the drizzle is getting heavier now. But they may just manage another hour or so as long as they get a move on.

"OK," he announces, raising his voice above the wind, "let's have one more push before we lose the light completely. It's going to be even colder tonight, so if Sasha is out there injured somewhere, we need to find her."

* * *

"So you're saying you texted Sasha at around 8:30 to say you'd finished your business dinner early."

"Right," says Blake. "She knew I was in Reading and I

promised I'd try to get over and see her, so I sent her the text on the off-chance she was around."

"I see," says Gislingham. "When we spoke to her friends they told us that it was after getting that text that she changed her mind about staying over with Patsie."

He looks flustered now. "Yeah, well—"

"*Yeah, well* what, Mr. Blake?"

"I told her that if her mother thought she was with Patsie, she could come over and spend the night at my hotel. I said I'd pick her up along by the bus stop at 10:00."

He looks from Gislingham to Everett and back again. "Look, it was nothing—you know—*dodgy*. She's my *daughter.*"

"Who you've barely seen since she was a toddler."

"What's that got to do with it? I'm still her father—and I resent your bloody tone. I am *not* a pedophile."

"Where was she going to stay, at the hotel?" asks Gislingham evenly. "Were you going to get her a separate room?"

Blake flushes. "No. It would have cost a fortune."

"So there was a spare bed in your room?"

"*No,*" he says sarcastically. "But amazingly enough there was an *armchair*. I was going to sleep in that."

Everett sits back and folds her arms. "So what happened, then? She never did go to that hotel, did she?"

Blake takes a deep breath. "No. As I'm sure the staff will confirm."

They sit there, staring at him, waiting. Come on, thinks Gislingham, spit it out.

"Look," he says eventually. "Something came up, OK? One of the people I was at dinner with called me and suggested we have a nightcap. It was an important client—I couldn't really say no."

And I bet you didn't try very hard, either, thinks Gislingham, who's just had a large bet with himself about which sex this super-important client turns out to be.

"So you texted Sasha again and blew her off?" says Everett. "Because you had a better offer?"

Blake doesn't dignify that with a response.

"We can check with your phone company," continues Ev. "They'll be able to confirm it, if you did."

"Then I suggest you do just that," Blake snaps, glaring at her. "And get off my back."

"What's this client of yours called?" asks Gis, pulling out his notebook. "Just for the record."

Blake hesitates. "Amanda Forman. But I'd rather you didn't bother her with any of this if that can be avoided."

Yeah, right, thinks Gis, several thousand imaginary pounds richer.

"And what time was your text to Sasha?"

Blake shrugs. "Amanda called around 9:45, so I must have texted Sasha just after that."

But as Gis well knows, Sasha's phone was already off by then—she'd never have received it. Did she get off that bus at Cherwell Drive, in the dark, on her own, to wait for a father who was never going to show?

There's a silence. Blake looks agitated and uneasy but Gislingham doesn't doubt he's telling the truth. He's just terrified about his other half finding out what he was really up to. That's what's got him so jumpy. Not his nineteen-hours-missing daughter.

"I'm afraid we will have to speak to *Amanda*," Gis

continues, injecting as much disdain into the name as he can get away with. "We'll need her to corroborate what you've said. Perhaps you could give DC Everett her details."

You're really bricking it now, aren't you, he thinks, looking at Blake's face as he writes down the number. His hand is shaking. Then Gislingham gets to his feet and Everett does the same.

"But don't worry, sir, we won't tell the missus. Unless, of course, we have no choice."

* * *

Adam Fawley
4 April 2018
17.32

"So where are we, Sergeant?"

It's 5:30, in the incident room. Twitter is alive with rumors of a missing girl and I'm going to be in front of a TV camera in half an hour so I'd quite like to have something I could actually say.

Gis looks up. He has a list, which is a good sign. But he's frowning, which isn't. "We haven't had any luck tracking down Sasha's boyfriend."

He glances at Baxter. "We don't have her phone, of course, which is making things a lot harder, and we haven't managed to crack the password on the laptop, but we've only had it a couple of hours—"

"Still nothing on social media?"

"Nope," says Baxter. "Sod all."

I turn to Everett. "What about Ashley Brotherton?"

Ev shakes her head. "We did check but nothing doing.

Seems he cut his hand quite badly at work yesterday and was sat in the A&E department at the John Rad until 10:00 last night waiting to get it stitched."

I frown; he still seems like a pretty good bet to me. "Has the hospital confirmed that?"

"Not yet, sir, but we've asked for the CCTV from their car park. Apparently the site foreman had to take him in, but they went in Brotherton's van so we should be able to find it on the footage if he's telling the truth. But I think we'll find he is."

She has one of those *I told you so* looks on her face now which prickles my irritation. But perhaps I'm just imagining it.

"And Jonathan Blake?"

"Nothing doing," says Gis. "We spoke to the 'client' he was having drinks with and she confirmed where he was. Though she was pretty pissed off to be dragged into all this so I can't see Blake doing business with her any time soon—"

"As opposed to doing *the* business," says Quinn with a smirk. "Which I reckon he's already managed."

"And there's nothing whatsoever to connect him to the assault on Faith," continues Gislingham, ignoring Quinn. "He's got a solid alibi for that morning, for a start—he was on a client call in Swindon."

I go up to the board and stand there, staring at it. At the pictures of the two girls. At the white space between the two that we still haven't found anything to fill.

"And we're absolutely sure they don't know each other?" I ask, without turning around.

"Yes, sir," replies Somer. "I asked Faith."

I pick up the marker pen and draw a circle slowly around Faith's picture. And then another, around Sasha's. And in the center, where they overlap, I put a question mark. Then I step back and snap the top back on the pen.

"You don't think Sasha's with her boyfriend, do you?" says Somer heavily.

"I hope she is. I hope they're having wild irresponsible teenage sex and haven't yet managed to come up for air. But we have to assume the worst. We always have to assume the worst. Unless and until."

* * *

THE CENTRAL CRIMINAL COURT

The Old Bailey
London EC4M 7EH

BEFORE:
THE HONORABLE MR. JUSTICE HEALEY

R E G I N A
v.
GAVIN FRANCIS PARRIE

MR. R. BARNES Q.C. and MISS S. GREY
appeared on behalf of the prosecution.

MRS. B. JENKINS Q.C. and MR. T. CUTHBERT
appeared on behalf of the defendant.

Tuesday, 9th November, 1999
[Day 18]

ADAM FAWLEY, sworn
Examined by MR. BARNES

Q. Name and rank please?
A. Detective Sergeant 0877 Fawley, Thames Valley
   Police.

Q. I believe you were the officer who
   questioned Ms. Sheldon after the attempted
   assault on 4th September 1998?
A. Yes I was.

Q. You were already working on the Roadside
   Rapist case?

MRS. JENKINS: My Lord—

MR. BARNES: I will anticipate an objection from
   the defense, my Lord. DS Fawley, were you
   already working to apprehend the sexual
   predator whom the media had by then
   nicknamed the "Roadside Rapist?"
A. Yes. The attack on Ms. Sheldon was the third
   such crime.

Q. But you were in no doubt that this attack
   was the work of the same man?
A. No doubt at all. The MO was the same—the
   plastic bag, the cable ties. It was all of a
   piece.

Q. But no DNA was discovered, I believe?
A. No. We believe the perpetrator was very
   careful not to leave biological trace.

Q. And how would he do that?
A. By wearing gloves, for example, and using a
   condom. We also believe he put down plastic
   sheeting when he abducted two of the victims
   in his brother's van, to avoid the transfer
   of DNA from his victims on to the vehicle.

Q. Because no DNA from either of the women was
   ever identified in the said van?
A. No. Only that of Mr. Parrie himself, his
   brother, and two colleagues who had worked
   with the latter on previous work projects.
   All three were categorically ruled out as
   potential suspects.

Q. To return to Ms. Sheldon—was she able to
   identify Mr. Parrie?
A. Not visually, no. She never saw her
   assailant's face.

Q. What about the van?
A. Again, she didn't see it. He placed the
   plastic bag over her face from behind.

Q. But she was able to identify him in another
   way, was she not? The identification which
   eventually led to his arrest?
A. Yes. She was.

* * *

Adam Fawley
4 April 2018
18.27

Fiona Blake handles the TV appeal remarkably well. I've
done more of these things than any police officer should
ever have to, but I can't remember anyone dealing with it

so steadily. Somer had warned me, as we drove over to Windermere Avenue, that there was a danger even asking her to do it might push Fiona over the edge, and I knew what she was getting at: for some people, in this situation, that's the moment the truth hits home. That their wife or child or friend or parent isn't just lost or confused or out of touch; they're gone, and they may never be coming back. But it wasn't like that with Fiona Blake. To say she took it calmly doesn't do her justice; she took it for what it is: a chance to ask the world for her daughter back. And for an hour this afternoon we sat there, she and I, going through what she should say, what I was going to say, and how to cope with the press, and she listened and asked questions, dry-eyed, but gray.

And she's still the same now, at the Kidlington media center, in front of the lights and the cameras and the crush of bodies. She's spoken clearly, and looked people in the eye. No evasive gestures, no glancing away, none of the involuntary signs our bodies betray us with. I remember the last time I sat here appealing for a missing child, and the instinctive unease I felt with every move the Mason family made. But not now. And when I spot Bryan Gow halfway down the room, all he does is nod: *This woman is telling the truth*. As if I didn't know that already.

And now it's my turn.

"If anyone has any information at all about Sasha or where she might be, please contact us as a matter of urgency. Either at St. Aldate's police station, on the phone number we gave earlier, or through the Thames Valley Police social media feeds. You can also contact us anonymously through Crimestoppers." I pause and turn to the photo of Sasha on the screen behind me. The one her mother chose. The two of them, laughing in the sun.

"And to repeat, Sasha is only fifteen. She's very much loved and her mother is desperate to have her home."

I look one more time around the room and sit back in my chair.

A man halfway down raises his hand. "Paddy Neville, *Reading Chronicle*. Is there anything to suggest this was an abduction?"

"We aren't in a position to rule out anything at this stage, but at present we have no actual evidence to suggest that."

"Have there been other recent incidents of this type, Inspector?" Another journalist. Bearded, glasses, one of those knitted ties. I don't recognize him. And he doesn't give his name.

"No."

"Are you talking just about Thames Valley or more widely?"

I fix his gaze. "There are none that I'm aware of."

He raises his eyebrows. "Really? What about the incident on April 1st?"

The other hacks start to look around at him; there's a stirring, a sense that there may be more to this than meets the eye. More than we're letting on. And there's nothing the hacks love more than a police cover-up. I can hear the murmurs rising: "What incident?" "Do you know what he's talking about?" And judging by their faces, a couple of the locals are pretty pissed off that an out-of-towner has scooped them; the BBC Oxford bloke for starters. At the other end of the dais, Harrison has started jiggling his leg up and down; I can feel it through the floorboards. Though thankfully the press can't see that behind the drapes and the large sign saying THAMES VALLEY POLICE: REDUCING CRIME, DISORDER AND FEAR. Something tells me I may not be doing very well on that last one.

"Inspector Fawley?" says the man as the noise in the room intensifies. "Was there or was there not an incident involving a young woman on Monday April 1st?"

"There was an incident, yes. But the young woman sustained no significant harm."

"Hang on a minute," asks a woman in the front row. "No *significant* harm—what sort of mealy-mouthed crap is that?"

And she's right. Some are born bullshitters; the rest of us just have bullshit thrust upon us.

"We have no evidence indicating a link—"

Knitted Tie pushes his glasses up his nose. "Don't you mean, no evidence *yet*?"

Harrison's leg-jiggling intensifies.

Knitted Tie checks back through his notes, but that's just grandstanding; he knows it and I know it.

"According to my sources, the victim of the attack on April 1st lives less than a mile from Sasha Blake." He looks up at me. "Now clearly I'm just a rank amateur when it comes to investigative policing, but that looks suspiciously like a *link* to me."

There's some laughter at that. But it's the hard, dry kind. The mood in the room has changed and I can feel Fiona Blake's eyes on me. She's wondering why we didn't tell her about this other girl, why we didn't do something to stop it happening again—

Knitted Tie is still looking at me. The room is growing silent.

"But perhaps I've got it wrong," he says. "You tell me, Inspector—after all, this is your patch, not mine."

He's holding my gaze now, watching my reaction. And that last comment was definitely a message, and a pretty thinly veiled one at that. This man is Fleet Street.

"As I said, we have no reason to believe there is any link between these incidents. Should that situation change, we will, of course, make an announcement at the appropriate time."

Hands are going up all over the room now, but Knitted Tie isn't giving up that easily.

"That first incident—is it true the victim was abducted in a van?"

A pause. Only two heartbeats, but that's one too many.

"Yes," I say. "We believe a van was involved."

You can almost hear the intake of breath. The woman in the front row glares at me. Everyone else is scrambling to write all this down. Everyone apart from Knitted Tie. He couldn't make it any clearer: all I've just done is confirm something he already knew.

The questions are machine-gunning now, no one is bothering to wait their turn.

"*What sort of van?*"

"*Who was this girl?*"

"*Why didn't we know about this before?*"

I hold up a hand. "As I said, we have no reason—"

"—to believe there's a connection," says Knitted Tie, who's still on his feet. "I know. I heard you the first time. But surely any reasonable person would think it was at least worth *checking*—"

"We are," I say quickly. Too quickly. I shouldn't show how rattled I am. "But, *as I'm sure you're aware,* I am not at liberty to divulge any information that might compromise an active investigation."

He nods, a nasty smile spreading slowly across his mouth. "But presumably we can take it as read that this 'checking' of yours also extends to other incidents employing a similar MO?"

I turn to fully face him. I can still see Harrison out of the corner of my eye, staring at me. Because I'm on thin ice here, and he and I both know it. I can't lie, but there's no bloody way I'm telling this pushy git of a journalist any more than I absolutely have to.

"Of course."

He nods slowly. "And that would include past cases too, I take it? Even—*theoretically*—those officially classed as closed?"

He stops; raises an eyebrow. Goads me.

"DI Fawley has given you your answer," says Harrison quickly. "I think this would be a good moment to bring things to a close. And let me remind you *all* that our sole priority—*my* sole priority—is to find Sasha Blake safe and well and reunite her with her family. And, in the meantime, we would ask you to respect Mrs. Blake's privacy, at this very anxious time."

It takes five minutes to clear the room. And throughout that whole time I feel the journalist's eyes on me.

He knows. Of course he bloody knows. But he hasn't got enough to go on. Not yet.

Back in reception, I see him go up to a woman who's clearly been waiting for him. The two of them speak for a moment then walk away toward the door, their heads bent together. The woman has light-brown hair twisted into a clip at the back of her head. Crisp, anonymous clothes, which sit oddly with her heavy crêpe-soled boots. She looks vaguely familiar.

And not in a good way.

* * *

"Why wasn't I told?" Fiona Blake is so angry she can barely speak. Fury is crackling around her like static.

Somer opens her mouth and closes it again. She can understand the anger; she's just not sure how it's going to help. She glances around nervously to check who's in earshot: there's always one or two press who think they might get a scoop if they hang about and eavesdrop. She takes Fiona's arm and steers her back down the corridor to the witness suite. As soon as the door closes Fiona yanks her arm away and turns on her.

"You got me to sit up there, in front of all those—those—*vultures*—answering their questions—letting them poke about in my life—and you didn't even tell me there'd been *another girl*?"

"I know it must look that way, but—"

"But what? *But what?*"

Somer hesitates. "The other incident. We were working on the basis that it was a hate crime. That's why we've been wary about saying anything to the press."

Fiona is staring at her. "A hate crime—what do you mean, a *hate crime*?"

Somer takes a chair, hoping Fiona will too. She doesn't.

"The girl who was attacked—she's transitioning."

Fiona opens her mouth to say something, then stops, breathes. "Transitioning? So she's a boy? Is that what you're saying?"

Somer nods; it's not as simple as that, but this woman has enough on her plate right now. "She's a trans girl, yes. We thought that was the reason she was targeted. At least initially. Now, we're not so sure."

Fiona sits down heavily, all the fight in her gone. "So what happened?"

"She was taken in a van. To the allotments on the Marston Ferry Road. The attacker—whoever they were—tied her hands and put a plastic bag over her head."

She sees Fiona wince.

"He pulled her underwear off, but then a police car went past on the road with the siren on and we think he got spooked."

Fiona looks up, her eyes wide. "So he just left her there? In that state?"

Somer nods. "She eventually managed to get free. A minicab driver picked her up."

Fiona takes a deep breath. "That poor girl, she must have been absolutely terrified."

"She was. She's being very brave. We've been trying to protect her privacy. As far as we can."

Fiona nods. "Of course," she says quickly. "You should have told me. I'd have understood. If it had been Sasha—"

But her daughter's name is too much for her. She bites her lip but the tears still come.

"Do you think it could be the same man?"

Somer takes a deep breath. "We can't rule anything out right now."

"And the place he took her—could Sash be there?"

Somer shakes her head. "I'm sorry. It was one of the first places the uniform team checked." She reaches forward and takes the woman's hand. "But we're not giving up. They'll be out again at first light. We'll find her, Fiona. We'll find her."

* * *

Abby Michelson @Hopscotch22098   19.07
Does anyone know anything about this attack on a young woman in #Oxford? Not poor #SashaBlake, something that happened before. Just saw a bloke from @ThamesValleyPolice talking about it on TV

Jimmy Post @JJP098456   19.09
Replying to @Hopscotch22098
I saw that too—something about a girl being abducted in a van? Can't remember anything about that in the news

Rona Mitchell @Corona1966765   19.11
Replying to @JJP098456 @Hopscotch22098
☹ Tagging @StaySafeinOxford to see if they know anything #Oxford

Stay Safe in Oxford @StaySafeinOxford   19.15
Replying to @Corona1966765 @JJP098456 @Hopscotch22098

217

We haven't heard any more than I've seen on here. Will check the news broadcast online. Does anyone know when and where it's supposed to have happened?

Micky F @BladeGamer   19.16
Saw a pic of that #SashaBlake online—no wonder she got picked up by a pervert—bloody asking for it, wearing kit like that

Scott Sullivan @SnappyWarrior   19.17
Replying to @BladeGamer
👍 stupid bint looked like a bloody tart

Rona Mitchell @Corona1966765   19.17
Replying to @BladeGamer @SnappyWarrior
That's a disgusting thing to say—you should be ashamed of yourselves. No one deserves to be assaulted or abducted, whatever they're wearing. And there was nothing wrong with what she had on in that photo anyway #SashaBlake

Scott Sullivan @SnappyWarrior   19.17
Replying to @Corona1966765 @BladeGamer
Here we go again—fucking lefty dykes poking there noses in

Micky F @BladeGamer   19.17
Replying to @Corona1966765 @BladeGamer
Bitches like that got no fucking idea and its blokes like us gets blamed when there off there tits and gagging 4 it

Janine Wheeler @MuddyBarvellous   19.18

Replying to @StaySafeinOxford @Corona1966765 @JJP098456
@Hopscotch22098

My mates OH is a copper. Apparently the other girl was
tied up & a bag put over her head. Like *serious* sicko
stuff.

Susan Hardy @LivingmyBestlife5761   19.19

Replying to @MuddyBarvellous @Corona1966765 @JJP098456
@Hopscotch22098

Shit—like that Roadside Rapist bloke? Remember,
back in 98 or 99? We weren't living in Oxford then but
I still remember it on the news.

Rona Mitchell @Corona1966765   19.19

Replying to @LivingmyBestlife5761 @MuddyBarvellous @JJP098456
@Hopscotch22098

Oh lord, you're right, I just looked it up online.
It's exactly the same #SashaBlake
#RoadsideRapist

Stay Safe in Oxford @StaySafeinOxford   19.22
Hearing reports of a serious incident of #assault
earlier this week in #Oxford which happened
BEFORE the disappearance (abduction?) of
#SashaBlake. We're contacting @ThamesValleyPolice
right now and we'll share anything we find out here +
on our FB page. In the meantime protect yourself and
#staysafe

*   *   *

"Are you sure you'll be OK?" says Somer, putting on the handbrake and turning to Fiona Blake. There's a uniformed officer on the doorstep of 87 Windermere Avenue, and two outside-broadcast vans parked opposite, but the press appear to be keeping a tactful distance. For now.

"If you need anything, you can call me. Any time, OK? Even if it's just for some company."

Fiona nods. "Thank you but I'll probably be OK. Yasmin's been fantastic and Patsie's going to stay over. It'll be nice having her around. Not sitting there in silence, wondering what to do with myself."

Somer nods. "She seems like a nice girl."

"She is. They all are."

"I promise I'll call you," Somer says as Fiona gets out of the car. "If there's any news."

* * *

Telephone interview with Charlotte Collyer
5 April 2018, 8:15 a.m.
On the call, DC E. Somer

ES: I'm Detective Constable Erica Somer—the
     switchboard said you have some information
     for us?

CC: I saw the TV thing last night—about Sasha
     Blake. I drive along there a lot, the Marston
     Ferry Road, I mean. What with the school and
     work and the gym.

ES: Did you see something? Did you see Sasha?

CC: No, sorry, I've never seen her before. No—it's
what people have been saying on Twitter—
about that other girl. The one they said got
taken in a van on April the 1st? I've been
thinking about it and I'm sure it was the
same day.

ES: What was the same day?

CC: I was a bit late for Pilates—I'd usually have
been going past there at least fifteen minutes
before. That's why I remember the time—I kept
looking at my watch and getting agitated—you
know what it's like. Sorry, I'm gabbling now.
What I mean is, I think I saw a van that
morning. Last Monday, I mean. I remember there
was a police car up ahead with the siren on
and everyone was slowing down, and then I
heard a screech of brakes and there was a van
coming past really fast on the other side of
the road.

ES: Did you see where it came from?

CC: No, sorry.

ES: Could it have been from the allotments?

CC: God—is that where it happened? Well, yes, it
could have been. I was a bit too far back to
see.

ES: Did you see the driver?

CC: Not really. Though I think he had some sort of
cap.

ES: A baseball cap?

CC: Yes—that sort of thing. Pulled down low.

ES: Was he white, black?

CC: Definitely white but that was about all. It all
    happened really quickly.
ES: What about the van—what do you remember about
    that?

* * *

"And that's it—that's all?"

Somer shrugs. "Sorry."

"OK," says Baxter with a heavy sigh, "tell me again?"

"It was a white van, with a logo on the side shaped like a shell."

"But no company name?"

Somer shakes her head. "Not that she saw. It all happened too quickly—I reckon we're lucky she saw that much."

"And it was shell as in the petrol station?"

"No, more like shell as in snail, she said."

Baxter frowns. "There's nothing like that on the CCTV from the garage, but I guess that doesn't prove anything." He sighs again. "All right, leave it with me. I'm still drawing a blank on the password for Sasha's laptop, so what the hell—why not alleviate the tedium with yet another hopeless and Herculean task."

Somer smiles. "I'll get you a tea."

"Three sugars," he calls to her retreating back. "And a Twix."

* * *

Fiona is spooning cereal into bowls when she looks up to see Patsie at the kitchen door. She's still in her pajamas and has her phone in her hand. But that's nothing unusual. She always has her phone in her hand. Like Sasha did— *Not "did,"* she tells herself, *"does." Like Sasha* does.

"You want milk or yogurt on this, Pats?"

The girl shrugs. There are dark circles under her eyes and Fiona suppresses the urge to ask if she's getting enough sleep. She's not Patsie's mum. Though sometimes, these last few months, she might as well be, the amount of time Patsie spends over here. Sasha hinted more than once that there might be a problem with Denise's new boyfriend, and Fiona was in two minds about asking Patsie if that was true, but she didn't want Denise to think she was interfering. And now—well, now she has more than enough troubles of her own.

She takes the bowls to the table and sits down. She isn't hungry—hasn't been hungry since it happened—but she'll be no good to Sasha if she doesn't eat. Something else she keeps telling herself. Along with how she's going to cut down on the red wine as soon as Sash is back. It'll be easy then, but today, this minute, it's the only thing that takes the edge off. Patsie comes slowly to the table and slides on to a chair, then reaches for the carton of milk in the center of the table. Fiona's stillness must have communicated itself to her because she looks up and smiles, a weak, brave, sad little smile. Fiona feels the tears burn her eyes and reaches out and grips the girl's hand. Thank God for you, she thinks. Thank God you're here. Because if you weren't, there'd be no one to stop me going over to the cupboard right this minute and opening another bloody bottle.

*　*　*

Everett is the only person in the ladies' loo on the first floor, staring at her reflection in the mirror. There's an odd distortion in the middle of her left eye that's been getting worse ever since she left the flat. Not blurring or double vision—it's more elusive than that. Almost as if there's nothing there at all; even though that makes no sense and she couldn't begin to describe what it looks like to someone else. But it's like that, all the same. She's never had a migraine before, but she's guessing that's what this must be. She doesn't have a headache as such—not the Nurofen-grabbing kind anyway. No flashing lights either, just a vague but heavy sense of unease. There's a noise at the door and Somer comes in. She smiles when she sees Ev, but something in her friend's face brings her up short.

"Are you all right?"

Everett does her best to smile. "Yeah, just feeling a bit off. Must have been that curry last night."

Somer frowns a little; she can't remember Everett ever eating curry. "You sure?"

Ev nods. "Absolutely. What about you, everything OK?"

Somer gives a wry smile. "Just dumped another crap job on poor old Baxter. He's exacting intravenous confectionery by way of recompense."

Everett manages a smile. "What is it this time?"

"We just got a new witness who saw a white van on the Marston Ferry Road the morning Faith was abducted. She remembered it had some sort of logo but it isn't giving Baxter much to go on. I mean 'a bit like a shell' could mean just about anything."

Everett turns from the mirror. "What sort of shell?"

"A snail, apparently. All I keep thinking is Brian from *The Magic Roundabout*——" She stops, mid-smile. "What?"

Ev fishes her phone out of her pocket, swipes to the web, then holds it out. "Is it possible it was this?"

Somer's eyes widen. "Oh my God. Shit—yes."

Ev takes a deep breath. "Email this over to your witness and ask her. And then we need to find Fawley."

* * *

Adam Fawley
5 April 2018
09.19

I'm still in the shower when the doorbell goes. By the time I make it downstairs ten minutes later Somer and Everett are standing awkwardly in the kitchen as Alex fiddles about with the kettle. Fussing is not like her, but it's obvious enough why she's doing it now: she wasn't expecting company and she's wearing a favorite but now tight-fitting jumper which makes it quite obvious she's pregnant. When Somer catches my eye she looks quickly away, her face flushed; she must be remembering what she said a couple of days ago. About the reasons people might not tell the whole truth.

"Oh, Adam—there you are," says Alex with manifest relief. "I'll leave you to it."

"Sir," says Somer as soon as the kitchen door closes, "the other day, I didn't mean—"

"Forget it—it's not important. What is it?"

"We may have something," says Everett. "Remember Ashley Brotherton?"

I frown. "I thought we'd discounted him?"

"We did."

"So what's changed?" I look at Somer and then back at Everett. "He had an alibi, didn't he? His bloody *van* had an alibi."

"A woman rang in first thing this morning," says Somer. "She said she saw a van on the Marston Ferry Road the morning Faith was attacked. She didn't remember much apart from the fact that the van was white and had a logo like a shell on the side. Baxter's been trying to track it down but it was looking like a wild-goose chase. Only then—"

"Only then Erica mentioned it to me," says Everett. She holds out her mobile. It's a picture of a van, and even though the logo on the side isn't a shell, I can see why you might remember it that way, especially if you only got a glimpse. It's a ram's head with a huge curling horn. In profile. And below it a five-bar gate surrounded by daffodils that looks like something out of Enid Blyton.

Ramsgate Renovations. The same company Ashley Brotherton works for.

"I emailed it to the witness," says Somer, "and she's fairly sure this is what she saw. Not a hundred per cent, but pretty certain."

"And the only Ramsgate van that could have been on the Marston Ferry Road that morning is the one Ashley Brotherton drives," Everett reminds me. "All the rest are accounted for."

"But even if it was his vehicle," says Somer, "it can't have been *him*. Fifty different people put him at the Headington crematorium that morning."

"So either he's worked out how to be in two places at the same time or he let someone else borrow that van."

"It's the most obvious explanation," says Ev. "Though he told me point-blank that no one else could have been driving it that day."

"Then it's someone he cares about—someone he's prepared to lie for. A relative? A mate? A mate who could be that mystery boyfriend of Sasha's we still haven't ID'd? Maybe *that's* the connection between those two girls."

"It wouldn't even need to be a boyfriend," says Somer. "It could just be someone she met once or twice—someone she thought it was safe to get into a vehicle with."

"Or he could have just attacked her from behind and dragged her off the street," says Ev grimly. "Like he did to Faith. He didn't have to actually *know* either of them. They could simply have been in the wrong place at the wrong time."

But I'm not so sure.

"Sasha, yes, absolutely. That had to be random—there's no way anyone could have known she'd be in that precise spot that night. But Faith was different: I think that *was* premeditated. I think the person who assaulted her planned it very carefully, and that may well have included making damn sure he wasn't in his own vehicle when he did it."

Everett nods. "If he wanted to cover his tracks—why not."

"Which leaves us with two possibilities," says Somer. "Either Brotherton knows *exactly* who borrowed his van that day but is protecting him or he doesn't know anything about it and never did. He was at the funeral for most of the day so it's not impossible."

The kettle has boiled but I'm not interested in tea.

"OK, let's get him in. The witness sighting is more than enough to justify that."

"Though we need to remember Brotherton has no criminal record," adds Ev, flushing slightly. "Not even speeding. As far as I can tell he just looks after his grand-dad and does his job—"

"So much the better. He has more to lose."

* * *

The search for Sasha Blake resumed at first light. It's been a grueling and thankless few hours since then, with nothing to show for it. Sergeant Barnetson is now directing the group working along the river; there are two more teams covering the fields to the north. At least they don't have the press breathing down their necks any more. Someone from the *Oxford Mail* tried to ambush him for a comment about the Roadside Rapist when he arrived, but Barnetson's not stupid. He's not going to get mugged into saying something that ends up on the evening news.

His mobile throbs against his thigh and crackles into life. He tugs his glove off and fishes the phone out from under his waterproofs.

"Barnetson? It's Gislingham—just wanted to check in. See if you've got anything."

"All I've 'got' is wet feet and a cold arse. But thanks for asking."

"How about the press?"

"Couple of hacks in the car park, one or two camera guys, but we're keeping them behind the tape. And right now, I can't see many of 'em volunteering to get up to their balls in mud. The weather's on our side on that, if nothing else. Though you know as well as I do how quickly that could change."

He doesn't need to spell it out: a search site thronged with hacks will mean only one thing.

* * *

We offer him tea, but he refuses.

"Granddad says you'd get forensics off it—prints and that. He says you have to be careful."

"We have to be careful too," I say, taking my seat opposite him. "And one of the things we're particularly careful about is checking our facts."

He looks confused. "I'm not with you."

I open my file. He glances at it, and then back at me. Something flickers across his eyes.

"You told my colleague DC Everett that you were at your grandmother's funeral on the morning of April 1st."

"Yeah—like I said—"

"You also said no one else could have had access to your van when you were in Headington, at the service."

He frowns. "Yeah, so?"

I glance up at him. "Which leaves me with a puzzle. You see, a witness has now come forward to say she saw your van on the Marston Ferry Road that morning. Perhaps you can help me with that?"

Brotherton opens his mouth then closes it again. "Do I need a lawyer or what?"

"You can have one, if you wish," I reply. "If you think you need one."

I stare at him; he stares at me. He blinks first.

"Yeah," he says. "I reckon that'd be a good idea."

*   *   *

Interview with Ashley Brotherton, conducted at
St. Aldate's Police Station, Oxford
5 April 2018, 12:42 p.m.
In attendance, DI A. Fawley, DC E. Somer,
J. Hoskins (solicitor)

AF: So, Mr. Brotherton, as I was saying before your lawyer arrived, you told DC Everett that no one else could possibly have been driving your van on the morning of April 1st, and yet it was spotted by a member of the public on the Marston Ferry Road. Perhaps you could explain that for us?

AB: They must've got it wrong.

AF: You're saying the witness was mistaken?

AB: Must be.

AF: It had to be your van.

AB: Ramsgate have loads of vans. Could have been any of 'em.

ES: According to Ramsgate they're all accounted for. They were all signed in at the Bicester site by eight that morning.

AB: Well, I've been thinking and I reckon Martyn was on holiday. It could have been him.

```
ES:  Martyn?

AB:  Martyn Ramsgate.

ES:  Your boss's son?

AB:  Yeah.

ES:  We'll double-check, but as far as Pauline
     Ramsgate is concerned all the vans were
     on-site.

AB:  Yeah, well she's going to lie for her own kid,
     ain't she.

AF:  Who would you lie for, Mr. Brotherton?

AB:  What the fuck does that mean?

ES:  You've never lent your van to anyone?

AB:  Nope.

AF:  No one else has access to the keys?

AB:  No. Like I said the first time—to that other
     bint.

AF:  All right, Mr. Brotherton. We'll leave it
     there for the moment. The officer will show you
     to a waiting room where you can be a bit more
     comfortable.
```

*   *   *

Adam Fawley
5 April 2018
12.58

The uniformed PC ushers Brotherton and his solicitor
out, and when the door closes behind them, Somer turns
to me. "What do you think?"

"What do I think? I *think* he's lying through his teeth."

Somer nods. "I know—I agree. I just can't work out
why. He has a rock-solid alibi for both attacks, and he

knows it. We can't touch him for either of them, so why take such a huge risk to protect someone else?"

We sit there for a moment in silence. There are muffled sounds of voices from the interview room next door. Whoever's in there, things are obviously getting heated.

"Perhaps the witness was wrong about the van," says Somer at last. "She did say she couldn't be completely sure about that logo."

And eyewitness accounts are notoriously unreliable. We all know that.

"OK, let's go through the motions of confirming where Martyn Ramsgate was that morning. I'd bet my mortgage he has nothing to do with it, but we still need to check."

She nods and makes a note.

"And start asking around—see if any of Brotherton's friends has any sort of record. And get Ramsgate's permission for a full forensic search of that van."

* * *

When Ev pops out for a sandwich the old man is sitting in reception, hunched on a hard plastic chair, in the cold draught from the front door.

"Mr. Brotherton?" she says. "It's Verity Everett, do you remember me?"

He looks up at her tetchily. "Of course I remember you. I'm not bloody senile."

He has a newspaper open on his lap, and Everett can see that his hands are trembling slightly.

"You must have been here for hours. Is there anything we can get you? Tea?"

He frowns. "I've had three cups already. How much longer is Ash going to be?"

"I'm not sure. I wasn't in on the interview."

He looks at his watch. It's an old-fashioned one with a snakeskin strap and a white face yellowed with age. "I've got an appointment at the JR in half an hour and we're already cutting it fine. Ash said he'd run me."

"Oh," says Everett. "I didn't realize. Let me check."

She goes over to the phone on the front desk and calls Somer, but when she comes back her face is rueful. "I'm afraid your grandson is still being interviewed. And his van is being taken in for forensic testing."

The old man frowns. "So how am I going to get to the hospital? It'll take me half an hour just to get to the bloody bus stop."

But this, at least, is something she can fix.

"Give me a minute and I'll see if we can sort you out a lift."

* * *

Interview with Ashley Brotherton, conducted at St. Aldate's Police Station, Oxford

5 April 2018, 1:50 p.m.

In attendance, DI A. Fawley, DC E. Somer,

J. Hoskins (solicitor)

AF: Mr. Brotherton, we've now spoken to Ramsgate again and they've confirmed all their vans were definitely at Bicester on the morning of April 1st. Martyn Ramsgate *was* on holiday, but

that was the week before, and both he and
his van were logged in at the hotel site by
8:00 a.m. that day. So I'm going to ask you
again—who else could have had access to
your van?

AB: No comment.

[*to his lawyer*]

I can say that, right?

AF: There's a big difference between being able to
say it, and it being a good idea.

JH: Inspector—

AF: I don't understand your reluctance, I really
don't. We know you were at your grandmother's
funeral that morning, and we have CCTV
footage of you at the John Radcliffe at the
time Sasha Blake went missing. Help me out
here, can't you, because I really don't
get it.

AB: Yeah, well that's my business, ain't it.

AF: Well, if that's how you want to play it, it's
your call. But you should be aware that we've
asked Ramsgate Renovations for permission to
search the van.

AB: You can't do that—it's my bloody van!

ES: I'm afraid we can, Mr. Brotherton. They're the
registered owner of the vehicle, not you.

AB: But I've got private stuff in there—

ES: That makes no difference. Sorry.

AF: I would also like to repeat our previous
request for fingerprints and a DNA sample. As
we said before, this is entirely voluntary, to

allow us to eliminate you from our enquiries.
Feel free to discuss it with Mr. Hoskins.

AB: [*confers with lawyer*]
OK, yeah.
[*pause*]
But only if you back off on the other thing,
OK? I'll give you the prints and stuff but
only if you drop the van.

ES: I'm afraid that's not how it works,
Mr. Brotherton.

AB: Well, fuck you—

JH: [*restraining his client*]
We agree to the DNA and fingerprinting. I trust
my client will be free to go home after that?

AF: In due course. The van, however, will be
subject to a forensic search. I'm afraid your
client will be taking the bus.

* * *

Adam Fawley
5 April 2018
14.09

"Do you still think he's lying?" asks Somer as we walk back up the stairs.

I shake my head. "No. We got the truth this time. Though more by omission than any wish to be actually helpful on his part."

Somer nods; she knows what I'm getting at. "There's something in that van, isn't there. Something incriminating. That's why he's so keen to keep us out of it."

"Well, let's bloody well hope so. And cross our

235

fingers that any DNA we do find is in the bloody database. Because otherwise we'll be going nowhere fast. Again."

* * *

"PC Atkins will give you a lift to the hospital and back, Mr. Brotherton. He's going to bring a car round to the front."

Everett offers the old man a hand getting up but he waves her away. "Thank you, young lady, but if I start taking help it won't be long before I can't do anything without it."

She smiles; he reminds her of her granddad. He was a bolshie bugger too.

Outside, the rain has stopped, but it's cold, and the old man's coat doesn't look thick enough to be warm.

"I'm sure the car won't be long," she says, feeling the need to break the silence.

He turns to face her. "Thank you. You didn't need to go to all that trouble, but you did. And it's appreciated. And tell Ash," continues the old man, "that I'll come to the station again when I get back from the JR. Someone needs to look out for him."

"He has a lawyer, Mr. Brotherton."

The old man's eyes narrow. "His kind of support costs two hundred quid an hour. I'm talking about someone who actually gives a toss. And the only one in that corner is me."

* * *

"And you're sure?"

I'm on the phone to Challow and the rest of the team are gathered around my desk. They can tell by the tone of my voice that it's not good news.

I finish the call and look up at them. "All they've got from Ashley Brotherton's van so far is one used condom and a quantity of what looks like semen on a tartan blanket. Our Mr. Brotherton clearly knows how to show a girl a good time."

Quinn's face falls. "And that's it?"

"There was also a plastic bag containing a princely fifteen grams of marijuana. Which won't even get the CPS out of bloody bed in the morning."

"But it could explain why he was so shit scared about the search," says Somer resignedly. "Perhaps none of this has anything to do with Faith. Or Sasha. He was just worried about us finding the drugs."

"And losing his job as a result," mutters Ev.

Ev is obviously a fully paid-up member of the Ashley Brotherton fan club, though for the life of me I can't fathom why. On the other hand, I'm starting to think Somer has a point—in fact, I'm not far off coming to the same conclusion myself.

"They're running the swabs for DNA but we won't get the results for at least a day or so."

"What about prints?" asks Gislingham. Ever the optimist.

"Nothing doing. There are a few partials but nothing

usable apart from Brotherton's own. They'll check his DNA against the profiles on the Tesco bag we found at the allotments but I'm not holding my breath. So if anyone else has any ideas, I'm all ears."

Quinn looks peevish. "So we're just going to send that bolshie little git home?"

I shrug. "We don't have any choice."

"What about the plaster dust?" asks Somer. "There must have been loads of it in that van."

"Good question. And yes, there was. But it'll take them a while to establish the exact chemical formulation. And Challow's already warned me building firms tend to source their plaster from a small number of big wholesalers, so the stuff Ramsgate uses won't be anything like unique. So even if what's in the van does match what we found on Faith, it won't be enough for an arrest. Not on its own."

"And Brotherton's just going to carry on insisting no one else could have borrowed it," says Gis with a sigh.

Baxter is frowning. "Well, he's right, isn't he? I mean, the van keys would either have been on him or in the house. How could someone else have got hold of them without him knowing?"

Ev shrugs. "Perhaps they keep a spare door key under a flowerpot? That's what my gran used to do."

"In *Blackbird Leys*?" says Quinn, openly incredulous. "You're having a bloody laugh. The place would be cleaned out in under a week."

"No, it wouldn't," says Everett. "That community— they look after their own. And Mr. Brotherton is one of them."

I get to my feet. "Well, that's one question we should at least be able to answer. Let's find out, shall we?"

* * *

It's pouring now, and at the search site Barnetson is up to his knees in dirty river and in danger of losing his footing at every step. He moves gingerly forward, feeling the mud slip under his waders as he steadies himself with his pole. The Cherwell is over its banks in places now, bleeding brown sludge across the fields on either side, where cows steam dejectedly in the teeming rain. With the water so high, all the rubbish and dead leaves and pleasure-boat litter is swirling downriver and catching in the overhanging trees. A few yards away Barnetson can see a bicycle frame, a shopping trolley and several old carrier bags caught in low branches and rimmed with white bubbles, one ripped against the bark, another bloated with—

No, he thinks.

Please

No

* * *

I'm not the first on-site; I can see Colin Boddie's car, and the CSI van is already parked up. But the two technicians are still sitting inside. They know I'll want to see the scene for myself before it's touched. Before it's disturbed.

I turn up my collar before I get out, hoping rain this heavy will give me some sort of anonymity, but the hacks have already worked out something is up. There are too many of us here now: however casually we play this, it's only a matter of time.

The uniform at the tape sends me in the right direction without (thankfully) being witless enough to stand there and actually point, and soon I'm over my boots in mud and slurry and struggling to keep vertical. We're in enough shit, frankly, without the literal version. Up ahead I can see a white tent, a scattering of search party members, and Ian Barnetson, standing unmoving, watching me approach. His face is bleak.

"Are we sure it's her?" I say as I draw level.

He nods. "As sure as we can be right now, sir, based on what she was wearing."

"Have we found anything else?"

"No weapon in the immediate vicinity, but we don't know where she went into the water, so it could be anywhere. Likewise there's no handbag and no phone." He holds my gaze. "And no underwear either. The state of the body—I don't think there's much doubt about what he did to her."

I swallow hard. Force myself to put up some professional protection. And then I think about Sasha's mother, who won't have that luxury. About her father, who's only just found her again. I wonder what I'd do, how I'd feel if it was me—if I had a daughter. And then I think—and it comes almost as a wonder—perhaps I already do.

*   *   *

In the gloom inside the CSI tent the only thing I can see at first is Colin Boddie crouched on the ground, his paper suit slightly luminous in the failing light. I say his name and he stands up and turns toward me and gestures to what they found.

There's no blood, because the river has seen to that, but there is damage. A cruel, relentless, again-and-again damage that would have taken time and intent to inflict. Dozens of cuts and contusions on her bare legs, and the washed-out stains of the same violence on her clothes. The flesh around her wrists sliced and swollen by the cable ties where she tried desperately to get free. And worse—worse than all this—the plastic bag, knotted hard behind her neck, clinging half transparent to the mess of brain and bone and hair.

A plastic bag. Cable ties. I can't pretend I wasn't expecting this. But it's a kick in the gut all the same.

"She took one hell of a beating," says Boddie quietly. "But you don't need a pathologist to tell you that."

"Please tell me at least some of those injuries are postmortem."

He makes a face. "Some of them, yes. But the way that bag is tied, it's possible she blacked out from lack of oxygen. We'll just have to hope so, won't we. At least before he started on her face."

*   *   *

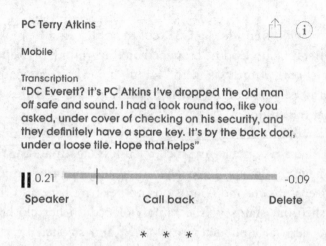

Voicemail

PC Terry Atkins

Mobile

Transcription
"DC Everett? it's PC Atkins I've dropped the old man off safe and sound. I had a look round too, like you asked, under cover of checking on his security, and they definitely have a spare key. It's by the back door, under a loose tile. Hope that helps"

▮▮ 0.21 ——————|———————————— -0.09

Speaker   Call back   Delete

*   *   *

"He must be the one who found her," observes Nina Mukerjee as a tall uniformed officer passes by where she and Clive Conway are unloading their equipment from the back of the CSI van.

Conway glances across. The man is up to his waist in mud. "That's Barnetson. Poor sod. It doesn't get any shittier than that."

There's a group of CID officers gathered a few yards away and Nina watches Barnetson go up and join them.

"Fawley doesn't look too happy either," she says.

"Well, are you surprised?" replies Clive, not bothering to look. "That's one pair of Hugo Boss brogues I wouldn't want to be in right now."

"It's not his fault the press are shits. Or that people have ridiculous expectations about clear-up times based on the crap they see on telly."

"It's not just that," he says, glancing up. "Word is there's another case—someone Fawley put away years ago. Apparently the similarities were already starting to look embarrassing. And now *this*."

He gives Nina a meaningful look, then turns to lift out the last case, banging the doors shut.

"You don't seriously think Fawley would fabricate evidence?"

Nina wouldn't say she knew the DI very well—not personally anyway. But she's never had the slightest doubt about his professionalism. Or his integrity.

Conway shrugs. "It doesn't have to be a conspiracy. Could just be a good old-fashioned cock-up."

At the far end of the car park, three harassed uniforms are trying to keep the press corralled behind the police tape, but there'll still be footage of Fawley on tonight's news. And of us too, no doubt, thinks Nina. There's always mileage in a white suit. Until, of course, the undertakers arrive.

She drags herself back to the task in hand. "So what's the plan?"

"One of the search teams has found what looks like drag marks on the bank. Could be where she went in."

Nina squints up at the sky. If it was dry, they'd be looking for footprints, blood, DNA, but now?

Clive makes a face, reading her mind. "I know, but if we wanted a cushy life we'd never have gone into this bloody job in the first place, now would we."

* * *

243

I get in the car and dial Somer. She must be expecting something like this—at some level we all have—but fearing it and knowing it are still worlds apart, and no one's going to feel that more than her.

"Somer? I'm at the Marston Ferry Road. We found her."

A breath in. And then out. If Sasha was alive I'd have said so by now.

"Look, I'm sorry but I'm going to have to land you with talking to Fiona."

This time, even I know I don't have a choice: I have to talk to the Super, and fast. Because the time it takes for this news to get out is measuring in minutes, not hours, and when it does, it's going to be open season on the Roadside Rapist case. Parrie's lawyers will see to that.

"I need to brief Harrison ASAP, so can you get over to Windermere Avenue? The press are all over us here and I'm worried Fiona will find out before I get back. Take Ev with you if you can."

"What do you want me to tell her?"

Her voice sounds dry, half-choked.

"Say we haven't yet made a formal identification, but given the age of the victim and where she was found, it's very unlikely it's someone else."

"OK, I understand. I'll make sure she's prepared. But you're certain, are you, sir? You don't think there's any doubt?"

"No. I'm sorry, but I don't think there's any doubt at all. It's definitely Sasha."

"OK, sir. Leave it with me." Her voice is stronger now.

The police officer in her is winning. At least for now. "Will you want me to bring her in for the ID?"

"Actually, I think—"

Again I hear the intake of breath; she knows what that means.

"Let's just say dental records may be the best bet. For all our sakes."

* * *

BBC News online

5 April 2018 | Last updated at 18:24

BREAKING: Body found in search for missing Oxford girl, 15

Residents in the Marston area of Oxford have reported that the missing local teenager Sasha Blake may have been found in an area of open ground close to where she was last seen. In the last hour, a number of people have tweeted pictures of a white police tent being set up on a site alongside the river Cherwell. An undertaker's van has also been spotted in the nearby car park, adding weight to speculation that it is indeed a body that has been found.

Thames Valley Police have not issued a statement as yet. *More news on this as we hear it.*

25 comments

Sylvia_Meredith_245

How truly terrible—such a tragic loss of a young life before it even began. My heart goes out to her family

Shani_benet_151

My daughter is at the same school as Sasha—her year group are just beside themselves. She was so popular and so talented. She even got some sort of internship with Vogue for next summer. They had 100s of applicants but they picked her

> **Amber_Saffron_Rose**
>
> They'll probably have a memorial service, won't they?

Johnjoe_84_Wantage

The mother was on the news on her own. So where's the bloody dad, that's what I want to know. He'll have something to do with it. Just you wait

> **Shani_benet_151**
>
> How can you say something like that? Don't you think her family and friends are going through enough without you chiming in—what if they're reading this, have you thought about that? You have NO IDEA what you're talking about so just zip it why don't you

> **Johnjoe_84_Wantage**
>
> Just because you don't like what Im saying doesn't mean its not true. You see if Im not right

* * *

As soon as Everett and Somer turn into Windermere Avenue they know they're too late. The press are three deep opposite the house already; cameras trained on the door, ready for the police, relatives, the Tesco delivery—they don't care who it is as long as it gets Fiona Blake to the doorstep. Others are homing in on anything that might be Sasha's—a bicycle just visible down the side return, a sticker in a bedroom window. There's no sign of life inside: upstairs and down, the curtains are drawn, but there are still people crowded behind the officers on the pavement, and on the top floors of the adjacent houses the neighbors are straining for a better look.

"Bloody vultures," says Somer, turning off the engine. "Can't they see the damage they're doing?"

"They don't care," says Ev, staring out of the window. "Why let tact get in the way of a good story?"

The Sky reporter is talking live now, gesturing back toward the house with a practiced one-quarter twist.

"Thames Valley Police have yet to issue a statement, but speculation is growing that the body of fifteen-year-old Sasha may indeed have been found, less than two miles from this house, which she shares with her mother, Fiona Blake, forty-three."

Ev looks across at Somer, who's gripping the steering wheel just a bit too hard.

"Look, Erica, I know this is easy for me to say, but try not to take it too personally. Cases like this—they'll break your heart if you let them. But that's not what Fiona needs. She needs us to find this bastard. That's all. Find him, lock him up and do our damnedest to lose the key."

Somer nods. "I know. Sorry. Didn't mean to—"

"It's OK. You don't need to apologize. Not to me, anyway." She loosens her seat belt and reaches for the door handle. "Right. Time for me to give those shits a piece of my mind."

* * *

"I don't have any choice, Adam. You must see that."

I nod. Though part of me doesn't see it at all. The angry, defensive, you-cannot-be-serious part.

"So what do you propose, sir?"

Harrison's eyes narrow. He's clearly picked up on my tone and he doesn't like it. But I don't care; if I sound pissed off it's because I am.

"I've asked the press office to prepare a statement confirming that there will now be an informal review of the Roadside Rapist case. That we believe it only prudent to assess the evidence again in the light of recent events, in order to ensure continued public confidence in the police. And if it becomes clear that a formal reference to the Criminal Cases Review Commission is appropriate—"

"Oh, for God's sake—"

"Come on, Adam. You know as well as I do that it's better to get out in front of a story like this. It's all over Twitter already."

"You can't seriously think that Gavin Parrie is innocent? That it was someone else all along—someone completely under the radar—who's started up again, all these years later—"

"It's not what *I* think that's important, Adam. We have to be seen to be doing the right thing. And all the more so if—"

"*If?* If what? If I got it wrong—if I fucked up. That's what you mean, isn't it?"

Harrison's fiddling with something on his desk now.

Anything to avoid looking me in the eye. "That sort of attitude isn't going to help. It's perfectly reasonable that the Chief Constable should ask us to demonstrate we've considered all the alternative theories of the crime."

If I wasn't so furious I'd laugh out loud. In fact, I'm almost furious enough to laugh anyway. Which would really land me in the shit.

There's a silence. An angry, fizzing silence.

Harrison sits back again. "In the meantime, I will, of course, have to bring in someone else."

"Someone *else*?"

"You can't possibly handle it any more, Adam. It's a manifest conflict of interest, surely you can see that?"

"Who? Who are you bringing in?"

"Ruth Gallagher, from the Major Crimes unit. She'll take on the Appleford/Blake inquiry, and liaise with whoever the Chief Constable selects to do the Parrie review."

It could be worse. In fact, it could be a lot worse. I've only met Gallagher at the odd police social thing, but I know of her. She's shrewd and she's uncompromising, but she's good. And she's fair. She'll call it how she sees it.

"And I will, of course, have to inform Parrie's lawyers."

I don't reply. I don't trust myself to say anything civil, but either way, the phone ringing saves me from myself.

Harrison seizes the handset. "I said I didn't want to be disturbed," he barks. Then he stops, glances at me, looks away. "Tell her that at this moment in time we have no statement to make, but one will be issued in due course."

He puts the handset down and gives me a heavy look. "That," he says, "was Jocelyn Naismith."

*   *   *

Outside, the rain shows no sign of easing, but there's no window on the weather in the morgue. Here, as always, the light is just a bit too bright, and the neon tubes hum beneath the low murmur of voices and the clatter of metal on metal. There are two CSIs and an exhibits officer in the room but Gislingham is the only one of the CID team present. He told the rest of them it's his turn and they're too busy to go mob-handed (which is true), but the real reason is because he doesn't want the women seeing this. And yes, he knows he'd have got labeled a sexist throw-back if he'd actually said so, but as far as he's concerned, it's just called "being considerate."

"Ah, just you, is it, Sergeant?" says Colin Boddie from the other side of the room. His assistant is behind him tying his gown.

"We've got a lot on."

Boddie gives him a wry look. "Likewise. So let's get on with it, shall we?"

*   *   *

The room is silent.

It has been, ever since Somer ran out of words.

Fiona Blake has asked nothing, said nothing. She's not hysterical, she's not frantic. She's just sitting there, in the cold and curtained room, her face running with tears she isn't even bothering to wipe away. Somer's never seen anyone so silent, and so still. She's never seen anyone in so much pain.

And as they sit there, in the deepening dark, from the pavement outside comes the drum of the rain and the low drone of the press; and from the kitchen, the sound of Everett doing her best to comfort Sasha's sobbing and inconsolable friend.

*   *   *

"I don't know the name—who is she?"

I'm in the car, on the phone. I got soaked running even the fifty yards across the car park, but I needed to talk to Alex and I wanted privacy more than I wanted to stay dry.

The woman I saw at the press conference; the woman I thought I recognized.

"Jocelyn Naismith works for The Whole Truth."

With anyone else, I'd have to explain. Anyone outside the criminal justice system, anyway. But my wife is a lawyer. She knows all about The Whole Truth—about their campaigns for people convicted on erroneous evidence, their dogged persistence in overturning miscarriages of justice. She's watched and applauded their work for the best part of a decade. But this is different: this time it's close to home.

"They've taken on the Parrie case—*seriously*?" Her voice is a note or two higher than usual. The pitch of anxiety. And she's breathing far too fast. This is not good.

251

"Apparently his lawyers have approached them before but they've always turned him down."

"Until now," she says bitterly. "That means they'll be looking at it all again—everything will be raked up and pored over. And then they'll start looking at these new cases—all those *similarities* you keep going on about."

That isn't exactly fair, but how can I blame her.

"They don't have access to that information, Alex. Not about live cases."

Which is true—for now.

"And we don't have postmortem results yet on Sasha Blake," I continue quickly, before she has a chance to reply. "If we're lucky, we'll get something from that which will put paid to this Parrie crap once and for all."

And stop the case review in its tracks before it even gets started. But what if all the autopsy does is prove that I'm wrong? Not just wrong right now, about these latest attacks, but wrong before. Wrong right from the start, when all this began.

What then?

* * *

Boddie cuts away the carrier bag and hands it to one of the CSI technicians to be tagged in evidence. She's wearing a mask but Gislingham can see how shaken she is. As for Gis, he's heard the phrase "beaten to a pulp" a thousand times—he's used it himself without even thinking. But he's never seen it. Not really; not like this. From one side Sasha Blake looks almost normal, but from the other—

He swallows, glad—again—that Somer and Everett don't have to see this. Half Sasha's face has broken in under the weight of the beating, the eye socket shattered and slivers of bone breaking through flesh swollen and stained by river water. The Sasha he's seen in her mother's pictures, the Sasha they were all looking for—she's never coming back. Boddie's team's ability to make the dead fit for the living to see is little short of legendary, but this—this is beyond even their skills to save.

"That wasn't just someone's fists, was it?" says Gislingham quietly.

"No," says Boddie, training the light closer and bending to get a better look. "The cuts were made by a knife, but the blunt-force trauma was caused by something else. I assume you didn't find any sort of weapon at the scene?"

Gislingham shakes his head. "Not yet."

"Then I'd look for something with edges to it. Something sharp but irregular. A piece of concrete, a rock—I'm sure you know what I mean."

Gis gives an inward sigh. Something like that—it could have just been lying around on the riverbank. And if that's what he used, what are the odds of finding it now?

"I'm assuming we haven't got a hope of DNA," he says, stifling the urge to retch. "The killer's, I mean."

Boddie shakes his head. "Afraid not. The water's put paid to that. And not just DNA. Fibers, skin. Plaster dust." He raises an eyebrow. "Just by way of example, of course."

* * *

"Can you tell me—did he, you know——?"

Somer knows what she's being asked. Fiona is staring at her now, with her hollowed, haunted eyes, begging to be told her fifteen-year-old daughter wasn't raped.

"There's stuff online—people are saying it might be that Roadside Rapist—that he's back. Please, tell me the truth—did he—I need to know——"

Somer bites her lip. Fiona thinks she wants the truth, but the truth won't set her free. It's a brutal one-way street leading only to grief.

"No one's told me anything," she says, even though she knows full well how Sasha was found. "It may be some time before we can be certain. But, believe me, there's *nothing* to suggest it has anything to do with the Roadside Rapist. DI Fawley is absolutely convinced that man is in prison. Where he belongs."

Fiona nods, the tears coming again. "It's just that I'm not sure I could bear it, if—if her only time was like that—if that was the only——"

Somer reaches across and clasps the woman's cold, dry hands. "Please—don't torture yourself with maybes."

It'll be bad enough, soon enough, without that.

"I can't," she says, her voice breaking, "I can't stop thinking about it—his hands on her—touching her—his disgusting disgusting——"

She breaks down now, and Somer moves quickly to her side, wrapping her arms around her as she sobs.

"Whatever happens," she whispers, "I'm here. I'm here."

* * *

It's nearly 8:00 when the phone rings in the incident room. It's the desk officer. Someone's come in with information, he says. About the Sasha Blake case.

Quinn sighs audibly and looks around the room, but there's no one junior enough to dump on. He hauls his jacket off the back of the chair and heads downstairs.

* * *

"Ah, Sergeant, good of you to rejoin us."

Gislingham closes the door behind him. "It was the boss. I had to take the call. I didn't realize it would take so long."

The body is on its front now, a sheet covering it from the neck down. The back of the head is a snarl of wet hair and gluey brain tissue, and near the crown of her head, a paler, rawer patch where the scalp is hanging away from the skull.

"I thought as much at the scene," says Boddie, seeing his stare, "and I was right: quite a large quantity of her hair was pulled out. And it was done before she died."

He moves further down the table and lifts the sheet, and even Gislingham, who's no rookie, who's done this many times before, has to turn away.

"The underwear was missing, as you know," continues Boddie. "I've taken vaginal swabs, but I doubt they're going to be much use."

"Because she was in the water?" asks Gislingham, keeping his gaze fixed on Boddie. "Or because he was wearing a condom?"

Boddie shrugs. "The first, absolutely; the second, quite possibly."

"But she was definitely raped?"

Boddie makes a face. "All the circumstantial signs say so—the missing underwear, the scratches on her thighs. But without DNA we may not be able to prove it one hundred per cent."

He looks down at the body and then at Gislingham. And then he pulls the sheet gently back in place.

* * *

It was worth shifting his arse down here, after all. The "informant" in reception is about twenty-five, with a sleek auburn ponytail and a leather skirt that only just escapes the word "mini." Quinn elects to ignore the knowing smirk from the desk officer and walks across to where the woman is sitting, staring intently at her mobile phone.

"Miss—?"

She looks up and smiles. "Nicole. Nicole Bowen."

"I believe you have some information for us? About Sasha Blake?"

"Yes," she says, still looking at him confidently. "I think I might have seen her."

Quinn sits down next to her, gets out his iPad and starts to make an entry on the system.

She looks across, straining to see what he's writing. "I thought policemen still used notebooks and manky old biros with chewed ends."

"Some do," he says drily. "But I don't."

"You have single-handedly shattered all my illusions. TV crime shows will never be the same again."

She smiles once more. She has her legs crossed and her fingers laced around one knee.

"The sighting, Miss Bowen?"

"I told you, *Nicole*," she says, leaning on the name. And leaning forward. He can smell her hair.

"OK, *Nicole*. When was it that you saw Sasha?"

"I think it was about two weeks ago. She was with two other girls."

Quinn looks up, sits back. "That was ten days before she went missing. What made you think it's relevant?"

She flushes. "Well, I just thought—"

His eyes narrow. What's this woman playing at? Or perhaps it's him she's playing. "You didn't see her at all, did you?"

Her chin lifts. "No, I'm sure I did—"

"Who are you, Miss Bowen? Assuming, of course, that really is your name."

"I don't know what you mean—"

He gets to his feet. "You're press, aren't you—"

She's shaking her head. "No—I'm not—not in the way you think, anyway—"

He's really angry now. "Don't you know what you just did is *completely* unethical? Not to mention wasting police time, which I could book you for if I could be bloody bothered. But I *am* going to report you to your bloody editor. Who is it—who do you work for?"

She gets up and pulls a lanyard from her pocket. The thick plastic card shows her face, her name. And along the bottom, ASSISTANT PRODUCER, POLYMUS STUDIOS.

That stops him in his tracks. "You're in film?"

She shakes her head. "TV, mainly."

"I'm not with you. What's that got to do with Sasha Blake?"

She puts her ID away. "We've been commissioned to make a series about the work of The Whole Truth."

Quinn makes a face. "Oh, for Christ's sake, that bunch of useless do-gooders?"

"Actually, they've put right some appalling miscarriages of justice—"

"And ruined some damn good coppers' careers in the process. You people—you have no bloody idea what it's really like—"

He starts to move away but she reaches for his arm. "Hear me out—please? Five minutes? I'll even buy you a beer."

He hesitates. It occurs to him that it might actually be useful to know what these idiots are planning. You never know, Fawley might even thank him for it.

"Please?"

* * *

Baxter, meanwhile, is up to his neck in paperwork. It's the first time he's managed to get to the Roadside Rapist transcripts today, but he can get in an hour or so now before he goes home. His wife is at that Body Balance thing of hers, so she won't know if he gets back late. And the plate of quinoa and avocado salad waiting for him in the fridge is hardly enticing.

He opens the cardboard file and starts reading. Judging by what he's been through so far, Gis's theory is holding up pretty well: there's more than enough detail for a potential copycat to fake Parrie's MO. Baxter starts to make notes, but the long day is catching up with him and he's soon stifling a yawn. Which makes him feel bad, because it's not as if what he's reading is boring; it's completely bloody awful. He sits up a little straighter and starts again. And that's when he spots it. He blinks, stares and reads it again. Then he crosses over to his PC and does a quick database search. He checks it against the transcript, then sits back and lets out a long slow breath.

He really didn't want to be right about this.

But he is.

*　　*　　*

He's technically off-duty, so having a beer is technically OK, but all the same Quinn opts for a pub where there's no danger of meeting anyone he knows. In fact, if he'd asked TripAdvisor for the seediest bar in a five-mile radius he couldn't have chosen much better: the one-arm bandit jangling in the corner, the packets of pork scratchings hanging by the bar, the ceiling still yellow with cigarette smoke more than ten years after the ban. And if this Bowen woman takes one look and concludes he's trying to tell her something, then so much the better.

Though to give her her due, she doesn't seem that fazed. So much so that she even braved the trio of builders' bottoms on the bar stools to get in a round. They're still eyeing her up as she comes back to the table and puts down the drinks.

"So," he says, picking up the glass, "shoot. And I want the truth this time."

"The Roadside Rapist case," she says. "That's what we're focusing on. In the series. You know about that, right?"

Quinn gives her a heavy look. He's not rising to that one. Does she think he just fell off the Christmas tree?

Bowen is still speaking. "The plan is for a fly-on-the-wall following the entire Whole Truth investigation, including full reconstructions and some eminent talking heads. Ex-judges, CSIs, psychologists. You know the sort of thing. Jocelyn is completely up for it, and we might even be able to include Gavin Parrie himself—the Beeb were allowed to record a phone call from prison for something similar last year—"

Quinn cuts across her. "The Parrie case is twenty years old. Why now?"

If she thinks he's being deliberately obtuse, her face doesn't show it. She has colour in her cheeks now—the flush of professional fervor.

"Well, obviously these latest cases put a whole new angle on it, don't they? And the timing really couldn't be better—what with Gavin Parrie coming up for another parole hearing. And, of course, he's always maintained he's innocent. He's never wavered from that. It makes for *such* an interesting angle."

"I think you'll find they all say that," says Quinn heavily.

Nicole Bowen raises an eyebrow. "They may all *say* it, but sometimes it's actually true."

"Yeah, right," replies Quinn. The beer has gone to his head already. He had no lunch and he's drinking rather more quickly than he should.

Perhaps she senses this, because she sits forward a little now. "This case review of the Roadside Rapist investigation—how's that going to work?"

260

He frowns; this is news to him. "Who told you about that?"

A shrug. "Oh, you know. The grapevine." She leans closer. "When's it all happening, do you know? Cos if we could feature that in the series as well, it would be *amazing*." She smiles. "Have you ever done any TV work? Because I can tell you now, the camera would *really* love you—"

"Investigations like that—they're confidential. They're not *entertainment*."

She's shaking her head. "It's not about that. Don't people have a right to know what's being done in their name? And with their taxes? And now there's new evidence—"

"You don't know that. *We* don't even know that."

She sits back again, eyes him, cooler now. "And then there's Adam Fawley."

Quinn's eyes narrow. "What about Adam Fawley?"

"Well, he was on the case, wasn't he?"

Quinn tries to play dumb, and manages it rather better than he probably intended. "You tell me."

There's a small sharp smile now, at the edge of her mouth. "*As I'm sure you know*, he was the DS on the original case. Same rank as you. Or rather, as you *were*."

She picks up her glass of sparkling water. Quinn stares at her. This woman shouldn't know that—what else does she bloody well know? If she's found out he was demoted for sleeping with a suspect—

Bowen is clearly finding his discomfiture distinctly amusing. A sly smile curls her lips. "I'm sure the public would like to know why Adam Fawley was assigned to the Sasha Blake inquiry, given it's such a clear conflict of interest."

Quinn frowns. "I don't know what you're getting at."

She looks at him disbelievingly. "Oh, *come on*. You aren't *seriously* telling me you don't know? About Fawley?"

But apparently he is. She gives him a meaningful look. "Well, I suggest you have a good look at the trial transcripts." She leans forward and puts a business card on the table. "And when you have, give me a call."

* * *

THE CENTRAL CRIMINAL COURT

The Old Bailey
London EC4M 7EH

BEFORE:
THE HONORABLE MR. JUSTICE HEALEY

R E G I N A
v.
GAVIN FRANCIS PARRIE

———————————

MR. R. BARNES Q.C. and MISS S. GREY
appeared on behalf of the prosecution.

MRS. B. JENKINS Q.C. and MR. T. CUTHBERT
appeared on behalf of the defendant.

———————————

Wednesday, 10th November, 1999
[Day 19]

ADAM FAWLEY, recalled
Examined by MRS. JENKINS

Q. Sergeant Fawley, I'd like to return to the incident you were describing to Mr. Barnes yesterday. Specifically the sequence of events which led to the arrest and detention of my client. You told us that you received a telephone call from Ms. Sheldon at 11:45 on January 3rd this year.

A. Yes, I did.

Q. She rang you on your mobile, I believe?

A. Yes.

Q. One might have thought that she would have called 999, in the circumstances.

A. I couldn't say.

Q. Someone in her situation would normally do so, surely?

A. I was the officer who interviewed her after the attempted assault. I would imagine that's why she chose to call me, but you'd have to ask her.

Q. And the reason for this call was that she believed she had identified the man who attacked her.

A. That's correct.

Q. But how could she have done that, if, as you have already told us, she never saw his face?

A. She had recognized his smell. She was queuing up to pay for petrol at a garage on the ring-road and noticed a distinctive odor. A sweet smell, like overripe fruit.

Q. From the man standing behind her?

A. Yes.

Q. And she recognized this?
A. Correct. She said she suddenly became extremely anxious while standing in the queue but it took a few moments for her to realize why.

Q. Had any of the other victims mentioned a smell?
A. No. But they had plastic bags tied tightly over their heads. In Ms. Sheldon's case, the perpetrator fled the scene before he was able to put the bag fully in place. We concluded that this would account for it. We also ascertained that Mr. Parrie suffers from type 1 diabetes. If the condition is not well-managed it can sometimes lead to a distinctive smell on the breath. A smell very much like what Ms. Sheldon described.

Q. What did Ms. Sheldon do next?
A. She followed him back out to the forecourt and started to follow his van in her car.

Q. She was putting herself in considerable danger, was she not?
A. She was. She was very brave.

Q. What happened next?
A. She saw Mr. Parrie park outside a garage off the Botley Road, open the door and go inside. She called me from her own car at that point.

Q. And help was dispatched?
A. Yes. I also advised her to go to an appropriate public place, where there were other people, and remain there until backup arrived.

Q. And that's what happened?

A. Yes. She went to the Co-op supermarket and I met her there approximately half an hour later.

Q. And where was my client at this time?

A. By the time we reached the scene, Mr. Parrie had adjourned to the Fox & Geese pub. We were able to secure the garage and van for forensic testing, and take him in for questioning.

Q. Some people might say you did all this on rather tenuous grounds. You arrested a man on the basis of a bad smell?

A. When I interviewed Ms. Sheldon immediately after her assault I found her to be intelligent, observant and articulate. It was my judgment that this potential identification of her attacker had to be taken seriously. And the items subsequently found in the garage bore that out.

Q. What were these items, Sergeant Fawley?

A. A quantity of pornography, assessed as category A.

MR. BARNES: Members of the jury, item 17 in your bundle is a schedule of these items, in the form of Agreed Facts. Both prosecution and defense accept that these items were indeed discovered in the garage.

MRS. JENKINS: What else was discovered, Sergeant Fawley?

A. Various cable ties of the same type and color as those used in the attacks.

Q. But not the item of jewelry taken from Miss Donnelly, which we heard described earlier in the trial?

A. No.

Q. And nothing linking Mr. Parrie to any of the other victims?

A. No.

Q. But there was one other, highly significant item, was there not?

A. Yes. The Scenes of Crime team found three strands of Ms. Sheldon's hair. The provenance was confirmed by DNA testing.

Q. And that testing was possible because the root was still present? Indicating that it was hair that had been ripped out, not cut?

A. That is correct.

Q. And you were certain, were you, that Ms. Sheldon did not go into the garage in the period of time between her call to you and the arrival of the police personnel?

A. I wasn't there. But there is absolutely no evidence to suggest that she did.

Q. But if she had done so, she could have planted the strands of hair herself, could she not? Specifically to incriminate my client?

A. Theoretically, but—

Q. You must acknowledge she had a motive to do so. She thought this man had not only attempted to rape her, but since that

266

incident had brutally assaulted several other women. It's only natural she would want him caught.

A. At the time of her assault, Ms. Sheldon had long hair. The hair found in the garage was over ten inches long. By the time of the events in question her hair had been cut short. Very short. Even if she had indeed wanted to tear out her hair and plant it to incriminate Mr. Parrie, it was far too short by then to be of any use.

Q. One final question at this time, Sergeant Fawley. You referred again, just now, to the fact that she called you that day. She called you direct, rather than 999 or any other police number.

A. Yes, as I said.

Q. And how did she come to have your number?

MR. BARNES: My Lord, if I may, Sergeant Fawley has already explained that he interviewed Ms. Sheldon after her assault, and that he gave her his card at that time.

MRS. JENKINS: Is that correct, DS Fawley?
A. Yes, I gave my card to Ms. Sheldon at that time.

* * *

"I didn't know either, not till last night."

Baxter, Quinn, Everett and Somer. Eight in the morning, in the coffee shop just along St. Aldate's, but upstairs, which is usually half empty and right now is completely deserted, apart from the four of them, sitting in the

267

corner furthest from the window by the only radiator. There's a pile of court transcripts on the table between them.

"The defense obviously thought there was something to it," says Baxter. "Even though they clearly didn't have enough to push it."

"And that Bowen woman definitely thinks there was something dodgy going on," replies Quinn. "Made us look like a right bunch of donkeys, by the way."

"Speak for your bloody self," says Baxter tetchily.

"Come on," says Ev, staring gloomily at her coffee. "That's not going to help. We need to stick together on this. Work out what to do."

"I'm not sure what we *can* do," observes Somer, "apart from come straight out with it and ask."

"But shouldn't Gis do that?" replies Ev. "As DS?"

"Well, that's why they pay him the big bucks," mutters Quinn sardonically.

"Shouldn't I do what?"

They all turn to see Gislingham at the door. And he doesn't look happy.

"I know it's Saturday but we've got a bloody murder on our hands. The incident room looks like the bloody *Mary Celeste*. What the hell are you lot doing skiving off up here?"

They look at each other, and Quinn gives Baxter a nudge and a meaningful look: *You're the one with the proof—you tell him.*

Baxter clears his throat. "It's the Parrie trial transcripts, Sarge. There's something you should know."

* * *

268

Sent: Sat 06/04/2018, 08.25   **Importance: High**

From: AlanChallowCSI@ThamesValley.police.uk

To: DIAdamFawley@ThamesValley.police.uk, CID@ThamesValley.police.uk

Subject: Case number 1866453 Blake, S

A quick heads-up on Ashley Brotherton. We've had the test results back. There was no DNA from either Faith Appleford or Sasha Blake in the back of his van, and the female DNA on the condom is not a match for Blake. Furthermore, Brotherton is <u>not</u> a match for any of the male profiles found on the plastic bag used in the Faith Appleford attack.

AC

*   *   *

Gis has already started the team meeting by the time I get there. I wait at the back, but I can tell the mood isn't good. An initial search of Ashley Brotherton's associates hasn't turned up any promising suspects, and the news from the scene is hardly encouraging either. A notice has been set up on the main road, appealing for witnesses, but there's still no sign of Sasha's bag or phone, never mind the murder weapon. They can't even be sure she went into the river where we thought. The rain is defeating everyone, dogs included.

Gislingham sums all this up neatly and concisely—he's

got a lot better at doing that recently, so it surprises me that he seems so tense. Perhaps it's just what he was forced to witness at the PM. He's made at least one good decision though: three other DCs who aren't usually on this team have been drafted in. And he's right: we need all the bodies we can get on this one. And no, I'm not going to apologize for the pun.

I wait until Gis's report is over then join him at the front.

"OK, everyone, I know this is all we need right now, but you should be aware that Harrison will be issuing a press statement on Monday morning. There's going to be a review of the Roadside Rapist case. Only informal, at this stage, but there's no guarantee it won't end up with a full referral to the CCRC."

People steal glances at each other, not sure how to react. It's one thing being aware there was a potential issue, it's quite another for the powers that be to go public on it. That makes a difference. To clean-up rates, careers, even to loyalties. At least that's what I'd be thinking in their place. And there's a definite undercurrent in this room, no question.

"I know this is going to put extra pressure on everyone, and there's bound to be a hell of a lot in the media. All of it inflammatory and most of it about Alastair Osbourne. Or about me. But none of it about *you*. So just stick to the job and don't let the shitstorm distract you. And don't speak to bloody journalists, even with the best of intentions. It never ends well."

"Actually, sir," says Gislingham. "About that—"

I open my mouth to answer, but the sound of the door at the back forestalls me. The woman who's just entered is mid-height, angular, in a neat tweed trouser suit. Her hair is shorter and lighter than when I last saw her. She looks rather like Lia Williams. As well as open, positive and confident. Everything I don't feel right now, in fact.

I look around the team. "Everyone, this is DI Ruth Gallagher. She's going to be taking over the Blake and Appleford inquiries from here on in."

You can hear the intake of breath, see the furtive looks, the glances at Gallagher they don't want me to spot. Two parts shock to one part embarrassment. I suppose it's only to be expected, but to be honest I haven't got a bloody clue what's "expected" in a situation like this. This is all new to me; I've never been taken off a case before.

I catch Gallagher's eye, invite her forward. "Do you want to say anything?"

She steps a little further into the room. "Not yet, I think. I need to familiarize myself with the case notes first. And I have a lot of catching up to do on the Parrie investigation. But this team has an excellent reputation; I look forward to working with you."

She handled that well, I'll give her that. Not throwing her weight about, not muscling in. Unassuming but businesslike. "Inclusive," as HR would no doubt say. But she must have picked up on the unease because she takes another step forward. "Let's all be clear. No one is saying DI Fawley did anything wrong or that Gavin Parrie's conviction is anything other than rock solid. But we all know what it's like these days with the press and social media on our backs all day every day—it's not fair, and it's a pain in the arse, but there it is."

She tries a smile, and I try one too.

I take a deep breath, feel my chest tighten. Because I've

finally reached it. The point of escalation. The Rubicon I won't be able to reverse.

I turn to the team. "There's something else. I should have said something before, I know, but there was always a chance it wouldn't come to this. Anyway, I hope you'll understand why I didn't. One of the women Parrie attacked—she was called Sandie Sheldon."

There's something wrong—I can't read their faces.

"Two years after the attack, she got married. To me. Sandie Sheldon——*Alexandra* Sheldon—is my wife."

Gis clears his throat. "Yes, sir," he says quietly. "We know."

* * *

THAMES VALLEY
POLICE

WE ARE APPEALING FOR WITNESSES

CAN YOU HELP US?

MURDER

A YOUNG FEMALE WAS LAST SEEN IN THIS AREA AT ABOUT 10pm ON WED 3rd APR 18. SHE MAY HAVE BEEN ABDUCTED IN A VEHICLE.

DID YOU SEE ANYTHING?
PLEASE CALL US
in strict confidence on
01865 0966552

Or at your local police station, or ring
CRIMESTOPPERS

* * *

"What do you mean, you *know*?"

Gis looks self-conscious, but only a little and only briefly. More than that, he looks annoyed. And let down.

Shit.

"When you first told us about Parrie," he says, "we thought—well, *I* thought—that it was possible we were looking at a copycat, in which case we needed to know how much of Parrie's MO someone could have picked up just from reading about the trial."

Which is exactly what I'd have done, in his place. Only I didn't need to. I was there.

"That's when we realized: the defense brief—he called her Alexandra."

"She used to shorten it to Sandie back then," I say, my throat cracking. "She doesn't any more."

I risk a look at Somer. And I can see: she understands that bit, at least. Just as Faith Appleford might understand, if she were here. The overwhelming need to start again. To have a new name, a clean slate. A chance to forget.

"You should have told us," says Ev softly. "We'd have been on your side."

And they aren't now, is that what she means?

I swallow hard.

"I'm sorry if anyone feels let down. I know I should have told you before. But I wanted to protect my wife. That's all. Not myself or my poxy career. My *wife*."

I turn to Gallagher, and I can see how uncomfortable she is. How much she'd give not to be in this room right now. "It's your case now—I'm not going to interfere. But I still care about getting this bastard. So if you need me, ask, OK?"

She nods. "Yes," she says. "I will."

*　　*　　*

Gislingham watches the door swing shut behind Fawley. And now everyone is looking from him to Gallagher and back again.

So now what? he thinks. It's not that he's unsympathetic—he'd have moved heaven and earth to protect Janet, if she'd been in that situation. But all the same—

"Sergeant?" says Gallagher, giving him a meaningful look. She's clearly expecting him to keep calm and carry on regardless of the amount of shit piled in the way.

He sighs inwardly; just his bloody luck. I mean, this Gallagher woman has a good rep, but you never know, not until the crap hits the fan.

"Right," he says, taking a deep breath. "Best idea for us is to stick to our knitting. Get this bloody case sorted once and for all."

He picks up the pen and goes over to the whiteboard. "Way I see it, right now we have four possibilities. One: what happened to Faith and Sasha—the plastic bag, the cable ties, Faith's ripped hair—it has nothing to do with Gavin Parrie and it never did. It's all just one hell of a sodding coincidence."

Silence. The whole team knows how Fawley feels about coincidences. But this time it's different: this time a coincidence is the one thing that would get the DI off the hook.

"Two," says Gis. "The man who attacked Faith and Sasha is the same man who committed the Roadside Rapes, which means the real killer not only managed not to get caught, but not even to get bloody questioned. Which, OK, has happened—we all know that."

"Peter fucking Sutcliffe, for starters," mutters Quinn.

"But in that case why did the attacks stop the minute Gavin Parrie was arrested, and where has this other bloke been for the last twenty years?" It must be pretty obvious, just from his tone, what Gislingham thinks about that as a theory. But, frankly, he doesn't give a toss.

He turns to the board again. "Number three: Faith and Sasha were attacked by someone who actually knows Parrie—someone who's trying to make it look like he was set up for something he didn't do. And the reason all this is happening now is because Parrie's up for parole. And because those Whole Truth people are suddenly poking their noses in. And we all know where *that* could end up."

Baxter mumbles something about *Making a Murderer*, and there's a ripple of agreement.

But Quinn is looking skeptical. "That's all a bit convoluted, though, isn't it? Who's going to go to that much trouble to get Parrie off the hook? It's like something off the bloody telly."

Ev agrees. "I could just about buy it if it was just Faith, but Sasha? Assault is one thing, but would someone really commit murder—a really brutal murder—just to put Parrie in the clear? Not even your own family's going to do that, surely?"

"I know blood's thicker than water," mutters Baxter, "but not that bloody thick."

Gis shrugs. "I'm with you, but we still need to take it seriously, at least until we can prove otherwise."

"I'll check who's been visiting him," says Everett. "Where did the boss say he was—Wandsworth?"

If Ruth Gallagher registers that "boss" she gives no sign. "Actually, I have that information," she says, opening a file. "DI Fawley already requested it."

There's a half-awkward moment as she walks up to Everett and hands her the sheet of paper, and Gis wonders for a second if she's about to take over, but her task done she returns to her place and gives him an encouraging nod.

"OK, Ev," he continues, "perhaps you could check where those people were on the days Faith and Sasha were attacked. Just so we can scratch them off our list."

"What about friends? Previous associates?" asks Asante. "He could have got a message out to someone via his family—it didn't need to be someone who actually visited."

"That sounds like something off the bloody telly too," says Quinn, rather louder this time.

"Let's start by eliminating the nearest and dearest," says Gislingham firmly. "See where that gets us."

He writes "4" on the board, and turns again to face them. "Last, but deffo not least, a copycat. Which is why Baxter was checking the transcripts in the first place."

Baxter looks up. "Right, yes. Basically, all the details of the MO are in there—the hair, the plaster dust, the cable ties, the plastic bag. And all that was in the press too. It might take a while to dig it all up, given how long ago it was, but I reckon anyone could get their hands on the right info if they were determined enough."

"What about Sasha's boyfriend, Sarge?" says Somer. "Are we still looking at him?"

"More like looking *for* him," says Baxter stolidly. "Because I for one am beginning to doubt the bugger even exists."

"Yes," says Gislingham firmly, glancing at him, "we are. Sasha had a half-empty box of condoms that didn't use themselves. Can you stay on that, DC Somer?"

She nods and he looks around the room again. "Anything else for now?"

But if there is, no one appears to want to raise it in front of Gallagher.

* * *

Adam Fawley
6 April 2018
14.49

"Can I have a quick chat?"

I look up to see Ruth Gallagher at my door, one hand still on the handle.

I sit back. It's not as if she's interrupting; I've been staring at the same report for the last half-hour and haven't got beyond the first paragraph.

I beckon her in. "Of course."

"You've got a good team there," she says, taking a seat.

"I think so."

She puts a thick cardboard file down on my desk. "I've just been reading through the Blake and Appleford material. That offer of help—does it still stand?"

I nod, but I must look wary because she hurries on. "Look, I know this is a shitty situation, but I hope you realize I didn't want this to happen any more than you did.

From what I can tell from the file, Alastair Osbourne did everything a good SIO would do. As did you. I don't see how any competent officer could have come to a different conclusion."

So she *has* read the file. She just didn't want to push it in the first five minutes. My respect for her inches up.

"Look, I know why you're here—you want to ask me about my wife—about what it says in those trial transcripts. But the defense were just fishing—trying to get me on the back foot. Alex and I didn't get together until long after the trial ended. At the time she was assaulted she was engaged to someone else. They split up a few weeks after it happened—he just couldn't hack it. If you spoke to Alex she'd confirm all of that. But I'd rather you didn't have to."

"I don't think there's any need," she says, looking me steadily in the eye. "But thank you anyway."

I sit back. "OK. So what did you want to talk about?"

She gets to her feet. "I don't know about you but I'm gagging for some decent coffee. And after that, we can get started."

* * *

Fiona Blake is sitting in the dark, alone, behind her drawn curtains. The TV is glowing in the corner, but the program she was pretending to watch has long since finished and she hasn't bothered to change the channel. On the plate in front of her, her long-cold lunch is congealing, uneaten. She can smell the heavy scent of the huge bunch of lilies stuck anyhow in a jug she hardly ever uses; she's never liked them but Isabel brought them around and she didn't want to upset her by throwing them away. Not after everything those girls have been through. The Family Liaison Officer is in the kitchen, no doubt making yet another cup of bloody tea. The sound of him moving about puts her teeth on edge.

"Mrs. Blake?"

She turns slowly to see Patsie hesitating at the door. It's gone 4:00 but she's still in a dressing gown, with that blurry look of someone who hasn't even bothered washing. It's the first time Fiona's seen her all day.

Fiona frowns a little. "Are you OK, Pats?"

The girl takes a step forward. And now it's obvious: there's definitely something wrong.

"Me and Iz and Leah," she says. "We've been talking."

Fiona puts her glass down. "OK," she says carefully.

"It was when I watched that appeal thing again that I thought about it. The one they did when Sash went missing. That bit when they asked people to get in touch—you know, if they'd seen her."

Fiona waits, barely breathing. Has Patsie remembered something? Has Isabel?

"It was that journalist—he said there'd been another girl, who got taken in a van." Her cheeks are flushed now. "We wanted to say something before but—"

"*But what?*" says Fiona. She doesn't seem to be getting enough air. "What is it, Patsie?"

The girl drops her eyes. "Iz says it can't be him because it isn't a van, not really—"

Fiona's on her feet now, gripping Patsie by the arms, shaking her. "*What isn't? Who are you talking about?*"

* * *

Ruth Gallagher takes her coffee black, no sugar, and she appears to like her discussions without sweeteners too. She gets straight to the point, and if she asks hard questions, she can take it as well as give it.

By the time we finish going through the Parrie case file I've become "Adam" and she's "Ruth," and I'm starting to think Harrison is a better judge of character than I usually assume.

"How did the rest of the team meeting go?" I say finally as she puts down her pen and closes her notebook. I've been itching to ask her that this whole time but didn't want to look completely paranoid.

"DS Gislingham seems to have it covered. Though I had a word with him afterwards and suggested he might want to do a reconstruction—for Sasha Blake, I mean."

In other words, she suggested it privately, so she didn't undermine him in front of the team. I'm starting to like this woman, which is hands-down the best thing that's happened so far today. Not that the competition is particularly stiff.

"And Harrison agreed to stump up?"

She gives me a dry look. "Let's just say I suggested he might owe you one."

Which, of course, he bloody well does.

"It has to be worth a try," she continues, "given how little we have to go on. And it will divert attention from the case review too, which is no bad thing either."

I'd been reaching for my coffee but I look across at her

now and I can't see any irony. Nothing underhand either in her tone or in her eyes.

"DS Gislingham is going to try to get it organized for tomorrow."

I wait for her to get up to go, but she doesn't. What she does instead is smile. Smile and sit back. "Now we've got those bloody files out of the way what I want to know is what never made it into them. I want to know what really happened."

And so I tell her. The truth, and nothing but the truth.

Just not the whole of it.

* * *

When Gallagher opens the front door she looks flustered. She has a box of hundreds-and-thousands in one hand and a tea towel in the other. There's a smear of what looks like flour on one cheek.

"I'm sorry," says Somer. "They said you'd gone home already, and I did try calling but—"

Gallagher laughs. "Sorry. I had to get back to collect my daughter. And then she mugged me into baking. I must have left the phone upstairs." She takes a step back. "Come in."

Somer looks tentative. "Look, if this is a bad time—"

She waves the objection away. "If it wasn't important, you wouldn't be here."

The kitchen is out the back. There's a tray of cupcakes cooling on a wire rack, and another batch still in the oven. The air is warm and sweet and chocolatey. A little girl of about eight is perched at the big wooden table, putting pale-blue icing-sugar flowers carefully on to the cakes; her little face is intense with concentration. From somewhere nearby, there's the sound of a TV. A football stadium roar.

"My son is at tae kwon do," says Gallagher, wiping her hands on her apron. "The football hooligan is my husband."

She goes to the fridge and pulls out a bottle of wine. "Are you driving?"

Somer nods.

Gallagher pours a large glass and a small one, and hands the latter to Somer. "OK, so what have you got?"

"I just had a call from Fiona Blake. Patsie Webb just told her something—something she hasn't mentioned before."

Gallagher raises an eyebrow. "Oh yes?"

Somer glances at the little girl and lowers her voice. "One of Sasha's teachers was showing rather too much interest in her. His name is Scott. Graeme Scott."

"Eliza," says Gallagher to her daughter, "why don't you take one of those cakes through for Daddy?"

The little girl looks up. "Can I have one too?"

Gallagher nods. "Just the one though."

When she's gone, Gallagher turns to Somer. "Didn't we speak to Sasha's teachers already?"

Somer makes a face and shakes her head. "All of them *apart* from this man Scott. DS Gislingham was told he'd gone home with a migraine."

Gallagher raises an eyebrow. "Had he really? How convenient."

"I just rang the head," says Somer. "Apparently he's suffered from them before. So it could have been legit."

Gallagher goes over to the oven to check the cakes, then turns back to Somer. "What exactly did Patsie say?"

"According to her, this man Scott has been trying to cozy up to Sasha for a while, but the girls were just laughing it off. Teasing her about it, calling him a creep—you know, like girls do. Apparently they call him Spotty Scotty. Among other things."

Gallagher gives a rueful smile. "God, I'm glad I never have to be fifteen again. Do we know if Sasha said anything about it to anyone?"

"Certainly not to her mother, and apparently not to any of her teachers either."

"What do we have on him? He must have been DBS-checked, surely?"

Somer nods. "Yes, but there's nothing flagging." She opens her bag and passes Gallagher a printout. The photo clipped to the top shows a man in his late thirties. He isn't that bad-looking, but he has a defeated, hang-dog air about him.

"Definitely looks a bit desperate," says Gallagher. "But he doesn't look dangerous—like he'd do you any actual harm. And I know teenage girls do sometimes go for older men," she says, making a face, "but I'd be absolutely staggered if this is that elusive boyfriend of Sasha's we still can't find. If you ask me, this man is about as far from a babe magnet as it's possible to get while still having a pulse."

Somer gives a wry smile. It's almost word for word what Ev said.

Gallagher scans down the rest of the page. "Lives

alone, never married, no criminal record. Not even a parking ticket." She looks up at Somer. "Have we sent this to Bryan Gow?"

Somer nods. "He's away till Sunday but he'll have a look and get back to me as soon as he can. And there's something else. We checked out what Scott drives." She gives Gallagher a heavy look. "It's a Morris Traveller."

Gallagher gets it at once. "Which is a lot smaller than a van but if you had a bag over your head and were shoved in the back, would you be able to tell? I'm not sure I could."

Somer shakes her head. "Me neither. And Faith did say she didn't think the vehicle she was taken in was very big."

"Right," says Gallagher crisply. "Do we have an address?"

"That's the other thing. It's 73 Grasmere Close."

The name alone gives it away. It's in the Lakes. No more than half a mile from the Applefords; even less from the Blakes.

"Oh dear," says Gallagher. "Oh dear, oh dear, oh dear."

"Baxter is trying to get hold of his employment records—to see if we can establish a link to Faith as well as Sasha. Whether he's ever worked at Faith's college or any of the schools she's been at."

Gallagher nods. "Good work. Exactly what I'd have done."

Somer flushes a little at the praise. "But even if we get nothing there, he could have seen Faith on the street any number of times. He'd have to drive past the bus stop she uses every day on his way to Summertown High."

"And what about the historical attacks," says Gallagher, taking a sip of her wine, "the Roadside Rapes—could we be looking at Scott there too?"

"He was eighteen in 1998," says Somer. "So yes, we could be."

"OK," says Gallagher. There's a sudden shout from the sitting room; someone has evidently scored. "Let's find out everything there is to know about Scott: everywhere he's lived since the late nineties, everywhere he's worked, and whether there's any reason why there might be plaster in the back of his car. *And* whether there's anything linking him to any of Parrie's victims."

Somer notes the last two words—notes and approves: Gallagher is still on Fawley's side. At least for now.

"And let's hope we turn up something, because right now, we don't have a warrant for either his house or his car, and we aren't likely to get one." Gallagher puts her glass down and gets to her feet. "But that's no reason not to have a nice little chat."

"Do you want us to bring him in?"

Gallagher nods. "Yes, I do. And take DC Quinn with you."

Somer frowns. "Quinn? I mean," she says quickly, "there's no reason why not, I just wondered—"

Gallagher smiles. "Horses for courses, DC Somer. I want Mr. Scott to be decidedly unsettled. And something tells me DC Quinn is going to get right up his nose."

* * *

The Old Bailey
London EC4M 7EH

BEFORE:
THE HONORABLE MR. JUSTICE HEALEY

R E G I N A
v.
GAVIN FRANCIS PARRIE

———————————————

MR. R. BARNES Q.C. and MISS S. GREY
appeared on behalf of the prosecution.

MRS. B. JENKINS Q.C. and MR. T. CUTHBERT
appeared on behalf of the defendant.

———————————————

Thursday, 11th November, 1999
[Day 20]

JENNIFER GODDARD, sworn
Examined by MR. BARNES

Q. Is your full name Jennifer Goddard?
A. Yes.

Q. Your daughter, Emma, was the victim of a
   sexual assault on November 14th 1998, is
   that right?
A. Yes.

Q. Did Emma live at home with you at that
   time?

A. Yes. She was only nineteen. We lived in Headington then. I moved to Wantage after, because of what happened.

Q. On the night in question, Emma was due home at her usual time, I believe?
A. That's right. She worked at the JR.

Q. The John Radcliffe Hospital?
A. Yes. She was training to be a midwife. She always got home between 6:30 and 7, unless she called to say she'd be late.

Q. But she didn't call that night?
A. No. That's why I started to get worried when she wasn't back by 8.

Q. Did you call the police?
A. Yes, but not till later. I was worried they'd think I was fussing.

Q. And what happened when you spoke to them?
A. They said they'd send someone over. That's when I knew it was bad. And then there was a woman in uniform at the door. They said I had to go with them. Em had been attacked and she was in A&E.

Q. What had happened to her?
A. They didn't tell me much then. Not till we got to the hospital. That's when I found out that she'd been raped.

Q. What effect did the assault have on your daughter, Mrs. Goddard?
A. It was devastating. She stopped going out— not just on her own, even with me or her

friends. She was just too terrified. By
December she was barely leaving her room at
all. They'd signed her off long-term sick
from the JR, but I was starting to worry
that she'd never be able to go back. She
said she couldn't bear being around babies.
It was enough to break your heart.

Q. And on December 24th last year, what
happened then?

A. I got back home from work and found her on
the bed. She'd taken pills. Pills and vodka.
She'd written this beautiful note saying she
loved me and she was sorry but she just
couldn't carry on any more. But she wasn't
the one who should be sorry. It's him—that
bastard over there—Gavin Parrie—

MRS. JENKINS: My Lord—

MR. JUSTICE HEALEY: Mrs. Goddard, I appreciate
how difficult this must be, but it is important
that you confine yourself to answering the
questions put to you. Do you understand?

MRS. GODDARD: Yes, my Lord.

MR. BARNES: Did your daughter succeed in her
suicide attempt, Mrs. Goddard?

A. I called 999 and they took her to the JR but
they told me in the ambulance it was touch
and go.

Q. And when you got to the hospital?

A. The doctor came out to see me about an hour
later. He said they'd done everything they

could but it was no use. Some of the nurses
were crying. They knew Em, you see.

* * *

You wouldn't know they were police, just from looking at
them. The woman is a real looker, for a start, and as for
him, well, he has that swagger-shagger look that's always
pissed Scott off. Men like him—they don't know they're
born.

"Yes?" he says, holding the door as close to shut as he
can manage.

"DC Erica Somer," says the woman. "I was wondering
if you'd mind answering some questions. About Sasha
Blake."

"Can't it wait till tomorrow?"

The man looks supercilious, like he knows something
Scott doesn't. "'Fraid not. We can do it here or you can
come to St. Aldate's. Your choice."

Scott hesitates. What's worse—letting them stick him
in one of those nasty little interview rooms or having
them looking down their noses at his house and making
excuses to go to the lav and snoop into his things. He
glances up and down the street. There doesn't seem to be
anyone about. And it's an unmarked car. At least the nosy
cow opposite won't be putting two and two together and
making forty-six.

"Give me five minutes," he says. "So I can lock up."

* * *

Interview with Graeme Scott, conducted at St.
Aldate's Police Station, Oxford
6 April 2018, 7:55 p.m.
In attendance, DC E. Somer, DC G. Quinn

ES: Before we start, I would like to thank you for
    coming here tonight, Mr. Scott, and especially
    so late and at such short notice.

GS: You didn't exactly give me much choice. But,
    of course, I want to do anything I can do to
    help. This is a terrible situation. For Sasha's
    mother, I mean.

ES: You taught Sasha art?

GS: That's right. For the last two years.

GQ: Since she was thirteen.

GS: Right. She was very talented. I kept telling
    her she should do A level.

ES: You were encouraging her?

GS: Of course. That's my job.

GQ: So, what—you gave her extra lessons? Personal
    coaching?

GS: [*laughs*]
    This isn't the private sector, mate. I just
    did what I could to bring her on.

GQ: Well, that's certainly the impression we've
    been given.

GS: [*frowns*]
    I'm not sure what you're getting at. I was
    just taking an interest. As her teacher.

ES: From what we've been told it was a lot more
    than that. The way it's been described to

us, it sounds like it was completely inappropriate.

GS: Now hang on a minute—

ES: You're what—thirty-eight? She was *fifteen*.

GS: It was *nothing* like that. Look, I don't know where you're getting this from—no, wait, I know *exactly* where you're getting this from. It's Patsie and Isabel, isn't it? And that Leah? They've been blabbing—

ES: "Blabbing," Mr. Scott? I believe I'm correct in saying that the meaning of that word is to "reveal information." Specifically, information people would rather wasn't generally known. Secrets, for example.

GS: [*red in the face*]
    I didn't mean that—there's nothing to reveal. Because there was *nothing going on*.

ES: But you'd have liked there to be, is that it? I mean, she was a very attractive girl.

GS: She was *fifteen*. Even if it were legal—which it wasn't—it would still have been une*thical*. She was a talented student. *That's all.*

GQ: Do you know a girl called Faith Appleford?

GS: [*frowns*]
    Sorry?

GQ: Faith Appleford. She's a talented student too. A very talented student.
    [*passes across a photo*]

GS: She's not in any of my classes. I don't know her.

ES: She used to go by another name. Perhaps that
    might jog your memory?

GS: I told you, I don't know her. Look, if it's all
    the same to you I have things I need to be doing.

GQ: This won't take much longer. And you did say
    you wanted to help.

GS: [*pause*]
    OK. As long as I can go in about ten minutes.

ES: We're asking everyone who knew Sasha where
    they were on Wednesday evening. Could you tell
    us where you were? For the record?

GS: I was at home. I'm at home most nights.

ES: No one was there with you?

GS: No. I was doing marking. I have a ton of it to
    get through. You have no idea.

GQ: Did you call anyone? Get any calls?

GS: Not that I can recall.

ES: What about the morning of the 1st? Where were
    you then?

GS: I'm sorry—I thought we were talking about
    Sasha?

ES: Just for our records, Mr. Scott.

GS: That was last Monday, right? I was in class.

GQ: Really? Because Summertown High told us you
    have two free periods first thing on Mondays,
    and often don't get in till after eleven.

GS: [*flushes*]
    Yeah, well, I go away a lot at weekends. I
    have a cottage in the Brecon Beacons. It makes
    sense to drive back Monday morning. Less
    traffic.

ES: Were you at the cottage last weekend?

GS: No. I wasn't.

GQ: So you were at home on Monday morning? You didn't take the opportunity to go in early—catch up on all that marking you were talking about?

GS: Look, if you must know, I didn't go in till after twelve that day. For obvious reasons.

ES: I'm sorry, Mr. Scott, I'm not with you.

GS: It was bloody April Fool's, wasn't it? And, believe me, I've been through enough puerile pranks to last me a lifetime. Last year the little shits covered the bloody car in shaving foam—it took me an hour to get it all off—in front of the whole sodding school. I told her—if you've damaged the bloody paintwork I'll have you up before the head quicker than you can say fixed-period exclusion.

ES: I see. So who did that? Who sprayed the car?

GS: [*pause*]
Some of the Year Tens.

ES: And this was last year? So that must have been Sasha's year group?

GS: [*pause*]
Yes.

ES: You said "her"—"I told her." Was it Sasha you were referring to?

GS: If you must know, it was that Patsie. I'd just given her 52 for a piece of work that frankly barely deserved 35 and she was getting her own back. She's a nasty vindictive little cow,

293

always has been. She was egging on the lads, her and that Isabel and Leah. Sasha had nothing to do with it. I mean, she was *there*, but I could tell she was embarrassed. Not like the other three. They're just complete airheads. You wouldn't catch any of *them* at MOMA.

ES: The Museum of Modern Art—in Pembroke Street?

GS: [*pause*]
Yes, I go there a lot. I'm a Friend.

ES: And you've seen Sasha there?

GS: [*flushes*]
Once or twice.

ES: I see.

GS: No, you don't "see." It's not what you're thinking—

GQ: Which is what, precisely?

GS: I wasn't *stalking* her or anything. I just happened to be there a couple of times. I'd recommended a couple of their shows to her. Things I thought she'd like. Look, have we finished now?

ES: Yes, I think that's all for now, Mr. Scott. Interview terminated at 20.17.

* * *

"I didn't believe a word that came out of his mouth."

It's Gislingham. Quinn and Somer have joined him and the rest of the team in the adjoining room, where they've been watching on the video feed.

Baxter shrugs. "Just came over as a sad git to me. I

294

mean, I can't see him abducting anyone. I just don't think he has the balls."

"I bet he likes looking, though," says Ev grimly. "I bet that house of his is stacked with porn."

"Perhaps that's why he went into art," replies Quinn. "All those tits and fannies."

"He doesn't want us to search the car though, does he," says Gislingham. "Can't see any good reason why not—not if he's really got nothing to hide."

Ev considers. "What if he gave Sasha a lift sometime? Perhaps that's what he's worried about—that we'd find her DNA in the car, even though it was actually completely innocent."

"If it was on the seat, yes," says Quinn. "But not if it's in the bloody back."

There's a silence. They're all remembering what happened to Faith. Whether it's her DNA they might find in the back of that car.

"I'm wondering," says Somer slowly. "It's a bit of a long shot, but—"

"Go on," says Gislingham.

"Well, we still haven't found any connection between Sasha and Faith, have we? And no connection between Graeme Scott and Faith at all, beyond the fact that they live quite close to one another."

"That may be all we need."

"I know, Sarge. But what Scott said about seeing Sasha at MOMA—I'd have to double-check but I'm pretty sure there was a postcard from there on Faith's pinboard as well. An exhibition she must have been to. On Manolo Blahnik."

Most of the men in the room look at her blankly.

"*Shoes*," says Everett. "Extremely posh and expensive *shoes*. Though I bet Quinn knew that already, didn't you?"

And evidently he did, though he's clearly not about to admit it.

"So you reckon Scott could have seen Faith there?" asks Gislingham, coming to Quinn's rescue.

Somer nods. "It has to be possible, doesn't it? And if he did, it would have been easy enough to follow her home. Then once he knew where she lived—"

Gislingham nods grimly. "All the bastard had to do was wait."

*　*　*

Adam Fawley
6 April 2018
20.55

She's not the person I was expecting when I opened the door. She doesn't have a pizza box for a start. It's raining again and Ruth Gallagher looks half drowned, her hair stuck to her head.

"Should have taken my umbrella," she says with a wry smile. "I never learn."

I step back and open the door wider. "Come in. I've got a takeaway arriving any minute if you want to join me."

She shakes her head quickly. "No—thank you, but no. I need to get back. There was just something I wanted to check and I thought it would be better done in person."

"It's through there," I say, gesturing toward the living room.

She shrugs off her mac and takes off her shoes, then pads after me in her stockinged feet.

The living room is empty, which I knew but she clearly wasn't expecting.

"My wife's having an early night," I say, sitting down. "She needs to take it easy right now."

She looks suddenly anxious, as if she's worried there's something she doesn't know.

"She's pregnant," I say. "Twenty-three weeks."

I've heard the phrase "face lit up" a thousand times but never seen it so suddenly and powerfully as I see it now. She is radiant with reflected happiness.

"Oh, I am so pleased—what utterly wonderful news."

"Thanks. It's been difficult, what with the Parrie case being dredged up again."

She's concerned now. "Oh, of course. What terrible timing."

I pour her a glass of wine, though she only accepts a small one.

"What did you want to ask me?"

She fishes in her pocket for her phone then scrolls down until she finds what she's looking for.

"This man," she says, handing me the phone. "His name is Graeme Scott. Do you recognize him by any chance?"

I frown. "No. Not at all. Who is he?"

Her sparkle has gone again and she just looks tired. Tired and dispirited. "One of Sasha Blake's teachers. And quite possibly her stalker."

"You think he may have killed her?"

She makes a face. "Let's just say he fits that psych

profile Gow gave you after the Appleford attack. Almost *too* well, in fact."

And if he fits that, he fits the Roadside Rapist profile too. I don't need her to draw me a bloody diagram: she thinks this man could be in the frame.

"How old is he?" I say, looking up at her.

"Old enough. But we don't yet know where he was living twenty years ago."

"Well, his name never came up at the time. That I do know."

She sighs. "I thought you'd probably say that, but I had to ask."

She finishes her glass and gets ready to get up. "I must be going. Science homework awaits." She smiles quickly. "My son's, not mine. But of course you have all that to look forward to."

Most people wouldn't say that. Most people would be too scared they might evoke the memory of Jake. I've seen that look on too many faces, these last two years. But not, perhaps, any more. Perhaps things really are going to be different now. The thought comes like a sudden rush of fresh sea air.

* * *

It's gone 11:00 but there's still a light under the door to Sasha's room when Fiona Blake goes up to bed. She hesitates, then knocks softly, but there's no reply. Patsie's fallen asleep with the light on, she thinks, but it's bound to wake her later. It was the same with Sasha—she loved reading in bed but was always dozing off over her book.

She pushes the door open slowly. Patsie is sprawled sideways against the pillows, her face turned away. Sasha's old teddy bear is clutched to her chest and even though she knows she's not her daughter, Fiona feels her heart buckle at the resemblance. The same ponytail, the same pajamas; Patsie must have bought an identical pair. It wouldn't surprise her—the two of them were completely inseparable. She wonders for a moment whether Patsie would like some of Sasha's things, to remember her by. The clothes would be too small, but there's the makeup, the handbags, the shoes. After all, Sasha has no need for any of them now—surely it'd be a good thing if they could make someone else happy. Especially someone who loved her.

And if Patsie doesn't want any of it she'll give it all to charity. She doesn't want this room turning into a shrine. Frozen in time, gathering dust, colder and bleaker and further away every time she opens the door. That's why she likes having Patsie here. She keeps the place warm, lived-in. *Alive.*

She moves quickly toward the bed, turns out the light and tiptoes back to the door, closing it gently behind her.

* * *

"No, that's fine. If you were out of the country I can confirm it with the Border Agency."

Everett puts the phone down and grimaces. She's had two coffees this morning but she could already do with another.

"Trouble?" asks Somer.

"Well, let's just say Gavin Parrie's family aren't overly pleased at being asked to confirm their whereabouts by the people they blame for banging him up in the first place."

Somer makes a face in return. "I bet they're not."

Everett sits back. "If you ask me, the idea of Parrie hiring a hitman is bloody ludicrous. Like *The Sopranos* in Aylesbury."

Somer grins and turns back to her screen. She's been liaising with the press office about the TV reconstruction. They'd been struggling to find a girl who looked enough like Sasha, but one of her classmates has just come forward. Or rather her mother has. On the basis—apparently—that it could be her little darling's big break: little Jemima wants to be an actress. Human beings, thinks Somer, they never fail to live down to your expectations.

"What do you think of her?" she says eventually, glancing across at Everett. "Gallagher, I mean."

"Seems OK. Fair. Bright. I don't think she's out to dump on Fawley if that's what you're asking."

"No, I didn't get that impression either. Poor sod—he doesn't deserve this."

Ev looks up. "Yeah, I know. And as for his wife—imagine what she's going through. As if losing your child wasn't bad enough, now all this shit is coming back to haunt her."

Somer bites her lip. It's what happened to Alex Fawley in the first place that haunts her. Even if it was only—even if that man didn't actually—

"And let's face it," says Everett, breaking into her

thoughts, "you can totally understand Fawley. Who wouldn't want to keep that man inside, in his position."

But that, of course, is the whole point.

* * *

Sent: Sun 07/04/2018, 11.15   **Importance: High**

From: DCGarethQuinn@ThamesValley.police.uk

To: DSChrisGislingham@ThamesValley.police.uk,
CID@ThamesValley.police.uk

cc: DIRuthGallagher@ThamesValley.police.uk

Subject: Graeme Scott—URGENT

Just heard back from the local council in the Brecon Beacons—we've got an address for Scott's cottage. It's near some godforsaken place called Ffrwdgrech (and yes, that is how you spell it). He's had it since 1995. The key point is that late last year he applied for planning permission for some fairly extensive renovations that include knocking down some interior walls. And according to the last Building Inspector's report he's doing the work <u>himself</u>.

We're bringing him in again. I've also applied for warrants for the cottage and the Oxford house, and for the car. And I reckon we're going to get them.

GQ

* * *

Interview with Graeme Scott, conducted at
St. Aldate's Police Station, Oxford
7 April 2018, 2:50 p.m.
In attendance, DS C. Gislingham, DC G. Quinn,
Mrs. D. Owen (solicitor)

CG: For the benefit of the tape, Mr. Scott was
    arrested at 1:15 this afternoon on suspicion
    of involvement in the abduction and murder of
    Sasha Alice Blake. A full forensic search is
    underway at Mr. Scott's home in Oxford and on
    his car, and Dyfed-Powys Police are carrying
    out a similar search at his property in Wales.
    Mr. Scott is accompanied for this interview by
    his solicitor, Mrs. Deborah Owen.

GS: I've already told you, I had absolutely
    nothing to do with any of this. I was at home
    Wednesday night, and I've never touched Sasha
    Blake. And as for that Faith Appleton girl, or
    whatever her name is, I told you before I've
    never even heard of her—

CG: [*pushes across a photograph*]
    She lives less than a mile from you and uses
    the bus stop on Cherwell Drive. You've almost
    certainly seen her in the vicinity, even if
    you don't know her name.

GS: [*pushing the photo away*]
    I *told you already*—I've never seen her before
    in my life.

CG: The cottage in Wales—you're renovating it,
    I believe.

302

GS: [*warily*]
   Yes, so what?

CG: You're doing the work yourself?

GS: It's the only way I can afford it.

CG: Including specialist jobs like electrics and plasterwork?

GS: Yes, with the odd helping hand every now and again. But I still don't see—

CG: When we did a forensic analysis of Faith Appleford's clothes, we found minute traces of plaster dust. I suspect we will find exactly the same compound in the back of your car.

GS: I'm sure you will. But all that will prove is that I've done some sodding plastering. What you will *not* bloody well find is any DNA from that Faith girl, or from Sasha Blake for that matter. Not unless you plant it your bloody selves. Because *they were never there*—

CG: Faith told us there was some sort of loose covering on the floor of the vehicle. We're assuming that her attacker laid down either plastic sheeting or a tarpaulin, to prevent the transfer of physical evidence. So even if we don't find the girls' DNA, it doesn't mean they weren't there.

DO: That's not *evidence*, Sergeant.

CG: No. But this is.
   [*shows witness an evidence bag*]
   Do you recognize this, Mr. Scott?

GS: [*silence*]

CG: Mr. Scott?

GS: [*silence*]

CG: For the tape, the item is a girl's hair
elastic. It's pink, with a small flower and a
bit of diamanté in the middle. This struck
us as a very odd thing for you to have,
Mr. Scott.

GS: [*silence*]

CG: Do you have a daughter? A niece?

GS: You know damn well I don't.

CG: So how do you account for it?

DO: Where was this found, Sergeant?

GQ: In Mr. Scott's locker at Summertown High. The
head gave us permission to search it.

GS: Look, I found it, OK?

DO: Has this item been conclusively identified as
belonging to either of the two girls?

GQ: We're awaiting DNA results, but Sasha's mother
says her daughter definitely had one just like
this, which she can't now find. So it's looking
pretty likely, if you ask me.

GS: Like I said, I found it. It was at school,
after a class. That's why it was in the
locker.

CG: Did you know it was Sasha's?

GS: [*flustered*]
I don't know. I might have done.

CG: So why not give it back to her? Or at the very
least hand it to Lost Property?

GS: I don't know. Look, I must have just stuffed
it in my pocket. I forgot all about the bloody
thing.

GQ: Er, I don't think so, mate.

GS: I'm not your "mate"—

GQ: You took it out of your pocket and put it in your locker, where you'd see it half a dozen times a day. That doesn't sound like "forgetting all about it" to me.

DO: Either way, it doesn't prove my client was involved in any way with Sasha Blake's tragic death. The fact that he was in possession of the hair tie—assuming it is indeed ascertained to be hers—would be significant if *and only if* she was wearing it when she went missing. Do you have any evidence of that?

CG: [*pause*]
No, we don't.

DO: But you must have a description of what she had on at the time? Does it include this hair tie?

CG: [*pause*]
No, it doesn't.

DO: In that case, I venture to suggest you have precious little evidence *at all*. In fact, I can scarcely see adequate grounds for arrest, let alone—

CG: Given the seriousness of the crime, your client's known association with Sasha Blake, and the physical proximity between his house and Faith Appleford's, we will be holding your client in custody pending further enquiries.

GS: You're actually saying I'm some sort of *suspect*?

GQ: We're *saying* we'd like to confirm you
    aren't one.
DO: May I have some time with my client?
CG: Absolutely. Interview terminated at 15:10.

* * *

"What do you think, Bryan?" says Gallagher.

They're in the adjacent interview room, where the pro-
filer has been scratching his observations into a Moleskine
notebook.

Gow pushes his glasses up his nose. "I think our
Mr. Scott may have genuinely believed he and Sasha were
in some sort of relationship. That all he had to do was
wait and eventually all the barriers holding them back
would be miraculously cast aside."

"Including the minor inconvenience of her being
underage," says Gallagher grimly.

"Precisely. Though that would have just added fuel to
the delusion. Scott could tell himself that was why they
had to keep it secret—why she couldn't say anything to
him in public. The problem comes, of course, when a
man in that position is forced to confront the fact that
the woman he loves doesn't reciprocate his feelings and
never will. In the face of that kind of rejection, well, let's
just say that things can escalate very quickly. Very quickly
indeed."

"So if he did see Sasha at the bus stop that night—"

"He might well have thought his moment had come—a
perfect opportunity to tell her how he felt. Only to find
her looking at him aghast like he's some sort of pervert."

"Or laughing at him," says Gallagher.

Gow nods. "That, of course, would have been even worse. His world was crashing in ruins and she was just laughing in his face. He loses his temper, lashes out –" He shrugs; he doesn't need to go on.

"Added to which," says Gallagher, "that Morris Traveller of his is chock-full with craft materials and decorating stuff. Including knives. Killing her may have been unpremeditated, but he had everything he needed to do it in the back of his car."

Gow makes a quick note. "Interesting, I didn't know about that."

He looks up again. "There's one obvious problem with all this, though, as I'm sure you've realized: Faith Appleford."

"I know," she says with a sigh. "The stronger we make the case for Scott's obsession with Sasha, the harder it is to explain why he'd have assaulted Faith. Or anyone else for that matter."

Gow is nodding. "Which any competent defense lawyer is going to seize on at once. And he—or she—will have a point. And if Scott didn't attack Faith, who did? You don't need me to tell you the chances of two different men carrying out nearly identical attacks at the same time, in the same confined geographical area, are vanishingly small."

On the screen, Scott is talking intently with the lawyer, jabbing at the table to emphasize his point.

"Do you think he could have done it before?" says Gallagher eventually.

"The stalking? Hard to say. If you forced my hand I'd

lean towards no. Largely because something would probably have flagged in his employment records by now."

Gallagher is still staring at the screen. "Then we'd better make sure he doesn't get another chance."

Scott's lawyer has now got to her feet and is gesturing up at the camera to attract their attention.

Gow nods toward it. "Looks like she has something to say. Or Scott does."

*　*　*

"Turns out he has an alibi," says Gallagher, looking around at the team. "For Faith at least. Less than ten minutes after she was abducted, Graeme Scott was buying milk on Cherwell Drive. Or so he claims. And it gets better: he used contactless, so there'll be an electronic record."

She looks around the incident room; at the weariness, the fatigue, the we're-getting-nowhere. She needs to turn this around, and fast.

"So the first thing we're going to do is check that alibi." She turns to Gislingham. "And in the meantime, have we had anything from the lab?"

He looks up. "They're testing the knives and plaster dust from Scott's car, and running his DNA against the Tesco bag from the allotments. I've put a rush on it."

"Right," she says briskly, addressing the room again. "And while they're doing their job, we carry on doing ours. We don't just check Scott's alibi for Faith, we also check his phone records to see if he really was at home the night Sasha disappeared. And we carry on running down Ashley Brotherton's known associates, because right now, we haven't ruled that out either. None of this is rocket science, people, so let's just get on with it, shall we?"

* * *

The reconstruction is going ahead as soon as it gets dark; by the time Somer and Everett get to Cherwell Drive there's already a considerable crowd along the pavement. The TV lights and cameras are set up and the bus company vehicle is parked up in a lay-by a hundred yards away. The driver is talking to a couple of uniformed officers.

Everett makes her way toward the BBC crew, but Somer stays where she is, scanning the faces of the bystanders, hoping Fiona Blake took her advice and hasn't come. If Sasha had still been missing there'd be a point; but not now. Now, the only thing here for her is pain. And not just because she's lost her daughter: Somer can see Jonathan Blake being interviewed on camera, and just behind him, the woman he must be living with now, rocking a small baby against her shoulder. Blake is speaking intently, a crease of earnest anxiety between his brows. And further away, behind the cameras, Sasha's friends. Somer didn't know if they were going to come—their parents were reluctant to agree, and the girls have been in such a state it was almost a cruelty to push it. But there's no denying it could make all the difference: Isabel's dip-dye, Patsie's red leather jacket—either might prompt a memory. But as Somer knows full well, what makes sense for a police investigation is a whole lot different for the people who have to go through with it, especially if you're fifteen and your best friend has just been horribly killed. Even from this distance Somer can see that Patsie is crying, and Isabel and Leah have their arms around each other. The girl who's playing Sasha can't be helping either. What with the clothes and the satchel and what they've done to her hair, the resemblance is unnerving. Thank God, thinks Somer again, that Fiona Blake didn't come.

"Erica?"

The voice is familiar, and Somer turns to find herself face-to-face with Faith Appleford. She's pale and even thinner than she was the last time they met, but she looks calm, which in the circumstances is little short of a miracle.

"I didn't know you'd be here."

"We thought we should come. It just seemed the right thing to do." She shrugs. "It's hard to explain."

"No, I understand," says Somer. "How are you? I'm so sorry we didn't have the chance to talk more when I called you a couple of days ago—"

"No, it's OK," she says quickly. "I know you're busy. And I'm doing much better. I know that sounds terrible after, you know, *this*." She flushes a little. "I guess I'm just realizing how lucky I was. How lucky I *am*."

Somer gives her a sad smile. "You're right—you are. Never forget that. You have such a great future ahead of you."

She can see Diane Appleford too now, standing with Nadine just beyond the BBC van.

"And even though all this is just horrible," says Faith softly, "at least it means that what happened to me—it can't have been someone I know."

Somer wants to agree, but she's not sure she can. Right now, it feels like they're back to square one.

The bus engine chugs suddenly into life, saving Somer from the need to reply. The bus door opens with a hiss and the two girls get in, first "Sasha" then Isabel. Leah and Patsie are standing watching from the curb, their eyes bright in the glare. A woman who must be Patsie's mother reaches out and puts an arm around her daughter's shoulders, but Patsie shakes her roughly away.

Somer turns back to Faith. "Do you mind if I ask you something?"

Faith shrugs. "Sure."

"I know you said it was possible it wasn't a van you were taken in. Do you think it could have been some sort of car? Quite a small car, even?"

Faith's eyes widen. "You think you know who it was?"

"There is someone we're talking to, but that's all I can say right now."

"Can't you test the car then—you know, forensics?"

"He claims to have an alibi for that morning, but we haven't been able to corroborate it yet. And in the meantime, yes, we are doing forensic testing on the car. But if there was anything else you remember, that would really help."

Faith looks troubled. "I'm really sorry, but I just can't be sure. I want to help, but—"

"No," says Somer quickly. "It's fine. I understand."

Faith looks back toward the crowd around the cameras. "Oh, I can see a couple of my mates over there—do you mind? I said I'd meet them."

Somer follows her gaze. Two girls are waving to Faith;

one of them is Jess Beardsley, the girl she talked to in the canteen.

"I'm glad you're making friends. That's really great. And Jess seems really nice."

Faith smiles, a little shyly. "Yeah, that's the one good thing to come out of all this shit. Turns out Jess's brother is trans too. She thinks it's no big deal."

Three small words, but a world of acceptance. The possibility of another life.

Somer watches her go, sees the hug she gets. Perhaps something good really could come out of all this pain. Against the odds.

* * *

Sasha watches as the bus pulls away, then goes back to the shelter and sits down on the bench. She checks her phone, and then gets to her feet again. She looks up and down the road, her face anxious. She appears to be looking for someone.

Then all the lights go out.

* * *

The cameras stop running and the girl playing Sasha turns and looks for her mother, avid for praise. And perhaps she deserves it—perhaps she really did look just like the girl she's impersonating, because Patsie and Leah are clinging to each other, sobbing their hearts out, and when the bus door opens Isabel steps down unsteadily and collapses, weeping, into Yasmin's arms. Everett watches as the woman drapes a blanket around the girl's shoulders, then leads her away like the survivor of an earthquake. And maybe that's not so far from the truth, thinks Everett; because the calamity those three girls have been caught up in has wrecked everything they thought they could count on, and even if that trust can be rebuilt the fault line will always be there.

A few yards away, Jonathan Blake is talking again, to another cluster of journalists. He seems to have found his vocation, thinks Everett scornfully, before remonstrating with herself for being so cynical. Perhaps the man just wants to help. One of the hacks interrupts to ask if Blake can pose for a picture with his new family and after a moment's modest demurral he calls his girlfriend forward. "Rach? Apparently they want you and Liam in this one as well."

"Fantastic," says the journalist as the cameraman arranges the couple and their child against the backdrop of the crowd. "The little brother Sasha never even got to meet. My editor will friggin'" love that."

* * *

After her husband leaves for work at 8:00, Alex Fawley allows herself another half-hour in bed before hauling herself into the shower and turning it on. She tests both the water and the pressure before she gets in: not too hot, not too hard. She soaps herself carefully, caressing the skin where it stretches over her child. The baby rises to her touch and she smiles. It's OK. Everything's OK. And it's not long now. Only seventeen more weeks. A hundred and nineteen days—

313

She doesn't hear the phone till she turns off the shower and steps carefully on to the mat. It's her mobile; she must have left it in the kitchen. She decides to ignore it and reaches for a towel to wrap around her hair. The ringing stops eventually, only to start again barely thirty seconds later. By the time she gets downstairs and tracks the phone down she's convinced herself it's only Adam checking she's OK, but when she picks up the handset it's her office number staring back at her. And they've already rung four times.

"Hello? Sue? It's Alex—were you trying to reach me?"

Evidently she was. It's about one of Alex's biggest clients. One of the *firm's* biggest clients. And an imminent deadline, and a problem with the tax, and the partner who's standing in for her being off sick, and—and—and—

Alex sighs: she's going to have to go in. But if she's lucky it'll only take a couple of hours. She'll be back long before Adam gets home. He won't even need to know.

"OK," she says eventually. "I've only just got out of the shower, but I'll get there as soon as I can."

"Oh, *thank you*," breathes the assistant. Who is, as Alex reminds herself, unquestionably very bright and very ambitious, but still terrifyingly inexperienced. "That is *so* kind of you."

"No problem," she says, trying to sound more animated than she feels. "Just hold the fort for an hour. I'll be as quick as I can."

*　*　*

Ruth Gallagher can't remember the last time she was in Alan Challow's office. Six months ago? Longer? She's run

314

three or four murder investigations in the last year but it's usually the DS who deals with the forensics. As for Alan Challow, he tends to come to you, not the other way around, so to be invited to his home turf is an anomaly, to say the least. She'd like to think he has something important to say, but if all these years in Major Crimes have taught her anything, it's not to get her hopes up.

There's no answer to her knock, and she pushes open the door to find the office is empty. It looks exactly as she remembers it—the view down over the car park, the meticulously tidy desk, the complete lack of any personalization whatsoever. Ruth is good at detail—at seeing the meaning in the supposedly trivial; she's learned as much about her temporary team from their desk detritus as she has from their personnel files. The toddler pictures stuck around the edge of Gislingham's computer screen; Everett's carefully tended pot plant and Somer's photo of a woman so like her they must be sisters; the casual scatter of Quinn's desk; the chocolate wrappers hidden in the bin under Baxter's. As for Fawley, he has a photograph too. His wife and son on a beach somewhere, tanned and barefoot, the sunset behind them redding their hair and making the resemblance between them even more striking. Jake Fawley is smiling, a little warily. It must have been taken the summer before he died.

"Sorry to keep you," says Challow, coming in behind her and closing the door. He has his thermal coffee mug in one hand.

"I thought it would be easier to do this one in person." He gestures to the chair and goes around the desk to his own seat.

"So what have you got?" says Gallagher, watching as he takes out a tub of sweeteners from his desk drawer and carefully counts out three.

"Let's do the dull stuff first. We've checked the samples we took from Graeme Scott against the plastic bag used in the Faith Appleford attack and none of the fingerprints are a match. The male DNA on it isn't his either, and there was no DNA from Faith in his car."

"We'd all but ruled him out for Faith anyway. His alibi checked out. What about Sasha?"

"None of the knives from the house, the cottage or the car were used in the attack, and there was no DNA from her in any of those places either. Sorry."

"You did check the front seat of the car, as well as the back?"

Challow gives her an old-fashioned look. "I do know what I'm doing, you know."

"Sorry—it's just that we were working on the theory that he might have offered Sasha a lift that night. But from what you just said—"

He's shaking his head. "*Highly* unlikely. It's extremely difficult to clean any car that well, and Scott's showed no sign of being vacuumed any time this millennium, never mind last week."

Gallagher sighs. "OK, so it looks like we can rule him out for Sasha too. But didn't you say you had some *non-dull* stuff as well?"

"Ah," says Challow, putting his stirrer down carefully on a napkin. "That's a good deal more interesting. The carrier bag features there too."

"OK," says Gallagher slowly.

"We ran the DNA profiles on the bag last week and didn't get a match in the database. But there was one thing we didn't do."

"And that was?"

"Comparing those profiles to one another. It wasn't a cock-up," he says quickly, seeing her face, "that's never been standard operating procedure—in fact, if Nina hadn't taken another look when we were doing the work on Scott—"

"You're losing me—"

"Two of the DNA profiles we found on the bag—turns out they're related."

"Related to what?"

He sits back in his chair. "To each other. Almost certainly mother and daughter."

Her heart sinks—wasn't he supposed to have something interesting? "That doesn't get us very far, though, does it. We've always known the bag could have been picked up at random. Off the street, from a bin, pretty much anyone could have handled it, frankly—"

But he's already shaking his head. "It's not as simple as that. The profiles aren't just related to each other. They're related to the victim."

Gallagher's eyes widen. "They're related to *Faith*?"

He nods. "We'd need to compare actual samples for it to stand up in court, but I'm as certain as I can be. That bag was previously handled by both Diane and Nadine Appleford."

* * *

"I'm Adam Fawley—they said my wife was here."

I'm struggling to get the words out, my heart is racing so hard I can hardly breathe, all the way in the car I've been telling myself—

The nurse at the reception desk glances at me, then checks a list. "Oh yes," she says crisply. "I think Dr. Choudhury is in with her now. Hold on a moment." She picks up a phone and dials a number.

My brain is in freefall—this woman, she's not meeting my gaze—she's not smiling either—wouldn't she do that, if everything was OK—so does that mean—

She puts the phone down. "Along the corridor on the right. Room 156."

Alex is sitting up in bed, in a hospital gown. And for a moment, that's all I can see—her pale face, the tears welling in her eyes—

"Oh, Adam, I'm so sorry."

I don't know how I get to the bed because my legs have gone, my lungs are iron—

"They called me—your office—they said you were there, that you collapsed—I told them they must be wrong—you weren't anywhere near that bloody office—"

"Your wife fainted, Mr. Fawley," says the doctor quietly. I hadn't even registered he was there. I turn and face him.

"We've run some tests, just to be on the safe side, but for the time being everything looks fine."

I stare at him like a dead man given a last-minute reprieve.

He nods. "The baby's fine. But your wife is going to have to take her own health much more seriously. Especially when it comes to eating properly and taking more rest."

I grip Alex's hand. Her fingers are cold.

"Why on earth did you go in today? You never said anything about it this morning."

"They were in a state—Sue rang me—I'm sorry, I'm so sorry."

The tears spill over now and her face crumples. "And then it happened and I thought—I thought—"

I pull her toward me and wrap my arms about her, stroking her hair. "It's OK. The baby's fine. *You're* fine."

"What you need now, Mrs. Fawley, is *rest*," says the doctor. "And I need a quick word with your husband."

"It's OK," I whisper. "I'll be back in a minute. Just try to relax."

Out in the corridor, Choudhury turns to face me.

"What you said in there—there's nothing wrong, is there? Nothing you're not telling me?"

He shakes his head. I think he's trying to look reassuring but it's not quite working. "We'll need to continue to monitor her blood pressure, but she's clearly extremely anxious and that's my principal concern at the moment. She's going to need complete rest, for at least the next two weeks. And absolutely no stress at all."

"I have been trying—"

"I'm sure you have. But you'll need to insist. I also spoke to your wife's GP. I gather she's received treatment for mental health issues before. Most recently in 2016."

I look away, take a deep breath. "Our son—he committed suicide. It was hard on both of us. Especially Alex."

"I see." His voice is softer now. "And before that?"

"That was completely different. And it was more anxiety than depression."

"What form did that anxiety take, do you remember? I know it was quite some time ago—"

Of course I remember. How could I not bloody *remember*.

"Trouble sleeping, one or two panic attacks. Listlessness, that sort of thing." I swallow. "Some nightmares."

Waking up terrified and screaming, the sweat pouring from her, her eyes dilated like an addict's, clinging to me so hard she drew blood—

"But it was nothing like this. Right now she's just worried about the baby."

He's looking at me. I'm obviously not making myself very clear.

"That first time—there was a reason."

* * *

"Shit, did that come out of the blue or what?"

It's Quinn. The team are gathered in the incident room.

"And Challow's absolutely sure?" asks Gis. "I mean, before we go crashing in like the bloody SAS?"

Gallagher sighs. "As sure as he can be. Both Diane *and* Nadine handled that bag."

"So what's he saying?" says Somer. "That Faith's *mother* did that to her? That her own *sister* was capable of something so—so—"

"We don't *know* they were involved," says Gallagher quickly. "As of now, it's just a theory. It's possible—though admittedly extremely unlikely—that the attacker just happened to find a bag the Applefords had thrown away."

But no one believes that, she can see it from their faces. Of course they don't.

"Well, there's one thing we *do* know," says Baxter, "and that's Diane Appleford's whereabouts that morning. We know exactly where she was when her daughter was attacked, and it wasn't the allotments on the Marston Ferry Road. And what about the bloody van—how the hell did she get hold of that?"

Ev is shaking her head. "Never mind *why*—why on earth she would even——"

"And Nadine's only fifteen," says Quinn. "No way she was driving any sort of vehicle—van, car, SUV, Chieftain tank——"

"She could have been with someone, though, couldn't she?" says Baxter, turning to him. "Not her mum—someone else—someone older who did the driving. And she could easily have taken a carrier bag from home."

Ev's eyes widen. "You really think she could have done that? Jesus."

Baxter shrugs. "How else do we explain it?"

"I could speak to the school?" offers Gis. "Make sure Nadine was definitely there that morning, like she said?"

"Yes, do that," says Gallagher. "But discreetly, please. If this gets out, the whole bloody sky is going to fall in."

* * *

I'm trying to do emails, but there's something about hospitals that numbs my brain. It's like muscle memory—an involuntary spasm of frozen recollection. All those times we had to take Jake to places like this. When he was self-harming, when we hadn't been able to stop him. The guarded looks, the careful questions. *Has he done this before? Can we speak to your GP?* Round and round and round again. All of us paralyzed in the face of something we couldn't explain, couldn't hope to understand.

I give up even trying to work now and toss the phone on to the chair next to me. On the bed, Alex stirs a little, but doesn't wake. She looks peaceful—more than she has for weeks. I wonder if that doctor has sedated her. There's a TV mounted on the wall in front of me, and I reach for the remote and turn it on, cutting the volume right down. It's the local news. They're running the reconstruction again, the last sighting of Sasha Blake. Her friends, her father, his new family. I've seen it before but I was cooking and distracted. Now, for the first time, I really watch.

*   *   *

Gislingham puts down the phone and looks up at Gallagher. "That was the head of Summertown High. Nadine Appleford *was* there the morning Faith was attacked."

"Thank God for that—"

But Gis hasn't finished. "Trouble is, they can't be sure what time she arrived. She missed registration, but she was there by 11:15—that was the first class she had that day. They initially assumed she was off sick—you know, that norovirus thing that's been doing the rounds."

"What time is registration?"

"Eight fifty. And when we first spoke to her, Diane Appleford said she dropped Nadine off at the school just after 8:00, on her way to work."

"So she was there with over half an hour to spare, and yet she still never made it to registration," says Gallagher thoughtfully.

She glances around and finds Everett. "Remind me, what time was Faith abducted?"

Everett looks up. "She left the house at 9:00, so probably about ten or fifteen minutes after that."

"And when did that minicab driver pick her up?"

"Eleven twenty," says Gislingham. "Give or take. But whoever attacked her was long gone by then. So if Nadine *was* involved she could easily have got back in time for that class. Whoever was driving the van could have dropped her off."

Gallagher turns to the map and looks again at the drawing pins marking where Faith lives, where she was abducted, where she was found.

"So her mother drops her off at school at just after 8:00, where she meets this mystery accomplice and they go back to Rydal Way together to intercept Faith?"

Gis gets up and joins her. He hesitates a moment then points to the sprawling site of Summertown High. "Or she could have just gone straight to the allotments from the school. That's no more than half a mile."

Gallagher is still staring at the board. "But whichever

way you play it, there must have been someone else involved. We just need to find out who it was."

* * *

Neither of them says much on the drive over. Whichever way they thought this case would go, they never dreamed it would bring them back here, to where it all started.

Somer pulls up outside and they sit there a moment, looking at the house. There's no sign of life, and she's half hoping there's no one in. But she knows that the most that will do is postpone the inevitable.

"What on earth are we going to say to Faith?" she says, turning to Everett now. "Hasn't she had enough to cope with, without this? It could break that family apart."

Ev reaches out and touches her on the shoulder. "You're catastrophizing. And even if the worst does happen, it's not *your* fault. And remember, we don't know Nadine did anything yet. There could be a completely innocent explanation."

"Oh, come on, Ev, you don't really think that."

Everett shrugs. "Until we ask, how do we know? All I *do* know is we have to do this, and if anyone can help Faith understand that, it's you."

They get out of the car and make their way slowly down the path. At the step, Everett turns and glances at Somer, then raises her hand to the bell.

Diane Appleford is clearly surprised to see them. "Oh, hello," she says. "We weren't expecting you, were we? I'm afraid Faith isn't here. She's at that new friend of hers. Jess something."

Everett can almost hear Somer's relief. She manages a thin smile. "Is Nadine in, Mrs. Appleford?"

"Nadine? Yes, she's upstairs in her room. Why—do you want to speak to her?"

"Something's come up, Mrs. Appleford. Could you ask Nadine to come down for a minute?"

A frown flickers across her brow. "OK."

She goes to the foot of the stairs and calls up. "Nadine? Are you there?"

They wait, but there's no sound of movement.

"Nadine!" calls Diane, louder. "Can you come down, sweetheart?"

Signs of life now; the creak of a bed, a door opening. A moment later Nadine appears at the top of the stairs. She sees them and retreats slightly. And Somer's heart sinks.

"What are they doing here?"

"They just want a word with you, darling. Can you come down?"

She starts down the stairs, slowly, pausing at each step.

"What's this about?" she says as she reaches the bottom.

"We've had some new information in from the forensic lab," says Everett. "So we need to check a few things, and talk to some people again."

Nadine seems to relax a little at this. "OK, what do you want to know?"

"It'd be better if you came with us. You and your mum."

"I don't want her to come," says Nadine quickly. "I'll do it on my own."

"What is all this?" says Diane, staring at her daughter and then at Everett. "You're worrying me now."

"We just need a quick chat with Nadine, Mrs. Apple-ford. It shouldn't take long."

What else can she say? *Your daughter could be there all night? This is looking really serious?*

"I can go on my own," says Nadine, stubborn now. "I don't want Mum there. I'm not a *baby*."

"Look, go and get your coat and we'll talk about it," says Diane. Nadine hesitates, then turns and makes her way back up the stairs.

* * *

Interview with Nadine Appleford, conducted at St. Aldate's Police Station, Oxford 8 April 2018, 6:15 p.m. In attendance, DI R. Gallagher, DC V. Everett, Ms. S. Rogers (designated Appropriate Adult)

RG: For the purposes of the tape, Ms. Sally Rogers is attending the interview as Miss Appleford's Appropriate Adult. Nadine is not under arrest, and has been told she can ask for her mother and a lawyer to be present at any time. At present, Mrs. Diane Appleford is observing in the adjacent room. So, Nadine, you must be wondering why you're here.

NA: [*shrugs*]

RG: Well, I'll tell you. We've done some more tests on the carrier bag that was used to choke your sister. There was DNA on it.

NA: [*silence*]

RG: Do you have any idea whose DNA it might be?

NA: [*looks away*]

    How should I know?

RG: You're absolutely sure about that?

NA: Look, stop *hassling* me—I told you I *don't know*.

RG: I'm afraid I think you do, Nadine. I don't know
    how much you know about DNA, but one of the
    things it can tell you is a person's gender. It
    can also show if two people are related to
    each other. Now we've done those extra tests,
    we know that two of the people who'd previously
    handled the carrier bag were related. Almost
    certainly a mother and daughter.

NA: [*folds arms*]

    So?

RG: You don't know who that mother and daughter
    might be?

NA: I *told* you—it's nothing to do with me. I don't
    know why you keep asking me this stuff.

RG: [*passes across a sheet of paper*]

    These are the results, Nadine. And they show—
    without the slightest possibility of a
    doubt—who that mother and daughter are. It's
    you, Nadine. You and your mum.

NA: No it isn't—it can't be. They must've got it wrong.

RG: Like I said, I'm afraid there's no possibility
    of a mistake. So I'm going to ask you again.
    What can you tell us about what happened to
    your sister?

NA: [*becoming distressed*]

    I *told* you—it *wasn't me*.

327

RG: You can't explain why that particular bag
ended up being used in the attack on your
sister?

NA: How should I know? Someone must have found it
or something.

RG: You must know that's extremely unlikely—

NA: I told you—I *don't know*—

SR: I think we should move on, Inspector.

RG: Where were you the morning Faith was attacked,
Nadine?

NA: At school. I told you.

RG: Do you know anyone who drives a van?

NA: No.

RG: An estate car, a four-by-four, anything like
that?

NA: No.

RG: Do you have a good relationship with your
sister?

NA: What's that got to do with it?

RG: There were times I could have scratched my
sister's eyes out, when I was your age. She
used to drive me completely mad. You've never
felt like that?

NA: No.

RG: Even though you've had to move schools
because of her? Even though you had to leave
all your friends behind? That must have been
tough.

NA: It wasn't that bad. And anyway, I've got new
friends now.

RG: Faith was very upset about the attack, wasn't she?

NA: Yeah, so?

RG: And since then, the whole thing has been really hard for her.

NA: I suppose so.

RG: I'm sure you never meant that to happen.

NA: I *didn't do it*—I told you already. It was nothing to do with me.

[*near to tears*]

Why do you keep on asking me this shit?

RG: We've spoken to your school, and they say you didn't make it to registration the morning your sister was attacked. They say you were in your Geography class at 11:15, but they don't know where you were before that. Can you explain that for us?

NA: [*silence*]

RG: Were you at the allotments, Nadine? Were you involved in what happened to your sister?

NA: [*silence*]

VE: Why should you take all the blame, Nadine? We know there must have been someone else involved. Someone who was driving the van. Who is it, Nadine? Why are you protecting them?

NA: [*to the designated adult*]

Can I go home now?

RG: I'm afraid you can't, Nadine. Not yet. But we can take a break if you want to do that.

SR: I think that would be a very good idea.

VE: Interview suspended at 18:35.

* * *

"It was like watching that TV thing," says Quinn. "What's it called? The one where they work out people are lying."

"*Faking It*," says Somer.

"But I'm right, aren't I?" says Quinn, turning to her. "She might not have been saying anything out loud but her body language was at full volume. If she was bloody Pinocchio her nose would be in sodding Birmingham by now."

"That's as may be," says Gislingham heavily, "but it ain't going to tell us who was driving that van, is it?"

* * *

It's raining in Blackbird Leys. A teeming, insistent, disheartening rain that only makes the surroundings more demoralizing. Everett parks her Mini under a street lamp—she's no fool—then turns up her collar and runs the last few yards to the Brotherton house. It takes a long time for the door to open.

"What do you want?" asks the old man. He's still wearing the same beige slacks, but there's a pinny around his waist now, and an oven glove in one hand. "Ashley isn't here."

"I'm really sorry to bother you, Mr. Brotherton. I just wanted to ask you a quick question. You—not Ashley."

He gives her a long look. "Is that an 'official' question?"

Everett flushes a little. Because he's right: she didn't tell anyone she was coming. She makes a rueful face. "Not quite."

"And is answering it going to land Ash in it?"

"No," she says quickly. "No, I'm pretty sure not. In fact, it might help."

He takes a step back. "You'd better come in then. You're going to catch your death out there."

* * *

The address Somer is looking for has taken some finding, especially in the dark and the rain, but she eventually pulls up outside a modern block just off the Iffley Road. She checks the flat number then splashes down the path to the main door.

She presses the buzzer and the entryphone crackles into life. "Who's that?"

"Erica Somer. Is that Jess?"

A pause. "Who gave you this address?"

"Faith's mum. She said Faith was coming over to see you this evening. Is she there?"

The door opens and a couple of girls come out, wrapped up snug in fur-hooded parkas and boots. They're both laughing. Somer is seriously tempted to dart in behind them before the door closes, but she forces herself not to: she needs Jess and Faith to feel they're in control.

She returns to the entryphone. "I just wanted to check Faith is OK."

There's a silence, and then the sound of the door lock being released.

"Come up."

The flat is on the top floor. The lift isn't working so Somer is slowing down by the time she gets to the right landing. But ahead of her a door is already open. Jess is standing there. It's only just gone 9:00 but she's in PJs and a long paisley dressing gown that looks like it was originally a man's.

She raises an eyebrow when she sees Somer. "We must stop meeting like this."

She has a mug in one hand. Steam is rising from it. Not coffee though, something earthy, herbal.

"How is she?" asks Somer.

Jess makes a face. "Not great."

They're keeping their voices low. As if someone's ill.

"Her mum called about twenty minutes ago," continues Jess. "She said you've arrested Nadine—actually *arrested* her."

Somer sighs. "I'm sorry—we really didn't have much choice. Not with the evidence we now have."

"Faith wasn't too bad before that, but she's been crying ever since. She can't believe Nadine could have done that to her."

"We don't know if she did. Not yet."

Jess shrugs. "You must think it's possible or you wouldn't be questioning her. Have *you* got a sister?"

Somer hesitates, then nods. "Yes. Actually, I do."

"Well then. How would you like it?"

* * *

"I don't know her name," says Mr. Brotherton, dragging the teabag out of the mug and dropping it in the bin.

"But Ashley does have a girlfriend?"

The old man snorts. "More like *had*, if you ask me. I don't think he's heard a peep out of her since all this started."

332

Everett's detective antennae flicker at this. It might mean nothing, but on the other hand—

"What's her name?" she says, taking the proffered mug.

"Search me. He doesn't bring 'em here."

Ev's heart sinks. "You've never seen her at all?"

The old man ferrets about in the cupboard for biscuits and comes up with garibaldis. She tries not to think about how long the packet has been in there.

He shuffles across to the table and sits down. "I did see her once or twice at a distance. A couple of months ago, maybe? But she had her back to me. Brown hair, longish."

Which could be almost anyone, thinks Everett. But it could also be Nadine Appleford.

"One thing I do remember though," he says, offering her the packet of biscuits. "He was teaching her to drive."

*   *   *

Somer takes a seat on the armchair opposite Faith. She has her arms wrapped around her legs and one cheek is resting on her knees. A waffle blanket has been tucked around her shoulders.

"How are you?" says Somer softly.

There's no reply. She can see the tears on the girl's face.

"I just came to see how you were doing. There isn't much I can tell you at the moment, I'm afraid."

Faith seems to register Somer's presence for the first

time. She raises her head and wipes her eyes. "Mum said that carrier bag came from our house."

Somer sighs. "I know. We still can't explain that. I'm afraid Nadine's not saying very much."

Faith drops her head again. Somer can't imagine what it must be like—to discover someone who's supposed to love you has betrayed you. And in such a cruel and deliberate and spiteful way.

"Do you know many of Nadine's friends?"

Faith looks up at her then shakes her head.

"Do any of them have a van? Any sort of vehicle that might have been the one you were taken in?"

Another tiny shake of the head; the tears have started again. She's begun to rock gently, her hands gripping tighter around her knees.

"I'm sorry, Faith, but I had to ask."

Jess slides down next to Faith on the sofa and puts a hand gently on her shoulder. "I'll put some food on in a bit," she whispers. "Mac and cheese, your favorite."

There's no acknowledgment from Faith, but she doesn't push the hand away.

When Somer stops at the front door a few minutes later and turns back to look at them, they're still sitting there, in the same position; the only sounds the patter of rain against the windows and the soft hiss of the gas fire.

* * *

Sent: Mon 08/04/2018, 21.55   **Importance: High**
From: DCVerityEverett@ThamesValley.police.uk
To: DIRuthGallagher@ThamesValley.police.uk

Subject: Ashley Brotherton—URGENT

Something's been bugging me about the whole
Nadine thing so I just went over and spoke to Ashley's
grandfather again. He told me Ashley had a girlfriend he
was <u>teaching to drive</u>. In car parks, places like that.
Mr. Brotherton doesn't know her name and only has a
vague description but from what he said, it could definitely
be Nadine.

So just because she's only 15 and doesn't have a license
doesn't mean she couldn't physically drive that van. And if
she was his girlfriend she'd know about the spare key by
the back door too.

I think it's possible Nadine got a bus down there the
morning Faith was attacked and "borrowed" the van while
Ashley and his granddad were at the funeral. The timing is
really <u>really</u> tight but I think she could just about have done
it. And Mr. Brotherton said Ashley parked the van in the
next street that day, to make sure there was room for the
funeral cars, which would have made it a lot easier for
someone to take it without anyone noticing.

I know it's a crazy long shot, but it <u>is</u> feasible. Remember
what that witness said about the van driver having their cap
pulled down low over their face? That would make sense, if
it was Nadine. She wouldn't want anyone to clock how
young she is.

And it would also give us a v. good reason why she's refusing to tell us who her accomplice was: she can't do that, because <u>she never had one</u>.

VE

* * *

"DC Everett? It's Ruth Gallagher—I just got your email."

Gallagher is on her hands-free in the car, at the traffic lights in Summertown. Everett is only a hundred yards away, if she did but know it, upstairs in her flat, tipping a can of cat food into a bowl with her free hand.

"That was a damn good hunch of yours—well done."

"Thanks—it just suddenly came to me—if someone borrowed Ashley's van, why not a girlfriend? Why not Nadine?"

"You're right about the timing though—she'd need miraculously good bus connections. And both ways: she didn't just have to collect that van from Blackbird Leys, she had to get it back there too, *and* get back to school."

"I know, but it's only five miles—it could be done. Just."

"Well, it may be we'll have to put that to the test ourselves, but first things first. Have you spoken to Ashley?"

Gallagher can hear a vague wailing noise in the background; not a baby though, more like a cat. A particularly insistent cat.

"I tried," says Everett, raising her voice a little, "but since he can't work with his cut hand he's gone up to Blackpool with some mates. I'm afraid he's not picking up his phone."

"Did you ask his granddad to have a go? Ashley's more likely to answer him than some number he doesn't recognize."

"Yes, I did, but it just went to voicemail. But don't worry, he's promised to try again first thing tomorrow. And if I have to, I'll go over there and watch him do it."

* * *

Alex is still asleep when I get to the hospital. But she stirs a little when I take a seat next to the bed, and opens her eyes. She smiles, that delicious slow first-thing-in-the-morning smile of hers that makes my heart turn over.

"Shouldn't you be at work by now, Detective Inspector Fawley?"

"I think community outreach can do without me for a while."

Yesterday it was a talk to the local Deaf Club about how the police deal with vulnerable witnesses; today it's a Careers session at Cuttleslowe Secondary. It's important stuff and someone should be doing it. I'd just rather it wasn't me.

Alex sits up now, slowly, pulling the bedclothes around her. Instinctively, without thinking. As if she's protecting the baby, even from me. Outside, in the corridor, I can hear the rattling trundle of the breakfast trolley.

I reach across and take her hand. "I can't stay too long but I'll come back later, as soon as I can get away."

She smiles, but this time it's a sad thin affair. "Ironic,

337

isn't it. All those years I wanted you not to work so late and now you're home early all the time, and it's all my fault."

"It's *not* your fault, and with luck it won't be for much longer. I heard on the grapevine that Ruth Gallagher may be near an arrest for Sasha Blake. One of her teachers. And if it *was* him, he was in north Wales in the late nineties, so there's no way he's a Parrie suspect we just failed to find. So try to put it out of your mind, OK?"

"You like her, don't you?" she says. "This Ruth Gallagher."

"Yes, I do. She's good at the job but she doesn't make a show of it. And she's managed to get the team doing what she wants without forcing them to work a whole different way. That's not easy."

"Even Quinn?" says Alex.

"Even Quinn. Probably because she's got a teenage boy at home and she's just transferred the technique."

We exchange a smile. I'm telling myself I can see a little more color in her cheeks now, and perhaps I can.

I get up and give her hand a last squeeze.

"Adam?" she says as I get to the door. But when I turn again she seems to have changed her mind.

"It's nothing," she says. "It'll keep."

* * *

"So that's as far as we've got," says Ruth Gallagher. "Full marks to Everett, but until we can speak to Ashley himself, it's all still supposition."

It's the morning meeting and the room is full. The sense of anticipation is now as palpable as the smell of

338

office-machine coffee. Perhaps they really are going to finally crack this bloody case.

"What's Nadine saying?" says Gislingham.

"Nothing," replies Gallagher. "No surprises there. Though her mother claims a) she's never heard of anyone called Ashley Brotherton, and b) Nadine doesn't have a boyfriend. Which, as any parent of a teenager will know, has no evidentiary value whatsoever. But that being the case, and with nothing else to fall back on, I had no option but to bail Nadine and send her home."

Quinn gets up and goes to the whiteboard. He's the only one with a proper shop-bought coffee; no surprises there either. He stares at the photos for a moment then turns to the group. "Well, if you ask me, we're barking up totally the wrong tree on this one."

No one *was* asking you, thinks Everett, her hackles rising. Typical bloody Quinn to stick a spoke in.

"Why do you say that?" asks Gallagher evenly.

"Well, you only have to look at her—Nadine, I mean. Ashley Brotherton's way out of her league. He wouldn't look at her twice."

There's a ripple around the room at that. Some of them may have been thinking it, but only Quinn would actually come right out and say it.

Gallagher raises an eyebrow. "One thing I've learned in this job, DC Quinn, is that if you base an investigation on your own personal assumptions, you're likely to land yourself well in the shit."

Somer and Everett exchange a glance: neither have worked for a female DI before, but it clearly has its upsides.

"So are we clear?" she continues, looking around the

room. "Regardless of DC Quinn's misgivings, we're going to assume there *is* a connection between Nadine and Ashley Brotherton, until such time as we prove there isn't. And while we're doing that, we're also going to work out if it was physically possible for that girl to get to Blackbird Leys and back on April 1st and still be in school for double Geography. Extra brownie points on offer for anyone who volunteers to do the buses, otherwise I just pick a victim."

* * *

Adam Fawley
9 April 2018
10.05

I see her as soon as I pull up in the car park. She'd be hard to miss anywhere, and even more so in this place. She's standing just outside the entrance, a messenger bag slung over one shoulder, her long dark-red hair in a jaunty ponytail. Over-the-knee boots laced up the front and a skirt that only gets halfway down her thighs. She looks at her watch twice in the time it takes me to lock the car. And then she sees me.

"DI Fawley," she says, coming quickly in my direction. There's no question in her voice, no rising intonation. She knows who I am.

"I'm busy. Talk to the press office."

She comes to a halt, directly in my path. "I already did. They won't tell me anything."

"Well, I'm not going to tell you anything either. It's not even my case any more. As you well know."

I start walking again, and she follows me. "But you're

340

still part of it—if they find the killer, that's going to have a direct impact on the Parrie case. That's what I'm working on—"

"Look, Ms.—?"

"Bowen. Nicole Bowen."

"It's DI Gallagher's investigation. Talk to her."

She makes a face. "I did. She told me to sod off. Unquote."

I can't help a dry smile at that. Then over the woman's shoulder I see a car signal and pull in from the main road. It's a red Jaguar coupé, which I'm fairly sure I've seen before. A hunch that hardens into conviction when I see who's driving. It's Victoria Parker; Isabel's mother. And I don't want Nicole bloody Bowen anywhere near her.

I turn away and start walking, but Bowen keeps pace with me. "I heard a rumor," she says. "They say you've arrested someone. For the Blake murder."

I stop and turn to face her. "Who told you that?"

She comes a step closer. "Word is it's one of her teachers. Graeme Scott?"

I don't control my face quickly enough—she sees the blow land. On the other side of the car park Victoria Parker is already locking her car and starting toward me.

"So it's true," says Bowen, her eyes searching mine. And one thing I do know: this woman needs to get herself a much better poker face if she wants a career in crime reporting—that knowing smirk of hers is going to get every copper's back up.

"Look, Ms. Bowen, I have better things to do than standing here listening to wild, uninformed speculation. If you want to keep your job, don't even think about doing that in public or putting any of it in your bloody documentary. Do I make myself clear? Good. Now, if you'll excuse me."

There must be something in my face because this time she doesn't try to follow. Victoria Parker has stopped at the main door now and raises an eyebrow as I approach. "Problem?"

"Press," I say. "Occupational hazard in a case like this, I'm afraid. Was there something we can help you with?"

"This terrible thing with Sasha Blake—the rumor mill at the school's gone into complete overdrive." She looks embarrassed. "I mean, I don't usually do the whole gossip at the gate thing, but I was talking to Leah Waddell's mum and I suddenly thought—I mean, I'd totally forgotten about it before that, but—"

She's a little flushed now. "Sorry, I'm gabbling, aren't I? It's probably nothing—"

"Mrs. Parker, there's one thing I've learned from doing this job: if people make the sort of effort you have to come to a police station it's very rarely for 'nothing.' So why don't you come inside and tell me what this is about and I'll find someone you can speak to."

Her eyes widen. "Can't I talk to you?"

I shake my head. "Not formally, no. I'm not part of the investigation any more. But there's DS Gislingham, or DC Somer if you'd prefer to talk to a woman—"

She hesitates, then nods. "OK. But I've only got half an hour. I told Isabel I was going to Waitrose. I didn't want her to know I was coming here."

* * *

Gallagher didn't have to dump the bus job on anyone in the end, because Asante volunteered. To a ripple of smirks and an audible mutter of "teacher's pet" from Quinn. But Asante doesn't care. He's always had a healthy respect for enlightened self-interest. And besides, the rain has finally stopped and he could do with some fresh air.

He parks the car in a side road near Summertown High, then walks up to the bus stop. There's one into town in five minutes.

*   *   *

Adam Fawley
9 April 2018
10.26

When I push open the door to the incident room, Gislingham is up at the front, gesturing toward the whiteboard. People are clustered close around him. They're all on their feet. And take it from me, as a snap indicator of case morale, the ratio of sit to stand is usually pretty reliable. "Up and at 'em" isn't just a cliché—not in this job.

Heads turn, people register it's me.

"We were just going through the latest developments, sir," he begins.

I move up toward the front. "I'm sorry to barge in but this can't wait. There's a witness downstairs who needs someone to take her statement."

Gislingham frowns slightly. "A statement about what?"

"About Sasha Blake. And Graeme Scott."

*   *   *

Interview with Graeme Scott, conducted at
St. Aldate's Police Station, Oxford
9 April 2018, 11:52 a.m.
In attendance, DC G. Quinn, DC A. Baxter,
Mrs. D. Owen (solicitor)

DO: I assume you've had a chance to check my
    client's alibi by now, so I'm at a loss to
    know what this is about.

GQ: The convenience store on Cherwell Drive
    has supplied us with their till receipts
    for the morning of April 1st, so we have
    confirmed that your client purchased milk
    at 9:16.

DO: Which means he couldn't possibly have
    committed the assault on Faith Appleford. Have
    you had the results of the forensic tests on
    his car?

GQ: We have.

DO: And? For heaven's sake, Constable, this is
    like drawing teeth.

GQ: There is no trace of either Faith Appleford or
    Sasha Blake in Mr. Scott's vehicle.

GS: [*slamming his hands on the table*]
    There—what did I tell you—I had *nothing to do
    with it*—

DO: In that case, perhaps you could explain what
    on earth we are doing here?

GQ: This is in relation to another incident.
    One that took place some days before Sasha
    died.

344

GS: I don't know what you're talking about.

GQ: Where were you on the morning of Saturday 17th
     March, Mr. Scott, around 10:45?

GS: I have no bloody idea.

GQ: Are you sure? You don't remember being on
     Walton Street that morning? That stretch along
     by the Blavatnik building? Because we have a
     witness who says you were.

* * *

Adam Fawley
9 April 2018
12.17

When I push open the door, Somer is already there, watching on the video screen.

"Sorry, I didn't realize anyone was in here."

I shouldn't be in here either, as I'm sure Somer knows. She looks as if she's tempted to say something but evidently decides against it. I move closer to the screen and frown a little.

"It's just Quinn and Baxter doing the interview? Didn't Gallagher want to be in on this?"

I glance back at her and realize she's gone very red. "Oh," she says, "didn't DI Gallagher say?"

"Say what?"

"We ruled Scott out. There was no DNA in his car—either from Faith or Sasha. It wasn't him."

I turn back to the screen so she can't see my face. I know Gallagher didn't do it deliberately but no one likes being made to look like a prat. Not in front of their own team. *My* team. Not hers; *mine*. The one I'm going to have

345

to carry on running, long after she's hauled her wretched stack of files back to Major Crimes.

"I'm sure she meant to tell you, sir. It's just, well, things got a bit crazy this morning."

"It's fine, Somer. Really." But I don't turn to look at her. And I'm not going to. Not until I feel the heat on my face subside. But then I realize what's quite literally staring me in the face and turn back to her again.

"Sorry, I don't get it. If Gallagher's ruled Scott out, why are you bothering to interview him at all?"

She holds my gaze this time. "DI Gallagher may want to charge him with stalking."

I frown. "Even though the person he stalked is dead? That's not going to be easy to prove."

"I know, sir, but she's worried he'll do it again. And given that he's a teacher—" She shrugs. "DI Gallagher's hoping that what Mrs. Parker told us might be enough to persuade the CPS it's worth a try."

All of which makes sense. But the "us" is still painful. Because I'm not part of it, even though it was me Victoria Parker came to see. It's them and me right now, not "we."

Somer turns back to the screen and sighs. "But even with a witness it's going to be yet another case of *he said/ she said.*"

I'm still watching the screen.

"Give the Blavatnik a call," I say slowly. "And ask them about their CCTV."

*　*　*

GQ: So, do you remember now, Mr. Scott?

GS: I suppose I may have been there. I shop in Jericho quite a lot.

GQ: Like I said, this was outside the Blavatnik building. You know where I'm talking about, right?

GS: Of course I do—

DO: What relevance does this have, Officer?

AB: Our witness saw Mr. Scott outside the building that morning. He was sitting in his car.

DO: There's no law against sitting in your own car. Or was he on a yellow line, is that it? You've run out of other options so you're resorting to minor parking infractions?

GQ: According to our witness, Sasha Blake was also on Walton Street that morning. But you already knew that, didn't you, Mr. Scott?

GS: I told you—I go there quite often at the weekends.

GQ: Our witness was in a coffee shop opposite the Blavatnik, waiting to meet her daughter. She was at a window seat and she remembers seeing a car just like yours parked on the other side of the road. And let's face it, we're not talking about a bog-standard Ford Mondeo here, are we? Your car is extremely distinctive.

DO: But it's not unique—was your witness able to identify who was driving? Because I have to tell you, I very much doubt it.

GQ: Oh, she can identify him all right. Because
    she's met him before, more than once. He
    teaches her daughter.

DO: [*pause*]
    All the same—

GQ: So let's try the question again, shall we, Mr.
    Scott? Where were you on the morning of
    Saturday 17th March?

* * *

Adam Fawley
9 April 2018
12.56

"They sent the footage over straightaway," says Somer as she opens the digital file on her laptop and navigates to the right place. "Baxter went seriously gadget-geek when he saw it."

And I can see why. The images aren't just high-res, they're full color; you can actually see people's features, the looks on their faces. The camera is angled down over the broad concourse in front of the Blavatnik building and the stretch of Walton Street immediately opposite. There's a time code on the bottom left of the screen; the date is 17:03:18.

Somer presses play and forward to 10:04. A couple of students are talking animatedly near the Blavatnik doors. On the opposite pavement, an elderly man is pushing a tartan shopping trolley. He's almost bent double, his head twisted to one side so he can see where he's going. And in the coffee shop, Victoria Parker is queueing up for a coffee before taking a seat on the bench in the window. She gets out her phone and starts tapping the screen, glancing up every few seconds to scan the road. At 10:14, a pale blue Morris Traveller pulls in on the opposite side of the street. The driver stops the car, but he doesn't get out. He looks up and down the street then opens a magazine.

"The latest edition of *Recreational Stalking*, no doubt," I mutter darkly.

Somer glances up but doesn't say anything.

She fast-forwards the footage again, then stops when we see a girl approaching from the left-hand side.

"It's Sasha," says Somer. "Looks like she must have come from the center of town."

We watch as the girl crosses the road by the coffee shop, hitching her pink satchel over her shoulder as she goes. She's wearing a fringed jacket, a beanie and a pair of black ankle boots. At this distance, and with her hair under the hat, she looks unnervingly like Somer, which judging from her face, isn't lost on Somer either. Victoria Parker looks up, and I know that what she told us was absolutely true: she did see Sasha that day, and she did see Graeme Scott.

We rewind and watch it again, and then again. Staring at Sasha as she dodges the traffic and heads straight into the Blavatnik building, disappearing out of view directly beneath the camera. And each time we run it we can clearly see the man in the car lower his magazine and stare intently at the girl. A few moments later Isabel, Leah and Patsie appear from the same direction as Sasha and stop outside the café. Victoria Parker gets to her feet and starts to pick up her things.

Somer presses pause and turns to face me.

"OK," I say. "If I'm Scott's lawyer I'm going to claim this is pure chance. He wasn't stalking her, he wasn't even following her, he was just innocently shopping for bog roll in the Co-op and suddenly, *bam*, there she was."

"But that's just it," says Somer, "he doesn't buy anything. He doesn't even get out of the car. He's only there for one reason and that's Sasha Blake."

"If that's true it had to be planned, right?"

She nods.

"So how did he know she'd be there? At that precise place and that precise time?"

"Actually, I think I may have an answer to that." She picks up her phone and flicks to a web page. "I did a quick check on the Blavatnik website and there was a talk that morning that was open to the public. *Art and Power in Renaissance Florence.* That's exactly the sort of thing Scott might have mentioned to Sasha. He's already admitted 'encouraging' her, the bloody creep."

But I'm only half listening. I've rewound the footage and I'm looking at it again.

"Here," I say, freezing it and pointing. "See that?"

Evidently she hasn't, because she moves a little closer.

"Just before Sasha crosses the road. That woman there, wheeling the bike."

She must be fifty, perhaps fifty-five, with longish blond hair and a turquoise coat. She's going in the opposite direction to Sasha, so there's a point when they have to pass each other on the crowded pavement. A few moments later the woman suddenly stops and stares at something, clearly startled, before turning and looking back toward

Sasha as she crosses the road. Then she shakes her head and carries on the way she was going.

"Is she looking at Scott?" says Somer.

"I don't think so. He's on the other side of the road, so I doubt he's in her line of sight. And he's just sitting in his car—there's nothing to provoke a reaction like that."

Somer looks more closely at the screen. "Victoria's on her phone—she wouldn't have seen anything. Damn."

"I doubt she'd have seen much anyway—not from inside the shop. The angle's all wrong."

"I suppose we could try to track down the woman with the bike," begins Somer, "but we're going to struggle to find her after all this time—"

"We don't need to. Whatever that woman saw, it must have been right outside the OUP building. What's the betting they have CCTV too."

* * *

It's the first really dry afternoon for over a week, and Ursula Hollis decides to take advantage. She hasn't been further than the end of the street for days and is starting to get a bit cabin crazy. Her elderly Labrador hasn't exactly complained, but they could both do with blowing the cobwebs away. She unhooks the lead from the rack by the door and smiles as the dog gets rather laboriously to his feet. You can almost hear him sigh.

"Come on, Bruno, it's not that bad. Just down to the Vicky Arms and back. There might even be rabbits."

It's a long time since Bruno chased anything, let alone a rabbit. There are silver hairs around that chocolate muzzle these days. She rubs him behind the ears and drops a quick kiss on his brow, trying not to think about what she's going to do without him, when he's gone.

Even if the weather's improved there's still hardly anyone about outside. In five minutes, the only people she passes are a man from BT doing something complicated with wiring in a green box and Jenny from number 4 wrestling with her bins.

She gets to the junction, zips her puffa jacket up a little further against the wind and heads down toward Mill Lane.

* * *

Adam Fawley
9 April 2018
13.13

"But the OUP didn't have anything?"

To her credit, Gallagher looked neither surprised nor wary when Somer turned up at her office with me in tow. I'm not sure I'd have been so sanguine about it, if the roles were reversed.

Somer shakes her head. "It's too long ago—they don't keep their CCTV footage that long. And they're not even sure the camera would have been pointing the right way anyway."

Gallagher sits back and her shoulders sag a little. "So we've no way of knowing what that woman saw, barring tracking her down. And even if we could find her it could be nothing—someone on a unicycle, that duck that got into last week's *Oxford Mail*—any bloody thing."

It's that sort of town; I saw a bloke dressed as a giraffe

on the Woodstock Road last week. *#OnlyinOxford* even has its own bloody hashtag. So yes, this could all be a complete wild-goose chase. But something tells me it isn't. That woman on Walton Street saw something—something that shocked her enough to stop her in her tracks. And I suddenly have a cold feeling in my gut about what it might be.

Somer makes a despairing face. "I don't think there's anything else we can do."

I look at her and then turn to Gallagher. "Yes," I say. "There is."

* * *

Interview with Graeme Scott, conducted at
St. Aldate's Police Station, Oxford
9 April 2018, 2:05 p.m.
In attendance, DI R. Gallagher, DC E. Somer,
Mrs. D. Owen (solicitor)

RG: For the purposes of the tape, DI Ruth Gallagher and DC Erica Somer will now be conducting this interview. I hope you enjoyed your lunch break, Mr. Scott; perhaps we could now return to the subject you were discussing with DC Quinn. Since you were last in this room we have obtained CCTV from the Blavatnik School of Government from the morning in question, and you are quite clearly visible on camera.

DO: I trust you will make this footage available?

RG: Of course. So, Mr. Scott, do you remember that morning now?

GS: If you say I was there, I suppose I must have been.

ES: There was a talk at the Blavatnik that we believe Sasha was going to. A talk about Renaissance Florence—is that ringing a bell?

GS: Now you mention it, I think I did point that out to Sasha. I'm on their mailing list.

ES: So you knew she'd be there.

GS: I didn't *know* she'd be there. I just mentioned it to her. My pupils don't keep me informed about their social lives, Inspector.

RG: But you knew there was a good chance she'd go, didn't you? Good enough for you to arrange to be there yourself. Just in case.

GS: Like I said, I often shop in Jericho.

ES: Only you didn't. You didn't even get out of your car. You just sat there. Watching.

GS: I wasn't *watching*. I'm not some sort of pervert—

RG: That's as may be. But you were watching her, all the same. And what I want to know now, Mr. Scott, is what *exactly* it was that you saw.

* * *

Adam Fawley
9 April 2018
14.37

"Do we believe him? Do we *actually* believe him?"

I don't think I've ever seen Somer's face so pale. Ever since she and Gallagher came out of the interview room she's been pacing up and down, trying to walk off the nervous energy, the sheer incredulity. Gallagher has gone the other way: she's sitting at the table, barely moving, but I can sense the din in her mind, even from the other side of the room.

Somer turns to Gallagher and repeats her question. "Well, do we? It's crazy—"

"But possible," says Gallagher quietly. "You know it is."

"But we can't go hauling people in for questioning based on *that*—even if it *is* true—even if he's not still lying through his bloody teeth, which he has *every* reason to do right now—"

I take a deep breath. "I don't think he is. I think he's telling the truth."

Gallagher looks across at me. "But Somer has a point, doesn't she. Even if you're right, we need a lot more than just his word. And without either the CCTV or that witness—" She shrugs helplessly. "We're stuck, aren't we?"

But I'm not so sure.

I get up and reach for my jacket.

"Where are you going?"

"Keep Scott here. There's someone I need to talk to."

* * *

Bruno picks up his pace as they get toward the turning for the pub. More bushes, more litter, more interesting smells. Ursula has to drag him away from a particularly well-loved lamppost, only to find him bounding off suddenly and ploughing into a ditch half-filled with blackish water. She goes to the edge and peers down, frowning at where he's worrying away at something. Which isn't like Bruno; he hasn't done anything like this for months. At first she can't see what he's got hold of, but then the dog moves and she catches sight of something pink. She recoils a little—she's had her fill of disemboweled rats over the years—but something about the shape, the color—

A moment later she's taking out her mobile phone.

"Is that Thames Valley Police? My name is Ursula Hollis. It's about that girl—Sasha Blake. I think you need to come."

* * *

We look at the footage again and then the woman sits back in her chair. She's in her seventies, with short thick white hair and a rather tired navy cardigan. But there's nothing tired about the look on her face. She's one of the sharpest people I've encountered in a long time. When I first met her, I told Alex she reminded me of that woman who used to play Miss Marple on TV in the eighties. I didn't realize then how close to home that was.

"It was a pretty good stab—for an amateur," she says, turning slightly toward me. I sense a little stiffness in her movement and sit forward so she can see me more easily. "Perhaps you should consider learning to do it properly. Looks like it might come in handy in your line of work."

I smile. "Only if you promise to teach me. But I was right, yes? That's what you're saying?"

She gives me a heavy look. "I'm afraid so. Judging from what I've just seen, there's something very wrong here, Inspector. Very wrong indeed."

* * *

The house is a new build on the outskirts of Marston, designed to look old in that Poundbury sort of way Somer always distrusts. It's tidy, well-kempt, but curiously lifeless, and the woman who opens the door is very much the same.

"Mrs. Webb? I'm DC Erica Somer and this is DC Everett. We'd like a quick word with Patsie if she's around?"

Denise Webb frowns. "She's not at the Blakes?'"'

"No. We did call Mrs. Blake, but she said she hadn't seen her."

"I suppose she must be here then," she says. "You'd better come in."

"You haven't seen her today?"

The woman shrugs. "You know what teenagers are like—if you see them at mealtimes you're doing well."

They follow her into the hall and through to the kitchen. The house has a slightly echoey quality to it, as if it's not fully furnished, not quite lived in. It feels like a show home, and the studiously monotonous color schemes aren't helping.

"Have you been here long?" asks Somer.

"A couple of years. Since my husband left."

Somer bites her lip; this job is strewn with bear traps. "I'm sorry."

"Life goes on," she says. "You don't have any choice. Not if you have kids."

"Patsie has brothers and sisters?"

"Just a brother. Ollie. He's at college in Cardiff. Engineering."

Everett looks around. "It's a big house for just the two of you."

She shrugs. "My boyfriend's here on and off. But Patsie spends more time at her friends' than she does here."

There was a quick bitterness in her voice, but then it's gone just as fast and she shrugs again. "Like I said, life goes on. Her room's upstairs. You can't miss it."

The staircase is carpeted in thick taupe-brown shagpile that seems to swallow their feet. The curious sense of muffledness grows even stronger as they make their way soundlessly up the steps, past pictures that are an odd mix of Ikea and Victorian kitsch. Somer frowns. She can't get a handle on this place at all. With her expensive blond highlights and Boden top, Denise Webb looks full-on yummy mummy, but when she turned away Somer could see the coils of a snake tattoo creeping up from under her sweater and across the back of her neck.

At the top of the stairs she stops and looks around, but Ev is already touching her arm and pointing. The door to the room on the left is half open. It's obviously the master suite, given the size of it. The bed is made, but there are clothes strewn across it. Male clothes. But again, not the ones Somer might have expected. No suits or shirts, but T-shirts, heavy-duty jeans, a tool belt. And on the floor, a pair of steel-capped work boots.

"Maybe it isn't a coincidence that Patsie's suddenly spending a lot of her time somewhere else," says Ev in a low tone.

They exchange a glance.

"Remind me, will you," says Somer softly, "to check where this bloke was the night Sasha disappeared."

Ev's eyes widen. "You don't think—"

"No, I don't. I just want to cover all the bases, that's all. We don't want anything coming back to haunt us, just because we couldn't be bothered to do a couple of routine checks."

She doesn't mention Fawley's name. She doesn't have to.

On the other side of the landing, there's the door to what must be Patsie's room. There's a bead curtain hanging from the lintel, and the strings are tinkling slightly in the draught of their arrival.

"Takes me back," says Ev. "My gran had one of those. I didn't think you could still get them."

Somer takes a step closer and reaches for one of the strings. The beads are pink, silver, blue; glittery, iridescent. And heavy. Much heavier than she'd expected.

"These must make a hell of a racket when you open the door," she says.

Ev joins her. "Perhaps that's the point," she says in a low voice. "There's no lock."

Neither of them likes where this is going, but they can't afford to jump to conclusions. Somer raises a hand and knocks. "Patsie? It's DC Somer, can we come in?"

There's the sound of footsteps and a moment later the door opens. Patsie is barefoot, in denim shorts and a black Ariana Grande T-shirt. She has a bruised look around the eyes.

"What do you want?"

"We've just got some new information. Something we weren't expecting. I know it's boring but it means we have to ask you some more questions."

Patsie's eyes narrow. "It's about that creep Scott, isn't it?"

"I'm sorry, Patsie, but we're not allowed to talk about it here. We need to take you back with us to St. Aldate's, so we can record the interview."

Patsie rolls her eyes. "*Seriously?*"

"I'm sorry. We wouldn't ask if it wasn't important."

She sighs. "Yeah, yeah. I get it. But you've got to promise me you'll actually nail that creep, OK?"

* * *

Interview with Patsie Webb, conducted at
St. Aldate's Police Station, Oxford
9 April 2018, 4:45 p.m.
In attendance, DC V. Everett, DC E. Somer,
Mrs. D. Webb (mother)

ES: So, Patsie, we're hoping you can help us by
    answering a few more questions.
PW: I've told you everything I remember already.
ES: This is about something that happened before
    Sasha died. The morning of Saturday 17th
    March.
PW: I don't get it—what's that got to do with it?
ES: The incident involves Mr. Scott, your art
    teacher.
PW: Oh right. That perv. I thought you said you
    arrested him?

VE: We did. Which is all down to you,
    incidentally—to the information you gave us.

PW: He deserves it, the bloody weirdo.

DW: Actually, I think you should be grateful to my
    daughter for all the help she's given you.

VE: Oh, we are, Mrs. Webb. In fact, Graeme Scott
    has been here answering questions today.

PW: He's *here*? Like, *now*?

VE: There's no need to be alarmed. He can't talk
    to you.

ES: So, can we talk about that Saturday morning,
    Patsie? Do you remember where you were?

PW: [*shrugs*]
    Not really. It's ages ago.

ES: Only a couple of weeks, surely? And if I said
    it was on Walton Street, would that jog your
    memory? Isabel's mother met her at the coffee
    shop that day—do you remember that?

PW: OK. Right. Yeah, I remember.

ES: There was a woman with a bike there too, and
    we're pretty sure she saw something. Something
    she found disturbing. Shocking, even. But we
    haven't been able to talk to her. In fact, it
    may be impossible to trace her at all.

PW: Well, I didn't see anything, so—

ES: But someone else did. Your teacher—Mr. Scott.
    He was there that morning. He saw you—all four
    of you.

PW: [*silence*]

ES: Do you know what he told us, Patsie?

PW: What's that creep been saying? The fucking *perv*—

DW: Patsie, there's no need for that sort of
    language.
PW: [*getting to her feet*]
    I've had enough of this crap. I'm going home.
VE: Sit down, please, Patsie. I'm afraid you're not
    going anywhere.
ES: [*to Mrs. Webb*]
    It seems Patsie doesn't want to tell you, Mrs.
    Webb, so I will. Mr. Scott saw the four girls—
    your daughter, Sasha Blake, Isabel Parker and
    Leah Waddell. They were walking up Walton
    Street from town and stopped at the junction
    of Great Clarendon Street where they talked
    for a moment. Then they all hugged each other
    and Sasha left the rest and crossed the road
    towards the Blavatnik center.
DW: So? What's wrong with that?
ES: According to Mr. Scott, as soon as Sasha
    turned her back on her friends, Patsie lifted
    her hand and mimed a gesture. And the other
    girls laughed. But Patsie wasn't laughing—
    Patsie was deadly serious. That's why it stuck
    in his mind—it wasn't just what she did, but
    the look on her face as she did it. He said it
    made his blood run cold.
DW: I still don't get it—
ES: She mimed a gun, Mrs. Webb. Shooting a gun.
    Your daughter play-acted killing her friend.
    And now that friend is dead.
DW: And that's the reason you dragged us in here?
    For *that*? They were just play-acting. Even *you*

362

admitted that. They're *kids*, for God's sake.
You know what it's like with teenagers, on one
day, off the next—

ES: I do know what it's like, Mrs. Webb. And I
also know how intense things can be at that
age. Small disagreements, imagined slights—how
quickly they can escalate.

DW: Sasha Blake was Patsie's *best friend*. They
spent all hours God sends together—they've
known each other since playgroup. Have you any
idea how terrible this whole thing has been?

VE: I'm sure it has, Mrs. Webb. And most
especially for Sasha's mother.

ES: Is your mum right, Patsie? Were you best
friends with Sasha?

PW: Of course I was—

ES: Because I've never pretended to kill one of my
friends. Even in jest.

PW: It was just a *joke*—how many more times—*it was
just a joke*—we did stuff like that all the
time.

ES: Was that what happened, Patsie? Did that start
as "stuff like that" too?

PW: [*looking from one officer to the other*]
Did what start? What are you talking about?

ES: I'm talking about the night Sasha died. Was
that just supposed to be another of your little
"jokes," only everything got way out of hand?

PW: What the fuck? Are you actually saying *I*
killed Sasha? Like, *seriously*? Why would I
even *do* that?

ES: I don't know, Patsie—you tell me. Did you have
     an argument? Or was it envy? That work
     placement she got at *Vogue*? The way she
     looked? Or just that she was clearly a lot
     more popular than you?

PW: You're fucking sick—you know that? *Sick.*

DW: This is outrageous—how dare you—

ES: Do you remember that reconstruction they did at
     the bus stop, Patsie? One of our colleagues saw
     a news report about that on the TV. It was in
     the John Radcliffe hospital so it was on mute.
     And you know what that's like—when the sound's
     turned down you focus more on the pictures. You
     notice more. He saw you and Leah talking to
     each other. It was when they were interviewing
     Sasha's father. But you were in the background.
     You were talking to Leah and she was looking
     very upset. Do you remember that, Patsie?

PW: So? Why shouldn't I talk to Leah? What's wrong
     with that?

ES: I suppose that rather depends on what you
     were saying.

PW: And anyway, we were miles from the cameras. No
     way anyone could've heard.

ES: Right. That's what our colleague said too.

PW: Well then, what's your bloody problem.

ES: But then he had an idea. He's done some
     outreach work recently with the local Deaf
     Club, so he took the footage over there and
     showed it to an expert in lip-reading. And she
     was in no doubt at all.

364

DW: What are you talking about? Patsie—what are
    they talking about?

ES: [*passing across a sheet of paper*]
    It's all here, Mrs. Webb. But the relevant
    part is highlighted halfway down. Leah is
    talking to your daughter—she's clearly in some
    distress but you can't see what she's saying
    because she has her back to the camera. But
    Patsie doesn't. Patsie can be seen quite
    clearly. She grabs hold of Leah's arm and
    says, "How many more times—it'll all be fine as
    long as you keep your fucking mouth shut."

PW: [*getting to her feet and moving toward the
    door*]
    I'm out of here.

VE: [*following and attempting to prevent her*]
    You can't do that, Patsie—

PW: [*pushing her away*]
    Don't you fucking touch me, you ugly bitch—

ES: Don't be stupid, Patsie—this isn't going to help—

PW: [*yelling and hitting out at DC Everett*]
    I said get your fucking hands *off* me—

ES: Patsie Belinda Webb, I am arresting you on
    suspicion of involvement in the death of Sasha
    Blake. You do not have to say anything. But it
    may harm your defense if you do not mention
    when questioned something which you later rely
    on in court. Anything you do say may be given
    in evidence. Interview suspended at 17:06.

* * *

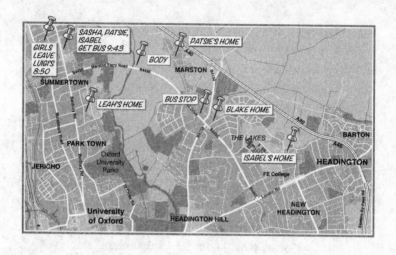

* * *

"I'm not saying you're wrong, Adam," says Gallagher. "I just can't get the timings to work."

We're standing in front of the whiteboard, in the incident room, looking at a map and a timeline scrawled in Gislingham's untidy capital letters.

8:33	JONATHAN BLAKE TEXTS SASHA
8:50	GIRLS LEAVE LUIGI's (till receipt)
9:43	SASHA, PATSIE, ISABEL LEAVE S'TOWN (bus ticket)
	LEAH STARTS TO WALK HOME
9:46	BLAKE TEXTS SASHA (not received/ phone off)
9:50 (approx)	PATSIE GETS OFF AT MARSTON
10:00 (approx)	SASHA GETS OFF AT CHERWELL DRIVE

366

10:05 (approx)	ISABEL SPEAKS TO DRIVER (C Higgins)
10:10 (approx)	PATSIE ARRIVES HOME, SPEAKS TO NEIGHBOR (L Chase)
10:15 (approx)	LEAH ARRIVES HOME, SPEAKS TO MOTHER

And it's all there, in black and white. The bus ticket, the driver, the neighbor, the mother. Things we can't get around. Things we know are true. And from the moment the girls leave Summertown the whole sequence is barely half an hour from start to end.

"However much I contort it," says Gallagher, "there isn't enough time. The CPS will never run with this—they'd get torn to shreds."

She's not wrong. I can hear the defense lawyer now, telling us we've got it all wrong—that it must have been a random predator, some pervert who happened to pass Sasha at the bus stop. Or someone else who knew her—someone who could have been stalking her. Like Graeme bloody Scott, for instance.

"But we *know* Patsie was involved somehow." I turn fully and look at her. "Don't we? Or am I on my own on this?"

Gallagher shakes her head. "No, I think you're right—not just because of what the lip-reader said but the way she reacted just now. I just don't see how we square the circle on *how*." She sighs. "And as for *why*—"

I turn back to the map and then the timeline. "OK, let's start with what we know. The bus arrived at 9:43, Patsie, Isabel and Sasha got on and Leah started to walk home."

She nods. "Which is supported both by Isabel's bus ticket and what we got from Leah's mother."

"Right. But we only have that one ticket, don't we? What if Isabel got on that bus alone? What if Patsie went off with Sasha much earlier than that—even as early as 9:00—and Leah and Isabel then hung around on their own for half an hour or so before going home?"

Gallagher's eyes widen. "You mean they did it deliberately? To create a fake timeline?" She gives a low whistle. "You're talking about a pretty sick conspiracy there, DI Fawley. But OK, let's play it through. Have we ever nailed down where they went after they left the pizza place?"

"They claimed they just 'hung out.' You know—on those benches up by South Parade. Which are conveniently out of range of any CCTV."

Gallagher nods. She knows the place, of course she does—she lives up that way herself. And there are always kids mooching about there in the evenings. Smoking, drinking cider. "Hanging out."

I take a step closer to the board; my head is buzzing. "What if this *whole thing* is a lie? What if Patsie and Sasha started for home straight after leaving the restaurant? Only they didn't get a bus. They walked." I trace the route—down the Banbury Road and then along the Marston Ferry Road toward Cherwell Drive. And then I stop and tap the map.

"Here," I say, turning to her. "This is where they stopped. This is where they turned off."

The footpath leading to the Vicky Arms. Barely a hundred yards from where Sasha's body was found.

Gallagher considers. "It would have been pretty dark along there at that time of night."

"Patsie could easily have brought a torch. If it really was that premeditated."

Gallagher glances at me. "But why would Sasha go with her?"

I shrug. "She didn't know Patsie intended her any harm, did she? They were supposed to be best friends—they'd known each other since playschool. Perhaps Patsie said she wanted to go to the pub. Perhaps they were supposed to meet some boys. Who knows."

"OK," she says. "Then what?"

"As soon as they're out of sight of the road, Patsie turns on Sasha and kills her, then drags the body into the river—"

"Sasha's phone," says Gallagher suddenly. "The last signal was at 9:35. We thought her battery had run out, but perhaps it wasn't that at all. Perhaps the phone went dead then because Patsie had just chucked it in the Cherwell."

It fits; it all fits.

Gallagher moves closer to the map. "And after that Patsie just heads off home on foot as if nothing had happened?"

I nod. "And when she gets there, she makes a big point of talking to someone in the street, so they'll remember seeing her. Meanwhile Isabel gets on the 9:43 bus in Summertown, making sure to ask the driver the time when they're approaching Headington."

"Perfect little alibis, gift-wrapped and ready to go," says Gallagher. "All they have to do after that is keep on insisting all three of them were on that same bus."

I sense someone come up behind me now and turn to see Gislingham at my shoulder.

"Good news," he says. "Someone called in—looks like we've found Sasha's handbag. It was up near the Vicky Arms. Quinn's on his way to the lab to take a look."

I stare at him. "Where was it—where *exactly*?"

He goes up to the map and points. "About there, I think—in a ditch on the corner of Mill Lane."

Halfway between where Sasha died and Patsie lives. This isn't just a hunch any more. This is evidence; this is a *case*. And for the first time since this all began, I'm staring at the photos of Sasha with a picture in my head of who did that to her. The body head-down in the water, the bound wrists, the jagged lacerations. The white and broken face.

"Something else occurred to me as well, boss," says Gislingham quietly. "What you were saying about Patsie Webb—no one saw anything on her clothes when she got home, did they? Perhaps that's why she used that plastic bag. Something to keep her clothes clean and tidy while she beat poor bloody Sasha's head in."

Gallagher looks across at him. "I suspect you're right, Sergeant. But I don't think that was the only reason. She didn't want to look at her. She couldn't bear to see her face."

* * *

Interview with Patsie Webb, conducted at
St. Aldate's Police Station, Oxford
9 April 2018, 6:45 p.m.
In attendance, DC V. Everett, DC E. Somer,
Mrs. D. Webb, J. Beck (solicitor)

ES: Interview resumed at 18.45. Patsie has been
     given time to consult with a lawyer, and
     Mr. Jason Beck is now present.

DW: I can't believe you arrested her—you can't
    seriously think—
ES: We don't "think" anything, Mrs. Webb. We just
    want the truth. Which is why I'd like Patsie
    to tell us what happened that night one more
    time.
PW: What *again*?
ES: Yes, again. You say you left Leah in
    Summertown at about 9:45, when the three of
    you got on the bus.
PW: I *told* you that—Iz gave you her bloody ticket,
    didn't she?
ES: Yes, that's right, she did.
VE: And then you got off on the Marston Ferry
    Road, and Sasha stayed on till Cherwell Drive,
    and the last time Isabel saw her she was
    standing at the bus stop, waiting for someone?
PW: Right.
VE: And Isabel stayed on the bus till Headington.
PW: Right.
VE: And she spoke to the bus driver. To ask him
    the time.
ES: You see, that's always struck me as odd. I
    mean, that she spoke to him at all.
PW: Don't see why.
ES: Young people like you—you don't bother with
    watches any more. You check the time on your
    phones. Why did she need to ask the driver?
PW: Dunno. Perhaps her phone was off.
VE: Good guess. You're right, it was. We checked.
    In fact, we've now established that *all* your

phones were off between 9:00 and just after
10:30. Yours and Leah's and Isabel's. And
that's odd too.

PW: [*shrugs*]

ES: So we started asking ourselves why. Could it
be, perhaps, that Isabel *wanted* an excuse
to talk to that bus driver—that she wanted
him to remember her? After all, she looks
pretty distinctive, doesn't she, with that
bright-pink dip-dye of hers? He wasn't likely
to forget that.

VE: When did she dye it, Patsie?

PW: [*shrugs*]
Can't remember.

VE: It must have been pretty recent because she
didn't have it when she met her mother on
Walton Street.

PW: Whatever.

ES: And that was just a coincidence, was it? That
she happened to dye it just before what
happened to your friend?

PW: I don't know what you're getting at. Look—what
difference does it make? We were on that bus,
you *know* that. Iz gave you her ticket.

ES: Precisely. We know Isabel was on the bus.
There's proof of that. But what about you,
Patsie? Where's your ticket? Or don't you
have one?

* * *

"What have we got?" asks Quinn.

The contents of the evidence bag are spread out on the lab table. A satchel. Soft leather, deep pink, with dark discolored patches where it's been out in the open and the wet for days. A pen with a bedraggled feather attached to the end. A purse. A makeup bag. A tampon wrapped in orange plastic. A packet of mints.

"It's definitely Sasha's bag," says Nina Mukerjee, opening the purse and taking out a series of plastic identity cards. She's wearing thick latex gloves. "These are all hers."

Most people use the same passport picture for everything, but not Sasha. A slightly different her stares out from each card. More and less of a smile, more and less of a playfulness.

"There was definitely no phone?" asks Quinn.

"Sorry. No notebook either."

"What about a bus ticket?"

"Not that I could find."

"So do you think we'll get any forensics?"

Nina nods. "There may still be some prints on the outside, and there are at least two here," she says, opening the bag out to reveal the inside. "This area under the flap was protected from the rain. We got lucky."

"But they're most likely Sasha's, though, surely?"

She shakes her head. "Actually, I don't think so. Not these, anyway. I think there are traces of blood here as well. And if that's the case, the prints are almost certainly *not* hers."

Quinn frowns. "Because—?"

"Because the person who made these prints had Sasha's blood on their hands."

* * *

```
ES:  Of course, there is another explanation.
     For why all your phones were off that night.
PW:  No comment.
     [turning to Mr. Beck]
     You said I could say that, right?
ES:  You knew we'd be able to use them to track
     where you were. You knew the only way to be
     sure you couldn't be traced would be to turn
     them all off.
DW:  Where are you getting all this from? My
     daughter is not a criminal—
ES:  And as far as I can see, there's no good
     reason why you'd want to do that, Patsie.
     Only a very, very bad one.
```

* * *

Adam Fawley
9 April 2018
19.15

The news has got around before we get to the incident room. One look at their faces tells me that. Quinn is at the front, an unusual flush to his face; and believe me, Quinn doesn't get that excited very often.

"So the bag was definitely Sasha's?" asks Gallagher.

He nods. "No question. And there's at least two finger-prints on the underside of the flap." He pauses; he knows

374

how to work an audience. "The prints were in *blood*. And we all know what *that* means." He looks around the room. "Forensics are running them against Patsie Webb's right now. Mukerjee said she'd call me within the hour."

Gallagher turns to me. The blood, the bag, the prints. Her face says it all.

We've got her.

*   *   *

VE: Interview resumed at 19:25.

ES: Why were you so keen to make us suspect Mr. Scott, Patsie? You went to a lot of trouble to direct our attention his way.

PW: Because he's a *pervert*—because he was *following* her—

ES: But he didn't kill her, did he? You knew that, and yet you went out of your way to make us think so. Why was that?

PW: What are you *talking* about? How the fuck would I know what he did? I wasn't *there*—

VE: I think you were, Patsie. I think you know exactly what happened. So why don't you tell us. Tell us the truth about how Sasha died—

PW: What are you *talking* about—Mum—they can't accuse me of stuff like this, can they?

JB: What actual *evidence* do you have to support this outrageous theory, Officer?
    [*DS Gislingham enters the room, confers with DC Somer*]

PW: [*breaking down in tears*]

```
         I didn't do it, Mum, I didn't do it—Sasha was
         my best friend—
DW:      I know you didn't, darling, I know you didn't.
         You couldn't do something like that, not in a
         million years.
```

* * *

Adam Fawley
9 April 2018
20.25

No one's quite opening champagne but the incident room feels like a surprise party awaiting the arrival of the guest of honor. There's some laughter, a sense of release; some of the blokes have loosened their ties.

When Mukerjee rings through Quinn puts her on speaker: we all want to hear this.

"So, do we have a match?"

The line is crackling a little, but her voice is clear. "Yes, we do."

There's some air-punching, some muted cheers; Gallagher is smiling. Someone claps Quinn on the back as if he waded into the ditch and found that sodding handbag himself.

"That's the good news," continues Mukerjee. "But I'm afraid it's not as straightforward as you were hoping."

The room falls quiet.

Gallagher moves closer to the phone. "Nina—it's DI Gallagher. Could you explain what you mean?"

"I did find some fingerprints from Patsie Webb on the handbag. The trouble is, there was no blood anywhere near those prints. They could have been made at any time."

And the girls were friends—Patsie could easily have handled that bag, even borrowed it. It's not enough. Nothing like enough.

"The prints with the traces of blood were only partials," continues Mukerjee. "It won't be good enough to stand up in court."

Gallagher moves a little closer. "But if they're partials for Patsie—"

The line crackles again. "Sorry, I wasn't making myself clear. They *are* a partial match, just not for Patsie Webb."

"So who—for Isabel?"

"No—we checked hers against ones on the bus ticket. It's not Isabel either."

Gallagher frowns—this isn't making any sense. "Then who—"

"Nadine," says Mukerjee, her voice clearer now. "The prints are a partial match for Nadine Appleford."

* * *

"You should be fucking *ashamed* of yourselves. And if you think you're getting away with this you've got another think coming."

Denise Webb is so angry she can barely speak without spitting. Everett's had her fair share of self-righteous abuse over the years, but this is up there with the most unpleasant. Patsie is a few yards away, her head down, hair falling about her face. It's impossible to see her expression. She hasn't spoken since they left the interview room.

"Keeping us here for hours on end," says Denise,

"accusing a *fifteen-year-old girl* of something so—so—it's *disgusting*, that's what it is."

The desk sergeant hands Everett the bail paperwork for Denise Webb to sign. It's clear from his face that he's keeping well out of it. Ev's on her own on this one.

"I'm taking my daughter home now, Constable, or whatever your damn title is. But this isn't the end of it. Not by a long way."

No, thinks Everett, as she watches the woman put her arm around her daughter and guide her to the door. I think you're dead right about that.

* * *

Adam Fawley
9 April 2018
21.35

Gallagher pushes open the incident-room door and sits down heavily on the nearest chair. She's just been briefing Harrison. I don't need to ask how it went: I've seen the look on her face too many times before—in my own mirror.

"Someone please explain to me how Nadine Appleford's prints got on that handbag," she says wearily, "because I am all out of viable explanations."

Gislingham shakes his head. "I don't care what forensics said, Nadine couldn't have killed Sasha—not on her own, anyway. She'd have struggled getting that body into the river on her own for a start, apart from anything else. Patsie could've, yes, but Nadine's a good three or four inches shorter."

"Oh, I dunno," says Quinn, "she may be small but she

looks pretty sturdy to me—and what with the slope of the bank, I reckon she could have just rolled it down."

"That *it* was a fifteen-year-old girl," says Somer curtly.

"And Nadine is fifteen too," replies Gislingham. "And why would she attack Sasha anyway? They didn't even know each other."

Baxter looks up. "Actually, they might. I just checked. They were in the same year at Summertown High."

Silence. More silence.

"Oh fuck," says Gallagher.

"So that's it," sighs Gislingham. "*That's* what we missed."

"Don't blame yourself," says Gallagher quickly. "We all missed it. It's been right under our noses all this time. We just never thought to ask."

"But even if they knew each other," says Somer, "they weren't *friends*. They can't have been. I went through Sasha's room, remember. There were loads of pictures of her and her mates, but Nadine wasn't in any of them. Not a single one. Why would Nadine kill someone she barely even knew?"

Everett shrugs. "Perhaps that's the whole point. Sasha had everything Nadine doesn't—friends, looks—"

"What—*seriously*?" says Quinn.

Ev shakes her head. "You were clearly never a teenage girl."

Baxter wasn't either, but he's starting to buy the theory. "I'm with Ev. And remember what Gow said—that it was almost certainly the same person who attacked both girls? We've got *evidence* linking Nadine to the assault on her sister, so doesn't she *have* to be the number-one suspect for Sasha too?"

"So she's a psychopath?" says Somer. "A serial predator who suddenly, out of the blue, for no apparent reason, brutalizes one girl and kills another, all in the space of a single week? Not to mention doing everything she possibly can to make those assaults look like the work of a sexual predator—I just don't think Nadine's that devious—"

"But Patsie is," I say quietly.

Gallagher holds up her hands. "Look, let's remember the prints were only partials. We might be barking up completely the wrong tree—it might have nothing to do with Nadine at all. I, for one, am clinging to that hope, however flimsy it feels right now."

Asante turns to her. "So what do we do now?"

Gallagher gets slowly to her feet. "There's only one thing we can do. But we have a lot of work to do first."

*   *   *

Adam Fawley
9 April 2018
22.09

It's gone 10:00. Gallagher and I are the only ones left in the incident room. After the tasks for tomorrow were divvied up she sent the whole team home, and frankly, I'd have done exactly the same. Adrenaline is a strange thing—it can keep you going for as long as you have no choice, but the minute that burning need disappears you go over an abyss. We were all flat-lining this evening. No one was thinking straight.

Gallagher drains another cup of coffee. I keep reminding her about her kids, and she keeps reminding me about my wife, but somehow or other we're both still here.

*   *   *

The following morning is bright and clear, with a slicing wind and thin high cloud.

They'd arranged to meet on-site rather than at the station, and when Gislingham arrives Quinn is already waiting for him in the car park.

"They obviously got the message," he says as Gis joins him. "The secretary has been out here already, telling me she will *personally* turn my car into a pumpkin if I even think about parking in the deputy head's space."

But Gis is in no mood for Quinn's brand of humor. "Let's just get this over with," he says.

* * *

I'm in reception when Nadine and her mother arrive, though neither acknowledges me. But it's quite possible they simply don't remember. Nadine is in jeans and a jumper, so her mother evidently doesn't expect her to be going anywhere near school today. She's pulling at the jumper, twisting the wool in her fingers and starting at every sudden sound, as if she hasn't slept in days. Whatever this girl did—or didn't—do, she's carrying something too heavy for her to bear.

Ten minutes later Bryan Gow joins the rest of us in the room next to Interview One. He looks as animated as I've ever seen him. He even has a tape recorder. Perhaps he feels a case study coming on.

On the screen Somer takes her seat next to Gallagher. The lawyer and the Appropriate Adult are women too, so there are no men in the room at all, which I have to admit is a good call on Gallagher's part. When they show in Nadine and her mother, even I'm shocked at the change in Diane in such a few short minutes. Her hand trembles as she reaches for the chair and her face is haggard, the unforgiving overhead light hollowing out her flesh. That's what it looks like to find out your daughter is suspected of murder.

*　*　*

Interview with Nadine Appleford, conducted at
St. Aldate's Police Station, Oxford
10 April 2018, 10:42 a.m.
In attendance, DI R. Gallagher, DC E. Somer,
Mrs. D. Appleford, Ms. S. Rogers (designated
Appropriate Adult), Mrs. P. Marshall (solicitor)

ES: Interview commencing at 10:42. Nadine is
    accompanied by her mother, Mrs. Diane
    Appleford, her lawyer, Mrs. Pamela Marshall,
    and Ms. Sally Rogers, who will again act as
    her Appropriate Adult.

RG: For the benefit of the tape, Nadine has now been
    arrested on suspicion of involvement in the
    death of Sasha Blake on the evening of April 3rd
    2018. So, Nadine, I want to start by asking you
    where you were that evening—did you go out?

DA: Will someone just please tell me what's going
    on? What on earth makes you believe Nadine
    could possibly—

RG: We'll come to that, Mrs. Appleford. Nadine—
could you answer the question for us, please?

NA: [*silence*]

I don't remember.

DA: Both the girls were at home when I got back at
11:00, I can tell you that for nothing.

ES: Both of them? Faith *and* Nadine?

DA: Faith went out I think, but she was back by
the time I got home. Like I said.

ES: And there was nothing unusual about that
evening? Nothing that stuck in your mind?

PM: [*preventing her from answering*]

What *evidence* do you have linking Nadine to
this crime, Inspector?

RG: Yesterday afternoon a member of the public
discovered a pink handbag a short distance
from where we found Sasha's body. It has been
positively identified as hers and carries
traces of her blood.

PM: That doesn't prove anything.

RG: I'm afraid there are also fingerprints in the
blood. Prints we believe may be Nadine's.

DA: But that's impossible—

PM: You said *may* be Nadine's. Are they a match or
aren't they?

RG: The prints are partials. Partial matches to
Nadine's.

PM: How many points?

RG: Five on one, four on the other.

PM: You know as well as I do that that won't stand
up in court. You'll need a lot more than that

```
      if you want the CPS to take you even half
      seriously. In the meantime, I need to
      discuss this new evidence with my client.
      I'm sure the Appropriate Adult would
      agree with me that that's entirely
      reasonable.
SR:   Yes, I agree that would be a good idea.
ES:   Interview suspended at 10:53.
```

* * *

It's the middle of morning break so the head teacher allows them to use her office, rather than fight for space in a crowded staffroom. She has a room around the back. From the window, Gislingham can see across the fields to a line of distant trees. Beyond that, as he well knows, is where they found Sasha's body. He just hopes the kids haven't made the same connection.

The head of year is a man called Dennis Woodley, who has a bright ginger beard, a lot of sincere eye contact and a deeply earnest handshake that requires both hands. Gislingham has him down as a born-again Christian before he's even let go. The other teacher is a small harassed-looking woman who gives the impression she's running permanently late.

Woodley makes a big show of offering to "do the honors" on the coffee rather than expecting his female colleague to do it. There's a poster on the wall announcing the school's values to be Teamwork, Diversity, Kindness and Equality, so Woodley's clearly aiming for the full house. Gislingham says yes, Quinn says no, and eventually they're all seated at the low table.

"So, Officers," says Woodley, turning on his big smile, "how can we help?"

* * *

The uniformed PC shows Nadine and the other two women out of the room, but Somer is still sitting at the interview table.

"What is it?" says Gallagher as she gathers up her files. "There's something on your mind, isn't there."

Somer frowns. "It was just something Diane Appleford said. About that night."

Gallagher stops what she's doing; she's already worked out that this woman's instincts are worth listening to. "Oh yes?"

"She covered it up really quickly, but there was just a moment—as if something had occurred to her—something she realized straightaway she wouldn't want us to know."

Gallagher considers. "Well, you've spent more time with her than I have. I say go with your hunch."

"But I can hardly come right out and ask her, can I? She's already clammed up—she's not going to tell me now."

"But you know Faith, don't you, and pretty well, from what I hear. If there was anything odd about that night, she would know. Why not ask her?"

Somer makes a face. "I'm not sure about that. The state she was in last time I saw her—I don't want to upset her more than we already have—"

"Then ask that friend of hers instead. Jess, isn't it? Perhaps she can do it for you."

* * *

"Well, if you ask me, that's our motive, right there."

It's Quinn, ballsing it out as usual. He's lucky Somer isn't in the room because I doubt she'd be letting him get away with it. But wherever she is, it's not here.

"As far as I'm concerned, what Woodley told us proves it—Nadine *did* have a motive to kill Sasha. And if you add to that the evidence from the handbag—"

"We don't *know* they're her prints," begins Everett. "They're just partials."

"Who else's could they be, for fuck's sake?"

The mood is getting fractious and Gallagher steps in to calm things down. "OK, DC Quinn, we've heard your view. Sergeant—what's your take?"

Gislingham looks up. "Well, it's pretty clear Nadine was desperate to get into Patsie's little clique. Woodley said she's been struggling to fit in ever since she arrived. Though it must have been tough, poor kid, arriving at a new school where everyone already has their own mates."

"But it was definitely Patsie's group Nadine wanted to be in?"

Gislingham nods. "They're the cool kids, apparently. The 'LIPS girls.' Everyone wants to be in their gang."

"Bet they don't any more," mutters Baxter, but he's at the back like me, and only I can hear him.

386

"And they rejected her?"

Gislingham nods grimly. "Worse than that. Apparently they'd started picking on her. Taking the piss out of her hair, her weight, stuff like that. Though it was mainly the other three—it sounds like Sasha tried to distance herself a bit."

"And the school didn't do anything about it?"

"Woodley said every time they tried Nadine bent over backwards to deny anything had happened. And the girls were way too clever to get caught."

"Surprise, surprise," says Ev darkly.

Gallagher turns to Gow. "What do you think, Bryan?"

He laughs. "About the teenage brain? How long have you got? Look, any parent will tell you the same thing: they don't function the same way we do. Nadine Appleford was under acute stress without the mental capacity to process it or the maturity to put it into context. All the usual peer pressures around looks and boyfriends and definitions of 'success,' added to a complete lack of any sort of supportive network at school and a home environment that's been thrown into complete disarray over the last few months."

Everett looks uncomfortable. "Faith didn't set out to cause any trouble—"

Gow nods. "I agree. But she has, all the same. Nadine's had to cope with a brother becoming a sister, moving house, starting a new school and a mother who's been understandably distracted. Being rejected by Patsie's group in such a spiteful and public way would have been the last straw."

"And yet she told her teachers nothing happened."

Gow shrugs. "That's how kids operate. She probably kept telling herself things would change—that if she hung on in there and didn't grass them up they'd come round eventually. And in the meantime all the petty little cruelties mount up until at some point it's all too much and she snaps."

"But where does Sasha come in?" says Gallagher. "If it's Patsie's gang, why would Nadine take it out on Sasha? Especially if Sasha was the only one who was nice to her?"

"Could just have been the wrong place at the wrong time," says Quinn. "Nadine happens to be on Cherwell Drive that night, sees Sasha at the bus stop and decides to have it out with her. Perhaps she approached Sasha precisely *because* she wasn't as much of a cow as the rest of them. But then something goes wrong, Nadine loses it—"

"And the cable ties?" says Ev. "The knife? She just happened to have that stuff on her?"

Gallagher looks grim. "I'm with you, Everett. I'm seriously struggling with that. The only possible explanation is that it was premeditated—that Nadine had planned it all in advance. But that doesn't make sense: how on earth could she have known Sasha would be there that night?"

"And even if she did, how did she get the body all the way from the road to the river?" says Baxter. "Because I can't see Sasha agreeing to go along that path with Nadine in the pitch-dark whatever excuse she came up with. *I* bloody well wouldn't, that's for sure."

"Look, we don't even know where Nadine was that night," says Ev. "She may have a perfectly good alibi—"

"She doesn't."

It's Somer. She's at the door, her mobile phone in her hand.

"I just spoke to Faith's friend, Jess Beardsley. Faith went to the cinema that night. *Phantom Thread* at the

Phoenix on Walton Street. She left the house at 7:15 and didn't get back until 10:45."

"So that's over three hours when Nadine could have been pretty much anywhere," says Gallagher wearily.

"I'm afraid it's worse than that. Faith said that when she got back home the washing machine was on."

Quinn frowns. "So?"

"That's why Faith's so sure it was the same night. It stuck in her mind because their mother's always on at Nadine about doing her own washing and she never does. That night is the one and only time Faith can remember her doing it without being nagged."

Gallagher shakes her head sadly. She's about to say something else when the door swings open again to reveal Tony Asante. He looks around until he spots Ev.

"Ah, DC Everett—there's someone downstairs who wants to talk to you. Looks a bit jittery about it though, so it might be a good idea to get down there before he has second thoughts."

* * *

He still looks nervous, an hour later, after they've finished. Even though they've told him again and again that he's done the right thing—that the truth would have come out eventually anyway, and on something like this it's far better to jump than be pushed.

Everett sees him to the main door and gives what she hopes is a reassuring smile.

"It'll be OK. Really. Though it probably doesn't feel that way right now."

"Yeah, I know. Just remember what I said, yeah?"
She nods. "Don't worry. I'm well warned."

* * *

Interview with Patsie Webb, conducted at
St. Aldate's Police Station, Oxford
10 April 2018, 3:19 p.m.
In attendance, DC V. Everett, DC E. Somer,
Mrs. D. Webb, J. Beck (solicitor), Mrs. M. Chandler
(designated Appropriate Adult)

ES: For the purposes of the tape, Patsie is
    accompanied by her mother, her lawyer,
    Mr. Beck, and Mrs. Monica Chandler, in the
    capacity of Appropriate Adult.

DW: It is *unbelievable* that you people have
    dragged us back in here. Patsie has
    already told you a hundred times that she had
    nothing to do with what happened to Sasha
    Blake, and even your own bloody scientists
    admitted the fingerprints on that bag weren't
    hers. I'm going to be making an official
    complaint—do you hear me, an *official*
    complaint. This is harassment, it's
    bullying—

ES: I can assure you that's not the case,
    Mrs. Webb. And we're not here to talk about
    Sasha. Not this time. Now, Patsie, do you
    remember what you were doing on April 1st?

PW: What the—?

DW: April 1st? That was the Monday before last,
right? I can answer that. She was at home, in
bed. She'd come down with that winter vomiting
thing.

ES: Is that right, Patsie? Were you sick that day?

PW: [*shrugs then nods*]

ES: We've checked with Summertown High and you
were definitely logged as off sick that day.
Just like Isabel. And Leah.

DW: The whole school had it—what are you
getting at?

ES: What time do you leave for work in the
morning, Mrs. Webb?

DW: 7:45. 8:00 at the latest. Why?

ES: So you can't actually be sure where Patsie was
that day, can you? Not 100 per cent. Unless
your boyfriend was there, perhaps?

DW: [*hesitates*]
No, actually he wasn't—not until later on—

ES: Did you talk to Patsie on her mobile during
that day?

DW: [*pause*]
I assumed she'd be asleep. She'd been up all
night being sick. I could hear her retching in
the bathroom but she wouldn't let me in.

VE: You didn't try the landline?

DW: No. Like I said, she was ill—she was *asleep*. I
didn't want to wake her. When I got back at 6:30
she was watching TV wrapped up in her duvet.

ES: That doesn't mean she'd been there all day,
though, does it, Patsie?

PW: You're just trying to make me think you know
    something, but you don't. Because there isn't
    anything *to* know.

JB: You're on thin ice here, Officer. If you have
    reasonable grounds for suspicion that an
    offense has been committed you should question
    my client under caution. As you well know.

ES: In that case, Patsie Belinda Webb, I am
    arresting you on suspicion of false
    imprisonment and assault occasioning Actual
    Bodily Harm on April 1st 2018. You do not have
    to say anything. But it may harm your defense
    if you do not mention when questioned
    something which you later rely on in court.
    Anything you do say may be given in evidence.
    So, Patsie, when DI Fawley spoke to Isabel on
    April 4th she said she didn't know anyone
    called Faith Appleford. But you do, don't you,
    all of you. You know her sister. Nadine.

PW: Nadine's in our year. But I don't *know* her.

ES: What happened to Faith—it was a lot like what
    happened to Sasha. So much so that we were
    convinced it had to be the same perpetrator.
    Faith was abducted and tied up and taken to a
    shed on the Marston Ferry Road allotments. The
    poor girl was completely terrorized—she
    thought she was going to be killed—they
    dragged down her underwear—

MC: Look, is this really necessary?

ES: And the attacker was really clever. They put a
    plastic bag over her head so she couldn't see.

They kept quiet the whole time so she couldn't hear anything that might identify them. The only clue we had was the fact that Faith was abducted in some sort of van. And even though we searched high and low we just couldn't find it. And then we thought perhaps it wasn't a van after all—perhaps it was an SUV, or even an old-fashioned estate car.

VE: And then *you* told us about Graeme Scott, didn't you, Patsie? About how he'd been taking an unhealthy interest in Sasha. And then we found out he drives a Morris Traveller and we wondered— perhaps *he* was the man we were looking for? Perhaps he attacked both Sasha *and* Faith?

DW: Like I said before, you should be grateful to my daughter, not treating her like some sort of bloody criminal.

ES: But then forensics told us that the bag that was used on Faith carried DNA from both her mother and her sister. Frankly, at that point, we didn't know what to think. We couldn't see how Graeme Scott could possibly have got hold of that bag. In fact, there was only one person it could have been: Nadine herself.

VE: But even that didn't add up. Because we knew she couldn't have been driving that van. She's only fifteen—I mean, that wouldn't have been legal, would it?

PW: [*silence*]

ES: And then we thought—hang on, just because it isn't legal, doesn't mean it didn't happen.

After all, someone can *know* how to drive even if they don't have a license.

PW: [*shifts in her chair but doesn't say anything*]

ES: We even tested it out—our colleague DC Asante did a dry run to see if there was enough time for Nadine to attack her sister and still be in school by 11:15. And you know, it is actually possible. Though she'd need to have a really good connection on the buses to Blackbird Leys—

PW: [*looks up, then down again*]

ES: Oh, didn't I say? We think the van involved belongs to someone who lives in Blackbird Leys. In fact, we don't think, we *know*. Because he came in this morning and gave us a statement. Ashley told us all about it, Patsie. There's no point lying any more.

PW: [*silence*]

DW: Patsie? Is this true?

PW: Look, it was just a *joke*, OK? An April Fool. I don't know why everyone's going so fucking batshit about it—

ES: You don't *know*? You're seriously telling us you don't understand why the police would take something like that seriously?

PW: [*sulkily*]
We didn't *do* anything to her.

VE: Yes, you did. You pulled out her hair. That's what makes it Actual Bodily Harm. And you did untold psychological damage. Faith thought she was going to be killed—raped—

PW: How can she be raped? She's not even a fucking *girl*—

DW: *Patsie*—

ES: So you are admitting to involvement in the abduction of Faith Appleford on the morning of April 1st 2018?

PW: For fuck's *sake*, it wasn't *abduction*, it was a *joke*.

VE: Just now you said "we" didn't do anything. Who else was with you?

PW: Iz. And Leah. They met me at the allotments.

ES: So none of you were really ill at all. You just told your parents you were.

PW: [*silence*]

VE: And you drove Ashley Brotherton's van. Your boyfriend's van.

DW: What *boyfriend*? Since when have you had a boyfriend?

PW: [*to her mother*]
Since *you* started spending all day every day with that creep Lee and stopped giving a toss about me, that's when.

ES: Ashley told us he had no idea that you were going to borrow it.

PW: Nah, well, I wasn't going to actually *tell* him, was I. He'd have hidden the bloody keys. He gave me all sorts of shit about it afterwards.

ES: So you planned it. You knew about the funeral and you planned the whole thing.

PW: Are you thick or something? It was an *April Fool*. It had to be that day.

VE: Ashley wanted to go to the police as soon as he found out, but you told him you'd tell us he had sex with you even though you're underage. He was frightened he might lose his job—

PW: Yeah, well, he's not that bright.

ES: Why did you pick on Faith, Patsie? Why her, in particular?

PW: [*shrugs*]
Dunno.

ES: I think you know very well. You see, when we first started investigating what happened to Faith, we assumed it must have been a hate crime. We thought her attacker must have known her secret and picked on her because of it. But however hard we tried we couldn't find anyone who actually knew about it. No one outside her immediate family had any idea.

PW: [*silence*]

ES: But that's the whole point, isn't it, Patsie? Nadine knew. And she told *you*.

DW: You can't prove any of that.

ES: Patsie just proved it herself. She said Faith "isn't even a girl." There's only one way she could know that.

PW: Like I said—it was an *April Fool*—

VE: Why did Nadine tell you about her sister, Patsie? Because she wanted to fit in? Because she wanted you to like her?

PW: We were just having a laugh, all right? We said she could be our friend if she told us a secret. Something no one else knew.

DW: Oh my God—

ES: But you had no intention of being her friend, did you? You were just using her. You took what she told you and used it to betray her. In the most vicious, unkind way imaginable.

PW: Stupid bitch was going apeshit. About her bloody sister and how she'd never have told us if she'd known. When we heard sirens we thought she'd called the fucking police.

VE: What about the carrier bag? Where did you get that?

PW: Iz nicked it off her. Dozy cow didn't even notice.

ES: So what about Sasha?

PW: I told you, that was *nothing* to do with us.

VE: Even though the details are almost exactly the same? The plastic bag? The cable ties? You did that deliberately, didn't you—so the police would think there was some sort of sexual predator on the loose—

JB: If I might say so, Officer, everything you've just said makes an extremely compelling case for *Nadine Appleford* as the killer of Sasha Blake. She knew exactly what had happened to Faith and was therefore in an ideal position to carry out a perfect copycat crime. She had the means, and she had an extremely powerful motive: revenge. She wanted to incriminate Patsie and the other girls, and get her own back on those who had rejected her and humiliated her sister.

PW: Yeah—*exactly*. That's *exactly* what must of
    happened—

VE: So you're saying Nadine planned it—that she
    deliberately set out to kill Sasha in a
    carbon-copy of what had happened to Faith,
    just to frame Patsie and the others?

JB: Can you prove she didn't?

ES: So why didn't she tell us Patsie and the
    others had assaulted Faith right at the start?
    Why wait all this time on the off-chance we'd
    work it out for ourselves?

JB: You'll have to ask her about that, Officer.
    Who knows what was going on in her head.
    She's clearly extremely disturbed.

PW: Right—Nadine's fucking *weird*—

DW: Patsie, please—

JB: Does Nadine have an alibi, for example?
    Because my client does. As well you know.
    Sasha, Patsie and Isabel were all on that
    bus together, and you have a ticket that
    proves it.

ES: It's a great theory, Mr. Beck. There's just
    one problem with it. How on earth could
    Nadine have known where Sasha would be
    that night? That *precise* place, that
    precise time—how could she possibly have found
    that out?

PW: That's easy. Because she bloody spied on
    us, that's how.

*   *   *

398

"Do you think that's true, what Patsie said?"

Gallagher is staring at the screen, her arms folded rigid and her foot tapping against the floor.

"That Nadine spied on them? I'm afraid it's only too feasible. Nadine was desperate to belong—I can easily see her eavesdropping on what they were up to."

"Let's see what Isabel and Leah have to say about that. Quinn and Gislingham are picking them up separately, so they don't get a chance to compare notes."

It should reassure me, but it doesn't.

"One thing I do know is that those girls will have got their stories straight long before this. Isabel and Leah are going to back up anything Patsie comes out with. Which means whatever Nadine says, it'll only be her word against theirs. And right now we can't even place them at the scene, never mind actually charge them."

Gallagher sighs. "A bunch of fifteen-year-old kids with half Thames Valley CID on to them, and we can't even break their bloody alibis."

* * *

"DC Somer?"

It's Nina Mukerjee, standing in the doorway of the Applefords' kitchen.

They started upstairs. Nadine's room, Diane's room, Faith's room, the bathroom. Bagging, tagging and taking away. And now they're in the kitchen, barely twenty feet from where Somer has been sitting with Diane Apple-ford, trying desperately to pretend she's interested in an ancient episode of *Law & Order*.

"Can you come in here for a moment?"

Nina's keeping her voice light but Somer isn't deceived. They wouldn't be calling her in otherwise.

Diane glances up, suddenly alarmed.

"It's OK, Mrs. Appleford, I'll just be a minute."

Nina leads her back down the hall. In the kitchen, the contents of the cutlery drawer are laid out on the table.

"I was just about to process these, but I thought you ought to see them first."

The knives have metal handles and serrated edges.

"What's going on?" Diane Appleford is hesitating at the threshold, her face bleached greenish in the overhead light. "They're just bloody steak knives," she says. "There must be hundreds in this sodding city. Thousands."

"I know," says Somer, "it's just procedure—"

"What am I going to say to Faith?" she says, her voice breaking now. "She's refusing to come home. She won't even talk to me."

"Look, that may be for the best," says Somer, moving toward Diane. "Give her time. This is tough on her—on all of you."

There are footsteps on the stairs now, and low voices in the hall. Low enough to be discreet, but still loud enough to be heard.

"You've got all the clothes?" It's Clive Conway's voice; he's talking to the junior CSI.

"Yup, I've got everything that was on the list. I've also bagged the shoes. One set of trainers have smears of dried mud, and I think there's other trace too, so we could get lucky."

"What do they mean 'trace?'" says Diane, turning to Somer, her eyes wide. "What are they talking about?"

Somer bites her lip. "Like I said, it's just procedure. Let's just take things one step at a time."

* * *

Adam Fawley
11 April 2018
10.08

The call comes through to the incident room at just after 10:00 the following morning. The stains on Nadine's trainers were blood. Sasha's blood. Most of us still can't believe it. But as Alan Challow always says, forensic evidence doesn't lie.

"This is going to destroy her mother," says Somer sadly. As if it needed saying.

"I still think there's more to this than meets the eye," says Gallagher. "Those girls—they have to be involved somehow—"

Ev makes a face. "Isabel and Leah just parroted 'no comment' to every single question we asked—it's like they're in some sort of bloody cult or something."

"Yeah, well," says Gis. "But I still think their finger-prints are all over this. *Especially* Patsie's."

"Not literally, though," observes Baxter. "The partials on the handbag don't match a single one of 'em."

"More's the bloody pity," mutters Quinn.

But something Baxter said triggers a niggle in my mind, and when the meeting is over, I take him quietly to one side. Because it's not worth making a song and dance about this in public. Not if I'm wrong.

* * *

Interview with Nadine Appleford, conducted at
St. Aldate's Police Station, Oxford
11 April 2018, 11:55 a.m.
In attendance, DC V. Everett, DC E. Somer,
Mrs. D. Appleford, Mrs. P. Marshall (solicitor),
Ms. S. Rogers (designated Appropriate Adult)

VE: Interview resumed at 11:55 on April 11th 2018.

ES: Now, Nadine. Since we last talked to you we've spoken to Patsie Webb, and she's admitted that she and her friends were the ones who attacked your sister. We've interviewed Isabel and Leah as well, and they're all going to be charged with Actual Bodily Harm. Do you understand, Nadine? We know it was them. We know what they did and how they tricked you.

NA: [*to her mother*]
I told you, Mum, I didn't do it—it wasn't me—

DA: I know, sweetheart, I know.

ES: And you still maintain you weren't at the river the night Sasha died either?

NA: No, I told you.

VE: You didn't see her—you didn't talk to her—

NA: No—I never even went out. I was at home all night.

ES: Your sister says the washing machine was on
    when she got home. Could you explain that
    for us?
NA: [*shrugs*]
    Dunno. I don't remember.
VE: As you know, we conducted a search at
    your house yesterday. Various items were
    removed and sent for forensic analysis. This
    included a pair of trainers found hidden under
    some other clothes at the bottom of your
    wardrobe.
DA: They weren't hidden—she's just messy—she's a
    teenager—
VE: Nadine? Were you trying to hide the shoes?
NA: [*silence*]
ES: Forensic tests on those shoes indicate that
    someone has tried to clean them with
    household bleach, which is a rather unusual
    thing to use on training shoes. Was that you,
    Mrs. Appleford?
DA: [*pause*]
    No. It wasn't.
ES: Was it you, Nadine? Did you try to clean
    something off your shoes?
PM: You're entitled to say "no comment" at any
    time, Nadine.
NA: No comment.
VE: Could you speak up, please? For the tape?
NA: [*louder*]
    No comment.

ES: [*passing across a piece of paper*]
    These are the results of the tests on the
    shoes, Nadine. There are traces of blood on
    them. Not very much. But it's there. And it's
    Sasha's.
NA: [*silence*]
ES: But that only proves you were present when
    Sasha died. It doesn't necessarily prove you
    actually *did* anything. So what happened,
    Nadine? How did you end up there that night?
NA: [*silence*]
VE: Patsie says none of the other girls were even
    there—that *you* killed her, all on your own.
    She says you knew Sasha would be going home
    that way that night because you'd been spying
    on them. Eavesdropping on their conversations.
    Is that true?
NA: It wasn't like that.
VE: So what was it like?
NA: [*shakes her head*]
ES: Why won't you talk to us, Nadine? Did Patsie
    trick you again, is that it? You shouldn't
    be taking all the blame, not if Patsie
    tricked you.
NA: It wasn't—
PM: [*preventing her*]
    You don't have to answer that, Nadine.
NA: No, I want to. It wasn't a trick.
VE: What was it then?
NA: She said to be there, that night. At the river.
VE: Patsie?

404

NA: [*nods*]

ES: You arranged to meet her.

NA: Not just her. The others as well. She said
they were sorry about Faith and this was a way
to make up for it. We were all going to be
blood sisters.

ES: Blood sisters?

NA: You know, like on the telly. They said to
bring a knife. We all had to bring our own.

ES: So you took one from the kitchen at home?

NA: [*nods, not looking at her mother*]

VE: What happened when you got there?

NA: I was waiting at the bus stop near the Vicky
Arms. They'd walked up from Summertown.

VE: Who had, Nadine?

NA: Patsie and Isabel and Sasha. Not Leah. Leah
wasn't there.

VE: And what time was this?

NA: About 9:15. They said I had to be there by
9:00. Patsie had torches and stuff in her bag.

ES: Did Sasha say anything when you all met up?

NA: No. But she didn't look happy, I don't think
she wanted to be there. She kept looking at
her watch like there was somewhere else she
was supposed to be.

VE: Then what happened?

NA: We went along the path to the river. Isabel
went first, then Sasha, then Patsie, then me.
Then suddenly Patsie was grabbing Sasha from
behind and Isabel was ramming a carrier bag
over her head, and then they got out some of

those plastic things and tied her up. Sasha
was falling over in the mud and she was
trying to scream but you could see she didn't
have enough air. Then Patsie got her phone out
and started filming it but she could hardly do
it for laughing, and then Isabel said "Don't
forget the hair."

ES: "Don't forget the hair?"

NA: [*nods*]

ES: Why did she say that—do you know?

NA: [*shakes her head*]

VE: What did Patsie do after Isabel said that?

NA: She pulled up Sasha's head by the hair and
yanked some out at the back. Sasha was really
really crying. She had really nice hair.

ES: Then what?

NA: Patsie told me to get out my knife and cut
her. Sasha. I didn't want to, I was scared and
I felt sick, but she said I had to and if I
didn't we wouldn't be blood sisters and I'd be
next. So I did. But it was just a little one.
On her leg. Patsie and Isabel were still
laughing—they were like, hysterical, like they
were on drugs or something. Then Patsie looked
at the cut I did and said it was pathetic and
I had to do another one. So I did and there
was more blood this time. Iz put some of it on
my face.
[*begins to weep*]
Sasha was crying really bad. Calling for her
mum. But they were just laughing and saying

things like "that'll teach you," "stuck-up
bitch," stuff like that.

[*wiping her eyes*]

She didn't know how much they hated her. She
thought they liked her but I heard them
talking about her when she wasn't there. They
were really pissed off because she was
prettier than them and Patsie thought she was
trying to get off with her boyfriend.

[*looking at each of the two officers*]

I'm not making this up—I don't know his name
but I heard Patsie talking about it. She went,
like, totally apeshit.

VE: We know, Nadine. We've spoken to him, and he
told us the same thing.

ES: So what happened next?

NA: Isabel started kicking her and Patsie joined
in. I tried to make them stop but Patsie said
they'd do the same to me if I didn't shut the
fuck up.

VE: How long did that go on?

NA: I dunno. It felt like ages but it probably
wasn't. Then Patsie said I was a useless loser
and gave me the handbag and told me to fuck
off. To fuck off home and dump it somewhere on
the way.

ES: What about Sasha's phone?

NA: She threw that in the river. There was a
notebook too and she threw that in as well.

VE: And then you went home.

NA: [*nods*]

ES: And Sasha was still alive at that point?

NA: [*nods*]

I don't know what happened after that. I thought they'd all just go home. I threw up on the way back, and I had blood on my clothes and mud and stuff, so I put it all in the washing machine.

[*weeping again*]

I'm so sorry. I'd do anything to take it back. I can't stop thinking about it—

ES: What happened the next day?

NA: When I got to school I saw Patsie and Iz but Sasha wasn't with them and didn't come to assembly either and I started to feel really sick. Then Patsie told me that if I said anything they'd give the police the video on the phone and I'd be the one who went to prison. Because I was the only one on the video.

ES: They'd have gone to prison too. The video would prove they were there.

NA: [*silence*]

I didn't think of that.

* * *

Adam Fawley
11 April 2018
12.19

Gallagher joins me at the video screen in the next room.

"Somer's doing really well," I say, glancing up. "I hope you're telling her that. She doesn't have enough confidence in her own abilities."

She gives me a look. "I have, but thank you, I'll make

408

sure to tell her again. I've also told her to take the afternoon off. She looks completely exhausted."

On the screen, Nadine is sobbing in her mother's arms, and people are getting to their feet. They must have decided to take a break.

"Have you heard from forensics?"

Gallagher nods. "There are small traces of Sasha's DNA on one of the Applefords' kitchen knives. Which ties in with Nadine's story, but as Patsie's lawyer will immediately point out, could just as easily corroborate Patsie's version of events. And without a murder weapon we'll struggle to prove which of them actually killed her."

"What about Patsie's mobile? Any sign of that video Nadine said she took?"

"The phone's gone to the lab, along with her laptop. I suspect the video she took is long gone, but if we're lucky she won't have deleted it so thoroughly that digital forensics can't find it."

I shake my head. "What if there never was a video? Because all their phones were off, weren't they—we know that. So it doesn't really add up."

She frowns; this obviously hadn't occurred to her. "She could have put the phone on flight-safe mode?"

"That's one possibility. But these girls are clever, especially Patsie. She'd know how difficult it is to really delete stuff. Especially anything to do with the Cloud."

"So you think Nadine is lying?"

"No," I say. "I think Patsie was bluffing—she just pretended to video Nadine so she could blackmail her into staying quiet."

She sighs. "And if there's no video, Patsie's lawyers will

just say that's yet more proof Nadine's the one who's lying."

She takes a seat next to me now. "What worries me is that even if we do manage to place Patsie and Isabel at the scene they're bound to say that as far as they were concerned it was just another 'prank.' That they left Sasha alive and well, and Nadine must have gone crazy after that and ended up killing her. Patsie's already telling anyone who will listen that Nadine's weird."

I nod. "And Nadine's got a far more credible motive. Even though Brotherton's evidence backs her up, it's going to be tough to convince a jury that those girls would have killed Sasha over something so apparently trivial. Not when they were supposed to be BFFs."

Gallagher smiles. "I'm surprised you know what that means."

I laugh drily. "I have hidden shallows."

She looks back at the screen again. Nadine is being led out of the door by her mother. "We need to find a way to help that girl, Adam, because right now, everything's against her. And as DS Gislingham continues to remind me, those bloody girls are playing us for fools."

There's a knock on our door now, and Baxter appears around it. "Ah, there you are, boss. I sent those prints over to forensics like you asked and got them to do a rush on them. They've just got back to me. I think you'll want to see this—looks like you were right."

As the door swings shut again behind him Gallagher looks at me and raises an eyebrow. "Care to share?"

* * *

410

> Looks like I may get off early—I'll leave my doorkeys at the front desk in case you get back before me. Can't wait to see you Ex

> Great—can prob leave in about an hour Gx

* * *

The incident room is crowded now. People are perched on desks, eating sandwiches from the Tesco across the road. And at the front, by the whiteboard, is Baxter.

"So," asks Gallagher, "what's all this about?"

Baxter turns and points at an enlargement of Isabel Parker's bus ticket.

"The DI asked me to get some more tests done on this and it turns out he guessed right. There are *two* sets of prints on this thing."

Quinn frowns. "Don't bus drivers hand the tickets out? So they'll be his, right?"

Evidently Quinn doesn't spend much time on public transport. As if you couldn't guess.

"The tickets are issued straight from the machine," says Asante quietly. "Only the passengers handle them."

"So one set are Isabel Parker's," begins Gallagher. "But the others—"

"The others," says Baxter, "are a perfect match for Leah Waddell."

But people don't get it; not immediately anyway. I can see that from the confusion in their eyes. I get up and turn to face them.

"OK. This is what I think happened. Patsie, Sasha and Isabel left Summertown on foot that night, just like Nadine said. They met up with Nadine at the footpath and then they all went down to the river. God only knows what they told Sasha to persuade her to go along with that, but whatever it was, she must have believed it. Meanwhile Leah Waddell waited in Summertown on her own, and eventually caught that 9:43 bus. That ticket there, on the board—that's *hers*."

"But it's a ticket for Headington," says Everett, evidently still confused.

"Right. *Precisely*. She bought a ticket for *Headington*. Only she didn't stay on that far. She got off at the very next stop, and walked back home from there, arriving—as we know—at 10:15. And the following day, at school, she gave that ticket to Isabel, so she had something to prove her alibi if she needed it."

Quinn lets out a long breath. "The cunning little mares."

"But that bus driver *spoke* to Isabel," says Everett, clearly still confused. "He identified her. I don't get it—she *had* to have been on that bus."

I nod. "And she was. Patsie walked home from the river but *Isabel* went back down to the main road and caught the bus to Headington from there. The *same bus* Leah had just got off only a few minutes before. I reckon Isabel probably had her hood up when she got on so the driver wouldn't notice her hair, but she must have taken it down later. She wanted to make damn sure he'd remember her."

"Fuck me," says Gislingham under his breath. "Someone remind me about this, will you, next time I say I want daughters."

* * *

Somer's flat doesn't have the space of Saumarez's house. Or the décor. Or the view. The sitting room is tiny, she has only the one bedroom and the bathroom doesn't even have a window. But it doesn't seem to bother Giles. It's one of the things about him that intrigues her. For someone who's clearly spent a pile of money and time on getting his own surroundings exactly as he wants them, he seems to have a talent for being at ease wherever he finds himself. Which, right now, is sprawled on Somer's sofa, watching TV.

He doesn't turn it off when he sees her, but he does get up, pulling her into his arms and burying his face in her hair.

"Missed you," he says.

"It's only been a few days," she laughs, but it's been a shit of a few days, and she feels suddenly on the edge of tears. She breathes him in, the heat of him, the smell. Sea air and skin and clean laundry. Perhaps this is what love is like, she thinks suddenly. Perhaps she's been searching for this—exactly *this*—all her adult life. She just never knew.

She pulls away now and hauls off her coat.

"I'm going to make tea," she says, heading for the kitchen. "And then I'm going to have a shower. Do you want anything?"

"No, I'm fine." He drops back on to the sofa and swings his feet on to the coffee table. If any of her previous boyfriends had done that she'd have seethed. But it's early days, as she keeps reminding herself—for this and many other reasons. Stuff like that only starts to jangle your nerves after at least six months.

It's a true crime show he's watching, surprise, surprise; Somer recognizes the woman doing the voiceover. A rich, arch American accent she can't quite place geographically. The west coast somewhere?

Her phone pings as she tips water into her mug. An email from Ev. She puts down the kettle and opens it up.

"Shit," she says. "Shit shit shit."

* * *

Adam Fawley
11 April 2018
13.35

"Have you got everything?"

Alex sighs. "God, Adam, I can't wait to get home. If I never see another cottage pie it'll be too soon."

I pick her coat up from the bed and hold it out. She's a little unsteady on her feet, after so long in bed. She brushes against me as I help her find a sleeve. Her hair smells different. Hospital shampoo.

"I've got chicken and chips ordered for tonight, by the way. From that French place."

That gets a smile. It's her guilty pleasure. Along with the Meursault she's not currently allowing herself to have.

She picks up her handbag and takes a last look around.

414

"OK, pardner. Time for you and me to get the hell outta Dodge."

* * *

"Show me that email again?"

Somer hands Giles the phone and watches as he scrolls down.

"We thought we had them," she says. "Fawley worked out it must have been Leah who got that bus ticket and gave it to Isabel. And he was right—her prints were on it. And we all thought, there we are, that's the proof."

"Only now Leah's saying she can explain how those prints got there," says Giles, handing her back the phone.

"Right. She says she looked for something in Isabel's bag when they were at school the following day and must have touched the ticket then. Which I don't buy for a single *nanosecond*."

He looks up. "But you won't be able to prove it either way, will you. That's the problem."

"We were already facing an uphill battle convincing a jury. The defense will be able to call a whole truckload of witnesses to say what great friends Sasha and the others were. And everyone's got a daughter or a sister or a niece who looks like one of those girls. No one's going to want to believe them capable of something like this."

"You wouldn't have any trouble convincing me—it happens a lot more often than you think. There was a bloody awful case in the States where a sixteen-year-old kid was stabbed repeatedly by two of her closest friends just because they 'didn't like her any more.'"

Somer wraps her arms around herself. "I just can't stop thinking about it, Giles. About Sasha—how she must have realized at some point that they weren't going to stop—that her *best friends* were going to kill her. Imagine that—imagine knowing that."

He reaches out and touches her on the shoulder. "You're doing your best."

"But what if it's not enough? What if we can't even persuade the CPS to run with it? Because right now, I don't think we have a hope in hell. It'll just be poor bloody Nadine carrying the can. And all this time that vicious little cow Patsie's been cozying up to Sasha's mother, eating her food, sleeping in Sasha's bed—that poor woman has no bloody idea—"

Saumarez stares at her. "Say that again."

"Patsie's been round at Sasha's house pretty much non-stop ever since she disappeared. We thought she was just trying to be nice—to give Fiona some support—but now of course it's starting to look like something else entirely—"

She stops. Giles has got his own phone out now and is tapping at the screen. "What is it?"

He holds out the mobile to her. "This is from the late nineties, in LA. The Michele Avila case. Any of it sound familiar?"

Somer reads what's on the screen and looks up at him, the color draining from her face. "What the—"

He nods. "Two of Avila's friends beat her to death, just because she was prettier and more popular than they were. And all the time the police were searching for her murderer, one of the killers was holed up in her house, 'comforting' her mother. They very nearly got away with it too."

Her eyes widen. "Are you saying Patsie and the others could have *known* about this? That they could actually have *copied* it?"

"Has to be a possibility."

She's reaching for her own phone now. "I'll ask Baxter to check the phones and laptops—"

But he's shaking his head. "Patsie's way too clever for that, Erica. Same goes for the school PCs—they keep records of what the kids look at online."

Her face falls. "Please don't tell me it's another dead end."

"No, not necessarily. The internet's not the only way they might have found out. You said Patsie and the others were well up on forensics and GPS tracking and stuff like that? Well, maybe I'm not the only one who watches too much crime on TV."

His voice trails off. He's looking at his phone again, frowning this time.

"What—what is it?"

"I'm just wondering—maybe the Avila case isn't the only one Patsie's been boning up on." He looks up at her. "Didn't you say Fawley thought this whole thing could be a copycat?"

She nods.

He holds out the phone again. "Well, looking at this, I think he might be right."

* * *

Voicemail

PC Andrew Baxter

Mobile

Transcription
"Got your message—I'll meet you there. And I've
checked all the phones and laptops again and there's
nothing on them, but like you said, that's hardly a
surprise. Oh, and I don't know if you've said anything to
Gallagher but I haven't either. Probably best to see what
we come up with first. See you shortly."

▌▌ 0.23 ━━━━━━━━━━━━━━━━━━━━━━━━━━━━ -0.07
Speaker   Call back   Delete

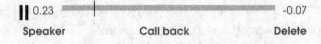

* * *

Baxter doesn't know who he is—not at first anyway. But
it doesn't take him long to work out it must be Somer's
new squeeze. He remembers Gis making snide remarks
about Saumarez when she first started seeing him, and
you only need to take one look at him to see why. All that
and a DI as well. Some buggers have all the luck.

He opens the car door and gets out as Somer comes up
the road toward him, her bloke a step or two behind.

"This is Giles," she says. "He's been helping me out."

Saumarez smiles and holds out his hand. "Good to
meet you. Erica's told me a lot about you. She says you're
the team computer ace."

"Giles is pretty good with computers, too," says Somer
quickly. Baxter eyes her—her cheeks are flushed and he's
never seen her looking so jumpy or trying so hard. As if

418

she's introducing Saumarez to her dad, not just some random work colleague.

"Oh yes?" he says heavily, turning back to Saumarez. "Digital forensics, is it?"

Saumarez smiles again. A clean smile, without sarcasm. Somer has to hand it to him: he's almost miraculously even-tempered.

"Nah, just a common or garden copper."

Somer looks from one to the other. "OK, so are we good to go?"

*　*　*

"You're not going in at all today?" says Alex, when I slide the mug of green tea on to the bedside table.

I shake my head. "I've done my bit on this one. And in the meantime, I'm going to take some of the pile of time in lieu they owe me and spoil you rotten."

Her lip quivers and I can see she's close to tears.

"Hey," I say, sitting down on the bed next to her, "it's not that dreadful a prospect, is it?"

But I can't get her to smile.

"I need to talk to you," she whispers, her voice breaking. "I should have done it before, I know I should. But there never seemed to be a good time." The tears spill over. "And then it all got out of hand and I didn't think I *could* tell you. I thought it would just make it ten times worse."

I take her hand. "It's about the trial, isn't it," I say softly. "The evidence you gave at the trial."

She looks at me. "But how—"
"I know. Alex, my darling, I've always known."

* * *

THE CENTRAL CRIMINAL COURT

The Old Bailey
London EC4M 7EH

BEFORE:
THE HONORABLE MR. JUSTICE HEALEY

R E G I N A
v.
GAVIN FRANCIS PARRIE

———————————

MR. R. BARNES Q.C. and MISS S. GREY
appeared on behalf of the prosecution.

MRS. B. JENKINS Q.C. and MR. T. CUTHBERT
appeared on behalf of the defendant.

———————————

Tuesday, 16th November, 1999
[Day 23]

ALEXANDRA SHELDON, recalled
Examined by MRS. JENKINS

Q. Ms. Sheldon, I'd like to ask you some
   further questions, if I may, about the
   events of January 3rd this year. I apologize
   for having to put you through this again,
   but this is, as you must be aware, a crucial

element of the prosecution's case. Indeed, quite possibly the single most crucial element of all. You, as a trainee solicitor yourself, must appreciate that.

MR. BARNES: My Lord, if I may interject, the witness cannot be expected to comment on such matters.

MR. JUSTICE HEALEY: Mrs. Jenkins, perhaps you might move on.

MRS. JENKINS: My Lord. So, Ms. Sheldon, it is still your contention, is it, that you did not enter Mr. Parrie's garage premises at any time that day?

A. That's correct.

Q. You didn't try the door before the police came, just to see if it was unlocked?

A. No.

Q. In fact, as we have heard, the door was indeed locked, but Mr. Parrie kept a spare key above the lintel—a key which anyone who might have been watching him that day could have seen him take down and use to open the door.

A. I told you, I didn't go in. They'd have found my fingerprints on the handle if I had. And on the key.

Q. Not necessarily, Ms. Sheldon. Not if you were wearing gloves. And according to Met Office records it was a bright but very cold day on January 3rd—the temperature barely exceeded six degrees.

A. I wasn't wearing gloves.

Q. So you didn't go in, and you didn't leave
   anything inside?
A. I told you.

Q. Like strands of your hair, for example? Such
   as were subsequently discovered by the
   police?
A. No, like I said. And I'd had my hair cut
   short weeks before. Where would I have got
   strands that long?

Q. You might have had some in your handbag? On
   your hairbrush?
A. How often do you clean your brush?

Q. That's hardly the point—
A. I clean mine every few days. Like most
   women. The assault had happened four months
   before.

MR. BARNES: My Lord, if I may, we have already
   heard evidence from the police forensic
   scientist that hair recovered from a brush
   would have been knotted in a clump, not in
   the long "free" strands retrieved from the
   garage.

MRS. JENKINS: One final question, Ms. Sheldon.
   The court has heard that you had never met
   Detective Sergeant Fawley prior to the night
   you were assaulted, on September 4th 1998.
   Is that true?
A. Yes, it is.

MRS. JENKINS: No further questions, my Lord.

* * *

It's a man who opens the door. His hair is wet and he has a towel wrapped around his waist and another in his hand.

"Who the hell are you?"

"DC Erica Somer, Thames Valley Police, and DC Andrew Baxter. This is DI Giles Saumarez. Is Mrs. Webb in?"

He stares at them all one by one. "Nah. She's gone shopping for Patsie. Something to 'cheer her up,' the spoilt little bitch."

His contempt is palpable. The last time she was here Somer came away wondering whether this man could have been abusing Denise Webb's daughter—so much so that she checked his whereabouts for the night Sasha died. But he was nowhere near the place.

"Can we come in?"

"What's this about? The Blake kid again?"

"Did you know Sasha, Mr. Riley?"

If he's surprised she knows his name, he doesn't show it. "Yeah, I met her once or twice. Nice kid. Quiet. Polite. Never could see what she saw in bloody Patsie."

He steps back and the three of them troop past him into the hall. There's a bag of tools on the floor by the stairs and a high-viz jacket hooked over the banisters.

"You're a builder, aren't you, Mr. Riley?"

He grins at her. "Fuck me, you really are a detective."

"Do you know someone called Ashley Brotherton?"

He starts a little, and a wariness creeps into his face. "Yeah. Worked with him a few times on jobs. Why?"

"Did you know Patsie was seeing him?"

"Seeing him as in shagging him? Yeah, I thought she might be. I saw them in town once."

Jesus, thinks Somer—if only they'd thought to talk to this tosser before—

"You didn't tell her mother? She's *fifteen*—"

A smile curls nastily about his mouth. "So fucking what? And in any case, Den's made it balls-achingly clear that Patsie is her business not mine. So as far as I'm concerned, what that little cow does or doesn't do is absolutely *nothing* to do with me."

He's toweling his hair now. He has tattoos all up one arm and a snake twisting across his shoulders—the same one, Somer suddenly realizes, that Denise Webb has.

"Didn't you search Patsie's stuff already?" he says. "Den said some of your blokes came and took her laptop."

Saumarez takes a step forward. "Does Patsie have a TV in her room, Mr. Riley?"

"No," he says, frowning. "Just the one down here."

"And you have, what, Sky? Virgin?"

"Sky," he says. "For the sport." He looks at Somer and then at the two men. "That's what you want to see? The *telly*?"

"If you don't mind," says Somer.

He smiles again. "Go ahead—knock yourself out. If you can find anything to incriminate that little bitch you'll be doing me a favor big-time. In the meantime, I'm going upstairs."

* * *

424

28 August 1998, 10:45 p.m.
Kubla Nightclub, High Street, Oxford

It's crowded in the bar. Friday night and everyone's a bit wired. Apart, that is, from the young man with dark hair sitting at the bar, who's had the same pint slowly warming up in front of him for over an hour. He hasn't been alone all that time—he had a mate with him until a few minutes ago—but whatever they were talking about, it must have been something serious because he hasn't been doing much smiling. But now his friend has gone and the young man has twisted around on his stool so he can observe what's going on in the rest of the bar. He's good at that—watching people, working them out. There's a scattering of couples—some at tables, a few dancing. One pair who've been needling each other all night are now on the brink of a row, another pair are definitely in the jittery stages of a first date. Groups of lads gripping fancy beer bottles by the neck and laughing just a bit too hard. And a group of women on a hen night in the far corner. Not teenagers—they must all be in their mid-twenties. No embarrassing inflatable body parts either, just satin sashes and tiaras and a balloon tied to the back of the bride-to-be's chair. He'd have known which one she was anyway, even without that: she's wearing a pink diamanté hairslide saying TAKEN in large glittery letters, which she's tried to take off several times, only to have it firmly reinstated by her friends.

Just along the bar, the hen-in-chief is now ordering a round of cosmos and something in a tulip-shaped glass that involves a cocktail shaker, a cherry on a stick and a sparkler. It's evidently destined for the bride-to-be, who catches sight of what's going on and gets to her feet. The young man at the bar isn't the only one to notice her: it's hard to ignore that long dark hair, the red heels she's probably now regretting, those violet-blue eyes.

She doesn't appear drunk—unlike some of her companions—but the young man has a hunch the wine has had its effect, all the same. She eventually makes it to the bar, after evading several attempts to get her to dance, and slides on to a stool next to her friend. She's six feet away from him now.

She gestures at the cocktail glass. "If you think I'm drinking that, you've got another think coming."

The pitch of her voice is low—lower than he'd have expected.

She looks at her friend and then at the barman. "Is she trying to get me pissed? She is, isn't she? So I'll do something appalling like dance on the table with no knickers."

The barman grins widely and shrugs. He's a heavy man, thickset. "Don't look at me. What happens on a hen night, stays in the coop."

She laughs out loud then turns again to her friend. "You haven't got a bloody stripper, have you, Chlo? *Please* tell me you haven't got a stripper."

Chloe opens her eyes wide and looks mock-offended: *Who, me?*

The woman gives her a narrow look. "Yeah, right. Well, let's just say I'm steering well clear of anyone in a bloody uniform."

She reaches across and takes the sparkler from the drink, then hands it, with a flourish, to her friend. It's all just a little too theatrical. As if she knows she's being watched. Which, of course, she is.

She picks up the glass and takes a sip.

"Actually, that's not too bad."

Her friend grins and gives the barman a high five. "Way to go, Gerry!"

"Though there's still no way I'm drinking it."

Her friend slides, a little awkwardly, off her stool. "I'll just take the drinks over to the girls. Amy's sending me manic distress signals."

Left to herself, the woman reaches for the hair clip to take it off. But it's got caught. The young man has to stop himself offering to help, but she finally manages to yank it clear, stuffing it into her bag, then rubbing the side of her head.

She must have seen the young man pick up his glass out of the corner of her eye because she looks straight at him now. She flushes and smiles, a little self-consciously.

"Bloody thing—it's been giving me a headache all evening."

There's a squeal of laughter from the girls' table now and Chloe starts to make her way, none too steadily, back to the bar.

"Sorry if we've been a bit loud," says the bride. "Blame it on the job. We work at a law firm, for our sins. It's hardly laugh-a-minute."

"You're a solicitor?" asks the young man.

She looks at him for a moment, then takes another sip of the drink. Her eyes are very bright. "No, just a legal secretary. Very, very, *very* dull. What about you?"

"Me? Oh, I'm just a civil servant. That's pretty dull too."

The woman laughs and raises her glass in a toast. "May universal dullness cover all!"

Chloe comes up and leans her arm around her friend's shoulders. She's having difficulty staying upright. "Are you coming, Sand? The girls want to move on somewhere else."

"In a minute. What sort of civil servant?"

He hesitates; perhaps there's something about his job he'd rather not divulge. At least to attractive women he's only just met. "At the council. I'm in Planning."

A smile curls her lips. "I *see*. So you're the man to ask if I want an extension?"

Chloe starts shrieking with laughter. "Oh my God! I can't believe you just said that!"

The bride is smiling too, but playfully, as if goading him. As if she's seen through his lie.

"You might be a useful man to know, Mr. I'm-in-Planning. Do you have a card?"

His turn to flush. "No, sorry."

She smiles a little more widely and reaches for a napkin. "I'm sure you have a phone number, though," she says. "Even *very* dull people have those. You can write it down for me. Just in case."

Chloe is looking at her, wide-eyed, as the young man takes out a pen and writes the numbers down.

The woman picks up the napkin, looks at it, and then at him. "Adam Fawley," she says softly. "For a dull man, you have a distinctly interesting name."

* * *

"There's nothing in the recordings," says Saumarez, staring at the TV. It's a huge flat-screen in the corner of the sitting room. So huge that it's hard to get far enough away from it to focus properly. "But let's have a look at the deleted items. We may get lucky—not everyone knows you have to erase stuff twice on these things."

He starts to scroll through the list—*Monday Night Football*, *The Big Fight Live*.

"Everything OK? Only I need to get going."

It's Riley, standing at the door. He's dressed now, a leather jacket slung over one shoulder.

"Yes, thank you, Mr. Riley, we won't be long now."

428

"What's this then?" he says, moving toward the TV. Saumarez has stopped scrolling; he's staring at the screen.

"Oh, just something we were checking," says Somer quickly, a little embarrassed.

"Patsie loves that crap," says Riley, gesturing at the list. "Watches it all the fucking time. *Faking It*, *A Perfect Murder*, *The First 48*. I asked her once why she was wasting her time with shit like that and she just gave me one of those looks of hers and said 'research.'"

He sees their faces change and laughs. "Yeah, like, seriously—she *actually said that*. I said to her, was she planning on killing me then, and she just did this weird smile. Bloody creeped me out, I can tell you."

He hitches his jacket a little higher. "Of course, when Den told me you were questioning her about the Sasha Blake thing I practically pissed myself. I mean—you couldn't make it up. She'd only been watching that sodding show two days before."

Somer frowns. "I'm not with you. Which show?"

Saumarez turns to her. "I know which one he means," he says quietly. "It's called *I Killed My BFF*."

* * *

Adam Fawley
11 April 2018
15.40

I can see it now, in my head. The colors slightly too bright, the focus slightly too sharp, like it is in dreams, or in fever. Parking the car outside the Co-op that day. The litter bin spilling over with rubbish, a magpie perched on the edge, something pink and glittery gripped in its beak, sparkling in the low winter sun. Something I thought, even then, I recognized. I remember my pace slowing, just for a moment; I remember wondering at the coincidence, if that's what it was. But I didn't put it together, not then. Not then, and not even five minutes later when I went inside and saw her and realized that she'd cut her hair.

And what about later, you're going to say, after they found what they found? If forensics had come to me first, if they'd showed me what was in that evidence bag, would I have put it together then?

Yes. No question.

And would I have said something? Would I have done things differently?

I think so, but if I'm honest, I don't know. I still don't know, even now. Because we knew it was him. *I* knew it was him. And this was the only way we were going to make him pay.

But it's all hypothetical, because they didn't come to me. They went to Osbourne, and he realized at once what they had, and the difference it could make, and by the time anyone told me it was far, far too late.

* * *

When Gallagher looks up from her desk and sees Somer her first reaction is to frown.

"Aren't you supposed to be off this afternoon?"

But then she notices there's a man standing behind her, and the thought half forms that this must be the boyfriend everyone's talking about, but then Somer's holding out her phone and there's no mistaking the look on her face.

Gallagher stares at the screen then looks up, frowning. "Sorry, I don't get it—what's this?"

"It's from the TV in Patsie Webb's house. A program she watched six months ago—a program she *thought* she'd deleted. This is why those girls ripped out Sasha's hair, and why they'd already done exactly the same thing to Faith. They knew about the Roadside Rapist all along. They wanted us to think he was back—they wanted us so focused on *him* we wouldn't go looking anywhere else."

TRUE CRIME TV

New: Britain's Most Notorious Predators
1h 3m HD

® ↕ Record series, Monday 11:00 pm

The Roadside Rapist: True crime author Walter Selnick Jr. takes an in-depth look at the case of Gavin Parrie, convicted of seven brutal sex attacks in the UK in 1999. But could the real rapist still be out there? (S3, ep8)

* * *

Adam Fawley
11 April 2018
15.45

"You knew about the hairslide."

Alex is staring at me, her face white to the lips.

"I remembered you wearing it. How it'd got tangled in your hair. And I remembered you shoving it in the side pocket of your bag. I thought, afterwards, how easy it would be to forget about something like that—how it might be weeks before you remembered it was there. Months, even."

"Why didn't you say anything?"

"There was no way to be sure." But the real truth is I didn't want to ask—didn't want to watch her face as she decided whether she was going to lie. Because by then I was already in love with her.

"And like you said, the longer it went on, the harder it got."

"You could have lost your job."

I take her hand. "I know."

There's a silence.

"I was terrified," she says, "all the way through the trial—I thought that barman at Kubla would say we were both there that night—that they'd find out I lied."

I don't say anything. I don't tell her I spoke to him. That I squared it away—told him about the girl Parrie assaulted in Manchester—that Parrie might walk because we couldn't refer to it in court and we had precious little else. The man was ex-army; he understood. But Alex doesn't need to know about that. Not now.

"It was him," she breathes now, her voice barely more than a whisper. "Parrie. I *know* it was him. I wouldn't have done—"

She swallows, forces herself to continue; she's not looking at me. "I wouldn't have done what I did if I wasn't sure. *Absolutely* sure."

"I know."

She raises her eyes to mine. "You do understand, don't you? Why I did it? I had to stop him. The papers kept saying there was never any DNA—that he was too clever to leave any proof. That poor girl who killed herself—she was scarcely more than a *child*. And then I found myself in that queue and I realized it was the same smell, and he was just standing there behind me like a *normal person*, but I knew, I just *knew* it was him, and I thought—this is my chance—this is my chance to make him pay—"

I hold her hand tighter. Her fingers are icy.

"I thought it was all in the past—that it was over and done with and he'd got what he deserved, and over the years I managed to convince myself that it was OK. That any reasonable person would have done the same thing I did. And then suddenly you were telling me that he might get parole—that he might be let out—and it all started up again. I thought you were going to lose your job—that it would all come out and it would all be my fault, and I—I—"

She's sobbing now. I pull her into my arms and kiss her hair. "Well, I didn't, and I'm not going to. It's over—really. Everything is going to be fine. You, me, our child. That's all that matters. And I promise you that nothing—*nothing*—is *ever* going to take that away."

* * *

Fiona Blake is woken by the doorbell. She reaches blindly for the alarm clock—7:35: she's been asleep less than an hour. Her eyes feel like they're opening into mud and her limbs are heavy but unstable, like wet cement.

They'd told her—the policewomen—that they'd do their best to keep the press away, but all the same it might be better if there was somewhere else she could go—

433

someone else she could stay with. But she'd told them no. There was nowhere she wanted to go, no one she wanted to see. She just wanted to be left alone. She wanted *them* to leave her alone. She'd almost felt sorry for them, by the end, when she finally got the two of them out the door. Especially the pretty one. Somer or whatever her name was. She looked really upset. As if she'd known Sash—as if she could even begin to understand what it felt like now—to know that—

The bell rings again. She rubs her face, feeling the skin coarse and unmoisturized under her fingers. She reaches for the dressing gown; it's the same one she's been wearing for days. Even she knows that it smells.

She daren't look at herself in the mirror by the front door, but she doesn't care. If there are bloody press out there, let them look. Let them see what it looks like—what it does to you to lose a daughter like that.

But it's not a journalist. It's Victoria Parker. She's holding a bunch of flowers in her hand. Lilies. Just like the ones her daughter brought. There's a sudden overwhelming wave of scent. Fiona feels nauseous.

"Mrs. Blake—I mean, Fiona," says Victoria, her voice dragging in her throat. Her face looks bleached, almost bruised. "I didn't know what to do. This is so awful—I just don't understand—they were all such friends—such great friends—"

Victoria swallows. Her knuckles are white where she's gripping the lilies to her chest. A small part of Fiona's deadened brain notices the smear of orange pollen on her beige jacket. She'll never get that stain out now, she thinks. There are some things that can't be retrieved.

"I'm sorry," says Victoria. She's blinking; too fast. Trying to push away the tears she knows this woman will not pity. "I'm just so very, very sorry."

Fiona stares at her for a long long moment, and then, slowly and quietly, closes the door.

* * *

Daily Telegraph

13th February 2019

OXFORD TEENAGERS FOUND GUILTY OF
"BRUTAL AND INHUMANE" KILLING

By Lisa Greaves

Four teenage girls were convicted at Oxford Crown Court today for the assault and murder of Marston teenager Sasha Blake. After an eight-week trial, Patsie Webb and Isabel Parker were found guilty of murder, and Leah Waddell of conspiracy to murder. A fourth girl, who cannot be named for legal reasons, was found guilty of Actual Bodily Harm. All four were fifteen at the time of the killing.

The court heard that Webb and Parker planned the murder for weeks, researching several similar crimes and focusing in particular on the 1999 conviction of Gavin Parrie, the so-called "Roadside Rapist." Nicholas Fox QC argued that certain details of the "brutal and inhumane" killing of Sasha Blake were specifically designed to lead police to believe that the perpetrator was a copycat sexual predator. The girls even went so far as to carry out an almost identical assault on another young woman a few days before the murder, to lend weight to the deception.

Sasha Blake was lured into woodland off the Marston Ferry Road, in Oxford, on 3 April 2018, and submitted to a brutal beating by Webb and Parker which resulted in her death. The jury was told how Webb had developed an intense and irrational hatred for Blake, despite the fact that they had been friends since childhood. She also believed that her boyfriend, Ashley Brotherton, wished to finish their relationship and take up with Blake instead. Brotherton gave evidence in court about Webb's volatile temper, and described various threats she made against him in relation to his supposed attraction to Blake. Mr. Fox told the jury that Webb had homed in on the Roadside Rapist case not only because the crimes had taken place in the Oxford area, but because Mr. Brotherton was a plasterer, and she knew any forensic evidence transferred from his van would give the police further reason to believe the assaults were linked to the Parrie case. Several witnesses attested to her fascination with true crime TV programs and investigative procedures.

Under questioning, Leah Waddell broke down in tears and claimed that she had been "bullied and intimidated" into going along with the plan, and Webb and Parker were "domineering": "I just couldn't say no—I was afraid of what they would do to me." After Sasha Blake's death, Webb went to considerable lengths to divert attention away from herself and Parker, including planting condoms at the victim's house to lead investigators to believe she had a boyfriend. When she overheard a CID officer tell Mrs. Blake that the police did not believe there was any connection between her daughter's death and the Parrie case, Webb came forward with another suspect, who was investigated but subsequently cleared of any involvement in the crime.

All four girls will be sentenced next month. Webb, Parker and Waddell are also due to face charges in relation to the earlier assault.

yougottahave

745 posts   **267k followers**   **629 following**

F A I T H Fashion | Beauty | Style
Sharing the passion, learning to love myself

Posted 10.27 16 February 2019

Headshot, interior, direct to cam

Hi everyone. I realized this morning that it's six months since I started sharing my personal journey with you guys. I didn't have the courage to talk about that when I started my channel, and I don't think I ever would've without my awesome partner Jess, and my amazing mum, who's been through so much herself lately, but has always always been there for me and loved me for who I am. Getting a bit emotional now because it's been such an overwhelming few months, but I just want to thank both of them from the bottom of my heart.

And I want to thank you guys as well, especially all the hundreds and hundreds of new followers I've got since last summer. I've had so much amazing feedback from you guys—both from my fashion passionistas and all the trans girls who are following me now. I love you all and I am SO SO happy that my own experiences are helping other people to feel as beautiful on the outside as they are on the inside.

Beckons to someone off-screen; Jess appears, smiling and waving. She's holding a cake with candles on it

So, that's it for today. A bit shorter than usual but it's Jess's birthday and we have a party to go to—yay!

This is Faith, signing off the same way I always have: Look good, be kind and love who *you* are.

Epilogue

HMP Wandsworth
23 May 2018

The car is waiting for him opposite the gate. His mother. He didn't want any bloody fuss, and certainly not the fucking kids. As for the press, there'll be time enough for that. His lawyer says they're queuing around the block. It's just a question of how much money they're prepared to cough up. A story like this—it's pure pay dirt.

His mother gets out of the car. Still the same shitty Fiat. That's something else he's going to bloody well fix.

"You all right?" she says as he crosses the road toward her. It's starting to rain. There are splashes on the shoulders of her coat.

"Just get in, Mum," he says. "No point getting wet, is there."

She doesn't hug him. Just looks him in the eye and hands him the keys.

"Thought you'd want to drive."

He smiles. "Yeah," he says. "Why not? Get back in the swing and all that."

He gets in, then leans over and pushes the passenger door open for her. He can smell her fag smoke, under the artificial pine. There's one of those air freshener things stuck on the dashboard. It makes him want to gag. All those years in prison seem to have sharpened his sense of smell.

His mother pulls the door shut, then turns to face him. "Well?"

"I'm not going to let them get away with it, you know."

He expects her to tell him to let it go. To move on. But she doesn't.

"That fucking copper," he says. "And that bitch wife of his. They fitted me up—you do know that, right?"

She looks at him, then nods. "Let's just go, eh? Get you home. You can think about the rest of it later."

But he's not finished. "I *know* there was no hair in the fucking lock-up, Mum. That bloody bitch planted it. She planted it to frame me."

His mother sighs. She's heard it all before; he's been saying the same thing for nigh on twenty years.

"I'm serious. Just you wait—those bastards, I'm going to make them pay."

Pay for all those years inside.

Pay for him not seeing his kids grow up.

Pay, above all, for playing him at his own game.

He knows there was no hair in the lock-up because he wasn't stupid enough to leave it there. Because he knows where to hide precious things like that. Because he knows places the police would never think to look.

And what he hid, all those years ago, will still be there, waiting for him. The long auburn strands he yanked out of that bitch's head. Emma's blond. Alison's red. The jewelry and the silk knickers and all the other things he took from those girls. He feels a stir in his groin just thinking about it. But that's for later. There's no need to rush. Not now. Thanks to Jocelyn Naismith and The Whole Truth and his dumb-arse lawyers, he has all the time in the world.

He sits a while, clenching and unclenching his fists, allowing his heart rate to slow. Then he puts the key in the ignition and starts the engine.

Acknowledgments

There are so many people in "Team Fawley" who have helped make this book what it is.

First, my team at Penguin, starting with my brilliant editor, Katy Loftus. A special thank-you to her this time, for pushing me into doing two final rounds of edits when I was very tired and really didn't want to have yet another go. But she was right, and it's a far better book as a result (it won't happen next time, I promise!). Also to editorial assistant Rosanna Forte, and my fabulous marketing and PR team Jane Gentle, Olivia Mead, Ellie Hudson and Lindsay Terrell, the mastermind behind the Cara Hunter newsletter.

I am also indebted to Karen Whitlock for her outstanding work as my copy editor, and to Emma Brown and the Penguin production team—I'm always giving them new challenges in my typescripts, from transcripts to Twitter feeds to the maps in this book, but they never fail to rise to them! Thank you likewise to the late, great John Hamilton and the design team who've developed such a striking and eye-catching look for the book jackets, to the Dead Good team, and to James Keyte and everyone involved on the audio side, particularly Emma Cunniffe and Lee Ingleby, who bring the books to life so brilliantly well.

Thank you also to my agent Anna Power, of Johnson &

Alcock, for her support, insight and her patience! And also to Hélène Butler—it's thanks to her that the Fawley books are now being published in over twenty countries across the world.

My team of professional advisers have given me invaluable advice on the technical and procedural aspects of *All the Rage*, as they have with the other books: Detective Inspector Andy Thompson, Joey Giddings, Nicholas Syfret QC and Ann Robinson. Any mistakes that might remain are entirely down to me.

Closer to home, I want to thank my husband, Simon, and the kind friends on my "early reader" panel—Sarah, Peter, Elizabeth, Stephen, Andy, Richard, Neera and Deborah.

Thanks also to KUCHENGA for providing such a brilliant read.

And finally I want to thank *you*—my readers. Penguin told me that someone buys a Cara Hunter book every fifty seconds (unbelievable!), and people get in touch on Twitter or Instagram every day to tell me they've enjoyed the books. I can't tell you how nice that is: being a writer is a wonderful life, but nothing beats that. I'm so grateful to everyone who's bought, borrowed or recommended the series in the last two years, and especially those who've taken the time to put a review on Netgalley or Amazon, and the bloggers who've given the books so much support.

A few last words on the book itself. As before, while there are some real Oxford places and roads in the novel, I have taken a few liberties with actual geography here and there, and some places are my own invention. For example, there is no "Summertown High," "Windermere Avenue" or "Rydal Way." The news items are also entirely fictional; none of the people represented is based on a real person and any similarity between online usernames in the book and those of real people is entirely coincidental.

And for the eagle-eyed among you, 1 April 2018 was actually a Sunday, but I had to shift it to a Monday for the purposes of the plot. But well done anyone who spotted it!

About the Author

Cara Hunter is the author of the *Sunday Times* bestselling crime novels *Close to Home*, *In the Dark* and *No Way Out*, all featuring DI Adam Fawley and his Oxford-based police team. *Close to Home* was a Richard and Judy Book Club pick, was shortlisted for Crime Book of the Year in the British Book Awards 2019 and *No Way Out* was selected by the *Sunday Times* as one of the 100 best crime novels since 1945. Cara's novels have sold more than three quarters of a million copies worldwide. Cara Hunter lives in Oxford, on a street not unlike those featured in her books.

READ MORE BY
CARA HUNTER

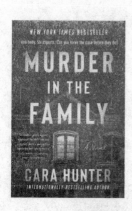

7